BLACK MOON

A ZODIAC NOVEL

BLACK MOON

A ZODIAC NOVEL

ROMINA RUSSELL

RAZORBILL®

An Imprint of Penguin Random House

RAZORBILL®

An Imprint of Penguin Random House
Penguin.com

RAZORBILL & colophon are a registered trademark of Penguin Random House LLC.

Copyright © 2016 Penguin Random House LLC

Penguin Random House supports copyright. Copyright fuels creativity, encourages diverse voices, promotes free speech, and creates a vibrant culture. Thank you for buying an authorized edition of this book and for complying with copyright laws by not reproducing, scanning, or distributing any part of it in any form without permission. You are supporting writers and allowing Penguin Random House to continue to publish books for every reader.

Library of Congress Cataloging-in-Publication Data

Names: Russell, Romina, author.
Title: Black moon : a Zodiac novel / Romina Russell.
Description: New York : Razorbill, an imprint of Penguin Random House, [2016]
Summary: Even though the Plenum declares peace in the galaxy, seventeen-year-old Rho continues her search for the master while she reunites with Nishi, who is working with the Tomorrow Party to unify the Houses by colonizing an uninhabited planet, and seeks out information about her Riser mother.
Identifiers: LCCN 2016042589 | ISBN 9781595147455
Subjects: | CYAC: Science fiction. | Fantasy. | Zodiac—Fiction. | Astrology—Fiction.
Classification: LCC PZ7.1.R87 Bl 2016 | DDC [Fic]—dc23 LC record available at https://lccn.loc.gov/2016042589

ISBN: 9781595147462

Printed in the United States of America

1 3 5 7 9 10 8 6 4 2

Interior design by Vanessa Han

For my sister, Meli,
whose inner flame could power solar systems.

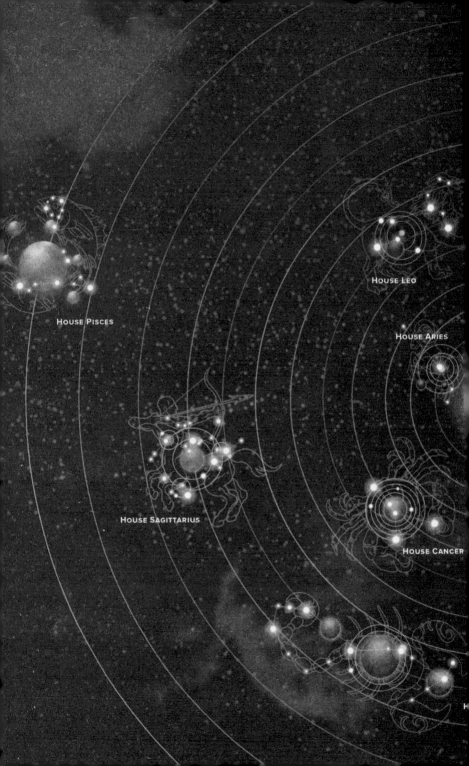

THE HOUSES OF THE ZODIAC GALAXY

THE FIRST HOUSE:
ARIES, *THE RAM*
CONSTELLATION
Strength: Military
Guardian: General Eurek
Flag: Red

THE SECOND HOUSE:
TAURUS, *THE BULL*
CONSTELLATION
Strength: Industry
Guardian: Chief Executive
Purecell
Flag: Olive green

THE THIRD HOUSE:
GEMINI, *THE DOUBLE*
CONSTELLATION
Strength: Imagination
Guardians: Twins Caaseum
(deceased) and Rubidum
Flag: Orange

THE FOURTH HOUSE:
CANCER, *THE CRAB*
CONSTELLATION
Strength: Nurture
Guardian: Holy Mother
Agatha (Interim)
Flag: Blue

THE FIFTH HOUSE:
LEO, *THE LION*
CONSTELLATION
Strength: Passion
Guardian: Holy Leader Aurelius
Flag: Royal purple

THE SIXTH HOUSE:
VIRGO, *THE TRIPLE VIRGIN*
CONSTELLATION
Strength: Sustenance
Guardian: Empress Moira
(in critical condition)
Flag: Emerald green

THE SEVENTH HOUSE:
LIBRA, *THE SCALES OF*
JUSTICE CONSTELLATION

Strength: *Justice*

Guardian: *Lord Neith*

Flag: *Yellow*

THE EIGHTH HOUSE:
SCORPIO, *THE SCORPION*
CONSTELLATION

Strength: *Innovation*

Guardian: *Chieftain Skiff*

Flag: *Black*

THE NINTH HOUSE:
SAGITTARIUS, *THE ARCHER*
CONSTELLATION

Strength: *Curiosity*

Guardian: *Guardian Brynda*

Flag: *Lavender*

THE TENTH HOUSE:
CAPRICORN, *THE SEAGOAT*
CONSTELLATION

Strength: *Wisdom*

Guardian: *Sage Ferez*

Flag: *Brown*

THE ELEVENTH HOUSE:
AQUARIUS, *THE WATER*
BEARER CONSTELLATION

Strength: *Philosophy*

Guardian: *Supreme Guardian*

Gortheaux the Thirty-Third

Flag: *Aqua*

THE TWELFTH HOUSE:
PISCES, *THE FISH*
CONSTELLATION

Strength: *Spirituality*

Guardian: *Prophet Marinda*

Flag: *Silver*

~~THE THIRTEENTH HOUSE:~~
~~OPHIUCHUS, *THE SERPENT*~~
~~*BEARER CONSTELLATION*~~

~~Strength: *Unity*~~

~~Guardian: *Master Ophiuchus*~~

~~Flag: *White*~~

PROLOGUE

WHEN I THINK OF MY adolescence as an Acolyte on Elara, I feel lighter. Like I'm back inside that semi-weightless world.

My memories from those years always wash over me in waves.

The first wave is the largest, and when it breaks, hundreds of Snow Globes bubble to my surface, showering me with memories of my best friends, Nishiko Sai and Deke Moreten. My life's happiest moments live in this wave's wake.

As the current carries Deke and Nishi away, a second, gentler swell always rolls in, and my skin ripples as I surf through a montage of mornings spent in the silent solarium, soaking in Mathias's presence and Helios's rays. When the warmth begins to recede from my skin, I always try to pull away, before the third wave can overtake me.

But by the time I remember to swim, I'm already caught in its riptide.

When the memory crashes over me, I'm submerged in a cement block at the Academy: the music studio where Nishi, Deke, and I used to meet for band practice. Where the first two waves flood my mind with my favorite moments from the moon, the third always brings me back to this exact moment, in this exact place, a year and a half ago.

Nishi, Deke, and I had spent the whole day in the studio, while Nishi taught us how to play a popular Sagittarian song called "Who Drank My Abyssthe?"

"Not good enough," she complained right after my closing hit, before the cymbals had even stopped echoing. "You guys have to stay present through the whole song. You've been fumbling through the bridge every time."

"I'm done," Deke announced, shutting off his holographic guitar in protest.

"No, you're staying, and you're going to *focus*," hissed Nishi, blocking his path to the door. *"We're going again."*

"You drank the Abyssthe if you think that's happening!" he shot back. Then, rather than trying to get around her, he flopped to the floor and sprawled out like a starfish.

"Wait, you're right."

Nishi's abrupt attitude reversal was as unpredictable as the pitch progressions of her vocals, and from the stunned expression on Deke's face, she may as well have started speaking in a new alien language. "Rho, please tell me you heard that," he said from the ground, "because I'm starting to think maybe *I* drank the Abyssthe—"

"There's a *bigger* problem than your focus," Nishi went on, staring at the cement wall as if she could see scenes within it that were invisible to our Cancrian senses. "I think we need a bass player."

Deke groaned.

"We'll post holograms in the music department," she went on, turning to me, her gaze hopeful and searching for my support. "We can hold auditions here after class—"

"Why does it matter how we sound?" I interrupted.

The tightness in my tone sent a new, tense charge through the air, so to soften the effect, I added, "It's not like we're getting graded."

We only started the band to improve our Centering. Our instructors at the Academy taught us that art is the purest pathway to the soul, which is why the Cancrian curriculum required Acolytes to rotate through diverse disciplines until we found our clearest connection to our inner selves. Only then, once we'd found that core connection, could we specialize.

Nishi had always known that singing was her calling, but it took Deke and me longer to figure ourselves out. It was only at Nishi's insistence the year before that we finally gave music a shot. I chose the drums because I liked surrounding myself with the armor of a booming beat and a shell of steel, sticks, and hard surfaces. Deke was a skilled painter, but he wasn't passionate about it, so he decided to learn guitar.

"Well . . ." Nishi looked from me to Deke, her features forming a familiar, mischievous expression. Deke sat upright in anticipation, watching her with reverence. "I kind of . . . signed us up for the musical showcase next week!"

"No way!" he blurted, his eyes wide with fear or excitement, maybe both.

Nishi beamed. "We've been working so hard the past six months, and I thought we could see what others think. You know, for fun."

"You're the one who just said our sound wasn't working," I said, only half-heartedly trying to keep the sharpness out of my voice. I stood up behind my set and crossed my arms, my drumsticks sticking out at the angle of my elbows.

"But we're nearly there!" Nishi grinned at me eagerly. "If we find a bass player in the next couple of days, we can totally teach them the song in time—"

I set my sticks down on the snare, and the rumbling note it made felt like punctuation to end the conversation. "No, thanks."

Nishi pleaded, "*Please*, Rho! It'll be a blast!"

"You know I have stage fright—"

"How can any of us—*you* included—know that, when you've never even been on a stage?"

"*I* know because I can barely address the classroom when an instructor calls on me, so I can't begin to picture myself performing for *the whole Academy*!"

Nishi dropped to her knees in mock supplication. "Come on! Just this once! I'm begging you to try it. For me?"

I took a step back. "I really don't like it when you make me feel guilty for being who I am, Nish. Some stuff just doesn't come in the Cancrian package. It's not fair that you always want me to be more like *you*."

Nishi snapped to her feet from her begging position. "Actually, Rho, what's not fair is you using your House as an excuse not to try something new. I came to study on Cancer, didn't I? And adapting to your customs hasn't threatened my Sagittarian identity, has it? Seriously, if you opened your mind once in a while, you might surprise yourself—"

"Nish." I spoke softly and uncrossed my arms, opening myself up to her so that she would see how much I didn't want to fight. "Please. Let's just drop this, okay? I really don't feel comfortable—"

"*Fine!*" She whirled away from me and grabbed her bag off the floor. "You're right, Rho. Let's just do the things *you* like."

I opened my mouth, but I was too stunned to speak.

How could she say that to me? Every time she or Deke wanted to do something foolish—sneak into the school kitchen after curfew to steal leftover Cancrian rolls, or crash a university party we were too young to attend, or fake stomachaches to get out of our mandatory morning swims at the saltwater pool complex—I always wound up going along with them, even when I didn't want to. Every single time I was the one who caved.

"Deke, what do *you* think?" shot Nishi.

His hands flew up. "I'm Pisces." Nishi rolled her eyes at the expression, which is what people say when they don't want to take sides in an argument. It comes from the fact that the Twelfth House almost always remains neutral in times of war, as their chief concern is caring for the wounded of every world.

"Forget it." Nishi stormed out of the studio. And for the first time following an argument, I didn't go after her.

Deke got to his feet. "I think one of us should talk to her."

I shrugged. "You go then."

"Rho . . ." His turquoise eyes were as soft as his voice. "Would it really be so bad?"

"You're telling me you actually want to play in front of the whole school?"

"Just the thought of it terrifies me—"

"Then you agree with me!"

"I wasn't finished," he said, his tone firmer now. "It terrifies me, yeah, but . . . that's what's exciting about it. It moves you toward the fear instead of away from it." In a gentler voice, he asked, "Aren't you bored with the redundancy and routine of being an Acolyte? Don't you ever want to escape yourself?"

I shook my head. "I'm fine with being predictable. I don't like surprises."

"All right," he said with a small but exasperated smirk. "You're obviously not listening to me, so I'm going to try Nish. See you at breakfast tomorrow, *Rho Rho*."

Alone in the studio, all I could feel was my anger. Did my friends seriously just abandon me for finally standing up for myself?

I blasted out of the room and charged through the all-gray halls of the quiet compound to my dorm-pod. Once there, I changed out of my Academy blues into my bulky, bandaged space suit with the colorful plastic patches covering snags in the outer fabric.

Curfew was closing in, which meant most people were already in their rooms for the night. But I felt claustrophobic, like the compound was too cramped to contain all my emotions. So I shoved on my helmet and, rather than stuffing my Wave up my glove where it could sync with my suit and provide a communication system, I spiked it on the bed on my way out the door, leaving it. I didn't want to hear from Nishi or Deke.

Then I shot out to the moon's pockmarked face without any of my usual safety checks, my anger so scalding it consumed every thought in my head. In my firestorm of feelings, I forgot Mom's final lesson.

For a moment, I forgot my fears were real.

1

TWELVE TOY ZODAI—DYED DIFFERENT House hues—are arranged in a row. All are missing limbs, a few have been decapitated, and the blue one is just a clay torso with an X slicing its chest.

It's the clearest message the master has sent us yet.

One world down, eleven soon to fall.

Squary is a cold cement bunker on House Scorpio that runs the length of the island it's built beneath. It used to be a weapons testing zone, until Stridents detonated a nuclear device decades ago, and the facility had to be quarantined. It's also where the Marad was working on its secret weapon when the Scorp Royal Guard barged in and arrested the handful of soldiers that had been living here.

Stanton and Mathias stand with Strident Engle at the other end of the room, studying the real star of the scene: the Marad's missile monstrosity, with its nuclear core that has the potential to devastate a whole planet, if operational.

But I hang back by the toys on the table, unable to look away from their mutilated bodies . . . until a blade stabs my arm, slitting my scars open.

I gasp and jump back, hugging myself. I know the pain is just a memory of the real thing, but it still makes me nauseous, and beads of sweat tickle my forehead. I snap my gaze to the guys, hoping they didn't notice.

They didn't.

They're still scoping out the weapon, the three of them indistinguishable from one another in their bulky black radiation suits and facemasks.

"So this is *everything*?"

Stanton's voice breaks the radio silence inside my heavy suit. "Aside from this weapon, five years' worth of compressed meals, and the creepy toys, you didn't find anything else? Nothing to tell us where the Marad's headquartered, or who's leading the army, or what the master's plan is?"

"We found the Risers we arrested." The second voice belongs to Strident Engle, a Zodai in Chieftain Skiff's Royal Guard who's been guiding our visit to House Scorpio.

"Have they said anything yet?" presses Stanton.

"They will, once we find a way to break them."

One of the figures flinches and takes half a step back. That must be Mathias.

"If you couldn't break them in two months, what makes you think they can be broken?" I identify Stanton's shape by his familiar stubborn stance, how he tilts his head and crosses his arms.

"Every man has his breaking point," says the Strident.

"That's ignorant." My brother looks toward Mathias. "Some men are unbreakable."

Mathias doesn't acknowledge the compliment as he ambles away from them. Stan's been praising him a lot since learning of everything he's been through. And yet, even now, my brother's warm words lack actual warmth. There's something else cooling their effect, only I can't tell what it is.

Mathias joins me by the table and stares at the toys. I wonder if he, too, feels Corinthe's blade cutting him open.

"None of the other Houses have any leads or ideas?" I say into the facemask's radio system, mostly to escape my darkening thoughts.

"We agree it's likely they knew we were coming, given they had enough time to make this macabre masterpiece for us," says Engle, recycling the same theory the Houses have been repeating to each other. He and Stanton stride over to join Mathias and me. "And if the Riser who betrayed you—*Aryll*—sent a warning, they had enough time to get rid of anything they didn't want us to find."

Stan turns away from the table. He still can't hear the name of the friend he loved like a brother.

But a different word jumps at me from Strident Engle's answer. This is the second time he's said *Riser* instead of *soldier* or *minion* or *terrorist*, as if the terms were interchangeable.

On every House, it's been the same reaction: a blanket vilification of all Risers out of fear they could become unbalanced.

Fernanda's warning that all Risers will be made to pay for the actions of the Marad grows louder in my head every day, as does Ferez's foretelling of a future forged of Risers. A minority of people who have been ostracized by every House may now decide the Zodiac's fate. Maybe my teachers were right: Maybe happy hearts start with happy homes. Maybe if Risers had been born into a world with a place for them, the master wouldn't be able to manipulate so many into committing murder in the name of hope.

"What's *this* about?" asks Mathias, gesturing to the tableau of toys. It's one of just a few questions he's asked all day. The old Mathias would have demanded to know every detail about the weapon and the captured Marad soldiers, even if it meant violating diplomatic protocol . . . like the time we visited Libra.

Thinking of the Seventh House makes my mouth go dry, and I clear my throat.

"We think it's a message," says Engle. "They're telling us to screw off."

His serious voice is identical to his sarcastic one, so I never know if he's feeling content or contentious. It's the same with every Scorp I've met so far, each one a mystery. But since these days it's impossible to know whom to trust, regardless of House affiliation, it's nice to know I'm in the company of someone Sirna trusts: Engle is a friend from her diplomatic travels.

Then again, maybe that's worse.

After all, friends make for frightening foes.

Mathias bumps my shoulder, and I look up. His facial features are hard to make out through the protective suit's thick membrane, but I can tell he's shaking his head, and he's right—we've searched the rest of Squary and found nothing. Every House that's been through here has yielded the same results. It's time to track down a real lead.

"I think we're done," I say.

"Then I'll take you back below sea level." Strident Engle directs us to an exit: round metal doors built into the floor of every room.

We descend a set of stairs to a canal system that runs beneath the bunker, and the four of us load into a small, unmanned boat that zips through a tangle of tunnels, toward Squary's transportation hub.

Even though Squary is considered one of House Scorpio's "above-ground" settlements, it's technically *in* the ground, since Sconcion's atmosphere isn't breathable. But from the perspective of Scorps who live in waterworlds deep within the ocean's depths, Squary is essentially the surface.

When our boat bumps gently into a dead end, we climb out and pass through a metal decontamination chamber that sterilizes our suits. Then we step inside a busy submarine station where Scorps are rushing along sleek silver floors to locate their gates and catch connecting rides. Timetables on wallscreens display routes and schedules for passenger subs, and a variety of holographic stands offer travelers options for private rentals and chartered trips.

The first thing we do is strip off our heavy suits and deposit them in a designated chute. Without the mask, at last my view is unobstructed. Across from us, floor-to-ceiling windows look into the dark blue ocean, and Stanton and Mathias immediately make their way over to watch the fish parading past, spanning every color in Nature's palette.

It must be nearly sunset because Helios's red rays are setting the top layer of water on fire. Normally I'd be running to the window to check it all out, too. But today I hang back with Engle, watching him as he consults the wallscreen nearest us. I'm still startled by the Strident's translucent skin and scarlet eyes; he hails from Oscuro, the deepest waterworld on Sconcion, which doesn't see sunlight.

"It's not racist to stare at the unknown," he says, suddenly meeting my gaze, "or to be astonished by it."

I feel my cheeks heating up. "I didn't—I'm sorry, it's just—"

"Don't finish that excuse. Just refer to my previous statement."

I wish there was a translation guide for speaking with Scorps. Once again, I've no clue where I stand with Engle.

A news report starts playing on another wallscreen, and my gut clenches as a montage of Cancrians in refugee camps across the Zodiac begins to play. I can't hear the narration over all the noise, but I can imagine what the anchor is saying.

At first the Houses were happy to take our people in and give us aid. One would think that with thirty-four habitable planets—well, thirty-one now—there would be more than enough space for all of us in the Zodiac Solar System.

Then news about Aryll broke.

When the Houses learned there was a Marad Riser hidden among the Cancrian survivors, nearly every government produced a list of reasons why they couldn't keep us anymore. How we're becoming a drain on their resources, how we're interfering with their laws by functioning as a sovereign nation on their soil, how we're selfishly accepting their handouts without working on any long-term solutions. But mainly they're afraid of more Marad soldiers hiding among us.

Virgo's planet Tethys is mostly uninhabitable, but its people had their choice of ten planetoids in their constellation to evacuate to. The Geminin who left Argyr landed on Hydragyr, where the largest number of Cancrians had settled, only now the planet doesn't seem to be big enough for the both of us.

Yet Cancrians have nowhere within our constellation to go. We've no choice but to beg the other Houses for their help. Our financial institutions were obliterated along with our planet, and a few weeks ago our currency was officially canceled across the solar system. So for now, our only options are settling into a refugee camp or moving to a community with a barter system, like Pisces.

"Our ride departs from gate six," says Engle, and I pull away from the broadcast. "Let's go."

I grab my brother and Mathias, and minutes later we're boarding a large passenger sub to Pelagio, one of Sconcion's shallower waterworlds, where Stanton, Mathias, and I have been staying. Engle booked us two rows of seats facing each other; I take the window, and Mathias snags the spot next to me.

My brother slumps into the seat across from mine, his gaze glued to the window as an emerald-green eel glides past. Strident Engle sits beside Stan and beams out a personal holographic screen from his Paintbrush—a fingertip device that's the Scorp equivalent of a Wave—and begins reviewing his messages.

"Good evening, this is Captain Husk speaking," says a man's voice over the intercom. "We anticipate smooth sailing to Pelagio.

Current tidal conditions have us arriving in a little over three hours. Once the seatbelt alert is off, please feel free to visit our restaurant and bar, located in the middle of the vessel. Now prepare for our descent, and enjoy your time on board."

Belt straps automatically slide across our chests, clicking into connectors in our seats. The sub's motion is so smooth that I only know we've started moving when I see the stunning sights swimming past the window. We soar over colorful corals that could be beds of candy, then thread through a forest of reedy underwater trees brimming with small sea creatures, until we arrive at a majestic clearing where the water is endless and diamond bright. Dusky red-purple rays pierce through the blueness like fiery arrows.

More than anything, I want to be out there.

I miss slipping into the Cancer Sea's folds, swimming alongside its turtles and seahorses and changelings, following its familiar currents to my favorite corners of the planet. I'd thought being on another Water House might be restorative . . . but it's only making me feel Cancer's absence more.

A pod of striped dolphins dances outside our window, twirling and playing and trailing along, until we gather speed and plunge into an abyss, leaving the sunlight behind us. Bubbles brush the sub's belly, and schools of fish scatter in our wake as we dive into deeper and darker waters.

I chance a peek at Mathias. His head is leaned back and his eyes are closed. He's been letting his wavy hair grow out, and a light layer of stubble covers the hollows of his cheeks and slight cleft of his chin. It's still hard to accept he's back, when being around him reminds me he's not.

What's up?

His voice tickles my thoughts, and my finger buzzes with the infusion of Psynergy. I look down at my Ring. When we wore the bulky compression suits, I couldn't reach it, but now I can touch the metallic silicon band.

Just not sure what happens next, I send back, staring at the fine black glove hugging my left hand—the one I keep on at all times, since the skin at my fingertips will stay tender until my nails grow back in.

Everyone urged me to heal my arm and get rid of every trace of Corinthe's torture, but that would have meant turning my back on the full truth of my experiences. And I won't do that.

Ferez taught me that the past can coexist with the present, but only if we remember it. So if I cheat the past by trying to change it, I'll risk forgetting it . . . and there are things I can't afford to forget. Like the fact that the young girl in the pink space suit floating on Elara's surface didn't have the chance to heal her body. Neither did the dead of Cancer, Virgo, Gemini, or the armada.

And neither do Risers.

Your brother's having a hard time, says Mathias. *Have you talked to him?*

I look across at Stanton. He's passed out with his holographic headphones on, and the new Wave Sirna was able to get him rests open-faced on his chest. I haven't seen him like this since Mom left—distant, sullen, suspicious. But at least then he had to set those feelings aside to raise me. Now they're just festering within him, sharpening his voice and hardening his heart.

I've tried, I whisper to Mathias through the Psy. *He feels guilty over how much he defended Aryll, and probably embarrassed about being used by him, too. But he won't talk to me about it, and I think that's because . . . because it's my fault.* I'm the reason Aryll used him.

It's the first time I've voiced this belief, and I'm glad it's only happening in my mind and not out loud, because a bubble of emotion blocks my throat.

I don't think that's it. Not at all. Mathias's musical voice is gentle, and he almost sounds like he used to—sure of himself and protective of me.

I think he can't talk to you because he feels he failed you. Aryll used him to get to you, and your brother didn't see him for what he was, so he didn't shield you. Rather than protecting you, he endangered you by bringing him into your life.

I frown at him. *Mathias, this isn't Stanton's fault—*

He shakes his head. *I'm not saying it is. I'm just telling you how he feels because . . . it's how I would feel. If I were him.*

His midnight eyes stare into mine a beat longer, suspending my pulse, and neither of us says anything more.

When my brother and I returned to Capricorn, Mathias stayed with his parents on Taurus for a month and a half, focusing on recovering from the Marad's torture by training with the other Lodestars at the embassy. Then, a couple of weeks ago, he reached out and said he was ready to help, so Stan and I invited him to join us. We haven't yet discussed our kiss or the words we exchanged the night of the celebration on Vitulus . . . which is a good thing, because I'm not sure what I'd say.

Not that it matters, since the note I sent him and Hysan after the attack on Pisces pretty much shut the door on any romantic discussions for a while. I guess I should be grateful Mathias is still talking to me, unlike—

"Apologies for this interruption." Captain Husk's voice over the intercom startles me. "If you'll look out the starboard side, you'll see a Scorpion whale making its way to the surface."

I press my face into the cold glass to get a glimpse of the massive mammal. *"Holy Helios,"* I whisper as its shadow swallows the submarine.

The jet-black whale is impossibly immense—at least ten times as large as this one-hundred-passenger submarine—and its six sets of flippers propel it forward so fast that the sub starts to sway in its waves.

The whale whooshes by.

One second I'm staring at an eyeball the size of *Equinox*, and the next all I see is a snake-like tail whipping past. The whole thing happens so quickly that it feels as surreal and fleeting as a vision in the Psy. I squint up at the hazy horizon to try keeping the whale within view, but it's already lost to the darkness above.

Disappointed, I lower my gaze, and at last I spy the silver lights of Pelagio twinkling in the watery distance.

2

THE SUB SLOWS DOWN AS a bright bubble the size of a moon blooms into being, its glass walls dotted with small lights that sparkle like stars.

On the way to Squary, Strident Engle explained the lights are mechanical *gills*, and they're part of a filtering system that uses electrolysis to split H_2O into particles of oxygen and hydrogen. The air is absorbed for breathing, while the hydrogen gets converted into fuel for powering the waterworld.

Planet Sconcion has a dozen of these waterworlds, each its own sovereign territory. Half of them, including Pelagio, are located in waters shallow enough that city tops crest the ocean's surface; the other half, like Oscuro, are buried in waters so deep that only special Scorp watercrafts can endure the pressure.

Nepturn, Pelagio's capital city, grows larger in the sub's window, looking like a reverse aquarium: Rather than fish wading in water, humans swim through air.

Scorps travel within waterworlds using *waterwings*—metal armbands with vapor jet pack attachments powerful enough to float a person off the ground. Scorps pair the wings with fins that slide over their footwear, enabling wearers to essentially "swim" through the heavy humidity in the air.

We dock into a port along the glass wall to disembark, and then we head down a narrow pathway that leads to Nepturn's transportation hub, where our identities are confirmed and belongings are searched before we're granted passage beyond. We follow the crowd of Scorps bustling along sleek silver floors to the wall of lockers where we stored our waterwings and fins before departing to Squary. Once we've got on our armbands—which are cold and a little constricting—we carry our fins under our arms and make our way to the exit.

"Wandering Star."

I turn to see Sirna, flanked by a Lodestar and a Strident. Smiling, I suppress my impulse to hug her and instead reach out to bump fists.

When I wrapped my arms around her after we arrived on Scorpio a couple of days ago, in front of her full entourage of Stridents and Lodestars, her stance stiffened disapprovingly, and I realized I shouldn't have done it. Sirna is a nurturer by nature, but like most Cancrians, she wears her shell to work and saves her softer side for her personal life.

I guess I just haven't had much affection the past couple of months. Or feminine company. And I miss Nishi more than water.

"How did your visit go?" asks Sirna, once she's traded the hand touch with everyone in our group.

"Uneventful," answers Engle on my behalf.

"No news then?"

"No," I concede. I didn't actually think I'd find anything the other Houses missed, but since the Plenum seemed so eager to arrange this trip when I asked for it, I'd hoped there might be a chance I could help.

Sirna turns to the Lodestar and whispers instructions. He nods and takes off with the Strident, and when Sirna straightens, she looks pleased about something.

"But I'm sure the master is far from done," I caution her. "I'd like to consult with the other teams of Zodai who came through here before giving my report to the Plenum, so please keep this to yourself for now. Anything new from the Marad soldiers in custody?"

Sirna sighs. "Representatives from every House have already tried interrogating them, but they're stoic. The only person any soldiers seem to have opened up to is . . . *you*."

I don't quite meet her sea-blue gaze. "I guess when you're about to murder someone, you stop thinking of them as a person."

Mathias's arm brushes mine, comforting me with his touch. He understands even better than I do how it feels when someone treats you like you're worthless. When they draw on your skin like they own it, reducing you to a replaceable canvas for their hate.

"You must be hungry," says Sirna, and I nod, blinking back my heavy thoughts. "How does dinner sound?"

"I'll tell Link and Tyron to join us," says Engle. "Your treat, right?"

Sirna's mouth twists into something like a smile. "And they say chivalry visited Scorpio and drowned."

"Who needs chivalry when you look this good?" Engle shoots me a wry glance. "Right, Rho? Tell your ambassador how you couldn't keep your eyes off me."

I start to flush just as Stanton steps in. "Is this banter on the agenda, or can we go already? I'm *starving*."

I stare at my brother, not recognizing him. There's no color in his cheeks, no bounce in his curls, no comfort in his pale green gaze.

"Yes, let's go," says Sirna, resuming her professional demeanor. As we're filing out after her, I try catching Stan's attention, but he stays out of my reach.

Outside we're swallowed by the hot breath of a sprawling, spongy city that's immeasurably high, the view softly illuminated by the starry glow of the gills on the glass walls. The landscape before us unfolds in a rainbow of colors, and once more I have a hard time reconciling the lighthearted look of this world with the dark nature of the Scorps I've met.

I slip my fins over my boots and hit the unlock sequence for my waterwings; the vapor jet packs jitter nervously for a moment, then my feet rise off the sandy ocean floor as I float into the humid atmosphere, like a feather flying against the wind. When I'm up in the air, my worries stay on the ground, and I finally feel free.

The four of us fall in line behind Sirna, and we merge with a school of Scorps headed downstream. It feels good to swim again, even if it is without water. But it's harder going from having the whole ocean to explore to being trapped inside an air bubble.

We pick up speed, swimming in sync with the Scorps around us, until we're a tightly woven team riding an air current we're creating together. With every corner we round, we shuffle and reposition ourselves; travelers who are exiting cycle to the outermost lane, while those who have a longer journey stay put in the middle.

Their bright colors make Nepturn's blocky buildings easy to avoid, and their spongy texture is pliant enough that even if a person flew off course and hit a wall, they'd be protected by its plushy pores. Once Sirna starts cycling over to the outer lane, the rest of us follow suit, and moments later, we peel away from the group, toward a blue building taller than the ones surrounding it: the visitors' burrow.

Scorps are the Zodiac's innovators; throughout the ages, they have been the inventors of our most groundbreaking and galactically coveted technology. The tech industry on Scorpio is so cutthroat that companies are intensely competitive with each other, making corporate espionage a constant concern—which is why the House operates under extreme conditions of confidentiality. And if there's anyone a Scorp distrusts more than a fellow Scorp, it's someone from another House.

Sconcion doesn't get many visitors because Scorps make it difficult for outsiders to obtain visas. Approved tourists are put up in a city's visitors' burrow, where a Strident is assigned as their guide to monitor their movements and limit their access to privileged information.

When we land on the burrow's rooftop, we stuff our waterwings and fins in lockers; air swimming is forbidden indoors. Up close the structure's spongy surface feels fuzzy yet sturdy, and random debris—shells, sand, stones—packs its pores. The temperature is refreshingly cooler inside, and we take a lift down to the dining hall in the belly of the building, an enormous room that spans the full floor.

The scent of fresh seafood tickles my nose as a cacophony of voices assaults my ears; even though the burrow isn't very booked, the hall is swarming with curious locals who want to hear the latest news from other worlds.

Long communal tables line the room. We grab drinks and silverware from a stand by the entrance, then we survey the space until we spot Link and Tyron waving to us from one of the tables near the back wall, the one closest to the hall's oceanic wallscreen.

As soon as I sit down, a holographic menu pops up in front of me, and I tap to make my selections—grilled blacktail filet with a peppered seaweed salad. When I submit my order, the hologram vanishes.

Link and Tyron already have their meals, but only Link has started eating. "So? See something the rest of us missed, *Wandering Star?*" he asks through his mouthful of food. "Find another secret message from your boogeyman? Planning to get more of us killed with an encore armada?"

When I open my mouth to answer, he obnoxiously slurps up an octopus tentacle and chews it loudly. Yesterday's Stanton and Mathias would have jumped in to defend me by now, but they're different people today, too busy fighting their own demons to shield me from my detractors.

"Ease off, Link," says Engle, studying me closely. "It's not her fault the person behind these attacks is messing with her head. She's just a little girl trying to play a grown-up's game."

I glare at Engle, though I don't get the impression he's being serious; more than anything I think he's trying to provoke me into a reaction. And if he's testing me, that means he hasn't formed his opinion yet—so I still have the chance to earn his respect.

"Give me your Ephemeris," I say.

"What for?"

"So I can call my boogeyman."

Engle's red eyes widen a fraction, but Link leans forward with interest. Since he and Tyron are from Pelagio, their sallow skin isn't as translucent as Engle's, and their eyes are a darker and less striking shade of red.

"My night just got interesting," says Link, nudging Engle's arm. "Do it. Give it to her."

Engle and I are still measuring each other, neither of us willing to look away first. "Why don't you use yours?" he asks me.

"Don't have it with me," I say. When he doesn't react, I lower my voice. "You're not scared, are you?"

He cracks a cold smile. "Not scared . . . just wondering what your game is."

"Thought you said this wasn't my game. That I'm just a little girl getting played." I cock my head and arch my eyebrows. "But grown men like you aren't scared of monsters, because you don't believe in them. Right?" The lines around his eyes harden, and I know I'm finally getting under his skin. *So pass me your Ephemeris.*

"That's enough," says Sirna, who's sitting to the other side of Engle. He flinches and looks at her suddenly, brows furrowed, and I get the sense she pinched his skin under the table.

Free at last, I lower my gaze and blink. Just then, a shadow falls over me, and I lean back as drones descend on the stone table, dropping off our dinner before flying back to the kitchen.

As I'm chewing my first bite of buttery fish, the enormous wallscreen beside us flickers on, and a holographic newscast begins. "We interrupt your night with breaking news: We've just been alerted that an announcement about the Marad is forthcoming from the Planetary Plenum."

The food slides tastelessly down my throat, and the whole place falls silent at once. I whip my face to Sirna's, but she doesn't meet my gaze. *What announcement?* Why didn't she mention that there was news earlier?

"Ambassador Crompton's transmission will begin at any moment," says the newscaster, "so stay with us as we await this latest update."

A montage of recycled news packages begins to play as the station fills the airtime. "The Marad first came on the galactic scene by instigating and later escalating the conflict between Sagittarians and migrant workers from Lune"—another Scorp waterworld—"but as our network was first to report, the Wayfare Treaty has at last quelled that conflict. So where did the army go after Sagittarius?

"The Marad—allegedly made up of Risers—brought its savagery to the others Houses, including our own, when they sabotaged the air supply in Oscuro, killing dozens of our people." I glance at Engle's downcast face, and as his hand clenches into a fist, I wonder if he lost someone in the attack.

"Given the random and inconsistent nature of their strikes, it's impossible to know what they're truly after. They've hijacked hostages and cargo from ships all across Zodiac Space, assassinated Elders on House Aquarius, set off explosions on Leo, blown up part of the Zodiax on Tierre, and, most recently, targeted Piscene planetoid Alamar, which fell victim to a technological strike that knocked out their communication grid and shut down their network for nearly two galactic months."

The screen cuts back from the montage of images to the somber-faced newscaster. "And now, silence. But have they finished with us, or are they planning their next attack? With no enemy to battle, and no new violence to point the way, how can our Zodai protect us? And how much longer must we hold our breath, waiting for our leaders to tell us what they know? This reporter believes if we don't breathe soon, we will drown."

New footage starts playing of an Ariean Zodai University student a few years older than me named Skarlet Thorne.

"New voices are emerging in our leaders' silence," says the newscaster as we watch the stunningly beautiful Skarlet speaking at a rally on Phobos, the Ariean planet where the Marad was first discovered. Zodai from all over the Zodiac have been scouting the location in the hopes of finding clues.

Skarlet's clear, strong voice rings over the gathered crowd of Ariean Academy and University students. "If it's true the Marad is comprised of Risers, then we already know what they want. It's what we would all want were we in their position: *acceptance*."

Even though I've seen this news clip before, I can't help nodding along to her words. Skarlet is one of the rare people proposing empathy for Risers, but unlike Fernanda, who deflects the issue of unbalanced Risers in favor of defending the whole race, Skarlet skirts the politics by narrowing her focus simply to finding a solution. "We're fighting to defend our homes, but Risers are fighting for their right to have one—"

Skarlet cuts out abruptly, her speech replaced by the image of a forty-something Aquarian man with pink sunset eyes who's standing beneath a holographic banner bearing all the House symbols. Standing in the background behind Crompton are a handful of Aquarian Advisors.

There's a small delay while he waits to speak, and then he beams a warm smile before beginning his announcement. "Brothers and sisters across the Zodiac, I come before you on behalf of my fellow ambassadors with happy news following a long season of darkness.

"For months, Zodai from every House have been investigating the Marad's hideout on Squary. I can now announce that we have found absolutely no evidence of future attacks, beyond the unfinished weapon that is no longer a threat, as it's currently in our custody. Consequently, today—which is a relative term, as we are scattered across the solar system, leading dozens of different todays—"

Some of the Elders behind him frown and clear their throats, and his smile falters. "As I say, on this day, in House Scorpio, our own Wandering Star, Rhoma Grace, has visited Squary—"

I gasp at my name, and trade startled stares with Stanton and Mathias.

"—and she, too, has found no concrete proof of anything to fear. Therefore, it is with great hope and relief that this Plenum is ready once more to declare Peace in our Zodiac."

3

I GLOWER AT SIRNA, BUT she keeps her gaze steady on the wallscreen.

I should be used to betrayal by now. And yet, each time it feels like a fresh slap across the face that I never saw coming.

Until this moment I actually thought I was here because the Plenum wanted my insight. I thought Sirna wanted my help. But what they wanted was a mascot.

I hate that Engle was right: Anywhere I turn, I'm stuck playing somebody else's game.

My stomach seals itself off, and I can't touch the food on my plate. I know I'll regret this in the middle of the night when my appetite returns with a vengeance, but I can't stay near Sirna another moment. She manipulated me, just like the other Ambassadors.

This whole time, she's been using me, and like a fool I thought we were friends.

"Rho, don't—" starts Stanton, but I'm already standing up.

"I'll see you upstairs."

I hear Mathias begin to object, but I move quickly so his words can't catch up. Each of us has our own room, so I take the lift to one of the burrow's higher floors, and then I lock my door with the controls on my wristband and drop onto the waterbed.

Rolling onto my side, I stare out the window; from this high up, I have a bird's-eye view of Nepturn's colorful buildings that's occasionally obstructed by schools of Scorps. Since there's no weather to worry about, the window is glassless, and thin privacy curtains are scrunched up on either side of the opening. The air-cooling technology inside the burrow is powerful enough that the outside humidity doesn't dampen it.

The window is outfitted with a laser alarm system, which can be activated from my burrow-issued bracelet. The black, rubbery band also controls the room's locks and lights. The mattress sloshes as I sit up and open my Wave, and once the holographic menus beam out, I call Nishi.

Unsurprisingly, she doesn't answer. I can rarely reach her anymore. Stan and Mathias keep telling me she needs space to deal with Deke's death. But what hurts is that no one seems to realize I lost Deke, too.

For five years, Nishi, Deke, and I operated as a single unit. I only left Oceon 6 because I thought I was fighting for a future for *all of us*. And now, Deke and Dad are gone, Nishi and Hysan are absent, and Stanton and Mathias are ghosts of their former selves.

Wiping away the tears from my eyes, I sigh inwardly, and though I promised myself I wouldn't, I hail 'Nox.

Some of my tension starts to melt away as my surroundings transform into the familiar glass nose of my favorite ship; at least my automatic access hasn't been revoked. A tall man with white hair and quartz eyes stands at the helm, his face revealing no surprise at my unannounced arrival.

"Lady Rho," says the Libran Guardian in his sonorous voice, "how wonderful to see you. I hope Scorpio is treating you well."

"It is. Thank you, Lord Neith." My heartbeat races as my gaze greedily scans the space beyond him for a glimpse of Hysan. "How is . . . everything?"

"I've been well since our last check-in, thank you for asking."

After Pisces was attacked, it was Neith who answered the message I sent Hysan and Mathias. The regal android informed me that Hysan would be out of reach for some time but assured me he would stay in touch in his stead.

"Have you come to discuss the Plenum's misguided Peace declaration?"

"I . . . have," I admit, and Neith's perceptive quartz eyes soften with pitch-perfect humanity.

"I understand. You were hoping Hysan would be here to comfort you, yet you've found me instead," he says matter-of-factly. "I realize I'm a poor substitute, Lady Rho, but if I may, I would like to say something."

I feel the muscles of my face relaxing, and I hear the smile in my voice as I say, "Lord Neith, you are *never* a poor substitute, and I would love to hear anything you have to say."

"That is very kind of you." He bows his head humbly before continuing. "I have always found it interesting that the symbol for Justice is a set of scales; the implication being that to achieve perfect harmony, good and bad must balance each other out. Rather than eradicating one, both must exist in equal quantities."

"That's depressing," I say flatly, remembering how Ochus once said something similar to me. "Why fight the Marad if the outcome can't change?"

"You fight them for the same reason they fight you—to tip the scales. Yet they hold an advantage over you: They're already aware that bad must exist alongside good, and they're equally aware that you don't want to accept that. Which is why their best strategy is to wear you down, to make you feel small and powerless and alone . . . because once you stop fighting them, they'll win."

I feel my head shaking involuntarily. "And how is that fair?"

A laugh—short, bark-like—escapes Lord Neith's lips. I had no idea androids could laugh. "And who said justice was fair?" he asks, his white teeth sparkling at the look of indignation that must be overtaking my face.

"Is it *fair* that for millennia most members of the Zodiac have had a home, a family, an identity, while we ignore the ugly fact that the stars like to quietly pluck people from our midst and curse them with a condition without a cure that changes them from the inside out? Is it *justice* if those cursed souls now band together to retaliate for what their people have endured, and continue to endure, due to the Houses' ignorance and prejudice and disinterest?"

Neith shakes his head sadly as he goes on. "There can be no universal standard for justice or fairness, Lady Rho, for they are concepts that can only be defined in context; a villain is only a villain from the hero's point of view. There is no universal right or wrong because there can be no universal judge. Existence is too complicated and nuanced for such simplicity. And that is why the bad must exist alongside the good . . . because to eradicate one is to eradicate both."

I blow out a hard breath as I process Neith's revelation. "Then . . . what's the solution?"

"If one exists," he says softly, coming around the control helm so there's nothing between us, "then it must be what the wisest among us have known all along." He towers over me, and I have to arch my neck back to keep my eyes on his. "The only way to have a just society is to *remember each other*. Down to the last individual, without discounting any person or population, without ignoring people we would rather not see, even those whose values we revile. Do you think this is possible for any civilization to accomplish?"

"I don't know," I whisper. "Do you?"

He doesn't speak, but the expression on his Kartex face is so compassionate that it feels like a reply, even if it's a non-answer. I guess the question was rhetorical.

Neith's ideas have left me feeling the way I do after speaking with Sage Ferez, like too many thought bubbles are multiplying exponentially in my head, and soon I'll run out of space. But before my brain bursts, my heart intervenes, and my mind moves from brilliant Neith to his beyond brilliant creator.

For weeks, I've been trying to wall off my memories of Hysan, but my feelings are impossible to forget. And as my heart rarely follows my mind's orders, it's now battering my chest, reminding me how much harder it beats in his presence.

"Where's Hysan?" Every muscle in my body tenses on speaking his name.

"I'm not permitted to say."

I frown. "We're supposed to be working together, not playing trust games," I say, hearing my words growing heated. "I need to know he's okay . . . and if he's found out anything that could convince the Plenum to change their ruling and take the master more seriously, he has to share it now. Please, Lord Neith, I really need to know where he is—"

"I'm not permitted to say," Neith calmly repeats. "I apologize, Lady Rho, I'm not trying to be difficult; I am simply programmed not to relay that information."

"Oh . . . sorry." I stare at the ground to keep Neith from seeing the depth of my disappointment, even though I'm sure he's already perceived it.

The truth is, even if Hysan were still talking to me, nothing has changed. Maybe he was right that I was too afraid to love him—but that doesn't matter now. As Wandering Star, I'm once again in the Guardians' ranks, even if I don't have an official vote; and while the Taboo technically only applies to Guardians, we'd still be violating the spirit of the law.

Our universal unity is too fragile to stir up over just two hearts. The Trinary Axis already proved that.

"If I might be so bold as to share yet another observation," says Neith, pausing until I've met his gaze and nodded for him to go on. "Sending that message to Hysan was the admirable thing to do.

As you said, there will be time to work out everything else that's between you, but for now, you each have different tasks that require your full attention. While I cannot provide more details on Hysan's whereabouts, I can at least assure you that he is doing his part. Whatever happens between you two personally, please trust that he and I will always stand with you and House Cancer."

His quartz eyes twinkling, he adds, *"I swear it on my father's life."*

After a heavy pause, I manage to say, "Thank you." How is it an android is able to restore my faith in humanity so much better than humans?

"Hysan aside," I add, "I hope you know, Lord Neith, that I am honored by your friendship."

"And I by yours, Wandering Star." He gives me a low bow, and as he starts to straighten, the smile on my face freezes.

His torso twitches jerkily, stopping at an odd angle, and the light in his eyes flickers. "L-lord Neith?" But before the words are even out, he's upright again, his eyes as lively and human as ever.

"Take care, Lady Rho," he says, as if nothing happened. Then the holographic ship disappears, and I'm alone again.

✦ ✦ ✦

Long after 'Nox's nose has faded from the room's walls, I'm still staring into them, thinking of Mom. I've been scouring the Psy for a sign of her every day since realizing it was *her* face Rising into an Aquarian, and not mine.

As much as I want to uncover and defeat the master, I've finally found something else I want just as desperately.

I want to find out what happened to my mother.

If she really took off to spare us the stigma of staining our family's reputation, just as Grey/Aryll did, then maybe she went to House Aquarius.

And maybe she's still there.

I'm desperate to discover if the black seashell Aryll gave me is the real thing, or if, like him, it's just a very convincing imitation. Then again, where could Aryll have learned so many details from my childhood if not from Mom?

I'd give anything to take off to the Water Bearer constellation and start searching for her this instant. Except my focus can't be love or revenge or even family anymore. I'm not allowed personal missions, not after the promises I made to everyone I met on Centaurion. So instead, I shake those thoughts off, shut the room's fabric curtains, and grab Vecily's heart-shaped Ephemeris.

Rho?

My finger buzzes as Mathias calls to me through the Psy. *Are you okay?*

Even though he hasn't knocked, I have a feeling he's outside my room. I bring up my wristband to unlock the door, but I stop short—I need all my concentration right now. And Mathias is one of my heart's favorite distractions.

I'm doing a reading, I send back through the Collective Conscious. *But thanks for checking in.*

After a moment, he says, *Find me after?*

Sure.

When I hear his footsteps fade away, I flick on the device in my hand. Silver light drowns the room as the twelve constellations of our solar system take form, and I focus on the Fourth House. Cancer's blue blaze is drowned by the rocky ring of rubble orbiting it, and the places where our four moons once shone are now dense patches of Dark Matter.

It looks like the planet is wearing a necklace, and I'm reminded of the pearls Mom gave me so many moons ago. My soul drifts back to that day on the Strider, and I can almost see Helios glinting off Mom's light locks and ivory features. Were her paling hair and skin signs of her transition into an Aquarian? How much more did we never know about her?

I'm so deeply Centered that I don't immediately notice when he appears.

Galactic gold coin for your thoughts, crab?

I suck in a quick breath as I turn and meet Ophiuchus's black-hole eyes. My body grows leaden with dread as the mist of Psynergy around him solidifies into icy skin and Ochus manifests in the star-dappled air.

I-I've been searching for you for months, I say, trying to sound stronger than I feel. *Where have you been?*

Only Helios may command her stars, he warns, the temperature in my room dropping rapidly as his full frigid form expands into being, taking up most of the space. I have to cross my arms over my chest to keep warm.

The last time you showed up, you told me Risers are descendants of your House. My voice quakes as I finally form the question I've been burning to ask since that day: *But if Risers really are Ophiuchans, why aren't whole bloodlines affected? Wouldn't whole families change Houses if they're descended from your line?*

Ochus's booming voice makes the air colder. *Only the truest Ophiuchans cannot fit into another House. Every time a bonafide Ophiuchan is born, he must eventually Rise.*

I exhale slowly, holding myself tightly while considering his answer. I don't know the values of House Ophiuchus—beyond Unity—so I have no way to evaluate whether I might also be a Riser. I guess I could just ask the Thirteenth Guardian himself.

I meet Ophiuchus's gaze again, but something in his expression silences me.

You've changed, he says icily, his black eyes growing larger as he takes me in.

Yeah, turns out torture, murder, and destruction can be pretty transformative, I shoot back before I can consider the consequences.

My stomach clenches preemptively, and to stave off punishment for my sarcasm, I quickly add, *If you still want me to help end your existence, tell me where the Marad is so I can stop the master.*

I don't know their location. His voice is like a low rumble that threatens thunder. *The master still has plans, and he cares as little for his soldiers' lives as he does yours. Every one of us is a pawn in his game. We are all victims here.*

I can't trap the cold, cutting laugh that escapes my lips; a sound so chilling it doesn't seem mine. *You don't get to wear the word victim. It could never fit you.*

Ochus shoots upward, taking over every particle of air. His form melts into a violent ice storm, and I bury my head in my arms to escape the wintry wind whipping against me, the glacial gales nearly lifting me off the ground.

Icicles stab my skin like knife blades, and I gasp, cowering close to the floor, my left arm and nail-free fingers scorching with pain, like the wounds are fresh. My eyes burn and my heart hammers so hard I'm sure it will give out, until I can't take it anymore, and I just want him to kill me already. I just want it to be over.

The violence vanishes at once, but I stay small on the floor, holding my limbs to my chest, trying to slow my breathing.

You are weak, he booms in a voice colder than his storm. *You have never shown fear in here, not even when you believed I would kill you.*

I refuse to look up, refuse to believe his words. He's trying to protect Risers. He's making excuses so he won't have to tell me anything about the Marad—

You are of no use to me now.

A light draft shushes past me, and the temperature rises. He's gone. Relieved, I unclench my muscles and lift my head.

Then I freeze again. Ochus is sitting down beside me.

I'm barely breathing as I gape at the Thirteenth Guardian, his body so close to mine that his icy Psynergy burns my skin. My gut fills with foreboding as his primordial eyes stare into me. *You believe personal loss and physical pain are the worst things you can endure?*

His voice is a whisper, so small it slips in through my pores, chilling me from the inside. *There is worse*, he says softly. *There is being* alone.

A feeling that isn't bloodlust or hatred pulls on his features. The mortal emotion makes him look less familiar and more frightening.

When you are an exile with no home, no personal agency, no living loved ones, no hope to keep you sane, no sign of an end to your despair— that *is when you are truly dead.*

I'd like to point out the hypocrisy of what he's saying, given *he's* the reason I lost my home and loved ones—he did to me the very thing he claims was done to him—but I don't want to provoke more physical pain. So instead, I say, *I'm not alone. I still have a few loved ones left you haven't killed.*

Alone has nothing to do with how many people surround us. He sounds distant, as if his Center is ebbing away from our conversation. *Loneliness is a condition of the soul. Once it infects you, you must suck it out, like Maw poison, before it reaches your heart. Especially* you.

His voice and gaze grow present again, and I feel his focus shifting from himself back to me. *Your soft, Cancrian heart could never survive true loneliness.*

I've been learning more and more what my heart can endure, I snap. *And it's not as soft as you think.*

I wouldn't say that so proudly, crab. Your soft heart is the very thing that makes you Cancrian. Lose it, and you lose yourself.

My teeth chatter not from the temperature but from the fear I've been harboring since I first saw the Aquarian face in my stars. The possibility that I could Rise.

A little unsolicited advice? Ochus expands again, growing more transparent as his ice starts to melt. *Trust someone. It's what I didn't have. And it might be what saves you.*

Where is the Marad? I demand as he fades.

You cannot help me anymore, he whispers, and soon all that remains of him is a mist of Psynergy.

4

THE LIGHTS OF VECILY'S EPHEMERIS glimmer in the darkness around me as I sit on the spongy floor and suck in deep breaths, trying to process my conversation with Ochus. Is he done helping me? Does that mean he's going back to the master?

"RHO!" My brother bangs on my door. "*Open up!*"

I unlock it with my wristband, and he barges in, shouting, "There's news!"

Then he rushes back out, and I scramble to my feet and run to catch up. "Where are we going?" I call after him.

"Sirna's stateroom!"

"Did you tell Mathias?"

I don't hear his answer because he's already rounded the corner, so just in case, I stop and turn toward Mathias's door.

I'm outside, I send, touching my Ring.

Come in, he sends back.

When I look inside, he's sitting on his waterbed, wearing a dreamy look on his face that I caught him wearing once before, on Tierre. "What's up?" he asks.

"Stan says there's news."

It takes a moment for my words to break through his expression, and then he grabs the Wave sitting next to him and joins me.

"Were you just talking to Pandora?" I ask as we hurry down the hall.

"I . . . was. Is everything okay?"

"I don't know," I say, feeling less comfortable than I was a moment ago. "They're waiting for us in Sirna's stateroom."

When an ambassador from another House or waterworld visits Pelagio in non-Plenum times, they're put up in a stateroom on the topmost floor of the visitors' burrow. The door to Sirna's suite is wide open, and inside we find her, Engle, and Stanton watching the same somber newscaster from earlier on a wallscreen. I avoid her gaze as I turn my attention to the reporter.

"We're coming to you with more breaking news, this time from House Pisces. We have just received word that an epidemic is plaguing Piscenes of all five planetoids. All we know of this illness so far is that it's causing people to fall into comatose states without warning. It's unclear how they're becoming infected, but healers are reporting new cases at an alarming rate, and quarantine procedures are already underway."

I exchange panicked looks with Stan and Mathias as my pulse triples its speed.

"Prophet Marinda has asked the Houses to send help," the reporter goes on. "Disciples from her Royal Guard believe the stars are punishing the Fish constellation for not foreseeing the Marad's threat; however, our viewers will be pleased to hear that our own Stridents are already en route to diagnose the *true* cause."

"We already know the cause—it's the Marad!" Stanton's shout is so loud and sudden that we all jump.

"Anything they touch, they destroy!"

"The Marad's attack was a targeted strike on one planetoid's communication grid," Sirna snaps at him. "*This* is a virus infecting Piscenes of every planetoid. There is absolutely no evidence linking it to the army, and you hurt our cause and Cancer's credibility when you make unfounded accusations like those."

I pointedly raise the volume of the broadcast.

"Those Piscenes who do not yet show signs of the affliction are asking for immediate sanctuary at other Houses," the newscaster continues. "An anonymous Advisor on Chieftain Skiff's Council has said our Guardian plans to propose a galactic quarantine of the Twelfth House, and I believe anyone of sound mind will agree. Whatever is happening on Pisces, it *must* be contained to that constellation. We are also hearing that there is no correlation between this epidemic and the Marad attack from a few months ago, nor Wandering Star Rhoma Grace's alleged Thirteenth House."

"This is a load of sharkshit!" snarls Stanton.

"Stan—"

My words die as he hurls his new Wave at the wall. Everyone flinches as the golden clamshell shatters into pieces.

"The only answer is war," he says savagely, passing a trembling hand through his blond curls, revealing eyes that are bloodshot from a lack of sleep. "We need to round up teams of Zodai from every House to form our own army, and then we need to smoke the bastards out and *end this*."

"That decision isn't up to you or Rho—it's for the Plenum to decide," injects Sirna.

Ignoring her, my brother comes over to me and actually meets my eyes for what feels like the first time since I showed him Mom's seashell. I'd thought for sure he'd want to discuss that discovery with me, but he's barely looked at me until now.

"Rho, use your Wandering Star status to convene an emergency session." He takes my hands in his. "I know I'm asking for too much, for you to set yourself against the Zodiac, **again**. But this time, I promise to be by your side through everything. You won't be alone."

Everyone is now watching us instead of the news. Looking into my brother's pale green eyes, my memory flashes back to the bioluminescent microbes from the inner lagoon on Kalymnos, and I see us dipping our feet in the cool water and tracing constellations in the microbes' designs. I never imagined my brother ever asking me for anything—and I certainly never envisioned myself denying him.

While the room awaits my answer, I scan the wallscreen again, and instead of the reporter speaking, it's Skarlet. She's broadcasting live from the Hippodrome on Phaetonis, addressing a crowd of Arieans that's made up of both Zodai *and* soldiers. For the first time in decades, the House's military government and the Zodai they've marginalized are sitting side by side.

Last week, it was reported that Guardian Eurek's house arrest had been lifted and that he was invited to a sit-down with the junta's twelve warlocks. Skarlet's hopeful words are healing her House's old wounds and bringing Aries back into the Zodiac fold.

"Most of us become who we are by living up to the standards set by our superiors, our role models, and our families," she begins, her clear voice cutting through the tension. "But Risers have no one to look up to. What kind of existence can they hope to achieve in our worlds when we've offered them no path to success? No home? No chance at happiness?

"We Arieans are warriors, and true warriors do not think of violence as a weapon. Violence is a shield we must sometimes put on to protect our loved ones, and it is always the final form of defense. It's now up to us to teach this to the members of the Marad. If we can offer them something they want—something hopeful—maybe we can find a solution without unnecessary bloodshed."

My heart swells at Skarlet's words, and as I feel the forgotten bond between Houses Aries and Cancer, my mind ticks toward a decision. I always thought Aries must be Cancer's polar opposite, but I was wrong—we're sisters.

Skarlet is right that war should be a last resort. But Stanton is right, too—we must take aggressive actions to stop the Marad . . . even if I don't like seeing my brother so violent and vengeful, and I'd rather not validate those feelings.

"I'd like to invoke my Wandering Star status to create a commission to open up a large-scale investigation into the Marad, and I'd like to invite Skarlet to join me in addressing the Plenum about this. I think if our Houses present our case together, we'll have a better chance."

"I'm sorry, but no."

It takes me a second to process Sirna's speedy rejection, and before I do, Stanton is already shouting, *"What do you mean NO?"*

"You lack the authority to call a Plenum meeting," says Sirna, looking at me and ignoring my brother. "Your role is symbolic only. The Plenum can call you in for consultations, but that privilege does not work both ways."

"THAT'S—"

"Peace has been declared," says Sirna, cutting off my brother's renewed outrage. "There are more pressing matters to attend to."

"Sirna," I say before Stan can respond. "You don't really believe that the Marad's threat is over, do you?" I point to Mathias, who's stoically watching us without giving any indication of what he's thinking. Beside him, Engle is just as inscrutably silent. "Mathias can tell you this isn't just a handful of terrorists. This is an organized army that has been planning these attacks for too long to stop now. We have to learn from each experience, or we'll never be ready for what's ahead. We can't reset to zero after every tragedy."

"All you have are words. Yet you know nothing of running worlds," says Sirna, hard lines cracking her smooth ebony face. "Right now we have to focus on taking care of the people who are still alive, not avenging the ones who are gone."

"Since when do governments focus only on one task at a time? We can divide our resources—"

"Our people are being pushed out of refugee camps on every House. The Piscene people are facing an epidemic we know nothing about. Food shortages from the attack on Tethys are affecting every House. And you want us to invest *what* resources into catching faceless, nameless bad guys, about whom we still know nothing, and who haven't attacked us in months?" Her dark skin is suffused with red undertones from her rising temper. "You cannot twist every bad thing that happens into fuel for your blood thirst. We are Cancrians, and it is our duty to be caregivers, not warriors."

"It's our duty to be protectors, not cowards," I counter as the same angry heat sears my own skin. "What about the agents from the Cancrian Secret Service? You embedded them into the Marad months ago, and now they've completely cut off communication and are most likely dead. What did they die for if we turn our backs now?"

Sirna glares at me, and it's as if the past few months never happened. I see the disappointment in her face, and suddenly we're back at our first meeting in the Hippodrome on Aries, when she accused me of trying to gain more followers for my "Ochus cult."

A loud sound rips my gaze away, and I turn to see Stanton abruptly blasting out of the room, leaving only his shattered Wave behind. Mathias and Engle follow him out, and then it's just Sirna and me and our oversized Cancrian feelings. They seem to take up physical space in the room.

"I know you don't agree, and I know it sounds heartless," she starts, her tone tight and tense, like she's working hard to pick out the right words, "but I took an oath to serve Cancer, and that oath comes before everything else. The person in power always changes, and that is why I don't serve people. I serve my House, and I will always act in its best interest. This is who I am, Wandering Star. I care for you, and I want us to be friends. But Cancer comes first. Always."

"I understand, Sirna—"

"Not yet you don't." She's still speaking slowly, as if she's trying to prevent her emotions from leaking out with her words. "You're young, and the young tend to take everything personally. But it's *imperative* that you learn to separate self from duty."

"You think I take this personally because I'm *young?*"

I try keeping my tone as restrained as hers, but my racing heartbeat makes my voice shake. "I've never been young, Sirna. I didn't have that luxury. I take my duty to Cancer personally because it's my life. *My life*. This isn't a job I trained and applied for. My whole world was taken over when House Cancer called me to serve. The stars asked me to step up, and I did, and then when I proved to be my own person and not a pawn who'd do the powers' bidding, my own people betrayed me and kicked me out to the streets.

"Then, a few months later, those same people changed their minds and asked me back to help them—and, foolish forgiving Cancrian that I am, I dared to believe it'd be different this time. That the friendships I made were real. That my faith in my own people wasn't misplaced. And then this morning you stuck a dagger in my back."

Sirna's nostrils flare, and she purses her lips, and I can tell she's working just as hard as I am to keep from shouting. I can't believe after everything we've been through, I still can't trust her. But I guess that's always been my problem—refusing to see people as they are.

"A word of advice before you go, *friend*," she says softly, and my gut hardens at her deadly tone. "You need to get your emotions under control. Because like it or not, you're in the public eye, and you represent something far greater than yourself. Your life is no longer your own. Do what you need to adjust to that reality, and then *adjust*—before the sea rises, and you find yourself unprepared. *Again*."

I glare at her, too afraid to speak for fear of shouting and proving her right.

"Taking things personally is another luxury you've not been afforded," she whispers, her sea-blue eyes flashing. "And if I were you, I'd go find your brother and give him the same message."

5

MY WAVE GOES OFF ALMOST the exact moment I slam the door to my room. I accept the call, and Nishi's holographic form blooms out.

The sight of her beautiful face is the only antidote to my anger, like a bolt of light chasing out darkness. Her hologram stays frozen a moment before activating, and I notice she's let her bangs grow out, and there's a shimmer of life in her amber eyes again.

"Rho! I'm so sorry I haven't been in touch. I got your messages, though. So you're on Scorpio? What's it like there?"

I hear how cheery she sounds, and now the delay in my reaction isn't simply from the transmission. Of course I want Nishi to be happy, but I just hope she's handling her emotions in a healthy way—as a go-go-go Sagittarian, she can sometimes take and do and feel things in extremes.

"It's a really stunning world, filled with spongy, bright buildings. We literally swim through air to get around, and earlier today I even saw a Scorpion whale. But what about you? Are you home?"

"No . . . I'm on Aquarius."

My heart stalls as she speaks.

"I've been hard to reach because I got tapped to join a new political movement of young people who are fighting for unity and acceptance across the Houses—basically, the same things we've been fighting for. It's called the Tomorrow Party."

It takes me a moment to hear her past my shock. Could it be coincidence that Nishi is on the very House I long to visit? Or is this the stars' idea of a joke?

"Now that the Plenum has declared Peace," she goes on, "which we both know won't last long, we have a window to woo more people to our cause. There are some big plans in the works, and I know you'll want to be part of this movement, so *please* say you'll come to planet Primitus!"

Her words are so perfect that I'm afraid to trust they're real. After so many months spent in pursuit of the smallest hint of hope, I'm not sure how to react when faced with so much of it.

Is it possible the stars aren't messing with me? Could they actually be answering my call? Could I have finally found the "right" reason to go to Aquarius?

Or, says a vicious voice in my mind, *maybe you're just looking for justifications to do what you want.* Maybe Sirna's right about me. Maybe I've been selfish this whole time.

"I'll . . . think about it," I say at last. "Let me check with the guys."

"When you're ready, let me know. I'll send for you."

She's obviously not being literal—Nishi's family might be rich, but not rich enough to arrange for private inter-House travel. Still, I agree to reach out soon with my answer. We have a few minutes left to catch up, so I fill her in on Squary and Stanton and Sirna, but before she can give me any advice, she has to jump off to attend a Party meeting.

"Rho," she says before going, "do you remember when I signed us up for the musical showcase at the Academy?"

Almost immediately I feel a tidal wave of fear pulling me under, the tug of that memory so powerful that I'm afraid of wasting what breath I have left on speaking.

"You were mad at me for leading us in a new direction," says Nishi, oblivious to what's going on inside me, "but in the end you loved our band. So trust me when I say that if you join me here, you'll find what you're looking for—just like I did."

Her voice and image disappear, and I let the memory drown me.

✦ ✦ ✦

I've never told anyone what happened that night. What I did was so foolish that I was afraid to confess it to Stan, Nishi, or Deke. Seeing their reactions would be confirmation of how recklessly I behaved, and I'd rather pretend it never happened.

After arguing with Nishi and Deke in the music studio, I was too consumed by my anger to think straight, and I stormed out of the compound fifteen minutes before curfew. I didn't take my Wave with me because I didn't want to hear from my friends, and without it, my space suit had no communication system.

I remember taking long leaps across the moon's rocky surface, beneath a starry sky, toward the crystal dome. The three other moons of our House formed a slightly jagged line above me that grew straighter every day. A year later, all four moons would align for the only time this millennium for the Lunar Quadract.

An alarm rang through the air, so loud it made my bones vibrate—the first of two warning bells before curfew. The doors to the compound would be locked on the third bell, and without my Wave to alert anyone I was out here, if I didn't make it back in time, I'd wind up outside all night.

Every cell within me knew I should turn back, but my gut clenched at the thought, so I pushed onward in defiance of my better judgment. Just a quick moonwalk and I'd be right back.

Behind the dome was an art exhibit created by the Academy's sculpture students—a Moonstone Maze. I half-skipped, half-glided my way toward the towering stone statues, so tall they obscured the horizon. All year we watched the artists work on them on Elara's surface, whittling while hovering in mid-air.

I entered the maze through the first entrance I spotted and floated down a narrow path; the long stretch of stone to my left featured a row of different trees from around the Zodiac, and to my right were giant-sized House symbols, beginning with Aries and ending in Pisces. As soon as my eyes landed on the Archer, I thought of Nishi again.

For all her daring, she'd never left the compound this close to curfew before, and especially not without her Tracker. My shoulders lifted a little at the thought of being braver than my best friend. Maybe she didn't know me as well as she thought she did. After all, wasn't my adventure tonight far more Sagittarian than Cancrian?

Deke used to love saying that the only way to change the norm was to break it. He used that line on our instructors every time he got in trouble for not following the rules. And wasn't that exactly what I was doing by breaking from my usual behavior? If I'd known how closed-minded and boring my friends had found me all those years, maybe I would have tried this s ooner.

The second bell chimed, and the network of lights surrounding the compound shut off, drowning Elara in darkness. My heart froze. I had only five minutes to get back to my room.

Inside the maze, the bell's echo seemed to ricochet through the rocky passageways, fading slowly, and the statues' shadows stretched around me. I brightened my helmet's headlights and stared at the sculptures in bewilderment. Instead of trees and House symbols, I was surrounded by larger-than-life representations of Cancrian wildlife—hookcrabs, crab sharks, sea horses. I hadn't paid any attention to where I was floating.

As fast as I could, I darted down the aisle and took turn after turn onto more paths I didn't recognize. Every time I rounded a corner, I hoped to run into an exit, but I couldn't find any way out. Then the third alarm went off, and I gasped in terror.

I was locked out.

But as I had the thought, I spotted the red light in the corner of my visor. The ringing was coming from inside my helmet, a warning my oxygen levels were low. I probably didn't have much to begin with, and the exertion and anxiety must have caused me to burn through most of my supply.

My headlights dimmed as my suit switched to survival mode to conserve power and air, which also meant rationing my oxygen. If I didn't make it back before the final bell, I wouldn't have to worry about surviving outside all night, because I'd only have enough air to last a few minutes.

I felt around and grabbed hold of the nearest statue, pulling myself forward from one to the next. We weren't supposed to touch the stone, but that didn't matter now. My brain already felt tingly from the reduced oxygen, and my muscles seemed to slow to half-speed; it didn't help that I could barely see in my helmet's lessened lighting.

My heartbeat, though slow, pounded too loudly in my ears, and as tears of defeat burned my eyes, a splash of light suddenly flickered ahead.

I frantically reached for the next sculpture, and the next, until at long last, I pulled myself out of the maze.

All around me, the moon's surface was inky black, and the only way I could spot the entrance to the compound was by the blue emergency lights blinking in the distance. From this far away, they looked like stars.

The curfew alarm could ring at any moment, so I urged myself forward, even as the reduced air made my mind feel Centered and half-asleep . . . like when I tried to hold my breath for too long in the Cancer Sea.

At the thought of home, Stanton's voice filled my head—*If you lose your oxygen and are far from the Sea's surface, don't panic. It will only cost you more air.*

The memory was almost a decade old, from when he taught me how to deep dive. I forced myself to stabilize my breathing as I moved forward, trying to recall his advice as I went.

Search for a surface you can push off from, so that you can preserve your energy for the final stretch.

Just as Stan's stories once saved me from my nightmares, hearing his voice now steadied my nerves and warded off despair. As I rounded the crystal dome, I launched myself at its surface, pushing off its wall and flying a good way before touching back down on the moon.

The blue stars of the compound grew a little larger, and I used my accumulated momentum to take a second flying leap, not as big as the first, but still helpful. And as I landed, my headlights shut off completely.

I was almost out of time, oxygen, and now, *power.*

Wrapped in complete blackness, fear gnawed at me from all sides. Until my brother's voice came to my rescue again.

Don't fear what you can't touch.

It's something he started saying to me after Mom left us, whenever sinister visions from the astral plane followed me home and haunted my mind.

Reinvigorated, I filled in the shrouded shapes around me from memory, and as the darkness lifted a little in my mind, I burned through every last reserve of life I had left, leaving no energy untapped, no part of me behind, until, unbelievably, my helmet bumped into the compound's metal doors.

The final alarm sang out as I cycled through the airlock. One more second, and I wouldn't have made it.

When the automatic locks clicked into place, I exhaled and slid to the floor of the dark and empty entrance hall, my back against the door, and I used my remaining strength to lift the helmet off my head. Sucking in lungfuls of air, my throat burning and brain throbbing, my body slowly revived.

I knew I ran the risk of a monitor catching me, but having just defied death itself, I felt invincible. As soon as I could move again, I dragged myself into my dorm-pod and shuffled out of my space suit. Then I snuck back out and crept a couple of hallways over to Nishi's room. I knocked softly on her door, and she opened it immediately.

"Rho!" She pulled me in quickly and shut the door. "What are you doing here? You haven't been answering your Wave!"

"I'm sorry," I said, taking her hand in mine. "You're right, I'm closed off to new things, especially if I think I'll fail. But I trust you . . . so I'll give the showcase a chance." But I couldn't help adding, "Even if I'm still pretty sure I won't like it."

Nishi laughed and pulled me in for a hug. "You really suck at fighting," she said near my ear. "And I'm glad because I can't stand being in a fight with you."

"Me neither," I said into her hair.

When I got back to my room, I sent Stan a message asking if he had time to talk the next day. I'd been missing his calls because of classes and band practice, but after what happened that night, I couldn't think of anything more important than seeing my brother's face.

As the memory ebbs away, and my eyes readjust to my Scorp surroundings, I'm left feeling the same way—like I need to see my brother.

Mom may have raised me to trust my fears, but Stan taught me to face them. It was his faith in me that made me brave enough to move to Elara, and it was his patient teachings that got me through those fatal minutes on the moon. He's the only person who's ever made me feel like maybe my fears aren't real. And now, he needs me to remind him that his aren't either.

My feet are already carrying me to my brother's room. I knock on his door, and when he doesn't answer, I try the handle. It's unlocked, so I peek inside, but he's not there. I try Mathias's room next.

"Come in," he says, and I find him sitting on the spongy blue floor, spinning through a carousel of holographic folders, each file a different color.

"Hi," I say from the doorway. He's wearing a plain white shirt and comfy pants, and I catch myself staring at the thick scar cutting down his neck. We haven't been alone together since Taurus, and the realization makes the room's cool air grow warmer.

"Any chance you know where my brother is?"

He looks up from the holograms to me and shakes his head. "How are you?"

I jut my chin out at the holograms. "What are you up to?"

His brow wings up at my non-answer, but he doesn't press me. "I'm reviewing reports my dad sent over. They're status updates from our eight refugee camps—Aries, Scorpio, and Virgo are the only Houses we didn't settle. Our Royal Guard is trying to get in touch with the Cancrians on Pisces to know if they've been infected."

A pang of guilt strikes my chest.

"It's not looking good for us anywhere, though," he adds with a deep sigh. "The Taurian government is demanding we join their workforce if we want to stay. Your friend Rubidum is defending us to her people, but as the Geminin government is a democracy this century, she's going to be outvoted, and we'll have to find a new home for our largest settlement. Sagittarius might be our best option, since they have such a large constellation and most Sagittarians don't live there year-round."

By now I feel the guilt all over, like it's a poison infecting my every organ. While I've been off obsessing about my personal problems, Mathias has been here, thinking of our people, doing what I should be doing.

But then, I've always known he's the better Zodai.

"Do you think Sirna is right?" I ask faintly, still standing in the room's threshold. "Have I lost perspective?"

He shuts off the holograms with a touch of his Wave, and when the floating colors vanish, the air is static and gray. I watch as a school of Scorps swims past the window, and I keep focused on their graceful, synchronized movements.

"When I was your Guide, I spent more time judging you than guiding you," he says softly, "and far from being helpful, I think I only made you question yourself."

"Mathias, that's not—"

"It *is* true, Rho." There's a resigned resolve in his tone, like he's been avoiding this realization for too long not to mean it now. So instead of arguing, I step inside and shut the door behind me.

"Rather than comparing you to the Guardians who came before, I should have trusted your instincts," he says as I sit beside him on the spongy blue floor. "When you became our leader, you had to adapt to a new galactic order, and you did so with admirable speed . . . but I held tight to the ways of the past, without realizing the world I was holding on to was already gone."

Images of Cancer flick through my mind, renewing my sense of loss. The master's taken more than just our home planet from us. He's taken our way of life.

On Cancer, most Cancrians lived on islands or pod cities overrun with our loved ones. As families grew and expanded and formed families of their own, we'd cluster closer together, like nar-clam colonies, and build bigger bungalows to fit more bodies.

Now families are irreparably broken, our people are spread out across the Zodiac, and a generation of Cancrians will be raised in orphanages. So much for *happy hearts start with happy homes.*

"Your parents," murmurs Mathias, "they didn't raise you and your brother on your maternal grandparents' land?"

"My parents started a new home in a new place . . . Stan and I never met the rest of our family." Mathias and I both know how decidedly un-Cancrian this is, so there's no need to say it.

"What did you want to do with your life before the Lunar Quadract?" I ask, mostly to avoid lingering on my family.

Mathias's expression grows wistful, the indigo of his eyes swirling like whirlpools of the Cancer Sea. "I hoped to distinguish myself at an early age in the Royal Guard . . . then retire young to return home and start a family."

It's a very Cancrian answer, and yet it's not what I expected of him. I think I envisioned Mathias being in the Royal Guard forever. "Did you have any marital prospects in mind?" I ask.

I meant it to sound playful, but somehow the question had less weight in my mind than on my tongue.

"I guess I just figured the right person would find me one day," he answers, his cheeks looking as pink as mine feel. The passivity of his response is very traditional for the heterosexual men of our House. That's because Cancer is—*was*—a woman's world: We're the House of motherhood, and that's why one of our most sacred images is that of the nursing mother. Ours is a maternal society where women run the households, women write the laws, and women make the first move.

"Did you—" My face flares like a just-lit match, and I'm not sure how I get the rest of my question out. "Did you ever notice me in the solarium?"

The fire catches and torches Mathias's features, too. "Not in the way you mean," he says, and my eyes study the porous ground. "You'd always been a kid to me, and I didn't want to encourage your crush. But something changed my last day of university."

I lift my gaze and find that his is unfocused, as if he's seeing yesterday. "I wasn't sad about leaving Elara. I didn't like it there. But when I woke up that last day, I wasn't looking forward to my freedom. I was upset about something, and I didn't know what it was until I walked into the solarium."

His eyes meet mine, and there's an intense clarity in their depths that feels safe and honest and Cancrian. "You were sixteen, but I hadn't noticed until then. I guess, in a way, that morning was the first time I really looked at you."

His baritone deepens, and I feel the rumble of his voice in my bones. "I realized then that mornings with you had become my favorite part of the day." He seems closer to me somehow, though neither of us has moved. "For five years, I'd been waking up and choosing your company over anyone else's . . . and what I didn't want to admit to myself was that I would miss you."

I feel my head shaking involuntarily, unable to reconcile his memory of that day with my own. "But that morning, when you walked in and saw me, you stormed right back out, like you were angry I was there."

I'll never forget that day. I'd been so depressed the months leading up to Mathias's graduation, knowing soon he'd be gone and we'd never share another morning together. For weeks I tried working up the courage to talk to him. Nishi threatened to invite him to my sixteenth birthday party if I didn't, and though I *really* wanted to . . . I just couldn't.

Behind my paralyzing fear of rejection hid a deeper reason: I liked the idea of him too much.

Mathias had become so important to me without ever saying a word. Because of him, I visited the solarium every day to read or meditate, and as a result I found a profound peace and concentration in Centering that I hadn't felt since the days of Yarrot with Mom. Every time I'd hear about another of his accomplishments in the Elara news, I'd work harder in class so I could become someone he would notice in a few years. He was my constant; I could bicker with Nishi and Deke, I could do poorly in class, I could suffer severe homesickness, but Mathias would be in the solarium every morning, as sure as Helios's rays would light up its glass walls.

So on his last day I finally resolved to speak to him. I thought it an auspicious sign that he actually held my gaze that morning, and just as I opened my mouth to say something, he blasted out of the room, and the moon, and my life.

"The moment I realized how I felt, I knew I had to leave," he says now, bridging what little space was between us. "I was still too old for you," he whispers, his breath brushing my face, "and we were in such different places in our lives, that I still think it would have been selfish to do otherwise."

"And now?" I ask, eyeing the slight stubble of his chin, the full shape of his lips, the sculpted lines of his cheekbones. I focus on every familiar feature of his face, forgetting my resolve to freeze my heart in hopes of finally figuring out my feelings. "Is what we feel for each other real . . . or is it a memory?"

I've wanted to be with Mathias since I was twelve. My love for him kept me steady during my homesickness on the moon, and his love for me kept him steady during his torture at the hands of the Marad. Whatever was between Hysan and me was wrong because it went against our laws and would have always had to stay hidden—but Mathias and I are fated. So what are we still waiting for?

My breath catches as I realize Mathias is leaning in, moving ever so slowly, until our lips lightly touch. His thumb caresses my jawline, then his hand slides to the back of my neck, and he pulls me into him, at last pressing our lips together.

The kiss is deep and breathless and all consuming—like first love. His mouth tastes like mornings in the solarium and afternoons in the Cancer Sea and yesterdays that came with guaranteed tomorrows.

"Whatever this is," whispers Mathias, "I don't think it's ever going away." He looks into my eyes, and the deep blue of his gaze feels as soft as clouds.

"Whatever happens, Rho . . . part of me will always be waiting to be yours."

6

I WAKE UP TOO EARLY the next morning and sit upright in bed, disoriented. As I survey my room for the cause, remnants from my dream flicker in my mind, and my body grows warm as I start to relive last night's kiss with Mathias. . . .

Then I hear it again. Someone's knocking on my door.

"Who is it?"

"It's Helios," says Engle's flat voice. "Rise and shine, crab."

I flop back onto the waterbed and pull the sheets over my head. "I'm sleeping."

"Chieftain Skiff has requested a meeting, since your party is leaving us so soon."

I pull the sheets down to my chin. "We are?"

"Your business here is finished. We expect you gone by tomorrow at the latest."

I'm really going to miss this House's hospitality.

I clamber out of bed and sleepily pull on a blue suit sewn from the same lightweight, stretchy threads everyone here wears—flexible enough for air swimming and thin enough to endure this world's humidity. My hair is a frizzy mess, but I have to hurry, so I just tie it into a sloppy bun. I should probably put more effort into my appearance when meeting with a Guardian, but if Skiff cares about that stuff, then he should have given me more time to get ready.

As we ride the lift up to the roof, I Wave Mathias a message, letting him and Stan know we're no longer welcome on Scorpio, so we'll have to figure out where to go next. I decide against mentioning Nishi's invitation, because we each have personal motives for wanting to visit the Eleventh House, and if we do go, I want to be certain it's not for one of those reasons.

"Where are we meeting your Guardian?" I ask as we retrieve our waterwings and fins from the lockers.

"Chieftain Skiff has a very busy schedule, so we'll be travelling to him. At the moment he's on my home world, Oscuro."

I snap my head up from the fins I'm slipping over my feet. "We're leaving Pelagio?"

"Where'd I lose you?" he asks as he activates his vapor jet packs. I roll my eyes as he floats into the sky, then I rise after him.

We merge into a school of air swimmers. The ocean around us is so clear that Helios's light illuminates the whole city of Nepturn, glinting off its glass walls and revealing a world of activity bustling beneath us. Crowds of Scorps hurry along sandy sidewalks, while families in small boats navigate networks of narrow canals outfitted with traffic lights and pedestrian bridges.

Unlike the visitors' burrow, most of the blocky buildings surrounding us don't have any windows. That's because the inventors inside are working on technology that's decades into the future, so they're less concerned with looking out than with outsiders looking in.

We board a submarine at the spaceport, and this time we bring our waterwings and fins with us and store them in the overhead compartments. I take the window seat and Engle sits beside me, promptly projecting messages from his Paintbrush and ignoring my presence.

A wiry, long-faced girl sits across from us, donning a black shirt and shorts sewn from the same lightweight material we're all wearing. Clipped onto her shirt is a scorpion-shaped metallic device; Scorps like to add strange pieces of technology to their clothing that are often their own inventions.

When we're underway the girl pricks her finger on the scorpion's stinger and a drop of blood dribbles out and gets absorbed by the metal. After a moment the scorpion's shell cracks open, and the girl wipes her hand on the hem of her shirt before pressing her Paintbrush inside the opening.

The scorpion's legs and tail clamp around her finger, and she shuts her eyes and goes completely still.

"They're called Crawlers," says Engle, and I turn to meet his red eyes. "Every Scorp designs his own version because the device is molded to his mind. The right DNA sequence unlocks it."

"What's it do?" I ask as I stare at the frozen girl.

"Organizes your thoughts."

"*How?*"

"When a person places his Paintbrush against the hidden sensor, the software syncs with his mind and runs a program in his head that sorts his thoughts into a processing system of his own design. Something compatible with the way his brain works but more comfortable than his mind's natural set-up."

"Where can I get one?"

With a glorious glare only a Scorp could pull off, he says, "You're sneaky."

"*I'm* sneaky?"

"You're good with words, I'll give you that. But all your talk of the Zodiac magically uniting against a mythical monster doesn't cut it on Scorpio. Here, we take *Trust Only What You Can Touch* more seriously." Brow furrowed and voice sharp, he adds, "And you're still too untouchable to do anything real."

The bite in his tone tips me off to the feelings behind his words; Engle's problem with me is more than just lack of faith—he doesn't *trust* me.

"What aren't you telling us?" he asks, proving me right. "What is it you really want?"

His questions are so ridiculously paranoid that rather than answering them, I retort with one of my own. "Who'd you lose in the attack on Oscuro?"

He doesn't respond, but I notice his hand clenching again.

"I guess I'm not the only one who's untouchable."

Engle returns to his holograms, and I go back to staring at the girl, who's now moving her hands through the air like she's conducting an orchestra. Just as I start to lose interest in her and decide to check my messages, the blue water beyond the windows darkens to a velvety black so opaque, we could be floating through Space.

The submarine's lighting system shuts off, and I turn to Engle. All I can see are his Maw-red eyes as he whispers, "Welcome to our darker side."

Beyond the glass, bright lights flit by, like showers of shooting stars. Once we slow down, I see they're really schools of glow-in-the-dark fish. Their colors draw patterns in the darkness, like shape-shifting constellations.

When I look back inside the sub, everyone has started to glow like the fish beyond the windows—including me. I look down at the blue tunic of my suit, and it looks as if bright blue light were pulsing from behind the fabric. Like I'm wearing waves of the Cancer Sea.

In the black water beyond, the silver stars of Oscuro's mechanical gills twinkle into view. Within the world's protective bubble, schools of Scorps wade through the air in glow-in-the-dark outfits, looking like fish showing off shiny skin.

"You'll need these," says Engle.

"I can't see what you're showing me."

He grabs my hand and presses something small into my palm. His skin feels thin and waxy, and I can't imagine it offers much protection from the outside.

"They're contact lenses."

"And how am I supposed to put them in when I can't see?"

He hits something on the armrest, and a dim light pops on over my head. I crack open my Wave and beam out a holographic mirror so I can see what I'm doing. Opting to ignore the cap of fuzzy frizz gracing my head, I hold up the eyedropper and squeeze out a single drop into each eye.

When the liquid touches each cornea, it solidifies into a pair of soft lenses that hug my irises, which have gone from green to red.

The overhead light suddenly blinds me, and I yelp, squeezing my eyelids shut against the pain. My eyes are streaming tears, and I cover them with my hands.

"It's off now," says Engle.

Very tentatively I spread my fingers apart on my face and peek out. There's no more illumination in the sub, and yet I can somehow identify every detail of the vessel. The shapes around me are all different shades of gray; I never knew there could be so many variations of the same color. It's like I've zoomed so far into a single wave of light that I'm seeing the particles that create it.

We dock at the station, and gaining access to this world proves to be exhausting. After the attack on Oscuro and the discovery on Squary, Scorps know there must be double agents within their ranks, and they've become even less trusting than they were to begin with—which wasn't much.

Once Oscuro's officials finally finish interrogating us, they grudgingly grant us passage past their borders, and we walk into a world where it's always night.

The gills above us sparkle like stars in a black sky, and curious sea creatures peer in through the glass walls, their neon bodies popping in and out of view every few feet. Unlike Pelagio, this waterworld doesn't have a network of canals; rather, the ground is buried beneath a sea of water. Boats abound, transporting people to the spongy buildings on the horizon, each vessel identifiable by the soft, golden glow of a candle-like light burning from its bow. The effect makes this place seem almost romantic, though that couldn't be further from the truth when it comes to its people.

"Do you want to visit your family while we're here?" I offer Engle.

His glower closes the subject, and I silently slip on my water-wings and fins before we take flight to join the swimmers in the sky. This world is so dark that soon the boats beneath us are visible only by the glow of their candle-like light.

Since I'm wearing the special contacts, the blocky buildings are easy to spot and avoid. I cycle to the outer lane when Engle does, and then we peel away from the group and land on the narrow rooftop of a green building. After stowing our gear in a locker, I follow him to what appears to be a gaping hole in the structure's ceiling. I peer over its edge tentatively. All I see below is darkness.

"Jump," he orders me.

"*Yeah, right,*" I say, backing up from the hole. "After you."

"Fine."

Before I can stop him, Engle steps off the ledge and vanishes.

"Wait!" I shout, too late. I drop to my knees and pop my head into the opening, but it's pitch black, even with these contacts. "Are you okay?" I call into the void.

No response. I can't hear anything, can't see any movement, can't even feel a waft of air. "Can't be as bad as the cannon," I say to myself. Then I jump.

I scream as I drop through blackness, but no sound comes out. Nor can I feel any air pressure affecting my fall. It's like I'm suspended in nothingness, even though logically I know I must be descending. An instant later, I feel solid ground beneath my feet, and Engle's dry muttering breaks the silence.

"Scaredy crab."

I look around. We're alone in an elegant waiting room decked with black spongy seats and ornate seashell accents. "What *was* that?"

"A scan to confirm our identity and inspect us. It's a requirement for anyone meeting with Chieftain Skiff."

"Inspect us for what? Weapons?"

"Anything dangerous." Glimpsing the curiosity still coloring my face, he sighs and starts counting things off on his fingers. "You could have embedded spyware in your skin, or your body could be carrying an undiagnosed disease, or—"

The only door in the room opens, and a wiry Scorp with white-blue skin and scarlet eyes appears. "This way."

The strange gadgets dangling from her belt jingle together as she leads us down a dark corridor to another door. "Only you are welcome," she says to me.

"I'll find you later," says Engle. He and the girl are already heading down the next passage without a glance back at me. I pat down my bushy hair, redo my bun, and then open the door and enter a mostly empty space.

It reminds me of a Sagittarian White Room, only there's an unidentifiable energy in the room's nakedness, as if the walls themselves are alive.

A gray-haired man with his back to me reaches *into* the white wall and pulls out a black holographic line. With wide eyes, I watch as he bends the line into a multi-sided shape and places it into a holographic model hovering before him. I start edging around to see what he's building, when the whole thing disappears.

"It's not very Cancrian to pry into a stranger's thoughts."

I freeze where I'm standing as Chieftain Skiff turns around. His hair and slightly stooped figure betray his elderly status, but his refined features and smooth, pearlescent skin give him an ageless quality.

I only met him once before, at the first armada meeting I attended on Aries, but I remember that while the other Guardians argued about strategy, he stayed silent. "Are you surprised I wanted to see you?" he asks.

"Yes." Tension tightens my nerves, reminding me of how I used to feel the mornings I'd awaken to Mom's whistle. It's that familiar braid of dread and readiness that comes from facing off with an opponent who's already a hundred knots ahead of you.

"You've taken private meetings with nearly every Guardian of the Zodiac, so why should I be excluded?"

"I . . . didn't think you'd want to meet me. Ambassador Charon hates me, and until recently, he represented you—"

"Charon is his own man and entitled to his own prejudices," injects Skiff. When Stridents discovered the soldiers on Squary, they reconsidered the proof of pay-offs Sirna had found before the armada and re-arrested Charon.

"Well, then"—I swallow, my throat suddenly dry—"so am I."

Skiff arches a gray eyebrow, a gesture that makes him seem both insulted and intrigued. "Are you admitting you purposely excluded me?"

I shrug to downplay my discomfort. "You and your House have given me no reason to trust you, so I didn't see a reason to humiliate myself before you again."

"Has anyone ever advised you not to take politics so personally?"

I almost ask if Sirna put him up to asking that. But then I remember the silver scrambler she set off in her Hippodrome office on Aries, and how she warned me then—My office is *always being watched*.

Instead I say, "You're spying on the staterooms at the visitors' burrows."

"You're paranoid," he says, sounding pleased. "Yes, the staterooms are bugged. Our first duty is to protect ourselves."

"But Sirna's an ambassador—she has diplomatic immunity from your laws. Does she know?"

"No one outside my Royal Guard knows."

I open and close my mouth. Unfortunately no words come out. He's willingly telling me something that's top secret?

"This is a test," I say at last.

"We Scorps are called a lot of things—suspicious, jealous, manipulative, ambitious." He takes a few steps closer, and I make out more details of his face: a small scar on his cheek and faint wrinkles along his forehead. "But there is one value we hold above all others, one I'm not surprised has been overlooked by the other Houses. *Loyalty*."

His red eyes burn like fire. "You have taken the name of Wandering Star, which means you may no longer put your House before all others. You are a citizen of every world now."

His gaze strays to my left arm, where the twelve scars are buried beneath blue fabric. "As a gesture of welcome, I have shared a secret with you. What you do with it now is up to you."

He turns around again, and the model he was working on reappears, visible from where I am only by its faint holographic halo.

"Safe travels."

7

SKIFF'S ABRUPT DISMISSAL DISORIENTS ME, and when
I leave the room, Engle is already waiting. We don't speak as he
guides me down a different direction, and we come upon a sleek
lobby where a handful of exhibits are displayed with holographic
tags. The largest by far is in the middle of the room.

Original Skiff

*A descendant of Strident Galileo Sprock, creator of the first
hologram, Chieftain Placarus Skiff is a great inventor himself. He gained renown across our worlds in his youth when
he designed this Skiff. The first of its kind, it's a one-person
rescue ship that runs on minimal energy, made from lightweight materials using sustainable resources. In later models*

Chieftain Skiff added a Psynergetic navigational system that allows the pilot's mind to sync with the vessel to steer it.

I flash to Hysan's face lighting up on *Firebird* as he marveled over the Skiff he was learning to pilot, how it handled like an extension of his mind, and I hear his voice in my mind—*I just wish I'd invented it myself. I'm building my own when we get home.*

Is he home now?

Is he building some amazing new invention in his workspace on Aeolus?

Does he think of me?

STOP, I command my thoughts for the millionth time. Hysan has obviously forgotten me, and now I need to forget him.

Once we've boarded the submarine back to Pelagio, I expect Engle to start projecting messages from his Paintbrush again, but he turns to me instead. "What did Chieftain Skiff tell you?"

"That was between us."

"And if it was Sirna or Stanton or Mathias asking?"

I reflect his frown. "You're not rattling me. I've been telling the truth for months, and no one's wanted to believe me. And it's cost me nearly everything. So I'm done trying to earn anyone's trust. It's now on you all to earn back mine."

We don't speak again after that, which is good because I need every single brain cell focused on solving Guardian Skiff's riddle. His test isn't over—it only ends when I tell or don't tell Sirna about the hidden microphones.

I *have* to tell her. She's the Cancrian ambassador, and I'm legally obligated to inform her. And even if I weren't, telling her would still be the right thing to do; it's wrong to invade people's privacy this way.

And yet.

Skiff has a point. I no longer belong to only House Cancer. Spying on politicians is a practice Scorpio has employed for a long time, and they do it with dignitaries from *every* House, so it's not actually an attack on mine.

I could opt to reveal Skiff's secret to the whole Plenum and not just my House, but that would only isolate Scorpio further. And alienating the Zodiac's House of Innovation might not be the optimal strategy when we're facing an enemy whose greatest advantage is their advanced technology.

To match the Marad's superior Veils and weapons will require our best inventors. If there's one thing I'm sure of, especially now that I've visited this world, it's that we won't win the coming war without them.

Lord Neith's words seem prophetic to me now. He was right: There can be no one-size-fits-all formula for measuring fairness because every situation needs context. Everything is a shade of gray.

Back at the visitors' burrow, Mathias and Stanton have gone diving. I'd love to join them, but I need this time to take Skiff's test. I can't wait for him to figure out how he feels about me, particularly as this is the kind of test he can drag out forever. We both know just because I don't tell Sirna today doesn't mean I won't tell her tomorrow.

But I need his trust *now*.

I have to share a secret of my own.

The answer comes so quickly that it's almost like it's been on my mind since Oscuro, waiting for me to acknowledge it. And for the first time in too long, what I have to do happens to be what I want to do, and without thinking it over, I Wave Crompton.

> *Ambassador Crompton, please call me as soon as possible. It's a private matter.*

Once I've sent the message, I leave my room and set off for Sirna's stateroom and knock on her door. As I'd hoped, no one answers. The suite is locked, but the sitting room in the lobby is accessible, and after making sure no one's around, I perch at the edge of the black levlan couch and wait.

My stomach is so squirmy that I'm starting to wonder if the squid I had for lunch on the sub is still alive inside me. I've been dreaming of making this call since discovering the face from my visions was Mom's, but I've been too scared to admit the truth about her.

My Wave goes off.

Hands clammy, I crack open the golden shell to accept the call, and an instant later, Ambassador Crompton's tall hologram beams out.

"Wandering Star Rhoma Grace," he says warmly. "It is an honor to hear from you." He makes a small bow before asking, "How may I be of service?"

"Hi, Ambassador." I'd love to begin by telling him off for using me in yesterday's announcement. But given that I'm in the process of using him, the words taste too hypocritical. "I'm sorry to reach out like this, but I wasn't sure where else to turn. I'd like your help with a personal matter, but first I need your word that you will not share what I'm about to tell you with anyone else."

When his next transmission comes through, he says, "I understand, and you have my silence."

I look up to the ceiling, to wherever Guardian Skiff might have hidden his bugs, hoping I can trust him, too. I hate sacrificing more of my personal life for political reasons, but it's the best secret I can offer.

How is it Sirna can't see how personal this is for me?

"I have reason to believe my mom, Kassandra Grace, might be alive. And I think she might be an Aquarian Riser."

When his hologram reactivates, Crompton looks astounded—like he can't believe I would admit something like that to a virtual stranger—and I'm momentarily mortified by what I've just disclosed. I must look crazy to be sharing such an intimate secret with someone I barely know, someone who isn't even from my House.

"I understand your need for discretion, Wandering Star. I will commence a search immediately."

As his answer comes through, I sense no judgment in his voice, no disgust in his warm gaze. I only wish I knew whether his honesty is real or just my wishful thinking; I've been wrong too many times to be certain anymore.

"Thank you, Ambassador."

"Of course. While I have you, I hear that you have been meeting with dignitaries at various Houses, and I would like to officially extend an invitation to you and your party to visit the Water Bearer constellation."

"*Thank you,*" I say again, and now my heartbeat picks up, because his invitation has sealed my decision. "I will consult my party and let you know."

✦ ✦ ✦

When Stanton and Mathias return from their dive, we eat dinner in my room to discuss our plans in private. I'd rather avoid Sirna's company and Engle's commentary for this conversation.

Mathias is first to arrive to my room, and the moment I see him, the reason for this meeting fades from my mind. "Welcome back," he says, standing closer to me than usual. My gaze finds his mouth, and I tilt up to kiss him, when Stan walks through the door.

"*Starving,*" he says by way of greeting.

Mathias and I pull away and join my brother at the stone table that I set for us with food I brought up from the dining hall.

"I think we should head back to Tierre and make sure our Cancrian settlement isn't in political danger," says Mathias as he pours water into each of our glasses while Stanton fills his plate.

"Ferez won't let that happen," I say. It's been a while since I've heard myself sound so assertive. "And I think there's somewhere else we should go."

Mathias sets down the carafe, and Stanton stops chewing the mouthful of seaweed salad he shoveled in there a moment ago. Both guys watch me with an air of ready anticipation, an expression

I recognize instantly because it's the way I've looked at them my whole life.

Like they're waiting for me to lead.

"Nishi called. She's been tapped to join a new political movement of open-minded people who want to unite the Houses. They call themselves the Tomorrow Party, and I think we should meet her there and look into it."

Stanton slides up to the brink of his seat, like he's a rocket ready to launch, but Mathias sits still and frowns. "Is she on Sagittarius?"

"No. She's on House"—my voice comes out coarse, and I clear my throat—"Aquarius."

As soon as I say the word, the guys' reactions reverse, and as Mathias's expression brightens, my brother's darkens. "Do you know which planet?" asks Mathias, his voice guardedly hopeful.

"Primitus."

"Pandora lives there," he says, and I hate how happy he sounds about that. "Maybe she's heard of Nishi's Party."

I force myself to nod. "It's possible."

"It's getting late there, so I should reach out now before she goes to bed." He stands up and adds, "I'll let her know we're coming and find out if she knows anything." Wave open in his hand and food forgotten, he strides out of the room without another word.

His reaction is a punch to my gut, but I can't wallow in it now, so instead I swallow my pain and turn to my brother. Once the door shuts, I say, "Talk to me, Stan."

He doesn't look up from his plate. "About what?"

"Don't do that." I stare stubbornly at his head of blond curls, until he grudgingly raises his face to meet mine.

"Rho, everything's *fine*—"

"*You threw your Wave at a wall!*" I slap my hand down on the stone tabletop for emphasis. "You're *not* fine, and since we're all either of us has left, why can't you just talk to me already?"

"And say *what?*" His voice is low and controlled, contrasting enough with mine that it makes me wonder if I'd been shouting. "I'm sorry I brought that monster into our lives? I'm sorry I made you distrust Hysan's warnings? I'm sorry I nearly got you killed? How much more could I possibly fail as your brother—*as a Cancrian?*"

"It's not your fault. We were *both* deceived." I reach out for his hand, but he pushes away from the table and cuts across to my room's only window.

Without looking at me he says, "The whole time we were apart, I kept thinking if I could just get to you, we'd be fine, because I'd keep you safe. But it turns out you were better off without me. Mathias has done a better job protecting you than I ever could."

"You're wrong, Stan."

I stand up, but I don't walk over to him, because he seems to need this space between us. "It's thanks to *you* that I've ever been able to face my fears—not just these past few months, but my whole life. You inspire braveness in me."

I don't know how many minutes pass, but eventually, he comes back to the table.

"I'm sorry," he says as we both sit back down. "I just think I need to join some kind of resistance effort or find a way to help the Houses somehow. I can't stand being useless anymore. Do you think Nishi's Party might have a real plan?"

He picks up his silverware and digs back into his dinner. "I'm not sure," I say, watching him wolf down his food and waiting for the chance to catch his gaze. "That's why I thought we could go check it out."

"It's just that Aquarius . . ." He chews for a few seconds, then swallows and spears another bite of fish with his fork. "I don't know. It sounds like you might want to go there for personal reasons."

"Well . . . don't you?"

He shrugs. "Just because you saw a vision of Mom as an Aquarian Riser doesn't mean it's true, or that she's alive, or that she'll be there. I don't want you getting your hopes up."

While he's yet to look me in the eyes, it's still nice to hear him sounding more like the overprotective big brother I know. And before I can stop myself, I start spilling everything that's been bothering me. "I'm worried about Nish, Stan. I don't know what's going on with her, and I want to make sure she's dealing with Deke's passing in a healthy way. I also want to check out the Tomorrow Party before she becomes more involved to make sure it's legit. And, yes, I would like to find a lead on Mom . . . if there is one."

Ophiuchus was right: It feels good to open up to someone again, and I think my brother would benefit from it, too.

"So how are you doing, Stan? How's Jewel? Have you talked to her since we left Tierre?"

"We're fine," he says vaguely, gulping down half his drink.

"Do you want to borrow my Wave to call her?"

"Rho, stop." He sets his glass down hard enough that water sloshes out. "Quit acting so naïve. The Houses are facing annihilation, and you want to gossip?"

"That's not how I meant it—"

"Pisces is under attack! I think we can find a better time to share our feelings, don't you?" Even though he's raising his voice to me, he still isn't looking me in the eye, and I feel like this whole time he's been trying to keep me from truly seeing him.

"I don't know what to do," I say carefully. "It's like everything sets you off—"

"Maybe that's why I've been avoiding this conversation! *You're* the one who cornered me into talking tonight, so don't make me feel guilty for not being ready." He snaps to his feet. "If you think going to Aquarius is the best way for us to get involved, let's go. But if this Party winds up being a bunch of school kids trading philosophies, I'm not sticking around."

I nod because I don't want to say the wrong thing again. Then he stalks out without so much as a *good night*.

For the first day in two months, I don't search the stars for Mom. There's no point in activating Vecily's Ephemeris; I already know I have no hope of finding my Center tonight.

8

I WAVE MESSAGES TO BOTH Crompton and Nishi, accepting their invitations to Aquarius. In her response, Nishi includes information for an early morning chartered flight to Primitus. Apparently she wasn't exaggerating about her new Party's resources.

When it finally hits me that I'm about to see Nishi again, my whole being feels lifted, somehow making even the pain of arguing with Stan feel less weighty. It's been too long since I've looked forward to tomorrow.

Before going to bed, I stop by Sirna's stateroom to let her know our plan. She meets me in the doorway and says, "Come in."

"That's okay. I only wanted to inform you we're leaving for House Aquarius first thing tomorrow."

Her sea-blue eyes examine mine curiously. "May I ask what's there?"

"My friend Nishi's working with a new political party, and she believes I could be useful to them . . . for a change."

Sirna's guarded expression softens. "Rho, I'm afraid my emotions got the best of me yesterday, which was the very crime I accused you of committing. I'm sorry."

"I'm sorry, too," I say, but my muscles don't unclench. I can forgive her heated words, but I can't forgive the fact that she and the Plenum used me again.

"Aquarians like their traditions," she says in her usual all-business tone. "You'll want to pack a good dress for your trip."

"Thanks." I don't bother mentioning that for obvious reasons I didn't bring any dresses with me.

As I look into the sea of her eyes, for a moment, I consider warning her of Scorpio's spyware.

"Take care of yourself," I say instead.

✦ ✦ ✦

When I wake up in the morning, I see a small black box resting by my nose on the pillow. It takes a second for me to register what I'm seeing, then I leap off the bed.

"Who's here?" I call out, my voice quivering.

I kick open the door to the lavatory, but no one's inside. I check the closet next, and under the bed, but I'm definitely alone.

I consult the settings on my wristband: The room is locked, and the window's laser alarm system is active. That means whoever came in had the power to override the system.

The package on its own proves my room's security can be breached—but placing it on my pillow feels like a warning of how easily I can be reached.

I shakily pop off the box's lid. Inside is a smooth black bangle sitting atop a bed of velvet.

Jewelry?

Unlike the rubbery wristband with the room's controls, this band looks to be made of black pearl, and it's about twelve sizes too big for my wrist—with one swing of my arm, it'd go flying.

I slide the bangle over my left hand and, as predicted, it dangles loosely around my wrist. Why would anyone—most likely Skiff—think this would fit me? I flick my wrist to slip it off.

And the band begins to shrink.

Shrieking, I flap my arm around violently, trying to toss the thing off. But the hard material has now become pliant enough to clamp around my wrist. Heart racing, I slam the bangle against my nightstand, again and again and again, trying to break it off, but nothing happens.

I search my room for something to use to try prying it apart—and then I remember.

Every House but Pisces has its own weapon of choice, and Scorpio's is one of the deadliest devices in the Zodiac. Stridents go to battle armed with the Scarab—a black bangle just like this one that, when triggered, fires tiny, poisonous darts toward its target. The paralyzing agent is so effective, it can even render electronic devices on the target completely useless, and it's fatal unless the antidote is administered within twenty-four galactic hours.

I go completely still and stop attacking the device so I don't accidentally trigger it. Thankfully it's on the hand that I usually keep covered with the black glove, so it's easy to conceal. If this is Skiff's idea of rewarding my loyalty, then I should have told Sirna the truth. I have no interest in a weapon, especially one this destructive.

Unbidden, a vision of Corinthe carving up my brother's flesh flashes in my mind, and hatred shoots up my throat like bile.

Maybe having a weapon won't be so bad.

✦ ✦ ✦

The interplanetary spaceport is located high above Nepturn in the uppermost layer of Pelagio, where the glass bubble breaks the ocean's surface. The endless landscape of sleek silver floor is filled with the rising and falling of spaceships; holographic flight information hovers over each vessel, and Engle guides us down a pedestrian corridor to gate seventeen.

Helios burns so brightly up here that the overexposed glass walls around us are almost invisible, and the view beyond is brushed with gradients of blue—the baby blue hues of the sky setting off the deep blue tones of the sea.

This time, it's Engle who wears protective eyewear; he slides on dark sunglasses that look like the ones worn by the Scorps who cornered me outside the Hippodrome on Aries. I can't help wondering whether he was among them.

When Stan and Mathias drift to the window to scope out the view, I say to Engle, "This might be the last time we ever see each other."

Despite the tinted lenses, the lines of his face betray his confusion. "I'm not hugging you."

"Tell me why you hate me so much."

He shrugs. "I don't care about you enough to hate you."

"Then tell me what you and Link have against me."

His wispy hair flaps in the wind as an orange Skiff is granted access through the glass ceiling and lands beside us at gate sixteen.

Shouting over the engine's roar, Engle says, "There was a delegate from Scorpio at your swearing-in ceremony."

I remember spotting the Strident as soon as I walked into the hall because of the strange technology that clung to his suit. "What about him?" I shout back, my curls whipping free of their bun and poking into my mouth.

The Skiff's engine finally shuts off, and in its echoing absence, Engle says, "He discovered you were colluding with Hysan Dax of House Libra."

Even my heart forgets what it's supposed to be doing.

Hearing Hysan's name knocks the air from my chest, and my gaze darts down to the silver floor so I can catch my breath.

"He reported that you and Hysan eyed each other all night. He said at one point the two of you even spoke surreptitiously, out of your Lodestars' earshot, and that it was clear from your familiarity you'd known each other for some time."

In my head I see Hysan's lips curving into his centaur smile and feel the Abyssthe-like rush of his touch, and the intensity of the memory keeps me from correcting Engle's suspicions.

"Later that night, our delegate spied you and Mathias boarding Hysan's ship. You might have the rest of the Zodiac fooled, but on Scorpio we see more than others. There's obviously a deeper agenda you and the Libran have yet to share, and until you do, we will not trust either of you."

Never in my life have I encountered this breed of paranoia. Engle's complete misreading of the situation is so bewildering that I'm not sure what to say. It's just like when Charon misrepresented everything about me by accusing me of abandoning Mathias to protect myself. "You know what the problem with you Scorps is?"

Engle cracks a scornful smirk. "Now you're *deflecting*—"

"You refuse to acknowledge that you're made up of as many feelings as the rest of us. You so badly want to believe you operate from a place of pure logic, but you forget that you're not Librans. You're ruled by the volatile sea whose tides change with the whims of the wind—*just like Cancrians*."

The smirk melts off his face, and I match his stony expression with one of my own. "You think emotions cloud one's outlook, but when you're so out of tune with your feelings, you won't see anyone clearly. *That's* why you always feel separate from the rest of us. It's not just your superiority complex keeping you apart. You're actually terrified you might not fit into this galaxy."

He shakes his head. "All this deflecting, and still you haven't refuted my report."

"Hysan and I didn't know each other before the ceremony, nor were we concocting any plans. What your suspicious friend witnessed is a scientific phenomenon we Cancrians call *chemistry*."

"*Right*. And rather than traveling to Gemini and Virgo on a Cancrian ship, you happened to board the Libran's—"

"When I saw Ophiuchus in the Psy after the ceremony, I ordered Mathias to commandeer the fastest ship available to fly me to Gemini and Virgo and warn them about the threat. It happened to be Hysan's ship." I look into Engle's dark lenses as though I can see the red eyes that lurk beneath. "I swear . . . the only beings in the Zodiac making plans for Hysan and me that night were the stars."

He crosses his arms over his narrow chest, staying sullenly silent a little longer, and I ask, "Is there anything I can say that would convince you to give me a chance?"

I'm so certain he's not going to answer that I start to turn away when he murmurs, "Tell me what you truly want."

I turn back toward him. "I want the Houses to start trusting each other—"

"No, not that." He shakes his head impatiently. "What do *you* want?"

"*I* want . . ." My vocabulary seems to be slipping away from me. "I want my loved ones to be happy, and—"

"*Helios!*" he growls, dropping his arms in frustration. "Are you actually that daft, or are you screwing with me? If you want me to trust you, then tell me what you want!"

"*I don't know what I want!*" I snap, and then I don't speak again because breathing becomes more important.

Mathias said he dreamt of one day returning home and starting a family. But even before becoming Guardian, I had no idea what I wanted to do with my life. It was Mom's dream that I join the Royal Guard, but it wasn't something I chose for myself. I've never known what's in my heart.

I'm not sure I've ever wanted to look.

"I guess I'm not the only one who's out of tune with his emotions."

I meet Engle's gaze, but this time there's only humor in his face. No distrust. "Who'd you lose on Oscuro?" I chance.

"I didn't lose anyone I know, but I was there when it happened."

I understand immediately; not many people have experienced the violence of a terrorist attack or witnessed how abruptly a living person can become a corpse. This is why Engle wanted so badly for me to earn his trust—he's been needing someone to talk to.

"Oscuro's gills stopped working for a moment, and our world had no air—not in our homes, not outdoors, not anywhere. It'd been so many centuries since any waterworld had an oxygen mishap that no one carried airmasks anymore."

His expression darkens, and he runs veiny fingers through his wispy hair. "Scorps fell from the sky, gasping for breath. It was . . ."

"Horrifying," I finish for him.

Engle's face looks paler than usual. "I wanted to help, but I had to block out what was happening to Center myself and preserve my air." He almost sounds like he's asking for forgiveness. "We were only out of oxygen for a couple of minutes, and Stridents were able to resuscitate most people . . . but not all."

I think of the frozen students floating on Elara's surface and the drowned families swallowed by the Cancer Sea, and along with the familiar sadness and survivor's guilt, I feel a renewed sense of purpose and resolve. "You couldn't have saved them, Engle. Nor did you kill them. And it won't help anyone if you stay stuck in that moment."

"I understand that, but"—there's a transformation in his features that makes him look fleetingly vulnerable—"what am I supposed to do with what happened?"

"Remember it," I say, and from his disappointed expression, it's clear that's the worst remedy I could have prescribed. "The only thing you owe the Scorps who drowned is to share their story. By never forgetting what happened, you'll be honoring them and ensuring another attack like that one never again takes your world by surprise."

He doesn't respond, but at least his silence feels less hostile than usual.

A shadow falls over us, and we look up to see a silvery star-shaped ship descending into our gate, sparkling in the sunlight as if it'd been painted with a paste of crushed diamonds. Its engine is a light hum, and small text lines its underside in elegant lettering.

Tomorrow Party

The four of us are ogling at the ship's splendor as it lands, when a loud voice behind us shouts, "HOLD IT!"

We turn to see Link and Tyron marching toward us with half a dozen armed Stridents in tow. "You three Cancrians are under arrest," booms Link.

The Stridents fan out in a semicircle, aiming the Scarabs on their wrists at our heads. "What's the charge?" demands Engle, standing between us and his friends.

"Theft."

My right hand involuntarily wraps around my left wrist where the black glove hides Skiff's Scarab. How can they know about that?

"Their belongings have been searched," says Engle, referring to the security scan we had to undergo to gain access to this transportation hub.

"We believe what they stole is hidden on their person and wouldn't necessarily draw attention to itself," insists Link, and my neck begins to burn.

This definitely has to be about the Scarab. Maybe this is why Skiff sent it—to set me up for this exact moment. Or maybe it wasn't from Skiff, but from a Zodai in his Royal Guard who wanted an excuse to arrest me. Who's going to trust me that the Scarab was a gift someone anonymously deposited in my room once they learn that I've been keeping it a secret?

"The three of you must submit to strip searches if you want to leave our borders," demands Link. "Otherwise we are taking you into custody."

My whole body breaks into a sweat.

"You're not touching me." Stanton steps up to Link as if he's daring him to say otherwise.

"Then you're coming with us." Link steps closer to Stan, too, and the Stridents around us tighten their ranks, their Scarabs still in firing position. I turn to Mathias to ask him for help with my brother, but his stance is stoic and his eyes are stony, and he seems to have completely withdrawn from this moment.

Engle suddenly faces his friend and says, "Stand down, Link."

"Can't. New protocol since Squary is that we investigate all accusations. They can't leave without official clearance."

"And what cause do you have for suspecting them?"

Link grits his teeth. "That's confidential."

"How convenient," says my brother, who's still standing too close to Link, like he *wants* the Scorp to arrest us. If they search us because of his antics, I'm the one who'll be screwed.

"I have the same level of security clearance as you," says Engle, drawing Link's scowl away from my brother and back to him. "So what's your evidence?"

Link doesn't answer, and Tyron edges forward, subtly establishing solidarity with him. But Engle doesn't cower from facing both of his friends.

"What's gotten into you?" asks Link, his voice a low growl.

Engle looks at me for a moment, then he turns back to Link and says, "I'm not entirely sure it's right for us to keep expecting trust without reciprocating it. We're never going to get along with the other Houses if we keep acting this way."

"Since when do we want to get along with the other Houses?" Link's tone is laden with disgust.

"Since looking out for only ourselves hasn't shielded any House from attacks, including our own. I think we could be stronger together. And I think Chieftain Skiff agrees."

At the mention of their Guardian, the Stridents grow alert, like the discussion has shifted into a graver gear. "He met with the Wandering Star yesterday," Engle goes on, "and has given her confidential instructions that she has not shared with me or even the rest of her party. So if you interfere with those plans now, you will have to face him and explain yourselves. And he's going to want to know your probable cause for this arrest."

Link's shoulders sag in defeat, and the Stridents lower their weapons and step aside. But before retreating, Link turns to my brother, like there's more he wants to say.

Stan speaks first. "I think this whole scene was just a way of projecting your guilt onto us."

"Guilt over what, Cancrian?"

"Over letting the Marad into Squary."

Link lifts his hand so fast that Stanton doesn't have time to dodge. The Scarab flies up in front of my brother's face, but before the Scorp can fire it, Mathias snaps to life and pushes Stan to the ground.

Engle leaps forward, too, and locks his arms around Link's neck, shouting, "Lower your weapon!"

Link struggles against Engle's hold, and Tyron and the other Stridents stare at them, too stunned to react. "He just accused me of being a traitor!" shouts Link, his face growing red in Engle's grip.

"Wandering Star, take your party onboard," calls Engle while he wrestles with Link.

I look over to the star-shaped ship and notice that two flight attendants have been standing in the doorway this whole time, watching us in bewilderment. Mathias pulls Stan up the ship's boarding ramp, and I follow behind. The flight attendants shut the door quickly behind us, and the sound of arguing is drowned out.

The instant I glimpse the glamour inside, I momentarily forget what's happening outside.

The vessel is sparkly and pristine, and it's shaped like a five-point star: The front wing holds the control helm; the back wings feature a lounge and lavatories, respectively; and each of the side wings holds a table, wallscreen, and luxurious levlan loveseat. The center of the ship is a vast open space, its floor made of glass so we can see the silver runway beneath us.

Stan claims one of the side wings for himself, leaving Mathias and me to share the loveseat in the other wing. A triangular window runs over us along the wing top, tapering to a point, and sunlight filters in through the glass.

I look to see what's happening down at the spaceport. The other Stridents have left, but Engle is still standing guard at our gate, arms crossed over his chest.

The ship begins its ascent, and an automated voice comes over the intercom. "The Tomorrow Party welcomes you onboard for this overnight journey. We should be landing on planet Primitus in approximately twenty-six galactic hours. Please ring an attendant if you need anything, and enjoy your time on board."

I stare at Engle's pale figure until I can't see him anymore. The wings shake violently as we pull out of Sconcion's atmosphere, and my teeth chatter so much that I worry I've chipped most of the enamel away. Turns out sitting in a ship's arm is much less fun than being tucked in its belly.

By the time we reach the blackness of Space, the ride smooth-ens out, and I watch the dark blue planet rapidly recede through the windowed floor. Of all the Houses I've visited, I think Scorpio was the most unexpected. I didn't imagine I'd find such a colorful world . . . or that I'd ever make a Scorp friend.

"How'd it go with Skiff yesterday?"

I look up from the glassy ground to meet Mathias's gaze for what feels like the first time since he left my room last night to call Pandora. His eyes have a hint of that lost look they wore when we rescued him from the Marad, as if the confrontation with the Scorps dragged him back to his abduction. If he's this shaken after facing a handful of his Zodai peers, how is he going to hold up before the master and his Marad?

"Unclear," I say, trying to shove back my concerns. "He's as indecipherable as any Scorp. I have no idea if anyone on that House cares what happens to any of us. But I do know we need them."

Mathias nods in agreement. "Engle seemed to be coming around back there."

"Yeah." I look past him to the other wing where my brother is sitting. He has his holographic headphones hooked into the ship's entertainment system, while his eyes search the blackness beyond the window, his thoughts lost among the stars.

"I wonder what made them think we stole something," says Mathias, following my gaze to Stan. "And what they think we stole."

I swallow back my guilt over the Scarab, and it dislodges other feelings that are clogging my throat. "Were you okay . . . back there?"

Mathias turns his gaze back to mine, and in his pained expression it's clear that the way he froze up is already tormenting him, and I wish more than anything that I hadn't brought it up. When the silence grows too long, I say, "You've been on Aquarius before, right?"

He blinks like he's adjusting to the new subject, then nods.

"What's it like?"

"*Mythic*," he says, and as the wrinkles fade from his brow, I know I picked the right topic. "The first time I saw that world, I thought I'd stepped into the pages of a storybook."

His gaze glazes over with the memory, and I let him relive it a bit before asking, "You were there when you were younger?"

"I studied at the Lykeion when I was eight, just like my mother and my grandmother, going back seven generations." His voice regains its musical quality, and its melody is like a song I never want to end. So I keep asking questions.

"And the Aquarian culture?"

"They're some of my favorite people," he says earnestly, and jealousy singes my neck at the thought that he might mean Pandora. "They're thoughtful, insightful, bookish, socially conscious . . . and they're also fun to talk to because they have a word for everything. Every feeling, every experience, every concept."

I think of Mom, and I wonder if she's truly changed Houses. Does Mathias's description apply to her now? What would it be like to meet her as an Aquarian?

When I was younger, I used to daydream that Mom was alive and had simply lost her memory. I'd picture her living in a cozy bungalow on a small island where she'd spend her days reading people's stars and her nights trying to remember the life she forgot.

Cancrians would sail from far away to have their stars read by this mysterious and prodigious seer, and in every future she charted, she'd search for some hint of her past. I'd imagine myself seeking her out to hear my fortune, and the instant her bottomless blue eyes met mine, her amnesia would be magically lifted.

One look at me, and she would know I was hers, and she was mine. She'd apologize for abandoning us and for the way she raised me, and together we'd return home to make new and better memories. Memories worth holding on to.

Mathias's Wave goes off, and when he accepts the call, the holograms of Amanta and Egon beam out. After we trade updates with his parents, the flight attendants emerge from the lounge to serve us lunch. Thanks to the ship's imitation gravity, we eat real food—a colorful tray of fresh cut sushi—and not a compressed meal.

They feed us again seven hours later, at what would be dinnertime on Sconcion, and afterward they dim the ship's lights so we can sleep. Stan passes out in his traveling suit, but I use the lavatory to change into my bedclothes, while Mathias changes in our wing.

When we recline our seatback, the couch converts into a bed, and we cover ourselves with the soft, cottony blankets the attendants gave us. The muffled white noise of the engine is the only sound in the pitch-black ship, and every now and then silver lights flitter through the glass. The atmosphere feels strangely charged . . . probably because I'm sharing a bed with Mathias.

I roll onto my side and meet his midnight gaze. Starlight glints off the whites of his eyes.

My breathing shallows, and I whisper, "Hi."

He reaches out and pulls me closer to him, hugging me to his chest and resting his chin on my head. "I'm sorry," he murmurs. "I don't know why I froze up when the Stridents stopped us. I think it was just easier knowing how to act before, back when I still believed there was a 'right' way to do things."

His voice echoes in my ear, and he slowly starts skating his fingertips up and down my back. A field of goose bumps blooms beneath my shirt.

"When the Marad took me, I watched them murder and dissect bodies from every House to find the thing that made us different— why *we* fit in but *they* didn't." Despite the warmth of Mathias's skin, my body grows cold. His hand pauses its movement along my spine, and I press a kiss into the neckline of his shirt.

As his words resume, so do his caresses. "The problem is we've *all* been brought up to view the Zodiac that way. The fact that ninety-nine percent of us marry *our own kind* assumes there is such a thing as a 'kind' of human—that we can be sorted into a filing system of Cancrians and non-Cancrians. But we're the same species. Not twelve, but one."

His heart is beating so rapidly in my ear that I pull away from his chest to look at him, and his hand goes still again. The vulnerability in his gaze makes me feel like the conversation is shifting from philosophical to personal.

"I don't know what's right for House Cancer or the Zodiac anymore, but I have figured something out about us." He swallows, and I can hear the dryness in his throat. "I think the only way we're going to find out if what we have is real or a memory is if you put aside the duty you believe you owe Cancer, and the loyalty and guilt I know you feel toward me, and listen to yourself. I think to know what you want, you have to let go of what you *want* to want."

I start getting up from the couch-bed. "Mathias, if you have feelings for someone else and are trying to let me down—"

"That's not it at all," he whispers, holding me so close that my chin is cradled in the crook of his shoulder. "I'm trying to be noble here," he breathes in my ear, "because . . . it feels like that's what the Libran would do."

Every muscle in me tightens, my body unprepared to hear Mathias reference Hysan. For the millionth-and-one time, the mere thought of him demolishes the weak wall I keep building and rebuilding to seal off my feelings, and once more I suppress those emotions.

Mathias's pulse quickens in my ear again. "I've been thinking of everything I admitted to you on Taurus about my capture. I don't want the guilt you feel for what I endured—and the loyalty we've always had for each other—to affect your feelings. That wouldn't be fair . . . to either of us."

"I don't know how I feel," I say, ashamed to admit the awful truth.

He pulls back from me, and I'm worried he'll push me away for my selfishness, just like Hysan did. "Mathias, please, don't—"

"It's okay, Rho," he whispers, tracing my jawline with his fingertip. "I'm not blaming you for being confused. When you sent that note about waiting for the war to be over to figure everything out, I think the old me would have approved. But this new me worries if we wait too long, we'll miss our chance."

His baritone competes with my booming heartbeat, and he takes my hand in his and squeezes it. "The *majority* of Cancrians we know have died. *The majority*. I died, too, only I've been given a second chance. And while I'd like to try leaving a better Zodiac behind me before I move on to Empyrean, dying has also taught me how important it is to *live* while I'm still here."

He brings our joined hands to his lips and kisses my skin. I've never heard Mathias sound so naked before, and every cell within me is paralyzed, sensing the significance of this moment.

"The other day I told you about the future I once dreamt of, before our House was attacked. But I didn't tell you about the future I dream of now."

His indigo eyes are so clear that it feels like his soul has risen to his surface. "I've realized the future is different for each of us. For some it's fifty years, for others it's ten months, and sometimes it's just a few minutes. I don't know how long mine is, but I know how I want to spend it.

"I don't just want to fight for what I believe is right. I also want to be *happy*. I want to love fiercely, I want to see new worlds, I want to start a family . . . and above all, *I don't want to wait*."

9

I WAKE UP WITH MY limbs sprawled across the full length of the loveseat. Picking up my head, I see Mathias in the center of the ship cycling through Yarrot. I stare for a few seconds, noting that something feels different about his movements. The choreography seems off.

I look around for Stan and spot him still sleeping, his body turned toward the window. I wonder how much longer until we land.

"How'd you sleep?" asks Mathias, dropping down beside me and breathing heavily from his workout.

"Good. Sorry if I hogged the bed."

"I've never woken up to an elbow in the face before."

I avert my gaze to hide my flush, feeling strangely shy around him this morning. Probably because we never concluded our conversation last night. Though I guess the point is we haven't chosen our ending yet.

"Was that Yarrot?" I ask, pulling up the menu of settings for the bed and bringing the backseat upright.

"*Aquarian* Yarrot. Pandora taught it to me."

I nod, trying not to dwell long on the weeks they spent alone on Vitulus when I went to Tierre.

"On Aquarius they use astrogeometry instead of astroalgebra to read the stars—"

"I know," I say, and I wish I didn't sound so snippy.

"Geometry carries real importance on House Aquarius. Since Yarrot poses are designed to mimic the twelve constellations, Aquarians are more precise about the shapes, so they perform the movements differently."

I nod and open my Wave to check messages, but the blue text before me blends into unintelligible shapes. Something about what just happened makes Mathias seem less familiar to me.

After so many years of watching him practice the same Yarrot routine, this change in his approach feels like yet another sign that the old Mathias is gone. And it's a reminder that I still don't fully know this new one.

✦ ✦ ✦

Soon the Water Bearer constellation comes into view. Seeing the Eleventh House makes my nerves tremble in anticipation, as if my blood has been replaced with jittery Psynergy. Like my heart knows I'm close to solving the mystery of Mom.

Aquarius has three inhabited planets—Primitus, Secundus, Tertius—all equidistant. The planets' atmospheres are amply oxygenated and perfectly pressurized, and a small moon orbits each one. When we're close to entering Primitus's atmosphere, one of the flight attendants emerges from the lounge and addresses us from the center of the ship.

"I apologize for this brief interruption," she says, and Mathias and I shut our Waves in unison. The blue screens floating before us vanish.

"Per protocol, we're now going to play a pre-recorded message from the leader of the Tomorrow Party, Lionheart Blaze Jansun." I can tell the flight attendant is Leonine by her wide face, toothy smile, and tattooed eyelids. Each time she blinks, the Lion constellation flickers in her eyes.

When she steps away, the Tomorrow Party's elegant holographic logo fades on and off over the glass floor, and in my peripheral vision, I spy my brother sitting up.

"Welcome to the Tomorrow Party."

A handsome holographic Leonine with a mane of blue hair bares his pointy teeth in a broad smile. "Who are we? A group of galactic unionists who believe passionately in our vision for a united Zodiac. We want to reshape our solar system into a place where we can be human beings first and House citizens second."

Holograms of all twelve constellations encircle him. "I'm Lionheart Blaze Jansun, and before I ask you to join us, I want to tell you a bit about myself. I was born into my House's Power

Pride, but even as a kid, I felt I didn't belong there. When we turn twelve, Leonines leave home to embark on a *walkabout*—we spend the next few years rotating through schools throughout our planet's nine nations. It's our choice how much time we want to spend in each place, or if we want to try all nine at all. But eventually we're expected to pledge ourselves to a Pride."

Blaze passes a hand through his puffy blue locks, and I spy colorful streaks of rainbow highlights hidden in the deeper layers of his hair. "It was in the Leadership Pride where I felt I'd finally found my place. There I learned about Leadership's prodigal son, the historical figure I was named after—Holy Leader Blazon Logax of the Trinary Axis. I was intrigued by the people of this Pride because they seemed the opposite of the ones I'd grown up with. Rather than prizing their personal interests above others, they prioritized others' interests above themselves."

The passion in his voice and his striking straightforwardness make him seem wild and untamable. A true Lion.

"It was there I had the realization that altered my life's course: A *powerful* man wants people to dream of him, but a *leader* wants people to dream of themselves."

Fire flashes in his russet eyes, and a feral passion infects his voice. "I wasn't born into the best world for me. I had to leave my first home to find my rightful one. So who's to say *any* of us have been born into our true House? How can we know where we belong if we don't know what we're missing?"

His words make me think of Ferez and his election to possess eleven technologies over one. And another memory slips in, something Hysan told me on Centaurion—*I've visited every House of the*

Zodiac, and I have the overwhelming sensation that not everyone would be happiest where they are. The Leonine, the Capricorn, and the Libran all seem to be saying the same thing: In a universe ruled by fate, our power is in our choices.

"When the Plenum honored Rhoma Grace with the title of Wandering Star, I felt something." My pulse quickens when I hear my name. "Her strength and passion inspired me to go public with a plan I'd only dreamt of—a plan to build bridges across the Zodiac.

"*We* are those bridges. The Tomorrow Party is actively searching for young people who want to help us reshape the worlds we'll inherit tomorrow. And I sincerely hope you will consider joining us."

The hologram winks out, and moments later, the ship's automated voice sounds through the intercom. "Please prepare for landing." As we buckle into our seats, I feel my first flicker of excitement for this new political party. Blaze's idealism reminds me of Twain and Candela and Ezra and everyone else I met on Centaurion a few months ago, and I'm eager to get involved and feel useful again.

At the memory of that trip, my mind immediately wanders to Hysan. *Has he heard of the Tomorrow Party? What does he think of it?*

But I force myself to leave those thoughts behind. If Mathias and I have any chance at a future together, I have to let go of Hysan as completely as he's let go of me.

The wings flap dramatically again as we cross the invisible barrier into Primitus's gravity, and then I feel the full weight of my body as the planet's colored contours swell through the floor's glass window. House Aquarius is a Royal Monarchy under the rule of the Supreme Guardian; Guardianship is a birthright here, so lineage is determined by blood. Since Supreme Guardian Gortheaux the Thirty-Third is only six years old, his Senior Advisor Untara—the House's best seer—rules in his stead.

Aquarius is made up of six Clans, two on each planet: the Nightwing Clan consists of the House's star readers (like Pandora and Mallie from Helios's Halo); the Literati, scholars and educators; the Fellowship, socially conscious activists and philanthropists; the Naturalists, environmentalists; the Visionaries, architects of tomorrow; and, finally, the Royal Clan, where the House's ruling Monarchy resides. Since Primitus houses both the Royal and Nightwing Clans, I'm hoping we'll get to see the royal palace. It's one of the Four Marvels of the Zodiac. The castle is supposedly so massive that on a clear day its silhouette can be seen from anywhere in the Royal Kingdom.

The ship lands on a grassy hilltop beneath an overcast sky, and the Leonine attendants assure us they'll deliver our bags to the Party's headquarters. Before disembarking, the three of us change into our Cancrian blue suits.

I deplane first and immediately wish I'd brought a thicker coat. I've never been this far from the sun before. The Eleventh House's orbit is farther out from Helios than any world I've visited—its three moons are even known for their famous ski spas.

I have just enough time to spot a wooden stable on the horizon when Nishi's arms engulf me, and we spin around and around on the field, clasped close together and laughing giddily into each other's ears. When we stop laughing, we tighten our holds, and I know we're both fighting tears.

When we pull apart, I get my first good look at my best friend, and I'm startled by how different she seems.

She's wearing a white levlan coat that probably cost three times as much as the red suit she wore to the Lunar Quadract, and a pair of brilliant gemstones dangle from each of her earlobes, so bright they look like stars. Nishi's always had expensive taste, but like me, she's generally more comfortable in casual clothes. Seeing her so uncharacteristically made up reminds me of my public appearances as Guardian, when I wasn't dressing up for me but for my cause.

While she greets Stan and Mathias, I notice a couple of silver-haired Aquarian men approaching us, and behind them trails a rainbow of horses—gray, aqua, pink, green. As the enormous creatures clomp closer, the aqua-colored steed steers away from the group to shake its head of hair, and a pair of gigantic, feathery wings stretch skyward from its sides.

"What are *those?*" asks Stan, and for the first time in too long, there's no shadow in his voice.

"Pegazi," says Nishi. "Members of the Royal Clan ride them to get around."

The pink horse trots up to Nishi, like it recognizes her, and the Aquarian men introduce Stan and Mathias to the green and gray Pegazi. I stare at the aqua creature that's still standing apart from us.

"That's Candor," says one of the men after he's helped Mathias onto the gray steed, referring to the aqua horse. "She's the head of her herd, so only a leader may ride her."

I consider mentioning that my Wandering Star role doesn't come with any *actual* power, but the silver-haired man is already clicking at Candor to call her over. She doesn't budge.

"Looks like she expects us to come to her." He grins at me, and I notice two of his teeth are missing. I really hope it wasn't Candor's hoof that knocked them out.

"It's the Pegazi's land, so I think we ought to heed her wishes," he says genially. "After all, the decision to bond must be mutual. She has to accept you."

I follow him over to the winged horse, and she looks down at me through onyx eyes; the longer I stare into them, the more colors I see within their depths. They remind me of the black opal Talisman.

"What do you mean *it's the Pegazi's land?*" I ask, still studying Candor's eyes.

"History tells us that when humans colonized Primitus, the Pegazi already inhabited the planet's northern hemisphere. To avoid disturbing their way of life, our ancestors designed the Royal Kingdom around them, and over the centuries the Pegazi grew curious about us and began befriending people, eventually learning our language."

I whip my face to the Aquarian, expecting to find he's joking, but he looks serious. "She can—understand us?" I ask incredulously.

Candor whinnies and bows low, and the man exclaims, "She's accepted you!"

My stomach is in knots as I take the hand he holds out to me and swing a leg around Candor's back. "There's a ridge in her spine that can cradle you," says the Aquarian, gesturing for me to slide up. As I edge along the Pegazi's smooth skin, I feel myself drop into a slight crest in the brackets of her back.

"Once you're bonded, it's for life," he says reverently. "A Pegazi never forgets a soul. She'll sense your presence any time you enter the Royal Kingdom."

"That's—*unbelievable*."

Looking down at him from high up on Candor's back, it occurs to me that though he seems to be some kind of shepherd for the Pegazi, the man doesn't touch the creatures, nor does he seem to have any control over them.

Without warning Candor clomps forward to join the others, and I turn around to wave to the Aquarian. "Thank you!"

The other Pegazi have formed a line to greet us, like soldiers saluting their captain, and as Candor surveys the winged horses, I gaze out at my friends. "Loosen up, Rho!" calls Nishi. "Try having fun!"

Candor's wings whoosh out suddenly, and the whole world starts shaking as she gallops ahead, and it's like going from zero to light-speed in a single breath. I hang tight to her neck as her wings flap at my sides, blowing frosty air in my face, and I hear the other horses' hooves echoing behind us.

We speed up as we near the cliff's edge, and I shriek as we leap off the hilltop. Then she straightens her wings, and we soar into the cloudy sky.

The wind whipping at my face would have frozen me by now if not for the Pegazi's body heat; the warmth emanating from her

hide combats the cold and makes the whole experience rather . . .
delightful.

I look down as we fly over a vast valley of widely spaced family
estates. The enormous homes sprawl along one side of a clear
turquoise lake, and on its other side is a Pegazi habitat boasting
sheltered shacks with barrels of hay and feather blankets. We rise
higher as we crest a steep hill, and then a forest emerges, swallowing the landscape in shades and textures of green, until the tapestry
of trees is cut off by the roaring blue ocean.

After a while, my neck starts to cramp, so I look up.

And I suck in a shocked breath.

Looming large over the gray horizon and hovering high above
the Royal Kingdom . . . is a castle in the clouds.

10

A MAJESTIC, MULTI-TOWERED PALACE SITS in the sky, covered with hundreds of waterfalls cascading down its walls.

I remember from Mom's lessons that the castle isn't really floating, not like Libra's flying cities; it's actually propped up on invisible ice that gets harvested from Primitus's moon. The ice is cold enough that it can't melt, and it's been holding up the castle since the Zodiac's earthling settlers originally built it millennia ago.

Candor gallops along the cottony clouds, which are actually swirls of frosty steam rolling along the ice's top layer. Since its surface is frigid enough to burn a person's skin off, the ice is buried beneath a bulky blanket of sand.

While I would love to see the castle, I can't help but wonder why we're headed there now, when we should be on our way to the Tomorrow Party's headquarters.

The Pegazi come to a halt in a waterfall plaza by the palace entrance, and the sound of rushing water echoes through the open space. All around us, Aquarian dignitaries decked in heavy layers of flamboyant fabrics go about their day, ostentatious Philosopher's Stones swinging from their necks. They have narrow faces, ivory skin, and glassy eyes with irises that span every shade of sky—black, gray, purple, blue, red, pink, orange, yellow.

A valet in a velvet top hat offers me a hand, and Candor bows low to let me slide off. But first I whisper in her ear, "That was *stellar*. Thanks, Candor. And, um, thank you for bonding with me."

My boots land on the sandy ground, and I head over to Nishi, who has climbed off her pink Pegazi. "What are we doing at the royal palace?" I ask.

"Aquarius was the first House—after Leo—to support the Tomorrow Party, so Blaze reached out to the Monarchy and asked if they would host our launch event. We've been here a few weeks, preparing for tomorrow night."

"What's tomorrow night?" I ask, as Stan and Mathias join us.

Nishi pauses dramatically, and I can't help but smile at her theatrics. "*A royal ball!*"

When none of our reactions match her excitement, she rolls her eyes and mutters to herself, "*Cancrians.* Anyway, it's our first formal event, and it's both a membership drive and a fundraiser. Blaze thought it would look best if a neutral world hosted us, since his own House would seem too biased. Besides, Leo endorses so many causes that their backing isn't taken all that seriously."

I feel hot breath on my shoulder, and I look up into Candor's onyx eyes in wonder. She blinks at me before trotting away, the other Pegazi following her at a respectful distance, and soon they all disappear around the castle's edge.

"There's a habitat for them on the palace grounds," says Nishi. "Now come see inside!"

We follow her through the rows of waterfalls, and I hug my chest as I walk, trying to return some feeling to my numb limbs. The chilly temperature of this world, combined with the coolness of the water cascading around us, is making me miss Candor's warmth.

The sand beneath our feet turns to stone as we step into a sheltered archway where a group of Elders—Aquarian Zodai—in aqua-colored suits guard the castle doors. They don't say anything as we pass them, and then we enter a round entrance hall with a ceiling so high I can't see it.

The sandstone walls around us are punctured with patterns of stained glass windows that are dyed and designed to reflect the Zodiac's twelve constellations. In place of the Thirteenth House is a massive rendering of Helios, its golden light so bright that it looks like it could be sunny out. I don't have long to admire the chamber's grandiosity, or the lavishly dressed courtiers who don cloaks of every color and fabric over their clothes, because Nishi nudges me onward.

We cut through countless common spaces where the textured ceilings are blanketed in arrangements of billowing fabrics, and every roof depicts a different sky—red sunsets, blue dawns, full moons, starry nights, cloudy mornings. Everywhere we turn, colorful, carpet-thick cloths cling to the walls, bearing elaborate mosaic patterns. Each cloth looks like it's encased within its own current of air, and they all undulate to the stone floor in rolling waves, creating the impression that the artwork is alive.

As we dive through more and more drawing rooms, a few times I glimpse the balcony of an upper level, but I haven't seen any stairs or lifts yet. It's impossible to tell how many stories there are because the castle's layout seems as intricate as the designs dancing along its walls.

Nishi stops walking when we reach a billowing burgundy-and-blue embroidered cloth. She presses her thumb to the wall sensor beside it, and I jump back as the fabric fluffs outward on its own and then ripples into a set of carpeted stairs.

"Aquarius is a stormy world," says Nishi, when she sees our stupefied faces, "and since the royal palace is so high up, it constantly gets struck by lightning. So Elders learned to harness the electric currents in the air to activate the stored static charges in these fabrics.

"It's completely safe," she adds, probably noting the hesitation on my face. "If you get a slight charge from a surface, don't worry. The worst that'll happen is you'll come down with a case of frizzy hair." She pulls me up the staircase with her. "And in your case, no one will know the difference."

"*Hilarious,*" I say, though her joke makes me think of Leyla and Lola and how much I wish they were here.

The steps feel unexpectedly sturdy beneath my feet, and when we reach the top of the staircase, we climb through an opening in the wall that had previously been hidden. We emerge in a brightly lit common area with a billowy ceiling depicting a violet twilight that's probably exactly how the Aquarian sky looked at the moment of Pandora's birth. A constellation of stars shines from the fabric in the shape of the Sagittarian Archer.

At least a hundred young people—all donning different House uniforms—gather together on plush, velvet couches, or review holographic screens at sandstone tables, or tune into news reports from the surrounding wallscreens. At least the temperature in here is warmer than the rest of the castle.

"This is the Tomorrow Party," says Nishi proudly, panning her gaze across the scene before us. "Aquarius loaned us this wing of the castle for our stay. We've been planning tomorrow's event for weeks. There's so much to do, from handling the invitations and RSVP's, to figuring out the decorations and catering and entertainment, to preparing our presentation and the night's agenda, to sorting out everything that happens next, and—I'll stop," says Nishi, pausing for breath.

"Wandering Star."

I turn to see a curvy and tight-clothed Geminin girl with lustrous, tawny skin. "*Imogen!*" I exclaim, and we run through her elaborately choreographed greeting, which involves knocking knuckles, bumping elbows, and slapping hands.

"Imogen and I joined the Party at around the same time," says Nishi, "and since we didn't know anyone else, we stuck together."

"You have to meet Blaze," says Imogen, and like last time, the red gloss of her lips is so shiny I can't look anywhere else. "He's really excited to meet you."

"I'd love to meet him."

"Holy Mother!" I'm startled to hear myself called by that title again, and I turn to see a group of blue-suited Cancrians. As I trade the hand touch with all of them, I learn they've come from refugee camps across the Zodiac. Most are survivors from Elara.

"We're kind of at capacity with rooms right now," says Nishi, once the wave of Cancrians has receded. "Especially since tomorrow's guests are also staying at the castle overnight. So if it's okay, Stan and Mathias"—she looks over my head to the guys—"you'll share a room, and Rho, you'll stay with me."

An irrepressible smile stretches my lips. Nishi notices my reaction and links her arm through mine again.

We cross to an alcove at the far end of the common area where a stone staircase spirals to higher floors. As we climb up, Imogen stops at a door on a lower level to give Stan and Mathias access to their room, but Nishi and I continue all the way to the very top of the tower.

When the staircase ends, Nishi swings the door open to reveal a round room encased in glass windows that looks out over the whole kingdom. If it weren't overcast out, we could probably see most of Primitus's northern hemisphere from this high up.

"This place is *stunning*." I spot my belongings on a bench at the foot of the bed. "How important are you to this Party?"

I survey the suite, which has its own lavish lavatory and a cordoned-off area that's probably a Lady's Lounge—a staple in the homes of Aquarian noblewomen. I remember reading about them at the Academy; through an opening in the gold-tasseled curtains, I can just make out its mirrored walls and velvet vanity.

Nishi perches at the edge of the large, feathery bed, and as she relaxes, her smile starts to falter. I sit beside her in silence, waiting for her to fall apart now that we're alone and can finally talk in private.

"When I got back to Centaurion," she begins, sounding more exhausted in here than she did out there, "I was a mess."

She rakes a slightly shaky hand through her thick hair. "My parents were so worried. They wanted me to apply to a Zodai University campus on another House, but I couldn't . . . ." Her amber eyes grow weighted down, and I take her hand, certain she's going to cry.

"Then, three weeks ago, I got a message from Blaze. He told me about this Party and asked if I would take a holographic meeting with him." She sits up a little straighter and blinks back the sadness with surprising ease. As I watch the heaviness fade from her eyes, I'm reminded of a morning on Elara four years ago.

Our class's first vacation from the Academy was approaching, and a couple of days before break, Nishi awoke to a recording from her parents saying they would be attending a festival on House Leo and wouldn't be able to join her at home. I remember watching as she blinked a few times, and I took her hand in mine, the same way I did just now, certain she was going to cry.

But then she turned to me with a smile and simply said, *"Guess who's coming with you to Cancer!"*

"When I met Blaze," continues present-day Nishi, her voice no longer sad, "he said he was a fan of the song I released, *Trust in Guardian Rho*, and that he thought it was a clever way to spread the word about Ophiuchus. He'd also heard from other Tomorrow Party members about the group we gathered on Centaurion and was impressed by my recruiting skills. He told me the Party was ready to bring its message to the Zodiac, but first he wanted to find the right co-director for the movement—and in particular, he wanted it to be someone from another House."

She breathes out deeply. "He's considering *me*."

"*Helios*, Nish!" I hug her tightly, and she squeezes me back. "That's amazing," I say into her hair.

"Nothing's decided yet; there are other candidates," she cautions me once we've pulled away, but her eyes are still bright with hope. "Can you imagine if the Tomorrow Party gains enough traction to be recognized at the Plenum? This could be *huge*. We could change the way the whole Zodiac operates, and not in the violent way the Axis did, but through leadership and communication. This could be my purpose in life . . . my way of contributing to our cause."

As her eyes grow bigger, my concern resurfaces. I'm thrilled her brilliance is being recognized, but I'm worried about how involved she's getting with this Party when I know so little about it. And most worrisome of all is the fact that she has yet to mention Deke.

The flint Tracker on her wrist starts vibrating, and she pulls up a stream of red holographic screens. I decide to check my Wave, too, and a blue message from Crompton appears; he's invited me to meet with him first thing tomorrow morning.

Even though I know it's too soon for him to have updates on Mom, I can't help hoping.

"Is that from Hysan?"

I shoot Nishi a dark look. "I told you already that he and I aren't speaking—"

"Sorry, sorry," she says quickly. "You just looked happy all of a sudden. Is it Mathias?"

To end the interrogation, I say, "It's Ambassador Crompton."

"*Crompton?*" She scrunches up her nose the way she does when her math doesn't match up with the Astralator's measurements. "He's our guest of honor at tomorrow's event."

"Impressive." As a galactic ambassador, Crompton isn't just an Aquarian political figurehead but a universal one, so his participation is very promising for the Party.

"It was originally supposed to be the Leader of Leo's Leadership Pride, but he had some scheduling conflict and bailed on us, so it totally saved us that Crompton agreed to step in." She tilts her head at me curiously. "Why are you meeting with him?"

"Well . . . there's something I've been wanting to tell you, and it's another reason I wanted to come to Aquarius. I think . . . I think my mom might be here."

Nishi grips my wrists, wringing my veins. "*What?*"

I describe the visions I saw of her Aquarian face, and then I take out the black seashell from my pocket and explain how Aryll had it. "I don't know what's real and what isn't. But being on this House is my best chance to find out."

"This is incredible, Rho," whispers Nishi, her eyes still taking up her whole face. "Is there anything I can do to help?"

"Thanks, Nish. Actually I've been consulting the stars as often as possible to search for signs of her. Is there a reading room I can visit, or should I just use my Ephemeris in here?"

"I'll take you. I have to handle some Party stuff anyway."

Midway down the stairs I stop by Stanton and Mathias's room. It's also got a great view, but it's smaller than ours. "I'm going to do a reading," I say from the doorway. "What are you two up to?"

"We're about to explore the castle," calls Stan from inside the closed lavatory. "Imogen is giving us a quick tour."

Mathias comes over to where I'm standing. "If you want to talk later and we're not here, try me on my Ring."

"Sure," I say, wanting to say more and yet not sure what I want to say. Then the lavatory door starts to open, and I dash down the stairs to find Nishi.

I watch from a distance as she delegates instructions to various people, then we both head out through the hidden hole in the wall and down the burgundy-and-blue cloth staircase. When we reach the ground, we've only walked a few steps when Nishi abruptly ducks down and pulls up on a bronze handle that practically blends in with the sandstone floor.

When the trapdoor opens, I peer into the blackness below. "Seriously?"

Nishi nods. "Good fortune!"

◆ ◆ ◆

I climb down, and I find myself at one end of a dimly lit, rocky tunnel. I follow it until I reach a cave that flickers with silver lights. I'm in the reading room.

Alone in the cave, I try tuning out everything else so I can access my Center. Sinking into my soul, it's no longer just the blues of Cancer I call up to steady myself, but a tapestry of faces—Dad, Deke, Stan, Nishi, Mathias, Hysan, Brynda, Rubidum, Twain, Leyla, Lola, Ferez, and so many others.

In a way, my definition of home has shifted. My soul no longer feels anchored to a piece of land or a body of water. It's now tied to all the people I love, across the Zodiac.

The Abyssthe in my Ring buzzes with the influx of Psynergy, and the map expands around me as I access the astral plane. Asteroids, white dwarfs, red giants, quasars, ethereal clusters of fire—the Zodiac Solar System unfolds before me in a beautiful dance of lights. As I survey the cosmic action, the air starts to tingle with instability. It's the way the Psy has been for months now.

I picture Mom's face, and my fingers find the black seashell in my pocket. I turn it over in my hand as I focus, using it like a lucky charm. After a while I survey the Water Bearer constellation, trying to pick up on her Psynergy, to trace her signature in the astral plane. But just like every time, I feel nothing.

I opt for a more generalized read. The Fire Houses—Aries, Sagittarius, Leo—are blazing brighter than ever, but that alarm has been sounding for a while now. I continue scanning our worlds, trying to glean any glimpse of tomorrow, and suddenly a sour and bitter taste settles on my tongue.

The substance spreads until it coats my mouth, and I fall into a coughing fit that burns my throat raw. When the sensation vanishes, I cup my neck, breathing in deeply and slowly.

I have no idea what kind of omen that was.

But it tasted like Death.

11

THE FOLLOWING DAY DAWNS AS dark and dreary as its predecessor. Nishi is still asleep when I wake up, and I lie in bed beside her, thinking of the Death omen that haunted me all night.

I barely spoke during dinner, and when Nishi asked what was wrong, I told her I was just tired, so we went to sleep early. I know I should tell her and the others about the omen, but I don't want to distract them from everything happening in the Zodiac right now. I'd rather wait and see if it appears again. Maybe I even misread it.

When Nishi wakes up, she orders that breakfast be brought to our room. Once we've filled our stomachs with flaky breads and sticky pastries and flavorful jams, we take turns bathing in the room's luxurious porcelain tub. After a long soak, I slip on a plush aqua robe and join Nishi in the Lady's Lounge. The mirrored room has a long, velvet vanity lined with a wide array of beauty products. I find a spray that looks to be in the same family as the ones Lola and Leyla used on my hair, and I spritz it on and exhale in relief as my glossy curls begin to dry.

Nishi plops down on a red couch smothered with gray feathery pillows and says, "Prepare to be blown away. Stand where that marker is."

I step up to a black line drawn on the sandstone floor, and a laser beams out from a pink box hanging on the mirrored wall across from me. It scans my body slowly, and when it's done, Nishi taps the spot next to her on the couch, and I crash beside her. Exactly where I'd been standing is an identical holographic replica of me.

"Eerie," I say, staring at myself.

"It's a *closet archiver* that uses a holographic simulation system for testing outfits, hairstyles, and makeup," explains Nishi as she pulls up a menu of options. "Once you're done and you pick out what you want to wear, the middle mirror opens and your outfit pops out."

"That's stellar," I say, taking over the controls and scrolling through an inventory of the items stored in this closet. We take turns making random selections for my hologram, and each time we assemble an outfit, the program rates our fashion sense by measuring our arrangement against what's currently in vogue in the trend-setting circles of every world.

In the end Nishi picks out for herself a pair of charcoal pants and a delicate lavender blouse that has a fine dusting of silver powder. These Aquarian fashions are all a bit too lavish for my taste, so I stick with my trusty blue Lodestar suit. Nishi hung it outside our door last night, and this morning we found it in a garment bag, the fabric so fresh and clean that the suit could be brand-new.

As I'm sliding my left arm into the tunic's long sleeve, I feel Nishi's gaze land on my scars. I don't wear a bandage anymore; the markings are now just red carvings covering my skin.

"How are you, Rho?" she asks from her seat at the vanity, where she just finished applying makeup.

"I'm okay." I perch at the edge of the feathery couch to pull on my boots, and she comes over to sit next to me.

"You sure?" she asks softly.

I shrug, keeping my head bowed while I speak. "At first, I was pretty impressed by how well I could compartmentalize Corinthe's torture. I just pressed down on the memory every time it floated to the surface of my mind . . . like I used to do with Mom."

Like I'm doing with Hysan.

I venture a glance at Nishi, realizing that what I'm saying applies to her situation, too. "But just as Ferez warned, the pain surfaced eventually. Nothing stays repressed forever."

"You're going to need a coat in case you go outside," says Nishi suddenly, and she activates the closet archiver again.

"Nish," I say gently, "how have you been since De—"

"I like this one!" The walls around us whir as she picks out a coat without consulting me, and when the middle mirror slides up, a garment bag pops out on a mechanical arm. Nishi swipes the hanger off its hook and unzips the bag to reveal a simple, deep blue feathery frock. It's exactly what I would have picked out for myself.

"It's perfect," I say, folding it over my arm.

"We should go or you'll be late." She grabs her expensive, white levlan coat and leaves the room so quickly that I have to run after her. By the time I reach the common room, she's already at the other end of the space talking to Imogen.

As I rush to catch up to them, Nishi turns and says, "I'm running late for a meeting, so Imogen will take you to see Ambassador Crompton. But I'll find you later for lunch."

There's no reproach in her voice, and I know she's just avoiding me to avoid the conversation we almost had. Still, she spares me a quick hug before leaving and whispers in my ear, "I hope there's good news."

✦ ✦ ✦

"How did you come across this group?" I ask Imogen as we're climbing down the static-powered, carpeted staircase.

"When you left Centaurion to meet the Marad, I volunteered to captain a rescue ship to come after you, but once we knew you were safe, Twin Rubidum took off to Taurus, and the rest of us were left looking for ways to help." Her spindly heels are so high that I don't know how she keeps balanced without a banister.

"What about your classes at Zodai University?"

"I can't go back," she says definitively.

In her answer, I hear Nishi, Mathias, Stan, and myself. "I understand."

Her copper-flecked eyes flick back and forth between me and the floor. "Some of my classmates had heard of Blaze, and when I looked into his Party, I liked what I saw and decided to get involved. I was really relieved to find Nishi here, and I figured it was only a matter of time before you came, too."

When we reach the sandstone ground, we wind through a collection of drawing rooms topped with billowy fabric ceilings and passages draped with undulating carpet-thick cloths. "When will I meet Blaze?"

"Probably today. I know he's just as eager to meet you."

The walls wilt around us as we cross into a space that's thoroughly mired in mist. The cool white steam blurs my vision, until all I can see is Imogen. "What—"

"I know, isn't it wonderful?" she cuts in. "It's a *thought tunnel!*" Through the fog, the shadowy shapes of Aquarians walking near us remind me of Psynergy signatures in the Psy.

"Aquarians like to stroll through here to take what they call *a walk in the clouds* whenever they need to think deeply about something. They use these tunnels to tune out the world around them and tune into the worlds within them."

Once the white smoke dissipates, we've crossed into another common space, and Imogen strides up to an extra-long, aqua-and-silver cloth. She presses her thumb to the wall sensor to activate the static stored in the fabric, and it fluffs out into a staircase.

"Do you know what Blaze's goal is with this Party?" I ask as we climb up. "Like, what kind of political plans he's envisioning?"

"I think Nishi wanted to be the one to tell you that stuff," says Imogen mysteriously. "She's an incredible leader. Blaze is really taken with her."

There are so many steps that we're quiet the rest of the way up, our breathing becoming labored. When we arrive at the hidden entrance in the wall, Imogen uses her thumbprint to gain us access into a marble passageway. Her spindly heels click-clack on the glossy floor, and at the end of the hall she comes to a halt outside a closed door.

"Thanks for what you did." Her red lips are so shiny they seem to be absorbing every photon of light.

"What I did?" I ask.

"You proved horrors like physical pain and personal loss and universal hate are survivable . . . as long as you wholeheartedly believe in what you're doing."

I don't quite know what to say; Imogen moved me with her strange and unexpected compliments last time we met, too. "Thanks . . . but conviction alone wasn't enough," I caution, thinking of how certain I was that Ochus was my enemy and Aryll my friend. "In fact, sometimes our strongest-held beliefs can become our worst enemies."

"How so?" she asks.

"I think conviction works against us when what we *want* to be true becomes more important than what's true."

"On Gemini we believe we create our own truths," she says, her voice growing sultrier as it deepens. "If you can imagine something, it can be done."

"That sounds fun but messy."

"Which sounds like us," she says with a smile. "This is as far as I can take you. Ambassador Crompton's office is beyond that door. Locate me on my Tattoo if you need help getting back to the ninth tower."

"The what?"

"The royal palace has twelve towers, and we're staying in the ninth," she throws over her shoulder as her heels click-clack away from me. "That's why the ninth constellation colors our common room's ceiling."

She hits the wall switch and climbs back out through the opening, and I turn to the door beside me. In place of a handle is a silver palm sensor, and I press my hand against its cold metal. Seconds later the thought tunnel's white fog floods the passageway until I can't see anything.

I stand still while the mist dissipates, revealing first my head, then my torso, then my legs, until a light layer of cottony clouds swirls around my feet. Instead of the marble passage, I'm now in a spacious stone chamber, and above me hovers a massive ball of blue energy that's sparking and buzzing and crackling with power.

"The royal palace's energy source," says a warm voice, and I turn to see a tall man with pink sunset eyes. "It's wonderful to see you again, Wandering Star."

"You as well, Ambassador." He's wearing a crisp court suit beneath a sweeping aqua cloak. From his neck hangs a Philosopher's Stone that looks less gaudy than the others, bearing the crown symbol of the Royal Clan.

We trade the hand touch, and I feel a jolt of static; instinctively I pat my hair to check for frizz. "I'm sorry," says Crompton, grimacing apologetically. "The energy in this chamber sometimes interferes with my Barer."

As he says the word, I look down at the interconnected rings on his fingers, recognizing the device—it's House Aquarius's quick-draw weapon. The Barer's bands convert energy from the atmosphere, emitting brilliant aqua arcs of electricity that can be molded into a series of lethal forms, including a sword, a bow, and a set of brass knuckles. Elders of the Royal Clan are always armed so they can be ready at all times to defend their sovereign.

I follow Crompton through one of the dozen doors outlining the chamber, and we enter an unadorned, windowless office with just a few choice pieces of vintage furniture. The only disruption to the plain sandstone walls is a rotating reel of holographic portraits, and I recognize the first face by his protruding forehead and nuclear fission eyes.

"Ambassador Morscerta," I say, a memory suddenly surfacing, "used to project a shade around him. I noticed it at the Plenum, and when I touched it, I felt an electric shock."

I look to Crompton who's nodding nostalgically at the portrait. "He was one of the most advanced Elders I've ever known. He could do amazing things with a Barer, including project an energy shield so powerful, it could deflect most attacks. He was never without it—not even in sleep." Meeting my gaze, Crompton shrugs and adds, "He was paranoid."

The Aquarian settles into a throne-like aqua armchair behind a gold-trimmed desk, and I take one of the velvet seats across from him. "Ambassador Morscerta was my mentor. This was his office before I inherited it, and those images are the faces of every dignitary who's inhabited this office, from the very first ambassador appointed by Supreme Guardian Aquarius himself in the earliest days of our House."

I can't help thinking of Cancer and all the truths and treasures and traditions that sunk to our planet's seafloor.

When Hysan told me the black opal was Cancer's Talisman, he said Guardians leave behind messages in their homes for their successors to find . . . only we'll never know the last words of our Holy Mothers.

The ambassador's velvety voice brings me back to his office. "Right away I want you to know that I have no leads on your mother's whereabouts yet."

Even though I was expecting this answer, my whole heart seems to crumble. I don't know how it could have contained so much hope when I only contacted Crompton a couple of days ago.

"I don't mean to be brusque," he says, "but I didn't want to pain you with what we Aquarians call *dullatry*—the courteous chitchat that delays important conversations—when this matter weighs so heavily on your heart."

"I appreciate that," I say, trying to sound unbroken.

But I must fail because Crompton continues in a too-cheery voice, "However, we've just started this search, and I don't plan to give up yet, and neither should you."

"I know, Ambassador," I say, at last lifting my gaze from the gold-trimmed desktop. "It's just—finding a single person who could be anywhere . . ."

"Is difficult, but doable." His pink eyes brighten with warmth as he says, "Without hope, tomorrow is just another day."

I want to believe his compassion is genuine, but I know better by now. The senators at the Plenum only care about me insofar as they can use me. If Sirna can't be trusted, no ambassador can. "There's something else I need to say. I don't mean to sound ungrateful—your help means a lot to me—but I won't be used by you and the Plenum anymore."

Crompton's expression goes from compassionate to confounded. "I don't understand."

"Your Peace declaration. You used my name to push an agenda I don't believe in. You put lies in my mouth."

Crompton's brow furrows with a show of consternation that could be completely feigned. "Ambassador Sirna contacted us with assurances that you were in agreement with our assessment. On my honor, Wandering Star, I would never use your name in vain."

His concern about my name reminds me of how meaningful the concept is on the Eleventh House; when an Aquarian becomes a Zodai, she loses her birth name and adopts a new one that's given to her by her Clan, consisting of a single, personality-embodying word.

I can't decide what to make of Crompton. On Vitulus, when I testified to Ophiuchus's existence, he was the first ambassador from the non-believing Houses to stand up and cross the aisle to my side. He was also the one who gave me the Wandering Star title. The pre-Aryll me would probably approve of Crompton, maybe even like him . . . but I can't trust my judgment anymore.

The ambassador rises to his feet. "I wish you a wonderful time at tonight's ball, Wandering Star, and safe travels wherever your journey leads. I will be in touch if the need arises."

"Oh." It takes me a moment to stand.

He gives me a quick bow, and I'm flustered by his abrupt attitude shift and my sudden dismissal. I half-consider apologizing, since I still need his help to find Mom, but then I freeze at the sight of the white-haired, willowy woman who's just entered the room.

"Supreme Advisor Untara," I say, reaching out with my hand for the traditional touch greeting. I met her when all the Guardians were summoned to Phaetonis; she came along with Morscerta and the House's six-year-old Supreme Guardian. "It's an honor to see you again."

She doesn't raise her arm, and behind me Crompton says, "Supreme Advisor Untara is a hologram." His tone, while tender, is tenser than before.

Untara looks so real that she must be transmitting from inside the castle, like Dr. Eusta used to do on Oceon 6. This kind of mobilized holographic projection is only possible in places that have been pre-outfitted with transmitters, like government buildings and corporate offices, and only the highest-ranking officials are generally authorized to move around so freely.

She continues to look at me for a long moment before bowing her head the slightest bit. "Wandering Star Rhoma Grace. You honor us with your presence." Her voice is strikingly high. "To what do we owe this pleasure?"

"I came here to learn more about the Tomorrow Party."

"How wonderful." Her eyes are as gray and heavy as this morning's sky. "And is Ambassador Crompton the one teaching you?"

"I was just welcoming her to our House is all," says Crompton, his tone still cautious. "However, we're finished here, so I am at your disposal."

At this second dismissal, I say, "Thank you for your time."

Untara watches me silently until I'm gone.

12

NAVIGATING THE PALACE'S PASSAGES AFTER my meeting with Crompton gives me flashbacks to the Moonstone Maze on Elara, and after hitting my twelfth dead end, I touch my Ring and reach out to Mathias.

I'm lost.

Do you seek physical or metaphysical guidance?

I grin, even though he can't see me. *Any chance you can beam a map of the palace into my brain?*

I can do better. Meet me in the Collective Conscious.

I close my eyes, and the sandstone walls around me are sucked into blackness. *I'm here*, I announce to the void.

There are a few shadowy forms nearby, but none of them pays me any attention. A small light grows larger on the far horizon, approaching me at breakneck speed, and before I can pull away, the Psynergy signature races right into me. With a jolt, I open my eyes.

Mathias's sculpted face is at arm's length from mine. "Hi."

Breathless, I touch his sleeve to make sure he's real, and my fingers feel hard muscle. "How—how did you do that?"

"It's a protective measure the Royal Guard employs when they need to find their Guardian urgently, but it only works if they're in close proximity." A dark lock of hair pokes into his eye, and instinctively I reach up and brush it back for him. "Thanks," he murmurs in a lower register, and I lock my hands behind me to resist doing it again.

"How does it work?" I ask to dissipate the tension.

He starts walking as he explains, and I fall in stride with him. "Guardians possess a close connection to the stars, which means they naturally attract more Psynergy than other people. Within the Psy, Psynergy possesses gravity-like properties; if someone commands enough of it, they can warp the network. So if a Zodai and Guardian have a strong connection, and they're both attuned to the Collective Conscious, that Zodai can allow himself to be guided by his Guardian's Psynergy."

"But I'm not a Guardian anymore—"

"I guess no one informed the stars." The playful look on his face makes me think of Helios's Halo, the last time I saw Mathias smile. I'd like to see that sight again.

"So what are you up to?" I ask as we approach the star-high entrance hall. I have no clue how he managed to navigate us here.

"I'm going to pick up Pandora and bring her to the palace."

Her name is an icy wall slamming down between us. Mathias seems to feel the cold front, too, because he adds, "She wanted to check out the Party. And Nishi said it was okay. Imogen said she could room with her tonight."

I shuffle my blue frock from one arm to the other. "Oh. That's good."

His shoulders sag a little, and his hair falls into his eyes again. "I was actually looking for you earlier to see if you wanted to come with me, but Nishi said you were meeting with Ambassador Crompton. What did he want?"

"Diplomatic stuff," I say evasively, not wanting to get into the whole Mom thing right now. "And I'd love to go with you." The thought of seeing Candor again is incentive enough, but I also feel a need to be there when Mathias and Pandora reunite. Maybe I've developed a taste for torture.

Mathias straightens, and his tone lightens. "Pandora will meet us at a marketplace on the border between the Royal and Nightwing Kingdoms. We'll fly the Pegazi over."

"How do we call to them?" I ask as we step onto the waterfall plaza and I pull on my coat.

"We don't. If we're meant to fly them, they'll find us."

Right as I'm about to ask what he means, a set of aqua and gray steeds trots over from around the side of the castle. "That's impossible," I whisper, staring agape as Candor approaches.

"Aquarians are very protective of the Pegazi, so it's hard to know much about them," says Mathias softly so the velvet-clad valets don't overhear us. "They don't allow animal experimentation, no matter how much scientists from other Houses offer to pay to study these creatures, but they do have a fascinating philosophy about them."

His indigo eyes seem to absorb the grayness of the horse's hide and the overcast sky, making them glint like lead. "They believe that since the Pegazi attract so much Psynergy, they're perpetually in sync with the stars and aware of everything that's about to happen. Aquarians think that's how Pegazi determine whom to bond with, and where to travel, and when to show up. They move not through space, but time." He gives me a hand climbing onto Candor. "Their movements are guided by *fate*."

✦ ✦ ✦

We soar over the vast ocean toward Primitus's southern hemisphere, and as I hug the Pegazi's neck, I wonder if it's true these creatures know the way everything will unfold. The thought makes me feel like I'm riding a shooting star.

Candor and I fly in companionable silence, and cradled into her spine I'm comforted by her warm hide, her gentle wings, her starproof heart. A primordial instinct begins to stir within my Center, like I've been touched by the essence of House Cancer, the survival skill at the core of every Cancrian: Candor's nurturing nature reminds me of maternal love.

I'm not sure how long we've been flying over the low-lying ocean when the horizon suddenly grows teeth: Mountains serrate the skyline, drowning the land below in shadows. If the Royal Kingdom was designed in a dream, Nightwing was born from a nightmare.

The spiky coastline of curvy and crooked peaks looks lethal, and it suddenly makes sense why the Pegazi only roam Primitus's northern hemisphere. Instructor Tidus touched briefly on Nightwing for her lesson on the Zodiac's best seers—since most come from here or Pisces—and I remember she said the people of this Clan live on mountaintops to be close to the stars.

Candor circles around the largest summit where there's a small, open-air market, a landing pad, and a Pegazi paddock—but no spaceport or fueling station or anything to hint at much inter-House tourism. The two Clans that share Primitus are notoriously insular, so I wouldn't be surprised if this planet doesn't get many visitors.

Candor's hooves thunder across the rocky earth of the paddock as she lands, and soon I hear the gray horse's echoing movements. There are no other Pegazi here, and as I look around, I realize every Aquarian face is staring our way.

The moment we dismount, a pair of aqua-clad Elders—a man and a woman—materialize at our sides. "Identification?"

Mathias and I each press our thumbs on the small screens they hold out to us, and when my holographic tag comes up—*Wandering Star Rhoma Grace of House Cancer*—they gaze at me curiously but don't ask questions.

"Where's Pandora meeting us?" I whisper to Mathias as we follow the Elders out of the paddock.

"She said she'd find us," he says, and we enter a sparsely attended marketplace. We cut through a grid of stands tented with heavy fabrics that sell everything from clothing to sustenance to Zodai supplies. Mathias dawdles by a delicate display of ivory

Ephemerii, and I cast my gaze around, only I'm not searching for Pandora.

I'm looking for the Aquarian face from my visions.

Could that be why Candor was destined to fly me here—to reunite me with Mom?

My eyes alight on a dark stand at the end of the row draped in a black fabric so opaque that it swallows all surrounding light. The material makes me think of Dark Matter.

"Wandering Star."

I turn to see Pandora, whose waterfall of auburn hair swallows everything but the amethyst orbs of her eyes. She bows to me before bumping fists.

"Nice to see you again, Pandora." She's wearing a charcoal frock that's almost identical to mine, and an overnight bag is slung over one of her shoulders.

Mathias comes up beside me, and Pandora's dusky violet gaze glides up to his. She shyly holds her fist up to him for the hand touch, and he smiles—*Mathias smiles*—and pulls her in for a hug instead.

Seeing his toothy grin, I'm sharply reminded of the boy I watched in the solarium, the one unburdened by death. Pandora's pale skin blooms with color, and I suddenly feel like I'm intruding on a private reunion. The air grows chillier, and I cross my arms to keep warm. I shouldn't have come here.

"So your parents were finally okay with you coming?" Mathias asks her, and from his tone it's clear there's a history to this conversation.

Pandora tips her head down, like her family's worries are a physical weight. "It wasn't easy," she says in a small voice. "My sister is trying to help them understand . . . ."

Mathias reaches over and gently brings her chin up, like he's helping her bear her burden. And I hear myself say, "I'm going to take a quick stroll to check out the stands."

"Rho, wait," says Mathias, his forehead furrowed with concern as I start to walk away. "We'll come with you—"

"*No.*"

The word comes out harsh, so I add, "You guys catch up. I'll be right back."

I head down the line of storefronts, and I pretend to be interested in a case of flashy jewelry a few stands over, until at last I hear the low murmur of their conversation resume. Then I carefully peek back at them.

Pandora is fidgeting with her Philosopher's Stone, but Mathias's stance looks noticeably relaxed, like he's comfortable in her company. Stan was like that with Jewel at first, and so was Deke with Nishi—before either guy recognized his feelings were more than friendly.

How could Mathias have said all those things to me on the flight to Aquarius when he and Pandora clearly have a connection? Mathias is the most honest person I know—I'm supposed to be able to trust him. And yet, like me, it seems he's anything but self-aware when it comes to his heart.

I force myself to keep walking, and when I get to the end of the row, I notice the black tent again. Only this time I spy a pair of white eyes within the folds of darkness.

A strange jitteriness infects the air between us, like a ripple in the universe's fabric.

I edge closer until I'm standing just outside the store's shadow. But I still can't make out anything inside besides those eyes.

My Ring finger buzzes. As I reach down into the icy energy, a raspy voice scratches at my mind.

Would you like to know your future, little girl?

I take a step back. It's considered extremely taboo to break into a stranger's consciousness uninvited; that usually only happens if a Zodai has a physical disability that makes telecommunication essential.

The seer's irises are a frosty blue, so light they look almost white. *I know the answer you're so desperately seeking . . . or should I say the person?*

A small gasp slips past my lips, and I step up to the tent's threshold, as close to the darkness as I dare. Maybe the stars did bring me here to find Mom.

"I don't have any money," I say softly, shame trickling up my face.

You attract a lot of Psynergy for one so young, the voice whispers into my mind. *Would you care to make a trade?*

I have nothing to trade, I say, this time speaking through the Psy, mostly so my voice won't give away my discomfort.

I'll tell you where you can find her . . . if you'll give me some of your Psynergy.

I shiver and repress a second gasp. I've heard stories about a black market for Psynergy, but I never believed it was real. I thought it was just something that happened in movies and holo-shows.

"No, thank you," I say out loud.

Are you so certain your Psynergy is more valuable than your time?

The eyes move closer to me, but I still can't see anything else. I've never heard of a fabric that can soak up light this completely.

Death is eager to have you.

The vision from yesterday paralyzes me with terror, and I can almost feel the omen's putrid flavor filling my mouth again—

"Rho."

Pandora's cold fingers close around my arm, and she pulls me into her stride, away from those frosty eyes. "Are you okay?" she asks in her misty voice. "You look green."

Death's aftertaste is gone from my mouth, and I try focusing on my surroundings: We're walking toward the Pegazi paddock. "Where's Mathias?"

"He spotted another Cancrian and wanted to talk to him."

"What . . . what was that black stand?"

"Dangerous," she says in a hushed tone. "There are seers who dabble in a deadly practice called Psyphoning—they channel another person's Psynergy so they can See more in the Psy. Only it's a very delicate process that requires lots of mental control, and too often the seer takes too much Psynergy, and the drugged person stays trapped in their mind forever."

I'm too revolted to respond, but thankfully we're at the paddock, and Pandora is distracted by the Pegazi. "I can't believe you bonded with your own Pegazi. They rarely do that with someone who isn't of the Royal Kingdom."

"*Hey!*"

We turn at the sound of Mathias's voice. "Sorry about that," he says, slightly out of breath. "There was a man here from the settlement on Secundus. He says the Fellowship Clan has been good to them, and they're going to petition the Monarchy to see if they can formally band together as a Cancrian village under the Aquarian crown."

"Identification."

The same man and woman from earlier stop us at the paddock gate, only this time they're addressing Pandora. When she presses her thumb to the screen, her holographic tag beams out—*Pandora Koft, House Aquarius, Armada Survivor*—and as the Elders scroll through additional details, I catch snippets like *Nightwing Clan* and *Academy Dropout*.

"What's your business in the Royal Kingdom?" the male Elder asks her.

Pandora opens her mouth to speak, but a familiar baritone beats her to it. "We're bringing Pandora with us to the palace," says Mathias, speaking in the firm but respectful tone I remember from when I was his Guardian and he was my Guide. "She's been invited to a royal ball tonight."

The woman Elder wrinkles her brow. "There is no indication of such an invitation on your astrological fingerprint," she says to Pandora.

"It's a last-minute invitation. We can have someone from the palace hologram over and confirm."

Mathias's assertiveness holds none of the hesitation he showed on Scorpio. Only rather than reassuring me, his newfound confidence makes me feel less secure.

"We have no way of verifying that whomever you contact is the true organizer," says the male Elder.

Pandora's shoulders sink, and her defeatist reaction makes me demand, "Why is it you don't need to see our invitations? Why are you only concerned with hers?"

The woman's storm-colored eyes meet mine. "The Pegazi chose to bond with you, so your arrival and departure must have been ordained by the stars. Yet the same cannot be said of her."

"This is Wandering Star Rhoma Grace," says Mathias, as if my name should settle the matter. "It's on her authority that Pandora is to come with us."

"Plenum politics have no bearing on matters of Aquarian royalty," says the male Elder, but he bows his head at me respectfully. "Apologies, but we must protect our sovereign and the royal family at all costs."

Pandora's staring at the ground, and Mathias and I trade questioning glances, each of us looking to the other for more ideas. I'm halfway tempted to contact Crompton himself to help us, when suddenly the Pegazi begin to move.

We all stare in awe as the gray and aqua steeds approach the paddock gate. The male Elder fumbles with the latch, and the woman helps him open the door for the Pegazi to step out. Then the Elders stumble back, giving the creatures a respectful distance as they clop over to us.

As if the horses have understood our whole conversation, Candor nods at the gray steed, and the latter bows before Pandora. The female Elder can't hold back her gasp.

"Looks like the stars are speaking through the Pegazi," says Mathias, and without waiting for permission, he helps Pandora climb on, showing her the dip in the horse's back so she can slide into it. The two Elders look like they'd like to disagree but can't find the words.

"Want help getting on?" he asks me, and I shake my head. I walk over to Candor, and she bows extra low for me so that I can climb on alone. I look back and see Mathias sitting behind Pandora, their bodies so close that her hair touches his chin.

Candor takes off first, which is a good thing since it means I won't have to watch them the whole flight.

The cold air whipping at my face clears my mind. Ophiuchus said the worst thing for us is to be truly alone—no friends, no family, no future. Yet since becoming a Guardian, I've spent as much time fighting against my heart as I have against the master.

Maybe Mathias is right that rather than repressing our feelings, we should be embracing them. None of us is guaranteed a future— so why shouldn't we seize the chance to be happy while we're still here?

A few months ago I thought love couldn't exist in times of war . . . only now I think I was wrong. Love is how we *win* wars. It's only when we're leading a life we want to keep that war becomes worth waging and winning.

Seeing Pandora enjoy Mathias's Cancrian care and protection makes me miss it more than I thought possible. It makes me want to reach out and secure it before it's gone. Except this time, Pandora brought out Mathias's strength . . . not me.

When the Marad captured them, they were thrown together in a situation so terrorizing that they still can't fully describe what happened. For weeks that must have felt like years to them, they clung onto one another to survive. They were broken again and again, and each time they had to repair each other, before the next beating happened.

After all they've been through, I've no doubt that the two of them could have something real and lasting.

But only if Mathias and I can let each other go.

13

WE MEET STAN, NISHI, AND Imogen for lunch at the dining hall closest to the ninth tower. Beneath a high-arched roof is a sea of round tables surrounded by throne-like chairs.

Nishi and Stan are waiting for me by the entrance with eager faces, and I shake my head as I approach. Letting Pandora and Mathias walk ahead, I say, "No news yet." The look on my brother's face makes me add, "but we knew this was too soon, and Crompton is hopeful."

"I'm hopeful, too," says Nishi gently. She seems willing to forget our awkwardness this morning, and I'm glad because I don't want to upset her, though my gut churns thinking of the moment when we finally do have the conversation she's so determined to avoid.

She links her arm with Stan's, and we join Mathias, Pandora, and Imogen at a table. "So what have you guys been up to?" I ask as we sit down.

"Watching the news," says Stanton, his voice tight. "There's been an update on Pisces."

I lean into the table, but our conversation is interrupted by the arrival of two velvet-clad valets with trays of food. They deposit massive gold and silver platters in the center of our table, enough food that it could feed a group twice our size. Holographic identification tags hover over each dish for a moment, and every ingredient sounds foreign to me—glazed oven roast, spiced porklings, sweet aquadile skewers—and accompanying the meats are bowls of the largest vegetables I've ever seen.

I learned my lesson last night not to pile my plate with too much food—it's good, but it's so rich that a few bites are more than enough. As soon as the valets depart, my brother picks up the thread again. "Healers from other Houses have gotten to Pisces, and the situation is worse than was first reported. They still don't know how the sleeping virus is being spread, but it's moving so fast that it's already infected over half the population. Prophet Marinda had to issue a decree confining people to their homes because bodies were dropping all over the place."

"What's being done to try to cure them?" I ask.

"First we have to know what's affecting them," he says darkly. "The Guardians have divided the care of the five planetoids among all the Houses. The first concern will be to protect those Piscenes who aren't showing signs of infection yet, so they'll separate the people of every planetoid into two camps."

"What could cause this?" I ask, turning to Nishi. She shakes her head like she's just as baffled as I am, only she's looking down at a holographic screen from her Tracker and typing a message.

"But there's a bigger problem," says my brother, and I snap my gaze to him.

"Worse than the whole Piscene population falling into comas—"

"The infected can't Center themselves," says Pandora, and a heavy silence falls over the table.

"They've been discussing this all morning on Nightwing," she adds in her soft voice. "Since the past two months have been peaceful, too few Piscenes are off world. Which means nearly the whole population is home."

She doesn't have to say more for the full horror to settle on me. Cancer lost its land, but a tenth of our people survived thanks to early evacuations. Virgo lost 50 percent of its population, and Gemini lost a third, but if 99 percent of Piscenes lose their connection to the Collective Conscious . . .

"House Pisces will be lost to the Psy," I whisper.

Just like House Ophiuchus.

The loaded silence that follows my words is broken by my brother. "Only good news is the Houses are now so preoccupied with Pisces, they've forgotten to kick our people out of our settlements."

He stabs a piece of meat with his fork, and I notice his eyes are bloodshot again. I turn to Nishi, who's barely picked at her food. She's still answering messages, probably having to do with managing tonight's event. Her complete focus on her duties reminds me of her intense dedication to our band. She's being *old* Nishi, from before we lost our school and our safety and our Deke.

"So when do we meet Blaze?" I ask, and the question finally pulls her away from her Tracker.

She winks out the red holographic screen. "Now, if you're ready!"

She's already pushing back from the table when Imogen says, "Just one thing. We should probably settle on dates for the ball first."

"Oh, right," says Nishi.

"Why do we need dates?" I ask.

"It's an Aquarian custom," says Pandora, and it's hard to miss the spark of hope in her voice. "We take an escort to most events. But *especially* a royal ball."

My gaze darts to Mathias, and a flush rises up my face when I find he's already looking at me.

"I'm not taking a date," announces Stan.

"We're guests here, so we have to follow Aquarian traditions," says Nishi, and the way she overrides him reminds me of how she used to override Deke at the Academy.

"But, the thing is," she goes on, her expression becoming apologetic as she turns to me, "since what we're doing with the Tomorrow Party transcends House divisions, Blaze wants tonight to be different from previous balls. So we each have to take someone from a different House."

The moment the words are out of her mouth, I can't look in Mathias and Pandora's direction again.

"Stanton, you'll have the honor of escorting me tonight." Imogen's invitation sounds less like a question and more like a declaration. Her confidence reminds me of Miss Trii.

I watch my brother's neck glow red with embarrassment, and then he brings his glass of water to his lips to avoid answering.

Knowing whom this night will be hardest on, I turn to my best friend and take her hand. "Will you go to the ball with me, Nish?"

She nods and rests her head on my shoulder, and I caress her long, black tresses, trying to ignore what's going across from me. All I can make out is Pandora's Philosopher's Stone, which she's turning anxiously over and over in her hands.

"Would you like to go together tonight?"

At the sound of Mathias's musical baritone, the Philosopher's Stone stops spinning, and I pull Nishi to her feet to tune out Pandora's reply.

"We should go," I say, leading the way to the ninth tower without looking back, my pulse rising and my hands becoming clammy.

I don't know how my heart got so twisted. Somewhere along the way I just started letting my emotions grow wild and tangled, without stopping to prune them, and now they've wrapped around my ribcage like vines, and they won't let me see what's going on in there.

I'd like to claim I've been too focused on all the lives threatened by Ochus and the master and the Marad to think of my own. But the truth Engle forced me to face is that I was neglecting my heart long before the Lunar Quadract. Even as a kid on Cancer, rather than facing the pain of growing up in a house without Mom, I chose to escape to the moon. Then as an Acolyte, rather than risking the pain of opening my heart to someone, I chose the safety of loving an older man who was too noble to love me back, finding solace in the riddle of knowing that if Mathias had feelings for me when I was too young, he wouldn't be the noble man I loved.

But I can't hide behind our age difference anymore because it doesn't matter. So is my fear once more trying to guide me down a pain-free path? And if so, what frightens me more: that I'm in love with Mathias . . . or that I might not be?

"Here we are," says Nishi when we're back in the ninth tower's busy common room. She knocks on a door at the far end of the space.

A voice from inside calls, "Come in!"

When Nishi swings the door open, I pause on the threshold to Blaze's office. I've never seen such a cluttered room in my life. Holographic posters cover every inch of wall space, and open boxes of every size are strewn throughout, spilling their colorful contents on the floor.

"Over here!" the same voice says from somewhere deep inside, beyond the stacks upon stacks of documents and decorations and devices. As we pick our way through the jumble, I see that the boxes are there for a reason—they're like flags indicating where one collection of items ends and the next begins.

My gaze pans across mounds of books, food baskets, Tomorrow Party T-shirts . . . and the longer I stare at everything, the more I realize that the seemingly haphazard placement is purposeful. There's some kind of unintelligible design in the chaos, a wild creature's organizational system.

"Just a little farther!" he calls out encouragingly.

Wending through the piles of possessions, I pick up on a territorial vibe. However temporary the arrangement, this office clearly *belongs* to its inhabitant.

We finally make it to the back of the room, where there's a slightly open area with a table and chairs. "Welcome!" roars a beaming, blue-haired Leonine, baring his jaws in a broad smile.

Rather than hold out his hand for the traditional greeting, he pulls each of us in for a hug. "It's an honor, Rho," says Blaze gruffly. After everyone's been introduced, he looks to me and opens his arms like he's offering another hug.

"So, Wandering Star. What do you want to know?"

Now that I've met him, I can understand the state of this office. Blaze seems like the kind of man who owns every room he walks into.

"What's your goal with the Tomorrow Party?" asks my brother before I can speak.

Blaze takes a seat at the head of the table and gestures that we should join him. "Our goal is to build bridges across the Zodiac so that we can stop viewing each other as strangers. We want to usher in a new generation of leaders who want to work together with the other Houses and encourage people to see beyond the walls of their own worlds. And we're doing that by focusing on a number of things.

"First, fundraising. Without money, we can't pay for things like tonight's event, which is when we're going to introduce ourselves to a small group of powerful people from the Houses and gauge what kind of support or resistance we're likely to encounter from the rest of the Zodiac. Second, we're researching the up-and-coming unionist leaders of every House to back them for upcoming elections." He looks from my brother to me, and I spy the rainbow highlights peeking out through his blue locks. "I don't think it's a coincidence that the past couple of decades the stars have chosen some of the youngest Guardians we've ever had. Guardian Brynda of Sagittarius, Prophet Marinda of Pisces, Gortheaux of Aquarius—and, of course, you."

Hysan, too, I think to myself.

"The stars have been choosing younger and younger Guardians because our galaxy is turning the page. A new order is needed for the Zodiac. A new vision for tomorrow."

"That sounds great," I say. "But every House has its own governance and election cycle, and building new political players and platforms—on twelve worlds—will take years. The Zodiac might not have that long. We need to come together *now*."

I didn't mean to sound so ominous, but from the way everyone's staring at me, I can tell they're all wondering whether I've had a vision. The taste of Death sours my tongue again, but I force myself to ignore it.

"You're right," says Blaze, his russet gaze so intense that I can't pull away. "And that's why we're not waiting."

Nishi and Imogen sit up, and an air of suspense settles over the table.

"The third and final task we've been working on will make sure that when this threat is over, our Zodiac's newfound era of peace will be even better—and more progressive. We're working with a privately funded team of scientists from every House to develop a terraform planet between the Leo and Virgo constellations. We're petitioning the Plenum to allow this settlement to become, on a one-year experimental basis, home to a mixed population of people from across the Houses."

Nishi squeezes my hand under the table, but I can't even blink.

"We want to create a model of Zodiac living where we aren't segregated by race. A system where we can just be a collection of individuals working together and celebrating a variety of cultures. A world where choice outweighs chance, where a man can change his stars.

"And we've named this new world *Black Moon*."

14

AN HOUR LATER NISHI AND I are lying side by side on the feathery bed, gazing up at the tower's pointy ceiling.

"Why *Black Moon?*" I whisper.

"It's a term for when there's more than one new moon in a month," she says softly. "So we're thinking of it as a chance for a new beginning."

I'm still in too much shock to string my thoughts into cohesion. The only thing I can think of is Ferez and his vision for our future. It's coming to fruition. Nishi was right. This Party is everything we've been fighting for.

Back in his office, Blaze showed us breathtaking designs for a major city that will one day be home to people from every House. He also spoke of having cultural centers throughout the city where people can go learn about each other's race through interactive workshops and exhibits. There will be a dozen temples where anyone who chooses can continue to celebrate her home world's traditions. Black Moon will have a democratic government: Residents will elect their own representatives, and anyone will be eligible to run for office. It will be a place where House affiliation won't matter, where everyone will have a home.

Even Stanton couldn't find anything objectionable. Once Blaze was finished speaking, my brother sat in the same bewildered silence as the rest of us.

"This is incredible, Nish," I finally say, a tear falling into my hair. She rolls onto her side to face me, propping her head up on her elbow.

"*I told you*, Rho! We're not just talking anymore . . . we're *doing*. We're changing the—"

Her whole face goes white, and she leaps to her feet, like she's been stung by a water-fly.

I know what she was going to say because I was thinking it, too. *We're changing the norm by breaking it*. Just like Deke wanted.

She marches toward the door. "I need to check on something—"

"Nish, wait—let's talk—"

I reach for her hand, but she swats me away. When she swings around to face me, her cinnamon skin is pale and her face is unrecognizably twisted.

"*Don't*," she warns.

"But—"

"I don't dwell in the past, Rho." I flinch at the hardness in her voice.

"I know," I say, "but you also can't keep running from it. If you want to move forward, you need to face what's happened and make your peace with it—"

"The same way you did with your Mom?" she asks, her voice almost icy. "Same way you're doing with Hysan?"

My mouth is suddenly parched. "So because I've mishandled the painful parts of my past, you're going to do the same with yours?"

"I'm not the one mishandling anything," she snarls. "I'm the one putting aside her personal problems to do what needs doing. But be honest with yourself—did you truly come to Aquarius to be part of this Party, or are you here to find your mom?"

I swallow down the awful feelings rising up my throat. "I came to make sure you were okay, Nish."

Her austere expression cracks, and she closes her eyes and inhales slowly, like she's Centering herself. When she looks at me again, she seems tired and sad.

"I don't want to fight," she says, letting me take her hand. "I found something to believe in here, something he would have wanted to be part of. Right now I just need to focus on that. This is how I honor him."

❖ ❖ ❖

After my almost-fight with Nishi, I decide to leave the room for some alone time before we have to start getting ready for the ball. From Black Moon to Nightwing to Pisces, today has been exhausting on every level. And yet, of everything that's happened, I still can't shake the sound of the seer's raspy voice.

She Saw my death, too.

I head down through the trapdoor to consult the Ephemeris, and just as she did on Vitulus, Pandora beats me to the stars.

"We really need to stop meeting this way."

She flicks her gaze over to me when I speak, but she doesn't look surprised. "On Aquarius, when two people's paths are constantly tangling, we say they're *soul-bound*—which means the same stars must be pulling our strings."

"I like that."

We meet in the middle of the room, like a couple of stars being drawn to the holographic Helios. "My parents couldn't believe I was invited to the royal palace," she says, a note of pride in her voice. "Usually only our senior Elders are welcome."

"Why is the palace so hard to access?"

"To protect the royal family. If the bloodline ends, so does our connection to the stars." The spectral map dapples the dark sandstone walls with light, and the shadows on Pandora's face remind me of how she looked when we discovered her in the Marad torture chamber.

"How was coming home?" I ask, for a moment almost envying her for having a home and a family and a planet to return to.

Her eyes grow cloudy. "I thought . . . I thought I'd never make it back. And in some ways, I haven't."

"What do you mean?"

"It was good to see my family, especially my sister. Only now I feel . . ."

She trails off, her airy voice dissipating into nothingness, and when she doesn't pick up her own thread again, I goad her gently. "Now you feel . . . ?"

"Like I've outgrown my life," she says, her amethyst eyes glowing as bright as the orbs of light surrounding us. "Like this isn't me anymore."

Her voice dips so low that I'm not sure if the words are for my ears or just for her own. "At a certain point the torture room where you found us began to feel more familiar than my own home."

The admission is so darkly personal that I'm taken aback by her easy trust, especially when it's hard to know where we stand with each other. Can we be both friends and rivals?

Before I can ask what she means, she asks me, "Do you think light can erase even the worst kind of darkness?" I start to nod *yes*, but I stop as she begins a new question. "Or do you think sometimes the dark can weigh so heavily on your skin that it seeps into your pores and becomes part of you?"

"I'm not sure what you—"

"After going so long without sunlight, I don't think I can return to an ordinary life. I can't stay here, on Primitus, pretending I don't know what lurks in the darkness. I need to be part of this fight . . . because this war is the only home I have left."

I nod, finally understanding her. "Sounds like we're soul-bound after all."

✦ ✦ ✦

An hour before the ball begins, Nishi and I are cozying up on the Lady's Lounge couch while she tries dozens of dresses on my hologram.

My doppelganger is caught in a whirlwind of gaudy gowns with corset-like torsos and full-formed skirts, in all kinds of colorful fabrics—embroidered taffeta accented with lace, sheer chiffon woven with pearls, brocade trimmed with silver, silky charmeuse studded with stones, crinkly crepe lined with fur, and more. Nishi's planning to wear a pale pink taffeta number, and when she modeled it for me on her hologram, she looked like a princess that belongs in this palace.

Nishi is tall, so she can pull off these elaborate Aquarian skirts way better than I can. My hologram just keeps getting swallowed by the fabrics.

"*None* of these is going to work," she snaps. The nice thing about having such an honest best friend is that I don't have to worry about her lying to make me feel better. "But don't worry," she adds quickly. "We'll find something."

There's a knock on our door, and we open it to find a couple of Aquarian lady's maids. One of them is holding a large garment bag.

"Good evening. We're here to help you get ready for the ball," says the older of the two. She has the orange eyes of a sunny afternoon. "We also bring a message for the Wandering Star from"—she seems to debate her words a moment—"a rather *unpleasant* woman who insisted we deliver this dress to you and seemed to imply we would be inciting a political incident between our Houses if we failed her."

"Oh. I'm . . . sorry?"

Nishi hears the laugh I'm biting back and mouths, "*Who?*"

"A thousand galactic gold coins says it's Sirna," I say as I accept the bag from the Aquarian. I carefully lay it out on the bed, and Nish impatiently reaches down and unzips it. She gasps at the soft, golden glow that beams out.

The dress is made of the most stunning material I've ever seen; it looks like millions of strands of liquid gold were woven together to create it. The structured bodice has a heart-shaped neckline held in place by a column of small diamonds that button down the back, and the skirt unfolds into a gown that's far less puffy than all the others I've just seen. There's no additional adornment or accent; the dress is simply a sea of gold without interruption, and it comes with a pair of matching, arm-length golden gloves.

"*Helios,*" breathes Nishi. "It's stellar, Rho."

The color makes me think of Hysan's golden Knight suit, and before I can punch them back, memories of him spill out of my subconscious and spread through my body.

My heart hurts the moment I allow my feelings for him to surface. I don't know what I miss more—his touch or his words. I've been trying so hard to move forward by going backward—taking back the passage of time, taking back my feelings for Hysan, taking back my years of silence with Mathias. But however hard I try, I can't seem to make Time move in that direction.

The dress's fine fabric feels as light as air, and as I run my fingers through it, a hand-written note topples out from the skirt's folds.

If the stars had called on me to lead when I was sixteen, I don't know how I would have fared. But I doubt I would have shown half your bravery or heart. Stay safe out there, Rho.

Your friend, Sirna

My gaze lingers on the last line . . . *your friend.* But is Sirna my friend, even after everything she said to me, even after betraying me to the Plenum? I twine my fingers through the gold chain around my neck with its single rose-colored nar-clam pearl—another gift from Sirna—while Nishi bathes and the lady's maids set up stations in the Lounge. Whether or not Sirna and I are friends, she does have a habit of swooping in and saving me when I need her to. I guess I owe her too much to hold a grudge.

I decide to leave the necklace on—it matches the dress, after all—and following a soak in the luxurious tub, I pull on my plush aqua robe and sit beside Nishi at the vanity. The younger lady's maid is already styling Nishi's black locks into an elaborately braided bun that makes her look like she's wearing a crown.

"The regal look suits you," I say, and Nishi winks at me in the mirror.

The woman with the sunny eyes brushes out my blond hair and sprays the strands until my curls grow wavy and glossy, then she starts pinning my locks into an asymmetrical up-do that makes me look slightly lopsided. When she leans over me to apply makeup, she blocks my view of the mirror, and to avoid staring at her chest,

I close my eyes while she works, bringing Nishi's commentary into focus.

"No, not that dark," she tells the lady's maid styling her. "Let's use a thin line of black eyeliner along my lashes and add just the tiniest dash of shine on the lids, but—no, not that color for the lipstick; I don't want to clash with the pale tone of the dress . . . ."

I start to tune her out, and my mind wanders to where Lola and Leyla might be. The last time we spoke was a month ago when I Waved Leyla to check in; she and Lola were accompanying Agatha on her visit to our Taurian camp, located on Vitulus's Flank Section.

Poor Agatha must be so overwhelmed with the situation on our settlements, especially now that she also has to deal with what's happening on Pisces. Maybe there's something I can do to help. I could call Sirna tomorrow to thank her for the dress and see if she can pass Agatha a message from me.

I hear Nishi getting to her feet. "Rho, I need to check in with Blaze and Imogen to make sure everything is on track, and I'll come back to get dressed with you."

I can't answer because my lips are being painted. Once the lady's maid steps back from my face, I open my eyes and see my reflection.

I glue my tongue to the roof of my mouth until I'm sure I have my emotions under control. Then I manage to say, "Thank you so much."

When I'm left alone in the Lounge, I study myself in the mirror. Now I understand why Nishi was so vocal earlier. My face is a disaster. I look like a fancy ghost: My skin has been painted a pale, powdery white, and my eyes are outlined in gold with glittering eye shadow. My gaze travels up to the cockeyed mess of hair on my head, and I know there's no way I can leave the room like this.

I start pulling out pins. There are hundreds, and by the time I'm done, my curls fall freely over my face. Then I go into the bathroom and wash the makeup off in the sink.

I return to the vanity and stare dejectedly at my reflection, then crack open my Wave and call Leyla. Rather than reaching out traditionally—which would send my hologram to her—I send a reverse request; if she accepts, her hologram will be transmitted here.

A few minutes later, Leyla's demure figure manifests in the air before me; like always, her red hair is pulled tightly away from her sapphire eyes.

"Wandering Star, it's an honor to hear from you," she says, bowing and sounding slightly out of breath.

"You, too, Leyla. If you're busy, we can talk another time," I send back, realizing how selfish I'm being. I don't know where she is, so I have no idea what time it is for her. "I don't mean to take you away from sleep or Holy Mother or any other obligations."

When her transmission reactivates, she's shaking her head at my concerns. "We're on Leo, and it's the middle of the afternoon." Her gaze pans across my surroundings, and she asks, "How may I be of service?"

"Well . . . I'm on Aquarius, about to attend a royal ball, and I was wondering if you had a moment to help me get ready?"

Leyla flashes her rare smile. "I would have been hurt if you didn't ask."

After I show her the dress, she makes me hold up various tins and tubes on the table, and then she starts instructing me. "The gold of the gown is flashy enough, so you should go with a more natural look, and maybe a little pop on your lips. Show me that foundation again."

Once she's picked out what I'm going to use, she directs me as I apply each item. While I work, she fills me in on what's happening with our refugee camps. "We're leaving our settlement on Hydragyr," she tells me, her face somber. "There are too many displaced Geminin, and it isn't right to ask them to split their resources with us when they need them just as much."

I lower my powder brush and stare at her. "Where will we go?"

After a transmission delay, she says, "We are negotiating with the Sagittarian government to create a permanent settlement along the coastline of planet Gryphon. Or at least, we *were*, until Pisces became everyone's primary concern."

"Have you heard any theories about what this epidemic could be?"

"No, but Lola found out that Stridents managed to isolate the agent in the blood of the infected, so now they can test conscious Piscenes to see who will develop the symptoms. They also synthesized a type of antiviral that protects visiting Zodai from becoming infected."

Again I'm reminded of how important House Scorpio is to the Zodiac. Their Innovation is what we're going to need to survive this war—and, just as significantly, to rebuild the Zodiac.

"Let me look at you," says Leyla, pulling me out of my reverie. "You can lose the headband now so we can figure out your hair."

My curls tumble loose, and while I wait for Leyla's hologram to reactivate, I stare at my reflection in the mirror. My sun-kissed skin glows, and there's a light dusting of gold bronzer along my cheekbones. Brown liner tops my eyelids, softened with a shimmer of creamy eye shadow. The beachy curls and understated makeup remind me of the natural look of the Cancrians back home.

I watch Leyla's eyes stray to the line of lipsticks on the vanity. "How do you feel about bold lips?"

"What are you thinking?" I ask, following her gaze.

"*Red.*"

Unlike the glossy red shade Imogen uses on her lips, Leyla picks out a matte shade that makes me think of rose petals. "Leave your hair down," she says, and I hear echoes of home in her voice, too. "You look more like you that way."

"Thanks, Leyla. I couldn't have done this without you."

"Yes, you could have. But you wouldn't look this good."

I laugh, and then we end our call right as Nishi walks into the Lounge.

"*Called it!*" she says the moment she sees me. "I saw your makeup as I was leaving, and I was sure by the time I came back you'd have washed it off. You did a good job on your own."

"I had help," I admit, following her out to the main room where our dresses are laid out on the bed.

The lady's maids are here waiting to help us into our gowns, and when the woman with the orange eyes sees that I've undone all her hard work, her brow dips with disapproval. I didn't think about the fact that I'd be seeing her again, and I feel my cheeks flushing with embarrassment.

"I'm sorry," I murmur as she holds the dress up for me. "I just didn't feel like myself. . . ."

She doesn't speak as she works, and it takes a lot of pulling and tugging to button every last diamond lining the bodice's back. I notice her eyes straying to the scars on my arm, and when she tries to remove the small black glove from my left hand to replace it with the long golden one, I pull my arm back.

"I can put the gloves on. Thank you for your help." She nods and leaves the room.

I turn away from Nishi and her lady's maid as I strip off the black glove so they won't see the Scorp weapon that hides beneath it. Then I slide my arms into the long golden gloves.

Once it's just the two of us in the room, Nishi and I turn to each other. She looks like the belle of the ball with her coronet of black hair, soft pastel makeup, and pink taffeta gown.

"Let's have fun tonight," she says, squeezing my hand. "No dark thoughts."

I nod. "It's a plan."

We duck into the Lady's Lounge to check ourselves out in the mirror, and almost immediately the flint Tracker on Nishi's wrist starts singing with alerts. "I need to head downstairs," she says, rushing out after a fleeting glance at her reflection. "Meet you there!"

I'm about to follow her, but I decide to look in the mirror first. And when I do, I see someone else.

The dress is out of this world; it looks like I've wrapped one of Helios's rays around me. And yet that's not what catches my eye.

My features reflect the effects of the shift from my sedentary days on Elara to this new adventurous life of racing through the

Zodiac. My cheekbones stick out more, my waist is more toned, and my hair hangs longer than it has in years. It's hard to find the girl I was in the woman I've become. But still none of these details are what's most striking.

The thing I can't get over as I look at my reflection . . . is how much I look like Mom.

15

I LEAVE THE ROOM, AND everyone is waiting for me at the foot of the spiral staircase. Everyone except Nishi.

I focus on the floor as I climb down in my high heels, but as I'm descending the last ring of steps, I steal a peek at Mathias. The sight of him in his black tuxedo nearly makes me miss a step.

Mathias sees me stumble, and when he steps forward to offer me his arm, I feel my cheeks heat up. The way he fills out a tuxedo makes me think the style must have been invented just for him.

"You look like you could light up the universe," he murmurs in his musical voice. His dark, wavy hair is combed back, leaving his indigo eyes front and center, and I'm reminded of how I felt the night he picked me up for my swearing-in ceremony, when it seemed like anything was still possible between us.

"You look . . ." I trail off, failing to find a word as beautiful as he is. Then I realize the others have gone quiet and say loudly, "You all look great!"

Stanton is wearing a disgruntled expression along with his navy-blue tux, and beside him Imogen is in a low-cut black levlan gown that makes her look like a sexy rock star. Pandora looks pretty in a turquoise gown that's simpler than the others, though she seems the least comfortable by far. I would have thought as an Aquarian she'd be used to this kind of opulence, but it appears the Nightwing and Royal Clans follow very different rules.

"Let's hurry," says Nishi, dashing over from the common room. "We're late, and if anyone notices, it's going to look bad for me and Imogen."

She takes my arm, and the six of us race through the sandstone halls of the palace, cutting through numerous drawing rooms, a couple of thought tunnels, and the star-high entrance hall with its stained glass windows, where some kind of scuffle is taking place by the main doors. A dozen valets in velvet top hats are blocking the commotion so I can't see what's causing it, but as I peek between the bodies, I think I spot a familiar face with a mane of brown hair. Yet before I can place him, we've turned the corner.

At last we reach the marble wall that marks the easternmost end of the castle, and a pair of Elders approach us to check our identities. After we've all flashed our thumbprints, an Aquarian presses his handprint to the wall, and a slab of marble slides down, opening a doorway into the ball.

We step onto the balcony of a grand staircase that descends into an enormous domed ballroom. The floor below is packed with couples dressed in formalwear, and a blanket of white, cottony smoke swirls along the ground, giving the impression that everyone is walking on clouds.

My eyes dart all over the place, taking in the room's grandeur. Intricate patterns in plated gold and silver are woven into the white marble walls, forming elaborate compositions that look like if you stared at them long enough, they might reveal a hidden design. There's a full orchestra playing a lively waltz at the far end of the hall, and ornate silver and gold trays bearing tall-stemmed glasses with a clear, fizzy drink float on their own among the partygoers.

The whole event feels enchanting but decadent, just like House Aquarius. The clothing is too busy, the lifestyle is too loud, the meals are too rich, the portions too large, the country too vast, and at times it's all too much. And yet it's also mythic and majestic and beguiling, and I can see how someone would never want to leave this place. It's the kind of world where fairy tales might actually exist.

And maybe even *happily ever afters*.

Once we've regrouped on the cloudy ground, Stanton says, "Pisces is on the cusp of extinction, our people are being exiled, the Marad could attack any moment, and here we are, having a royal ball."

I don't say it out loud to avoid agitating him further, but I can't help agreeing. I wonder where all this money came from, since I'd gotten the impression the Party's backers were young and idealistic people, not older wealthy types; this level of opulence feels almost in opposition to the Party's philosophy of acceptance and open-mindedness.

Still, it's only natural that as different cultures come together, we're going to clash. Traditions will rub us the wrong way, people will be misunderstood, arguments will arise—but we can't jump to judgment, or we'll never make any progress.

"Stan, they couldn't accept Aquarius's support while dismissing its customs. This is how the royal palace throws parties, and the Tomorrow Party had to respect that."

"Hear, hear!" says a voice behind me, and I turn to see a smiling girl with a headful of braids reaching out to bump fists with me.

"Ezra!" I say at the sight of the brazen and brilliant fifteen-year-old from Centaurion. She's wearing a silver tulle gown revealing feet that are clad in clunky combat boots.

As we trade the hand touch, she asks, "Have you come to join the Tomorrow Party?"

Before I can answer, a mournful voice injects, "Or are you here in your capacity as Wandering Star?"

I look up to see her friend, the philosophical Gyzer, smiling at me, and I feel a smile warming my face, too.

"Or both?" asks Ezra.

"Or neither?" asks Gyzer.

"Helios, is that what I sound like?" asks Nishi, turning to me with a preoccupied brow.

I look at the three sets of long-cut eyes staring at me, awaiting answers, and all I can manage is, "You Sagittarians are exhausting."

"Thank you!" says Ezra, as Nishi laughs.

"You know you were supposed to bring a date from a different House, right?" asks Imogen, after Ezra and Gyzer have traded the hand touch with everyone.

"Try telling *him* that." Ezra rolls her eyes toward Gyzer.

"What's wrong with bringing someone from our own House?" he asks, and in the depths of his soulful eyes I spy a challenge. "I find it troubling that a Party founded on a foundation of choice would forbid us from bringing whoever we wanted."

"It wasn't meant to be taken that way," says Nishi defensively. "It's about celebrating the spirit of the Party. It's not like anyone's going around enforcing it."

"That's not the point," says Gyzer. His lavender bowtie—the color of Sagittarius—pops against the dark gray of his tux and the coal-black of his skin. "Freedom shouldn't move like an arrow, in a singular direction. It should flow like an ocean, swallowing the whole horizon."

"I like that," I say, and noting Nishi's frown I turn to Ezra. "What's been going on since Taurus? I remember your invention traced part of the Marad's transmission. So does that mean you're working for Brynda now?"

Ezra looks at Gyzer before answering. "Well, she wants us to finish our Acolyte studies first, but we're done with that life. We can't just go back to school after everything that's happened."

"So what then?" asks Stan. "What will you do?"

"That's what we're trying to figure out." She looks like she might say more, but again she looks at Gyzer, and this time I notice his reaction—a slight shake of his head. And she stops talking.

Just then another couple approaches our group, and I recognize more faces from Centaurion. "Numen!"

The blond Libran flashes me a charming smile. "Lady Rho, it's wonderful to see you." She bows before bumping fists with me, and

I have to look away from her gray eyes to avoid seeing the painfully familiar golden star.

"This is Qima," she says, introducing me to an olive-skinned, mossy-eyed girl whom I remember from Twain's crew.

"Nice to see you again," I say, trading the hand touch with the Virgo. "And I'm . . . I'm sorry about Twain. And Moira," I add, thinking of the still-comatose Guardian.

"And planet Tethys, too?" she asks, one brow arched. "Seems like our House has lost a lot since you came onto our soil."

"I—"

"I'm not blaming you." There's no threat or sarcasm in her voice; she's just stating facts. "I'm simply pointing out that our House has suffered as much as yours. So if you need help, you need to come to us."

"I will," I say, if only to escape the intensity of her gaze.

"Virgos have been cooped up on their constellation for so long, they've forgotten how to socialize," says a sunny Numen. "I guess politeness isn't a function on their Perfectionaries."

"What's wrong with what I said?" asks Qima, who looks to be fighting back a grin, while the Libran laughs openly and melodically.

As the others introduce themselves, and I watch my expanding group of friends, I feel like I've become part of a new family, one made up of more than just Cancrians. Diversity doesn't weaken us—it binds us closer together. Numen and Qima come from opposite cultures, yet rather than being polarizing, their polar perspectives keep them in balance. This is what Black Moon will be like—a place where our inherited prejudices will fall away because we'll have a chance to personally interact with people of every House.

Skarlet Thorne is right: The only way to combat the Marad's violence is to replace the soldiers' hate with hope. And tonight it feels like Black Moon is hope made tangible.

The festive orchestra starts to play their first slow number, and Gyzer and Ezra peel away to the dance floor. Mathias moves closer to me and murmurs, "Would you like to dance?"

Confused, I dart a glance at Pandora, who's hovering near Nishi and Imogen but isn't participating in the group conversation. She looks miserable.

"Sure," I say, though I don't sound it.

He leads me to the dance floor near the orchestra, and I slink a gold-gloved arm around his neck as he takes my other hand in his. Mathias's fingers brush along my lower back, and he says, "I liked everything about this new Party until this ball. It feels more like a celebration of the old ways than the new."

"Yeah," I say, my mouth dry, "except we're here with partners from different Houses. That would have never happened before."

He goes quiet, withdrawing into his mind, but not in an injured way. Rather than looking lost, his eyes are focused, like he's been doing a lot of thinking. "What do you imagine would have happened," he whispers, his musical voice wistful, "if I'd spoken to you my last day of university?"

Picturing the scene and trying to envision a different outcome, at last I understand the true tragedy of Mathias and me.

We're a couple of Cancrian clichés: More than our hearts, we've always trusted our fears. Even if we couldn't help falling for each other, it was the decisions we made after we fell that mattered.

If either of us had dared to speak up any of those mornings in the solarium—if he hadn't shut down my feelings on *Equinox*, if I hadn't shut the airlock door on him on *Firebird*—today, we wouldn't be these same people. The stars set us on the same path . . . but our choices diverted us.

This whole time, I've been trying to find my way back to those mornings on Elara when life was so simple and my feelings were so clear. But when the opportunity presented itself—when Mathias opened his heart to me on our way to Aquarius—I didn't take it.

I may not like the thought of him being Pandora's, but I haven't claimed him for myself either.

When I look into Mathias's midnight eyes again, I feel the decision taking over every cell in my body, even though there's a small piece of my heart that hasn't given its consent yet. There's a part of me that will always love Mathias—but I've been hiding behind the memory of what I once felt for him to avoid admitting that I'm not in love with him anymore.

The truth is my heart already made the choice between Hysan and Mathias . . . my brain just didn't want to hear it.

"I didn't mean to upset you," murmurs Mathias, reeling me in a little closer. My feelings stick to my tongue, but they won't become words yet. I don't know how to say what needs to be said.

On Vitulus, Miss Trii told me that sometimes the best way to love someone is to let them go. So I inhale deeply and say, "I-I don't think these feelings are real anymore, Mathias." My voice has never sounded less mine. "I think they're memories."

He pulls away enough to look at me, and I see sadness swimming in his eyes, the same sadness I'm fighting down within myself.

But in the depths of that sadness, I think there's also freedom.

We pull away before the song ends, and when we return to the others, Nishi comes over and links her elbow with mine. "Are you okay?" she asks softly, and there's no point in answering because I feel a tear rolling down my cheek.

She pulls me in for a hug, and I rest my face against her collarbone, content just to breathe for a moment. My heart feels fragile, like it's recovering from a major operation, so I keep a good distance from my feelings and try focusing on my inhales and exhales.

A few feet away Numen and Qima are filling Stan and Imogen in on news from their worlds, and Mathias and Pandora stand at opposite ends of the group, neither one looking at the other. An ornate golden tray of clear, fizzy drinks floats past, and Mathias takes one.

It's amazing how he can be so attuned to my emotions and yet so deaf to his own. How can he not realize his feelings for Pandora are more than friendly? I hate to admit it, but Cancrians can be so hard shelled sometimes.

Nishi and I pull apart, and she squeezes my arm in encouragement as we rejoin the group. Eager not to cross gazes with Mathias or Pandora, I look up to the top of the grand staircase, where more couples are appearing on the upper balcony and descending into the ballroom. Among the new faces, I spot a stunning Ariean girl in a show-stopping red gown who looks familiar. As I squint at her warm, bronze-brown features, I recognize Skarlet.

Excitement flutters in my belly. Of course she'd be invited; she's exactly the kind of rising leader the Tomorrow Party would be interested in wooing. I take a few steps toward the stairs to position myself close enough to talk to her, and I notice a man's arm circling her waist. Curious to check out her date, I pan my gaze up to see his face.

And I shatter.

16

WHEN I SEE THE GOLDEN hair and lively green eyes, everything seems to just *stop*.

The music.

The Zodiac.

My heart.

Sporting an immaculate white tuxedo and his trademark centaur smile, Hysan descends the staircase with Skarlet on his arm, commanding the attention of what feels like the entire ballroom.

"Breathe," whispers Nishi, her hand gripping my shoulder. "I'm so sorry, Rho—the Party invited him, but he never responded, so I figured he wasn't coming. I didn't see a point in bringing him up to you for no reason."

My pulse is pounding so mightily that I'm scared my heart might be trying to break away from my body. If it keeps punching this hard, it's going to crack open its cage.

"What do you want to do?" asks Nishi in my ear. But I can't think, can't answer her, can't turn away from him as he moves in my direction.

"Rho, if you don't want him to see you, maybe we should—"

"Wandering Star!"

I force myself to look away, and I see Blaze parting from his entourage to greet me, his date in tow. He's donning a flashy, royal purple tuxedo, and as he comes closer, I notice the pair of pants is actually a floor-length skirt.

"You look luminous," he says, planting whiskery kisses on my cheeks. His breath smells sweet; he's been drinking the fizzy Aquarian cocktail everyone's enjoying. Then he spots Nishi and roars, "By the muses! Is that Nishiko Sai?"

After kissing her smiling cheeks, he holds her hands in his. "You did a brilliant job organizing tonight."

Nishi jokingly curtsies. "Why thank you."

Blaze slides his arm around the waist of his date, a woman with short red locks. "This is my friend Geneva. Two years ago, at age nineteen, she became House Taurus's youngest Promisary."

Geneva rolls her eyes but smiles. "You keep talking like this and everyone will think my best years are behind me."

Nishi and I shake hands with her, and my gaze strays to the faces beyond them as I search for Hysan again. He and Skarlet haven't made it very far; they're still near the foot of the staircase, and at least a dozen partygoers surround them. Laughter breaks out from their group, and I see other partiers ambling over to listen in.

"Don't you think, Rho?"

I look at Nishi, whose eyebrows are nearly at her hairline. "I . . . sorry, what?"

She links elbows with me and spins me to face Blaze. "I was complimenting Blaze on his style. What do you think?"

"Yeah . . . I love the skirt," I say, trying to smile. "How did you settle on this outfit?"

"I requested a room with a Lady's Lounge, and when I tried on all the gowns and tuxedos in the archiver's database, I thought this number looked best." He speaks like he's never owned an inhibition in his life.

Nishi and Geneva laugh, and in my periphery I notice a rippling in the crowd. Hysan and Skarlet are on the move again.

My temperature seems to rise with Hysan's every step, and beads of sweat tickle my skull. Whatever I'm feeling, I've never felt it before. It's like my brain has signaled my organs to self-destruct, and I worry that at any moment I'll spontaneously combust.

"Well," Nishi starts to say, her voice a pitch higher than usual, "Rho and I should probably—"

"*Hysan Dax!*"

When Blaze roars Hysan's name, my heart stops so completely that I think it's finally punched a hole big enough to escape my ribcage.

"Over here, playboy. You're too busy to return my calls now?" Blaze brings Hysan in for a hug. "I've been trying to tell you about the Tomorrow Party for weeks!"

I glue my eyes to the white clouds on the floor, unable to look up from the foamy swirls.

"I've come to make it up to you."

At the sound of the charm-filled voice, I give in and look up.

"That's a start," says Blaze, slinging an arm around Hysan's neck. "Now come greet my other most important guest—I believe she's a friend of yours."

Blaze wheels him around, and Hysan sees me at last.

The instant his leaf-green eyes meet mine, solar systems are ignited inside me.

I feel frozen in place, my body buzzing from being back in Hysan's orbit. As we stare at each other, I forget where I am, what I'm doing, why I'm here—I forget the whole Zodiac. And all I remember is the tingly feel of his electrifying touch. The Abyssthe-like taste of his confident kisses. The sunny brilliance of his beautiful mind.

He looks at once the same and completely changed. He's still the best-dressed man in the room, but there's a gravity in his gaze that makes the clothing seem like just a costume. It makes me think of the way light from far-flung stars takes billions of years to reach us, so that when we stare up, we're seeing the star as it was and not as it is. While I know I'm seeing the real Hysan, I also know he isn't this person anymore.

Nishi squeezes my arm, bringing me back to the ball, and as I blink back my stupor, I realize Hysan hasn't reacted yet either. His eyes look as dazed as I feel.

"My . . ."—his voice falters, and he tries again—"My lady."

He holds out his hand for the greeting, and I hesitate because I know what I'll feel when he touches me, and then my heart will give me away. But Blaze and the others are all staring, so I start to extend my hand.

Suddenly, Nishi tugs on my arm. "Sorry, Hysan. I just spotted a potential donor we're trying to court, and I'll need my date's help with the wooing!" And before I know what's happening, she's whisked me away.

"Where are we going?" I ask over the thudding of my heart. She pulls me along with her at such a swift pace that I'm tripping over my heels.

"You should be thanking me," she says as we elbow our way through the crowd. "You two were like a couple of firebursts facing off—and Helios knows how flammable these Aquarian fabrics are!"

We go through a door marked "Lady's Lounge" and enter a wide, mirrored space filled with velvet couches, sandstone tables, wallscreens, and refreshments. Even though the party just started, at least a dozen women—mostly Virgos and Scorps—are already draped over armchairs, their gown skirts crumpled and their up-dos loose, enjoying each other's company.

Nishi finds us an unoccupied couch. "How are you?" she asks the moment our heels are off. Without giving me time to answer, she fires off more questions. "What was that dance with Mathias? And how about that tension with Hysan? Please start talking, or I'm just going to keep asking you more questions—"

"Mathias and I are . . . done," I say, keeping my voice low so no one else can hear. "Seeing him with Pandora was painful, but . . .

losing him felt more like letting go of the girl I'd once been, and a future I wanted to keep believing in."

"And Hysan?" she asks gently.

I shake my head. "In another stunning display of my heart's perfect timing, I *just* realized he's the person I want to be with. I'm completely in love with him."

Now she shakes her head. "It's a good thing you Cancrians are pretty, because you're dumb as a bag of nar-clams." At my glare she shrugs unapologetically. "You love me because I'm honest."

"I love you *in spite* of your honesty." I'm annoyed that she's being sarcastic when I'm in real pain; it's not like her. Then again, she's right. I have been dumb as a nar-clam.

"I've been such a coward, Nish." I drop my head in my hands. "Not in the ways Charon said, but in my personal life. This whole time, I've been brave enough to risk my life but not my heart."

She wraps her arm around my shoulders. "Rho, there's no reason for you to feel this way. Hysan's in love with you. That's not something that changes from one month to the next. And if it has, then he wasn't in love with you in the first place. But based on the tension I just witnessed between you, I don't think that's what happened. So cheer up."

Her tone grows tougher as she goes on, like she's flitting too close to doors she's desperate to leave closed. Discussing my love life must make her think of her own; here I am dwelling on my feelings for a guy who's just outside this room, while the man Nishi has loved her entire adolescence is gone forever.

"You have no reason to pout, Rho. So leave the dark thoughts in here, and then let's go back out there and have some fun." She grabs our heels from the floor and hands me mine. "I promise to keep an eye out so you don't have to run into him again."

I would much rather stay in here the rest of the night, but for Nishi's sake I get to my feet. I can't drown in my heartbreak now, not when her heart is barely hanging on.

◆ ◆ ◆

When I leave the Lounge, I survey the ballroom for Stan and Mathias and the others, but by now the place is so crowded that it's hard to find anyone. Every few steps we take, Nishi flags down another dignitary or Party member to introduce me to, and between the fear of running into Hysan and the stress of interacting with so many new people, I feel drunk on my emotions, even though I've yet to try the House's fizzy drink of choice.

Eventually a round of dinner trays begin to float among us, and Nishi and I fill up on finger foods—porkling burgers, aquadile cakes, falcon poppers. While we're talking to a group of Aquarian, Scorp, Geminin, and Capricorn dignitaries, I feel a tap on my shoulder and turn around.

"Wandering Star," says a dark-skinned, middle-aged woman with fine, short hair. She's wearing a striking gown comprised of glossy green feathers.

I grow alert when I recognize the Taurian Guardian. I wasn't expecting to see anyone from such a high level of government at this youthful soiree.

"It's an honor to see you again, Fernanda—I mean, Chief Executive Purecell."

"Fernanda is still fine." She transfers the drink she's holding to her other hand so she can reach out for the traditional Taurian handshake. "Are you joining the Tomorrow Party?"

"I think so." As I say the words, a fantasy unfolds in my mind of Nishi and me living together in our own home on the Black Moon settlement, of Hysan and me dating out in the open, of Stan and Jewel marrying and starting a family—and I feel myself smile. "How about yourself?"

"I'm one of the Party's financial backers."

"Oh—I had no idea." Strange that with everything going on in the Zodiac, she took the time to travel here for a ball.

"I think any movement that embraces inclusivity and choice deserves our consideration and support, don't you?" The focus of her sharp eyes reminds me of the horned hawks on Tierre.

"Yes, and having your support will mean a lot down the line." The more I think about it, the more I like the Tomorrow Party's experimental approach to uniting our solar system. After all, it's unlikely we'll convince every House to drop its walls and start welcoming everyone at once, so this small-scale trial run is far more sensible.

Fernanda leans closer, and her terse, no-nonsense voice brings the ball back into focus. "Nobody knows yet, but the Plenum has convened a confidential, multi-House tribunal to investigate me and my ties to Risers. If found guilty, they'll try me for treason."

My drunken emotions sober fast. "Why?"

"Because I've spoken out in support of Risers? Because my father was a Riser?" She shakes her head. "Because, as you well know, those in power always need a new boogeyman. It's how they stay in power."

Chieftain Skiff comes to mind; the last time a Guardian shared a secret with me, strings were attached. "Why are you telling me this?"

"Because if they ask you to testify to what I discussed with you in my office—about my correspondence with Risers—I need you to lie."

I feel my face blanching, and I look around us to see if anyone's listening. Nishi's still entertaining the same group of diplomats, and everyone around us is engrossed in their own conversation. When I turn back to Fernanda, I barely move my lips as I form my answer. "Don't you think this should be a more *private* discussion?"

"I don't trust any quiet rooms that aren't my own," she says, taking a slow sip of her drink.

"Fernanda, I'm not a good liar. I want to help you, but even if I tried, they'd probably see right through me. And anyway, from everything you've told me, you've done nothing treasonous. The only thing they can blame you for is that you didn't bring your concerns to them sooner, but you couldn't have known—"

"*The only thing they can blame me for?*" she repeats, her voice sour. "Don't you realize yet that they can do anything they want? You yourself are proof of that. They can sell any story they please, they can rewrite history, they can make me out to be the Marad's master!"

"If the system is this broken, why didn't you and the other Guardians try fixing it before the attack on Cancer?" I burst out, anger shooting through me.

"Who says I haven't been?" she asks, and a flash of power surges through her dark features, a glimpse into her fearless core. "But a chemical reaction requires more than energy. It needs a catalyst."

"You mean a *sacrifice*."

There's something new in her eyes tonight, a darkness I didn't see on Vitulus. "On Cancer you believe the loss of one life is as unacceptable as the loss of ten thousand," she says, and I nod. "But on Taurus we are team players, and we believe in making sacrifices for the greater good. I'm sorry for the people we've lost, but I can't pretend something like this wasn't bound to happen. You can't crush an entire race of people and think you'll hold on to power forever; Nature will balance herself out."

I glare at her. "That doesn't sound like balance. It sounds like a tug of war."

"Are you saying *no* then? You won't help me?"

I sigh. "I won't lie. But I won't betray your trust either."

She quirks her head. "What then?"

"If they come around asking," I say, the answer coming to me as I'm speaking, "I'll tell them what we discussed was just between us. That's all."

Her expression is unreadable, so I don't know if this is good or bad news to her. With her hawkish eyes and feathery dress, she looks more than ever like a bird of prey.

"You know," she says, taking another slow sip of her drink. "I think we might make a politician out of you yet."

17

WALKING AWAY FROM FERNANDA, I'M thinking it's definitely time to investigate the Aquarian drink situation.

Nishi's circle of admirers has grown, and rather than rejoin her, I decide to hunt down one of the floating trays. She's far better at the small-talk stuff than I am; I'd rather skip this kind of *dullatry* and go straight to working on the Black Moon project.

The ballroom is so packed that I can't spot any drinks, so I edge toward the outskirts of the crowd to get a better vantage point, knocking into elbows and shoulders along the way. When I reach the white marble wall, there's a massive, gold-embossed mirror where a handful of women are checking themselves out. Their chiffon and satin and velvet gowns are so puffy that they can't get very close to the glass.

I stand near them as I scan the room for the glint of tall-stemmed glasses.

"You look like you're on the hunt," says a clear, confident voice to my left, and I look up to see statuesque Skarlet Thorne holding two drinks in her hands.

It seems impossible, but upclose she's even more stunning. Her skin is a shimmering bronze brown that seems to produce its own light, her eyes are curved and cat-like, and the folds of her red silk dress roll off her like watery flames.

She offers me one of the glasses. "Thanks," I say, taking it. "How'd you know this was what I was hunting?"

"I figured if it was a guy, you would have checked your lipstick first."

I stare at her questioningly, then I lean over to peek at myself in a corner of the mirror. The red paint has mostly smudged off my mouth, probably from eating.

"I think we're wearing the same shade." She draws a red tube from a barely noticeable pocket in the folds of her dress. Beside us, competition for space in front of the mirror has intensified, and she says, "I've got you."

She hands me her glass but holds onto the napkin that was wrapped around its stem. Then she takes my chin between her fingers. "Part your lips."

Her cat eyes study my mouth as she paints my top lip. "I'm glad we're getting this chance to meet because I think there's a lot we can do together to improve the situation for Risers," she says, moving on to my lower lip. "I heard that Chief Executive Purecell is here, too, and since she's such a vocal Risers' rights advocate, it could be even more effective if the three of us combine forces. If you want, I'll get your information from the Party so we can get organized."

She slips the napkin between my lips. "Blot." Then she steps back and admires her work. "Perfect."

"Thank you. And yes, I'd love that," I say, handing back her drink. "I've been really inspired by how you've bridged the divisions of your House."

She clinks her glass with mine. "Well, it's an honor to inspire the woman who inspired me." Then she takes a sip of her drink, and I bring mine to my lips.

The liquid's sweet fizz seems to invade my mouth, eyes, and nose all at once, and I cough a couple of times. To cover my mortification, I take a long sip. The drink is a mix of fruits I've never tasted before, and another flavor that's familiar but I can't place.

"I met Corinthe."

The sweetness sours, and I nearly choke on it. "W-what? How?"

"She and the other Risers are being held in The Bellow on planet Phaet." It's the highest security prison in the Zodiac. "Since she's the only soldier without a mask, most interrogations are directed at her, but she hasn't spoken yet. The Majors felt since I've been advocating for Risers' rights, and since I've been effective at addressing our people, I might stand a better chance."

My mouth suddenly dry, I ask, "Did she . . . talk to you?"

"No—but I'm the only one who's elicited a reaction from her." Skarlet leans a little closer, and I catch a whiff of a spicy, floral scent that makes me think of a field of firebursts. "I did it by mentioning you."

The glass slips a little in my fingers. "Me?"

"I asked if she'd rather talk to you." The Ariean's gaze trails down my gloved arm, where my scars are hiding, then flicks back to my face.

"And she *smiled*."

I take another sip of my drink to drown the visual of Corinthe's leering smile. As if she could see what I'm thinking, Skarlet adds, "She's finished her transition. Want to know what House she's in now?"

Somehow, I know before she says it.

"Cancer."

So the person who doesn't believe in love now looks like she belongs in the House of love. I can't imagine a worse punishment for Corinthe.

"Actually . . ." Skarlet scrutinizes my face closely. "She looks a lot like you."

My left arm suddenly starts to boil. I rub it against my dress to calm my skin, as the thought of Corinthe wearing my face burns me from the inside.

"Strange, isn't it?" whispers Skarlet.

"What's strange?"

Her fireburst scent grows stronger, like she's about to spark. "The stars' sense of humor."

She walks away before I can say anything, leaving me to stare after her as she goes. And I'm not the only one looking.

Heads turn wherever Skarlet passes: She's like a blaze of fire you want to keep your eyes on at all times in case the wind changes direction, and her flames blow your way.

◆ ◆ ◆

When I find Nishi again, she clutches my arm. *"There you are! Let's go! It's speech time!"*

I run with her to the grand staircase, and we come to a stop next to Blaze and Geneva and the rest of his entourage. "Oh, good, you're here," he says, seeing Nishi. "Stay close."

"I will."

Blaze hands his date his drink, then hitches his purple skirt up on one side so he can climb to the middle of the staircase. At his signal, the orchestra stops playing, and in the absence of music, everyone looks around.

"Welcome, trailblazers!"

His voice comes from all corners of the room, and I notice a small *volumizer*—a black ball that's a sound amplifier—hovering in the air near his head. He waits for the wild cheering and clapping to calm down before speaking again.

"Everyone who came here tonight is a pioneer of a new tomorrow. A different tomorrow. A *united* tomorrow. One that looks like this." We look up to see holographic captures materializing in the air above us.

All the images are of the party attendees as we descended into the ballroom, each of us walking alongside a person from a different

House. Mossy-eyed Virgos with dark-haired Sagittarians with tawny-skinned Geminin with broad-faced Leonines with athletically built Arieans and so on. No divisions among the Houses.

"If you're here, you've heard me give plenty of speeches already, so I'm going to cede the floor to someone far more eloquent than myself. But first, I would like to give special thanks to a few guests who—despite everything going on in the Zodiac— still made it a priority to come here tonight and support our cause. Chief Executive Purecell, Wandering Star Rhoma Grace, and, of course, our guest of honor, whose hospitality we're testing tonight, Ambassador Crompton."

The room breaks into applause as Blaze steps down, and Ambassador Crompton climbs the stairs. When they meet, Blaze and Crompton trade the hand touch and then the Ambassador turns to face us.

I hear Nishi and Blaze murmuring as he returns to our group, but I'm not paying attention. I just spotted Hysan in the crowd.

He's standing with Skarlet to the other side of the staircase, and she's whispering something in his ear. My gaze lingers on how his hand hangs off her hip, and I take another sip of the sugary drink. Almost immediately, I start to feel a little lightheaded.

"Thank you, Lionheart Blaze, for this generous invitation to address tomorrow's leaders. I am honored to be honored by you." Crompton bows in our direction, toward Blaze. "I've thought a lot about what possible wisdom I could impart to such a talented group. What can I offer you in return for awarding me this distinction?"

My gaze keeps straying to Hysan. Each time I look over I feel like his eyes have just been on me. And yet he seems so completely immersed in whatever Skarlet's telling him that it seems impossible his sight would have strayed, even for a second.

"*Assurance.*"

Ambassador Crompton's voice booms through the space, bringing my attention back to him. "There is nothing humans fear more than change, and that is why, from here on out, you are going to face profound opposition. The best thing I can try to give you before you set off is *assurance* that what you're doing is worth doing. That you are not living your life in vain."

The whole ballroom has gone silent, and I'm happy to see even Skarlet has stopped talking.

"Helios forgive me, for I am an Aquarian!" Laughter breaks out across the room at Crompton's cry. "And as a Philosopher I must beg you to allow me this moment to philosophize."

His pink eyes shine brightly, reflecting the room's colors back to us. "Why are we crawling one year and walking the next? Why is it that one birthday we're asking our parents for toys, but the next we want an Ephemeris? Why does a shirt that fits us today not fit us tomorrow? Because we are ever-changing organisms. We were not meant to be static. Change is the universe's only currency, and that is why it is futile to stand against progress, for evolution will always prevail."

Clapping breaks out, and Crompton waits for it to die down completely before continuing. "So why do we fear our own growth?"

He takes a long pause as he pans his gaze across the room, like a teacher waiting for a brave student to raise her hand. "Because in order to change, we must relinquish control; we must momentarily lose ourselves. And in those moments, anything is possible—the best of us or the worst.

"When we're younger, we leap across this divide with ease, eager to see what the next year brings. Yet as we grow older, we begin to fear the pain of the changing process, and we worry more and more about the person we will become on the other side. So we claw onto time, trying to keep it from ticking onward and moving us forward—and in doing this, we stunt our personal evolution."

The place is so silent that he could be whispering and we would still hear him.

"Somewhere along the way," he continues, "our misguided hubris hitched human pride to humanity's progress. That is why you face such steep opposition. Because if you succeed in designing a stronger, better, fairer system, *you* will be the founding parents of the new world. The old thinkers will be displaced as flawed philosophers from an earlier era, caged within the confines of the past, falling further from relevance.

"So I want to use this moment to *assure* you that your work here is important. What you're doing reminds us that while the past must be remembered, it cannot come at the cost of the future. Change keeps our species alive, and that is why we must shed our fear and allow ourselves—and our solar system—to grow with the times. Our eyes are in the front of our heads because what's coming ahead means more than what we're leaving behind. Where we're going means more than where we came from. And as we say on Aquarius, *Only when we let go of today will we be living in tomorrow.*"

I set my now empty glass on the floor and join the others in a round of applause. It's a while before our clapping dies down, and Crompton looks less comfortable accepting our praise than he did speaking. Eventually, he holds his hands up to signal us to stop.

My vision has gone blurry from drinking, and when I look at Hysan, I can no longer make out his features.

"And speaking of *tomorrow*," says Crompton, "I have been asked to welcome to the stage the Tomorrow Party's new co-captain, who will help Lionheart Blaze lead you into a hopeful new morning—*Nishiko Sai of House Sagittarius.*"

I turn to Nishi with wide eyes, and she grins at me, her amber irises filled with light. "I found out earlier but wanted to keep it a surprise!" she squeals.

Wrapping her in a huge hug I say into her ear, "I'm so proud of you, Nish."

Blaze offers her his arm and escorts Nishi up the steps to where Crompton is standing. They trade the hand touch, and then he descends, leaving Nishi with the room's attention. Watching her up there, my heart bursts with pride. After all she's endured these past few months, Nishi has found herself and her place in the Zodiac.

"I'm going to keep this short," she says, her voice carrying across the room. "First, I need to thank Ambassador Crompton on behalf of everyone present for that incredibly inspiring speech." The room claps in solidarity, but tamps down quickly. "I also want to thank the incomparable Blaze Jansun for bringing us together for such a magnificent cause. And on a personal note, for trusting me to help bring his revolutionary vision to life."

People applaud again, and I'm awed by the graceful ease with which Nishi handles having hundreds of eyes on her. There's something comforting about the scene in front of me; it feels good being in the background again while Nishi takes center stage.

"Finally, I want to thank the person who means the most to me and whose courage inspired my own." I feel Nishi's gaze cut across to me, and, astounded, I stare back at her semi-blurry face. "Wandering Star, thank you for reminding us that we are not powerless, that we are the future. You sacrificed so much when you set out to warn the Houses about Ophiuchus, and you risked your life when you went out in that Wasp to bait him, and then you put yourself on the line again when you faced the Marad.

"By refusing to compromise your beliefs, you proved to everyone that we all have access to a powerful weapon, one that can change worlds with a single sound: *our voice*. By standing up, and speaking out, and refusing to go quietly, you showed us how change gets done."

I feel everyone's eyes on me as they clap, and my cheeks heat with color.

"Our system only exists because we subscribe to it; and that means we have the power to change it. The people making the rules today won't be the ones inhabiting our solar system tomorrow—but *we will*. Don't we deserve a say in what kind of worlds we want to inherit?"

As we break into more applause, a flicker of white-blond hair catches my eye. An Aquarian woman who seems familiar somehow is a few feet away, but I can't see her face. I keep looking between her and Nishi, waiting for the chance to glimpse her features.

When at last she turns to talk to the person next to her, I hazily trace high ivory cheekbones and brilliantly blue eyes.

Everything goes still inside me.

Mom.

18

MY BODY IS AN ECHO chamber for my heart, and all I hear are its thudding beats.

I start moving closer to the woman, my skin clammy and mind blank, and as her features sharpen, I realize it's not my mother.

The shock wears off slowly, and as the warmth of my relief lifts the cold from my skin, I decide I'm done drinking for the night.

The orchestra starts playing again, and Nishi descends the stairs to another round of applause. She's immediately bombarded by people who want to offer their congratulations, and soon they pull me into the celebration. We trade the hand touch with what feels like hundreds of people, and I scan their faces for Stanton or Mathias, but they don't show up. This kind of ball isn't a very Cancrian scene, so they're probably in a corner somewhere, hanging with a smaller crowd.

Once Nishi and I extricate ourselves from her admirers, I draw her to a quieter area to give her another hug. "You were extraordinary!"

Her cinnamon cheeks are rosy, her eyes bright. A silver tray of clear drinks floats past us, and she swipes a couple of glasses. "To us!" We clink them together, and she takes a huge swig.

"I think one drink was enough for me," I say without tasting mine. "How can you have so much of this stuff when the alcohol is so strong?"

"There's no alcohol in it," she says, after polishing hers off. "It's called a *Spacey Spritzer*. It's spiked with Abyssthe."

"*Abyssthe?*"

"It's only a few drops. Since it comes with no hangover, Aquarians prefer it to alcohol. It's only supposed to make you feel a little floaty, nothing more."

"Then why is it making me . . . *see* things?"

Nishi's up-do is starting to fall, and flyaway strands of hair fold over her forehead. "It affects people differently based on their tolerance. Since the best seers naturally draw more Psynergy to themselves, they feel it more, so—yeah, actually, you're right. You've definitely had enough."

She reaches for my drink, only I'm no longer sure I want to give it up. Maybe my eyes weren't playing tricks on me. Maybe when I thought I saw Mom, I was Seeing an *omen*.

"Nishi!" Imogen runs up to us and gives Nishi a huge hug. "You were perfect!" A string of prospective Party members are with her, and while they introduce themselves to Nishi, I draw away to consider the glass in my hands.

I haven't had any luck finding signs of Mom in the Ephemeris, and I have no other leads. So why not try a little more of this Spritzer and see what I can See? Besides, it's not like anyone needs me right now. Nishi has found her place, Mathias and Pandora have found each other, and Stan is once more nowhere to be found.

I sneak up beside Nishi and say into her ear, "I'm going to look around, see if I can find Stan. I'll be back in a bit."

"Wave my Tracker if I'm not here," she says, and I nod, not bothering to point out that I didn't bring my Wave with me.

Sipping the fizzy, fruity Spritzer, I edge along the room's outer perimeter where it's less crowded. Though obviously old, this room somehow seems newer than the rest of the castle, more pristine. Maybe it's just been used less often.

I cross under the static-charged staircase to the other side of the marble ballroom where fewer people are gathered. My sight grows shakier the more I drink, as if the molecules of oxygen around me have transformed into erratic Psynergy.

Spying a whirl of blond hair ahead, I speed up to see a blurry woman in a white dress turning a corner.

I chase after her until I reach the far end of the room, but there's nowhere to turn. She disappeared into the wall.

Heart racing, I step back to survey the gold-and-silver-streaked marble, and I spy a faint, shadowy archway. But when I touch it, I only feel cold stone.

I look around me to make sure no one is watching, then I trace the designs in the stone with my finger, trying to find a hidden key. Soon I start to feel a strange pull toward whatever lies on the other side of the wall, and my body hums with curiosity to get through it.

Instinct seems to be whispering instructions to me, and, remembering that Abyssthe is strongest when first taken, I swallow what's left of my drink and concentrate on the archway in the wall.

My Ring finger buzzes as I pull in Psynergy to Center myself, and slowly the shaded archway begins to darken.

I touch it again.

Immediately I'm transported to something that looks like the shadow world of the Collective Conscious, only I don't see the Psynergy signatures of other Zodai. I can't see or feel my body, and panic spreads through my thoughts as I sense someone's Eye on me, like I'm being examined and my identity is being confirmed.

Suddenly the castle reappears around me, only now I'm inside a cold sandstone hall, and the music from the party sounds faint. This must be some kind of advanced security measure, like the drop with Engle on Scorpio.

My knees are too shaky to risk moving, so I stand still as I cast my gaze along the tall empty space. I must be on the other side of the marble.

"Untara warned you this morning not to do this."

My heart shoots into my mouth at the sound of a man's voice. It seems to be coming from right behind me, only when I spin around, no one's there.

"You already knew she was upset about the Tomorrow Party coming to the castle. She meant for our House's endorsement to be symbolic, not practical."

I scan the dim, dusty chamber again, and this time I notice a spiral staircase at the far end of the place where a long, thin beam of light spills down the steps. For a moment I keep still, torn between spying and going back to the ballroom.

"She didn't want some silly youthful movement staining our ancient walls, and—"

"As Ambassador it is my right to recognize new leaders and movements."

At the sound of Crompton's voice, I make my choice. I pad quickly toward the stairs and peek up at the spiraling steps.

Maybe it's the Spacey Spritzer, or maybe Skiff was right and I'm not just Cancrian anymore. But I'm tired of being taken by surprise by the people I want to trust. If Crompton is duplicitous, I need to know.

"Please, sir," I hear the other man say. "You're only hurting yourself."

"I'm grateful for your concern," says Crompton, his voice warm yet firm, "but engaging in new conversations and exploring different viewpoints is the soul of Philosophy. Since when does House Aquarius not welcome new ways of thinking and leading? What happened to our revered Guardian Aquarius's immortal words, *Man needs a brain to live, but a mind to be alive?*"

I climb up the stairs as slowly as possible. Thankfully, the dust in the space muffles the sound of my heels.

"I'm not disagreeing with you on philosophical grounds," says the other man, his words taking on a pleading tone. "But Untara isn't happy. You knew the Wandering Star's presence hadn't gone unnoticed, nor the fact that you agreed to be this event's guest of honor. And yet, despite her warnings, you went through with it!"

The first door I come across is ajar, and the room beyond it is dark, so I continue climbing up. "They're kids, Crompton. They're only going to be a distraction at a time when the Zodiac's focus should be on stopping this Riser army and finding the person in charge of them. This group will be painting a target on their heads when they go public with this nonsense, and mark my words, the Marad will come after them for daring to bring hope to the Houses. That's how terrorism works."

I freeze midway to the next floor. The door is open just a slit, and the line of light guiding my way is coming from in there, as are the two men's voices.

"So you would sacrifice our galaxy's hope for the sake of a sense of safety?" asks Crompton, somehow sounding both patient and frustrated. "Even when that safety is only an illusion? I understand and even share your fear, Pollus, but if we let that feeling rule us, then we have already let the terrorists win. The truth is that *hope* is the most powerful weapon in our arsenal . . . and recent events prove that change is necessary to achieve it."

"What I heard you saying tonight didn't sound like change," says the other man—Pollus—cautiously. "It sounded like revolution."

There's a long silence, and then Crompton says, "That is your fear speaking again, Pollus, and it does you a disservice. The system isn't perfect, and it doesn't help us to pretend otherwise. Do you know what Rhoma Grace told me yesterday? She never agreed to the declaration of Peace. In fact, she believes the Marad is still very much a threat. And yet when I suggested to the Plenum that we invite her to give testimony before making Peace official, I was told there was no need because she'd already signed on. Does this sound like a system worth preserving?"

Pollus sighs loudly, and I hear him pacing the floor. "Do you realize what's happening? They made you the face for the Peace declaration, just as they made you the face for crowning that girl as the Wandering Star. They're using you just as they used her. You're the newest member and, frankly, you're too trusting. And now they're setting you up so that when everything backfires, you can become their scapegoat!"

"If you're right, that's all the more reason to support change!"

"*I do!*" says the other man, raising his voice to Crompton for the first time. "But I'm trying to look out for you, too. We both know Untara feels threatened by you."

"But *why?*" asks Crompton, sounding like he's finally found a question he can't answer. "Have you asked yourself that?"

"She's jealous of your talent, and she worries if you challenge her to a duel in the astral plane, you might actually win, making you the rightful Supreme Advisor to the Guardian. She's afraid you're the better seer."

"Or," says Crompton, his voice so low I have to strain my ears, "maybe there's just something she's afraid I'll See."

"Listen to me. You have to go to her right away and apologize; she's probably already heard your speech, and she'll use it as grounds to—"

"That's enough."

Crompton's voice is still kind, but it carries an irrefutable finality. "I am grateful for your friendship and honored by the depth of your concern. But I will look out for myself."

I see the door opening, and as more light spills out, I dart away quickly, slipping through the open door on the first floor and hiding in the dark room.

I hold my breath as Crompton and the other man climb down the stairs. And as my heart hammers in my chest, the same phrase circles through my mind: *Maybe there's just something she's afraid I'll See.*

◆ ◆ ◆

I tail them back out through the archway quietly, keeping a careful distance. On the other side of the wall, the party is over. The orchestra has stopped playing, and as the crowd funnels up the staircase to exit the ballroom, the hum of their conversations sounds like ocean waves that are becoming more distant.

Crompton and Pollus walk toward the staircase side by side, the latter still speaking surreptitiously while Crompton busies himself drinking a Spritzer.

"Ambassador!"

They turn around. "Wandering Star!" says Crompton warmly, and from the sound of his voice, I think he's relieved to have a reason to leave Pollus's side. Pollus, on the other hand, looks incensed by my approach, and he turns on his heel and strides off.

"You look lovely," says Crompton, giving me a low bow. His pink eyes are aglow with the Abyssthe in his system, and now that he's away from Pollus's warnings, he seems pleasantly buzzed and pleased with tonight's event.

"Thank you. Your speech was fantastic. And it meant a lot to the Tomorrow Party that you even agreed to speak here tonight. I mean, it's like you said, progress always has its opponents, right? And I'm sure you dealt with your own share of difficulties when you agreed to do this . . . didn't you?"

I'm hoping the drink dulled his senses enough not to notice the lack of subtlety in my fishing expedition.

"Oh, I'm not worried; everything will work out," he says, smiling merrily. "It's in the nature of a disagreement to want to resolve itself."

His optimism reminds me of when I was Guardian, before the Plenum stripped me of my title. "Are you enjoying yourself?" he asks.

"Yeah, this has been great, thank you." Unwilling to give up so easily, I say, "I thought maybe I'd see the Supreme Advisor here tonight. You know, since I saw her in your office this morning."

"*Untara?*" Crompton laughs. "That woman couldn't find tomorrow on a calendar!" His expression tightens as he realizes what he's said, and his eyes grow more alert. "I didn't mean that, of course—"

"It's okay," I say, smiling. "She didn't seem like the most . . . *progressive* person."

"That she is not," agrees Crompton, though he still looks concerned by his own behavior. He sets his drink down on a golden tray of empty glasses floating past. "So much talk of tomorrow has got me acting like it's yesterday," he says, chuckling at his own joke, "but I'm not a young man anymore."

"Ambassador, why is the Plenum pretending the Marad isn't a threat?" Judging by my boldness, maybe I'm still under the Abyssthe's influence, too.

Crompton stares at me, his face sobering fast. "I don't think that's true—"

But he cuts himself off, like his heart isn't in the excuse, and he sighs, pinning me with a particularly paternal stare. "Rho, be careful. If they don't think you're with them, you know better than anyone what can happen."

Funny how he's giving me the same advice he himself refused to take from Pollus. "But why are they willfully blinding themselves?"

"Because they have no progress to offer their people, and the longer we extend the purgatory period of waiting for the next attack, the further morale falls among the Houses. It doesn't mean Zodai aren't still searching for signs of the army. But surely you'd agree that Pisces takes precedence over everything at this moment?"

"Of course."

He looks abruptly behind me, and when I turn I see Nishi coming up to us; beyond her the ballroom has almost cleared out.

"Hi, Ambassador," says Nishi. "Thank you again for your amazing speech."

"Same to you," he says, bowing to Nishi. "Watching you speak tonight, I saw a brilliant career ahead of you, Nishiko. My door will always be open—to the both of you—for anything you need."

As soon as he goes, Nishi turns to me. "Party's over, but there's an after party. I need to go finalize a few details first. But don't move from this spot!"

The instant she darts off to confer with other Party members, my brother appears. From his exact timing it seems like he's been waiting for me to be alone. "We need to talk," he says in a low voice.

"Where are Mathias and Pandora?" I ask, scanning the mostly empty ballroom for a sign of them.

"I saw the two of them leaving a while ago," he says, and the stab of those words cuts less deeply than I'd have expected. "I've been eavesdropping on a lot of people tonight, Rho, and there's stuff about the Party that Blaze and Nishi didn't mention."

"You're *eavesdropping?*" I ask loudly, even though I've just returned from doing the same thing. "Stan, seriously, you have to stop being so cynical about everything. It's not like you, and it's changing you into someone you're not."

"Listen to me." He grips my arm. "All their talk about unity and acceptance was a load of crap. Black Moon is actually as elitist and exclusionary as it gets." He gestures to our surroundings. "You saw the people who came tonight. Only the richest, or best educated, or most talented members of the Zodiac were invited."

"Stan, tonight was about raising funds and attracting attention to the Party. That has nothing to do with who's going to the new settlement. That project is still top secret, remember?"

"Well people are talking about it." Stan's voice is tighter and lower.

"I don't believe that people would be openly discussing it. Nishi wouldn't have waited to bring me all the way here to tell me about Black Moon if it was something that could be discussed casually at a party."

He rolls his eyes in frustration and pulls something out of his tuxedo pocket. It looks like a metal Scorpion. "What's that?" I ask, thinking of the Crawler device that organizes a Scorp's thoughts.

"It's what I stole from Link that got him so ticked off."

"What you *stole*?" The Scarab around my wrist seems to tighten, reminding me that this is my second hypocritical statement in under two minutes.

"After I broke my Wave, I told Engle I wanted to buy a new communication device and asked if he'd show me some Scorp tech so I could decide what to get. But he said there was no point, since Cancrian money is no longer accepted. So I decided to try the line on someone stupider instead.

"Link was thrilled to invite me to his quarters to boast about his favorite gadgets. But since most of them operate on DNA or fingerprint technology, they were useless to me. Except for the *Echo*."

Stan holds up the device, and I notice small red dots on the scorpion's shell. "At one point Tyron came in to tell Link something, and I pretended to be eavesdropping so they'd move their conversation outside. Since I'd seen where he stored the Echo, it was pretty easy to slip it into my pocket."

I shake my head, unable to process that my brother has become a thief. And worse, a remorseless one. "Stan, I don't like how you're acting. This isn't you—"

"You can program specific keywords into a holographic menu," he says, barreling past my concerns, "and when you activate the device, it scans every electronic transmission within a specific radius and echoes back any mentions of your keywords."

"*Stan—*"

"Rho, *listen*. There are lists being passed around among top Party donors. They're the names of the members of each House chosen for Black Moon. They're guaranteeing people spots in exchange for financial sponsorship and political favors."

My heart outracing my thoughts, I whisper, "You have to stop this."

This isn't my brother. What if everything we're going through affects him on a soul-deep level—would that trigger some kind of Ophiuchan gene? No one really understands how or why Risers Rise . . . but if Mom was a Riser, that means Ophiuchan blood runs in our veins. So if Stan twists his soul too far, is it possible his body could assume a new shape?

"Stan, even if you have your doubts about the Party, you can at least trust Nishi," I say, making my voice as reassuring as I can. "She would never be part of an elitist and exclusionary organization, and she investigates *everything*, so you can be sure she's vetted these guys."

Stan just shakes his head, and it feels like for the first time in our lives, we're not understanding each other. "Maybe you haven't noticed, but Nishi isn't herself right now. She's not thinking clearly. She just lost the love of her life, and she's acting like he never even existed. Does that sound healthy to you?"

"She'll face her pain when she's ready, but that doesn't mean she's had a personality transplant. Whether or not she's suffering, Nishi would never stand for a discriminatory system of any kind." I flash back to a picture of the three of us on *Equinox* just a couple of months ago, dreaming of Nishi and Deke's future children. "She's doing this for Deke, to create the kind of world they wanted for their kids. She's mourning him her own way."

"Think about it, though," pleads my brother. "The Tomorrow Party must have made promises to most people here. Otherwise, how did a bunch of young, open-minded kids like Nishi pull this off? How did they afford the ship we flew here on? They're showing a lot of money—"

"They have sponsors, people with means, like the Guardian of Taurus."

"Actually," he says, his voice dipping further, "I have something to tell you about her—"

"Okay, let's go to the conservatory!" announces Nishi, interrupting us, and Stan doesn't finish his sentence. Ezra and Gyzer come up behind Nishi.

"I'm heading to bed," says my brother, and he takes off without another word. Nishi looks at me curiously, but I shake my head so she won't ask.

I'm not sure whether to chase after him or stay with her, and as if she knows what I'm thinking, Nishi says, "Come to the after party! You can talk to your brother in the morning."

Ezra suddenly raises her mahogany face to us, her eyes wide with a hopeful expression. "Somebody say *after party?*"

✦ ✦ ✦

The castle's conservatory is a grassy park with a giant garden attached, and the whole place is encased in glass walls. The Aquarian sky above is heavy and black, but small lights are strung along the glass ceiling, showering the place in a subtle, starlit glow. The lights remind me a bit of the gills from Sconcion's waterworlds.

About a hundred people gather on a field filled with high tables and lined with Spacey Spritzers. On the grass are fluffy blankets covered with baskets of finger foods, and those partygoers who aren't standing by a table are lounging on the blankets in their formalwear, snacking and drinking like they're at the world's fanciest picnic.

"There's Blaze!" says Nishi, spotting him with Geneva and half a dozen others, sharing an aqua blanket. She heads over to where he is, and Ezra and Gyzer go with her, but I hang back and stare out at the overgrown garden that looms just beyond the park.

A stone path disappears into the foliage, and I follow it to the towering plants. In the garden's mouth is a collection of silver benches where a couple dozen partygoers have gathered. I consider cutting past them to stroll through the greenery, but since this golden dress isn't very inconspicuous, odds are I'll get roped into someone's conversation. Maybe I should just join Nishi.

When I'm turning to go, I spy a glimmer of gold amid the green.

Hysan is leaning against a bench talking to a small group of people, wearing a lazy smile that says he's probably tired but having too much fun to go to bed. I don't see Skarlet nearby.

Before I've decided what to do, he spots me.

We stare at each other across dozens of partygoers for I don't know how long. His hair is tousled, and his bowtie is askew, but the more he comes undone, the more handsome he becomes.

I watch him excuse himself from the others, and then he comes over to where I'm standing. He stops a few feet away, leaving a devastating buffer between us.

As he takes me in, I flash back to the other times we've met at parties, and I realize how much I love the way he looks at me. He makes me feel like I can be more than I am—like I could be *anyone* I've ever dreamt of becoming.

I think that's what scares me most about him.

"That's quite a dress," he says, without offering me his hand for the traditional greeting. "How are you, Rho?"

I want to answer his question, but I can't summon my voice. Words are funneling together in my throat, fighting each other to come out, and I wish I really had a Crawler to help me sort through them.

"I'm . . ."

There's a weird creak in my voice, and I stare down at the stone path I'm standing on, mortified to hear it. Even worse, Hysan hears it, too, because he shifts his weight on his feet.

"I'm sorry," I finally say.

And I so badly want to stop there, but the buildup of words has reached a critical mass, and before I can seal everything in, a flood of feelings gushes out of me.

"I *hate* not speaking to you. I know it's my fault things got to this point, but I really miss you. If there's anything I can do to make things right between us, I want to try. I can't apologize enough for how blind I've been, and how cruelly I've behaved. You're right—I *was* afraid—but I'm not anymore."

I take a couple of careful steps forward, closing the distance between us. "And even if it's too late"—my voice dips now that we're closer—"I need to say this." Gazing deeply into his lively green eyes, I feel myself sinking into my Center. Like I'm looking at my new home.

"I'm in love with you, Hysan. *Only you.*"

His eyes brighten and widen, and I move in, lured by the familiar cedary scent caressing my skin. I spy his gaze sweeping over my lips and the low cut of my dress, and I'm millimeters from his mouth when he murmurs, "Rho . . . I can't."

I feel the color drain from my face, and my chest caves with the weight of my mortification. I back away too quickly and trip on a stone, nearly toppling over.

Hysan steps forward like he's ready to catch me if I fall. "What I mean is, I'm here with Skarlet."

"Right . . . of course you are. I'm sorry, I don't know what got into me—"

"I should probably go," he says, shoving his hands into his white tux's pockets. "I hope you enjoy the rest of your night, my lady."

As he walks away from me, I feel like he's taking my whole world with him. I can't believe how badly I've messed up. I'm a joke—a Cancrian who's an absolute failure at love.

I press my hand to my stomach because I feel like I've just lost a vital organ, one I'm not sure I can survive without.

Then my finger buzzes with Psynergy, and Hysan's voice cuts through my pain.

Meet me in the entrance hall in thirty?

19

TWENTY MINUTES LATER, I'M STANDING in the dim and seemingly ceiling-less entrance hall with its stained glass constellations shining overhead. Nishi was so excited for me when I told her what happened that she practically kicked me out of the after party so that I wouldn't get lost and show up late.

I feel Hysan before I hear him; now that I'm not fighting against my feelings, I can sense him more clearly. Something changes about a room when he enters it.

Though it's been a long night, he still looks like a work of art. I study his windswept golden locks, sparkling emerald eyes, and wrinkled white tux; and as he gets closer, I notice he's carrying a black coat on his arm.

"Want to get out of here?" he asks when he's in front of me.

"And go where?"

He holds the coat open, and I slide my arms into the warm sleeves. Then he approaches the castle doors and beams a schematic out from his Scan. A moment later one of the doors pops open.

"Are you allowed to do that?" I whisper.

He steps out to the sandy plaza with its rushing waterfalls, and when he looks at me, that irresistible centaur smile tugs on his lips and dimples his cheeks and lights up the Aquarian night.

"You scared, Grace?"

Grinning back I say, "You're dreaming, Dax."

I slip off my heels, drop them into the coat's oversized pockets, and join him outdoors. It's nice to feel sand under my bare feet again, and I'm surprised to find it's not freezing.

"They keep it toasty for the Pegazi," says Hysan, observing me. He locks the door again, and then we stroll around the palace's perimeter and alongside the waterfalls.

"Where are we going?"

"This castle was constructed by the planet's first settlers, and Aquarians have built so many secret additions over the millennia that it's unlikely anyone knows it completely. So whenever I visit, I like discovering something new—"

"I found something tonight!" I say suddenly, cutting him off. "In the ballroom, there was this archway—"

"The thirteenth tower," he says, turning to me eagerly. "I saw it, too!"

"The *what?*"

"It's because of you the Aquarian Royal Guard discovered it." His golden skin glows with excitement, and his eyes seem to take up even more space than usual. "When the House's Elders considered your story about Ophiuchus, they realized if it was true, there must be a thirteenth tower in the palace. But since there's no thirteenth turret jutting from the castle top, they had to assume most of the tower had been demolished, and it was a matter of locating its base, which had to have been sealed off. I hear that when they finally found it, they worked for weeks to get through its security measures."

"So how did I get through tonight?"

"You went *inside*?" When I nod, Hysan's gaze grows distant, a line forming between his eyebrows. "Interesting."

"How'd *you* get in?"

"I thought I'd hijacked the code," he says, shrugging, "but maybe I didn't." He falls deep into thought for a few strides before he says, "Maybe the person who sealed off the tower programmed a loophole that allows access to anyone with a Guardian's astrological fingerprint. But we'd need a third Guardian to test the theory."

"Well, while I was in there, I overheard something," I say, relating Crompton's conversation with Pollus.

When I've finished, Hysan says, "I'm not surprised there's dissent. Morscerta came from a traditionalist school of thought, but Crompton is younger and idealistic and far more progressive than anyone who's held his role in recent history. The past few decades, divisiveness among the six Clans has intensified, so this House has been headed for a political shake-up for a while now. Though I agree it's bad cosmic timing."

"What do you think of the Tomorrow Party?" I don't mean to barrage him with questions, but there are few things I enjoy more than hearing Hysan's mind at work.

"I think Blaze always has a cause," he says, sounding like he hasn't committed to an opinion yet. "I don't know much about the Party, so you can fill me in if you'd like. Mostly I've been concerned with what's happening on Pisces. I sent a team of Knights to work with Stridents on planetoid Naute to study the virus and try reversing its effects. I also sent Miss Trii to help Prophet Marinda, since as an android she can't contract anything. Neith has been called to attend so many emergency meetings that he's perpetually running on low charge; I had to take him away from Libra just to apply updates and sync him with 'Nox."

He sounds like he's relieved to be able to share all these things with someone, and it hits me how much harder our period of not speaking must have been on him. At least I had friends by my side—Hysan can only talk this openly with me.

The heaviness of House Pisces wraps us in sad silence until we round the castle corner, and a whole new vista is revealed. A man-made lake runs the length of the palace, and across its sandy shore is a massive Pegazi habitat with sheltered stables. Dozens of the colorful creatures are sleeping on feathery blankets laid out along the sand, while others are standing around chewing hay.

I'd love to go find Candor.

"You like them?" asks Hysan, who's observing me again.

"Yeah," I say, as we walk between the lake and the castle's waterfall walls. "And you?"

"They're my favorite animal of the Zodiac. I bonded with a wild Pegazi five years ago and ever since, any time I visit Primitus, he finds me." Hysan comes to a stop by one of the waterfalls and sticks his hand into the stream of water.

"What are you doing?" I blurt, looking around to make sure we're alone.

"There are three hundred waterfalls on the palace grounds, but this one is special. I know because I've investigated them all."

After a moment the water stops running, and we watch the last of it swirl down a drain embedded in the ground. Where the waterfall had been there's a column with a control panel jutting from a long slab of stone on the floor. Hysan takes my hand and pulls me across the drain onto the stone; even through the glove's fabric, his touch delays my pulse a few beats.

He hits a sequence on the control panel, and the sound of rushing water starts again. I look up in awe as the white crystal drops crash around us, blurring the whole world except Hysan.

We're standing extra close to keep from getting splashed, and our hands are still interlocked. There's a wet curl sticking to my forehead, and Hysan reaches up to free it, his touch melting my skin. Then he lets go of my hand and drops to the ground, feeling along the outline of the stone slab.

"Now what are you doing?" I ask.

"Showing you my favorite secret I've uncovered so far."

When he finds what he's looking for, he digs his fingers in and lifts, sliding half the stone to the side and revealing dark steps that descend underground.

He blasts light from the Scan in his eye, and I see that the drop isn't deep. "You should go first, so I can illuminate the way for you."

He helps me stuff the folds of my gown into the tunnel's opening, and then he shines his light on me until I've climbed down to the stone floor. He descends next.

"Where are we?" I ask, pulling the coat tighter around me.

"Technically the sewers, but this tunnel isn't functional. It's a fake." With his Scan's light he leads us down an echoing stone passage. "There's a legend, one of my favorites, about an Aquarian princess who lived during the turn of the first millennium. Her name was Zenith."

I see a door looming ahead where the passage comes to a dead end. "Zenith was next in line to be Supreme Guardian, which meant she had to marry someone noble from the Royal Clan to continue the bloodline. After graduating from Zodai University, she returned to the palace and joined the Royal Guard to ready herself for the day the stars called on her to step up. Since the Houses were under galactic rule then, there was an ambassador from every House stationed at the castle, each in a different tower; it's why the common rooms represent the different constellations.

"The youngest ambassador was Paloma from Capricorn, and she and Zenith became fast friends. Every week Zenith brought Paloma with her to the royal balls hosted by her father, the Supreme Guardian, who hoped his daughter would find her future spouse among the gathered suitors. But year after year passed, and she never picked anyone."

We reach the door, which is crudely crafted from stone, untouched by modernity. Hysan doesn't have to unlock anything; he just shoves it, and the stone scrapes open, revealing a cave-like space that's covered in carvings.

He removes a metal grate in the floor and uses a lighter to stoke a low fire. When he puts the grate back in place, light flickers through its ridges and plays on the stone walls, bringing the drawings to life. Hysan shuts off his Scan.

The only piece of furniture in the room is a large, feathered bed in the back. I'm awestruck as I take in all of the art around me; colorful canvases hang over some of the carvings, creating a collage effect that gives the place a sacred feel, like we're touring a person's mind. Or *heart*.

"Zenith was an artist, so the walls tell her story."

Hysan stands before the depiction of a small girl with charcoal eyes wearing a crown too big for her head. The design beside it shows a slightly older version of the same girl, and while her classmates leap through the air, unburdened, she lags behind, bent beneath the weight of the Aquarian constellation she carries on her back.

"Zenith couldn't give her heart to any of her suitors because she'd already given it to someone—Paloma, the Capricorn ambassador." On canvas are a series of semi-nude portraits of a dark-skinned woman with sand-colored eyes who must be Paloma.

"But the Supreme Guardian grew impatient and gave his daughter an ultimatum: She must choose a husband by the end of the year, or he'd choose one for her." Beneath the canvas is a carving of a man bearing an Aquarian crown, his eyes as dark as night.

Hysan turns from the flickering designs to me, and in the cave's warm glow he looks like he's made of gold. "Zenith knew she couldn't put off her duty to her House any longer, but before succumbing to her fate, she first ordered her servants to build her this secret chamber, swearing them to a lifelong secrecy they never broke. It's said that even after she married and gave birth to a line of heirs and became Supreme Guardian, she and Paloma never stopped meeting here."

"How . . . how do you know about this place?" I ask, my heart pounding against my ribcage.

"It's hard to keep something this big hidden forever when you're in the spotlight." Firelight dances in Hysan's eyes. "Whispers followed Zenith, which became rumors that got handed down over time, until they became part of the historical canon about the royal line. These stories get mostly dismissed as myths because it's hard to come by tangible proof about people who lived millennia ago. But when I was nine, I was fascinated by everything to do with Aquarius, and I loved reading about this castle and the line of royals that graced its halls. Zenith's story in particular stayed with me, so when I became Guardian, I used every visit to the palace to search for signs of this chamber. I found it two years ago."

His voice loses some of its sunniness, and I recognize the tone as the one he adopts whenever he shares something about himself. "Seeing a myth come to life changed something about the way I look at the universe. It made me curious about what other stories we've lost to time." Regaining his charm he adds, "Of course, none of my discoveries have been quite as exciting as a Thirteenth House."

My stomach tickles from the way he's looking at me, so I fill the air with more words. "Are you the only person who knows about this place?"

He shakes his head. "It's definitely been found; otherwise it'd be in disrepair by now. I'm betting plenty of Royal Guard regimes have located it through the ages, but why would they publicize a discovery confirming a sensational story about the royal line? They'd probably prefer no one ever finds it." His mouth curves into a sad smile that's shyer than his usual one. "But I hope other star-crossed lovers have found this place over the centuries. It'd be nice to think there's a corner of our galaxy where love has always prevailed over prejudice."

He stares at Zenith's carvings, and his ears look a little pink. But that could just be from the firelight.

It takes every ounce of self-control to refrain from reaching out to him. At least now that he's facing away, I finally feel brave enough to ask about his date. "How did you meet Skarlet Thorne?"

"She and I have known each other for years. I wasn't going to attend this event, but she asked me to escort her. I guess I needed a break from everything." My skin tingles as he turns to me again. "And I couldn't come up with a good reason to say no."

I nod, suddenly eager to move on. "Neith wouldn't say what you were up to whenever we'd talk. Have you found something on the Marad?"

He takes a long moment to answer. "No, not yet. But I might have more news soon." I want to ask him for details, but rather than display distrust, I decide not to press him. He's more than earned my faith.

Only now I've run out of words to stack between us, and in the absence of conversation, the room's fire seems to burn hotter. I slip the black coat off and turn away to lay it on the mattress.

I don't know how to be around Hysan without touching him.

His mind seems to be in the same place, because when he's in front of me again, he takes my hand. I wish I'd removed the gloves so I could feel his skin. "When Nishi pulled you away in the ballroom, it was only out of consideration for Skarlet that I didn't run after you."

I'm not sure I heard him correctly.

"That's why I went to see her before meeting you tonight. To tell her I just want to stay friends."

"You did?"

His eyes flicker with light. "I told you on Centaurion, Rho. You're the only person I've ever loved."

Something splits open inside me, filling my body with so many feelings that there's no room left for the oxygen I need to breathe.

"I'm not going to ask you for a date," he goes on, "since that hasn't worked so well for me in the past. All I'm going to ask you for is tonight."

He cups my face in his hand, and the feel of his skin on mine gives my pulse a sudden burst of speed. "I know our heads have to be elsewhere these days, but for a few hours, let's let this place be what it was always meant to be . . . a haven for the star-crossed."

I wrap my arms around him, and when his lips touch mine, nothing in the universe has ever been as right as this kiss.

Just as I've let go of my fear, I feel Hysan giving up his control. Unlike the measured kisses I remember, this one is free and unrestrained, powered by an irrepressible force, as if for tonight at least, neither of us is willing to let anything come between us.

His fingers dig into my curls, and I tug down on his collar, pulling his suit jacket off. I peel off my gloves and toss them onto the mattress, but before I can wrap my hands around him again, Hysan takes my left arm in his hands and stares at the twelve red scars.

When he looks up again, there's so much tenderness in his green eyes that I know he's traveled back to the scene on 'Nox, to the way I must have looked when he found me.

"So how many girls have you brought down here?" I tease, trying to distract him.

"You'll be number one hundred and four," he says, flashing his dimples.

"Ha. Hilarious—"

"What is that?" He frowns as he notices the black bangle on my left wrist.

"New bracelet," I say dismissively, freeing my hand from his and circling my arms around his neck again. "You know, I've been wondering about that night you came to my bedroom at the Libran embassy."

"I already like where this is going. . . ."

I hold him closer so he can't see my face. "Were you—did you bring protection with you because you knew what was going to happen between us?"

He laughs softly in my ear, and mortification singes my skin. "Are you asking if I consulted the stars to See if you'd sleep with me?"

"No—that's not—" But I can't think of any justification for my idiotic question, so I bury my face deeper into his dress shirt, my cheeks burning like coals.

Hysan kisses the top of my head, and I can hear the smile in his voice when he says, "I didn't know what would happen, Rho; I only knew what I *wanted* to happen." His voice huskier, he whispers, "And, since you've brought that up. . . ."

"Unfortunately this dress will require the assistance of a lady's maid to remove," I say through still-flushed cheeks.

"Well, since they're all asleep by now . . . ." He pulls away, and when I see the hungry look in his eyes, my blood buzzes in anticipation. "I insist you allow me to serve you in their stead."

My mouth dry, I swallow.

Then I gather my curls to one side and turn around.

Hysan stands so close behind me that his breath nestles into the crook of my shoulder. I feel his fingers working deftly down my spine, patiently undoing every diamond button, until at last air brushes across my exposed back.

His hand skates along my skin, tickling every nerve ending, and I turn around to face him. His gaze has this way of taking in everything about me, as if he can see how my pieces puzzle together.

"*Helios*, you're beautiful," he breathes, his lips temptingly close to mine. He kisses my jawline and traces his way down my neck, while his fingers hook into my dress's heart-shaped neckline and slowly slide it down. The bodice dips beneath my breasts and hangs around my waist.

Hysan drops to his knees, still feeling his way down my curves with his mouth. He keeps sliding my dress lower, until it crumples around my ankles, and goose bumps ripple across my skin.

I gasp as he kisses my hipbone, and his green eyes dart up to meet mine as he pulls gently on the band of my underwear, lowering it slowly.

My eyelids close as my muscles yield to Hysan's touch, and my mind grows floaty, like I'm Centered. I've never felt my body more intensely than in this moment; it's like I can sense everything happening to me on a microscopic level, down to the oxygen atoms' whispery brush against my skin.

The world tips sideways, and now I'm lying on a constellation of clouds, every part of me pulsing with pleasure. The exhilaration builds inside me like a rising rhythm that makes my bones quiver, the feeling sweeping through my blood so swiftly it takes my breath away. My heart pumps blissful music through my veins, its drumroll beat growing louder and louder with every rising breath, until—

Until my chest bursts open and my soul soars free and I touch the stars.

20

WE LEAVE OUR HIDEOUT BEFORE sunrise, using the cover of darkness to surreptitiously shut off the waterfall.

The castle doors are still closed, but Hysan unlocks them with his Scan, and we slip into the deserted entrance hall. He takes my hand as we dart past dim drawing rooms, and when we pass through a thought tunnel, he pulls me into him, and we make out in the mist.

We might as well be walking in the clouds because I don't remember life on the ground ever feeling this good.

"There's something I want to tell you," I say once the white smoke dissipates. "A couple of months ago, I saw a vision of my mom."

Hysan turns to me, shock written all over his face. "What was it?"

"It was her face . . . morphing into an Aquarian." I don't look at him as I say it, and I realize I'm *ashamed* she's a Riser. And the realization shames me even further.

"Was there any indication of where she might be?" he asks, and I shake my head. He tips my chin up. "You'll find her." His eyes seem so sure. "*I promise you.*"

We turn down the hall with the undulating burgundy-and-blue carpet, and Hysan halts mid-stride. I turn to see why he's stopped, and I notice his expression has hardened into a frown.

"What is it?"

"Neith," he says, the green of his gaze growing distant. "Rho, I'll fill you in later—but right now I have to go."

My happiness fades as quickly as the thought tunnel's fog. "What's wrong with Neith? Is he okay? Where is he?"

"He'll be fine," says Hysan, pressing his thumb to the sensor on the wall; the thick fabric flaps out and then ripples into steps. "It's not what happened last time. He just has some leftover glitches I haven't worked out yet, but it's nothing for you to worry about. Focus on learning what you can about the Party, and I'll be in touch later."

"Hysan—"

He presses his mouth to mine but pulls away too quickly. "I'm sorry, Rho—I have to go."

I watch him until he disappears, and then I make my way to the ninth tower, my worry over Neith rising with every step. The common room is crowded with sleeping partygoers in formalwear who didn't make it back to their beds last night; this must have been the *after* after party. I tiptoe through the bodies on my way to the spiral staircase, and then I climb to the top of the tower and slip into my room.

Nishi is facedown on the bed, still wearing her pink taffeta dress. I shake off my black coat and reach back to undo the handful of dress buttons Hysan hooked; I asked him to only do a few so I could slip it off easily.

I take a long bath, using the foamy, floral beauty products, and then I smooth my curls with the glossing spray. Rather than wear my Lodestar suit today, I play around with the closet archiver to put together an outfit that looks like Cancrian formal attire. I settle on a long, flowing, cream-colored skirt with a fitted sapphire blazer, and the program rates my fashion sense a six out of ten.

I grab the black glove for my left hand but before pulling it on, I stare at the Scarab clamped on my wrist. I caught Hysan's gaze straying toward it a few times last night, but as much as I wanted to confide in him, I couldn't bring myself to ruin our reunion. I decided I'd just tell him today, since I thought we'd be spending it together.

I didn't realize he'd be off before the sun came up.

When I slip out of the Lady's Lounge through the gold-tasseled curtains, the air in the main room is tinged with rays of brilliant blue. Dawn is breaking over Primitus.

For the first time since I arrived, Helios has managed to cut through the constant cloud covering, revealing a skyline like none I've ever seen before. Since all three Aquarian planets orbit closely together and maintain equidistance, the massive round silhouettes of Secundus and Tertius press into the atmosphere on either side of Helios, and below, the picture is reflected in the deep blue ocean.

"Stunning, no?"

I turn to see Nishi lifting her head off the mattress, her black locks mussed over her face. I go sit beside her and start unhooking the back of her dress's corset-tight bodice. She folds her arms under her head and rests her cheek on her hand, looking up at me through her tangle of tresses. "Did you sleep?"

"Nope."

"Skarlet?"

"Over."

"Happy?"

"Very."

"Prepare to relive every detail . . . *after* I've caffeinated." She sits up and shuffles into the Lady's Lounge, clutching her dress's neckline as the loose fabric falls off her lean frame.

While she showers and gets dressed, I send Sirna an encrypted message to thank her for the gold dress. I also confide what I've learned of the Tomorrow Party and ask her to consult her sources about Black Moon, but to make sure the information stays confidential. Sirna is better positioned to navigate the political sphere in which the Party operates; and while we may disagree philosophically, I do trust her instincts.

"Blaze just sent a message; we're expected at a Party meeting for senior officers," says Nishi hurriedly, rushing in from the Lady's Lounge with wet hair and wearing the same lavender shirt and charcoal pants she wore yesterday. "Stan, Mathias, and Pandora are also invited; Imogen will tell them."

"Perfect." I pocket my Wave, and we dart downstairs to meet my brother and the others in the common room. They all look far better rested than Nishi and me.

Despite my sleeplessness, I have more energy this morning than I've felt in a long time. Memories of Hysan hum through my mind, turning the sandstone beneath my feet into cottony clouds, and I find myself imagining what it'd be like to stroll with him through the grounds right now, feeling the sun on my face and his hands on my skin—

"Why are you smiling like that?" asks Stan, frowning at me.

My gaze darts to Mathias, who's also studying me, and I shrug. Then I hurry to catch up to Nishi and Imogen. Even though there's a quiet tension between Mathias and Pandora, they're walking together, so some kind of understanding must have passed between them.

The meeting is in Blaze's office, and a few dozen people are already gathered around the conference table—some in chairs, some standing, and the rest sitting on the floor. Blaze stands at the head of the table next to an empty seat. He waves Nishi over, and while she weaves her way to her appointed position, we hang back among the outermost ring of people.

"Welcome, everyone," says Blaze, the bags beneath his eyes matching the blue of his hair. He's wearing a red shirt, and I watch as a small holographic lion prowls across his chest. "Sorry for cutting into your recovery sleep," he says as the lion disappears around his ribcage, "but I've just been informed that now that the party's over, so is our stay on Aquarius."

He sounds more than a little bitter, and I'm reminded of our abrupt dismissal from Scorpio. "We'll need to immediately identify our next base of operations, and then we'll have to be ready to move over the next couple of days. I'll be meeting with the Locations Committee right after this meeting to review our options, and we'll have some updates on that front tonight."

Was Untara upset enough about Crompton's speech that she revoked the Party's welcome? And if so, what kind of punishment awaits Crompton?

"I will now shift the spotlight to the fierce Nishiko Sai, your new co-captain, to update you on the Black Moon front."

Blaze sits as Nishi stands, and everyone breaks into applause. A smile overtakes Nishi's sleepy features at the warm welcome, and she grows more alert.

"Thanks, guys. I'm amazed by how much we've been able to accomplish on Aquarius in just a few weeks, and I can't wait to keep working with you wherever we land next! Like Crompton said so eloquently last night, we're going to face opposition, so we have to be ready to put in hard work. And the first issue we have to tackle is that our permit for planet XDZ5709—or, as we know it here, Black Moon—only provides us with a scientific right of exploration.

"The hard part comes next, when we have to convince the Plenum to allow us to form our own experimental society, free from a single House's rule. The only precedence for something like this involves medical trials and psychiatric studies, but what we're doing goes further than any experiment preceding it. So we'll want to explore a wide array of potential legal arguments to pursue. And on that note, June, how's the Legal Committee doing?"

"We've drafted a dozen dockets," announces a blond Libran in a medical hover-chair with a yellow blanket covering her legs. Most healers can regrow a person's limbs, but there are some congenital conditions technology can't cure yet.

"Right now our favorite approach would be to argue that the Plenum has no jurisdiction over the unaffiliated planets of our solar system, so we shouldn't have to get their permission to do any of this. It's a broad argument, and it's failed before in other cases, but we have a far more progressive Plenum now than we did then, and we also have the benefit of studying where previous cases went wrong to make ours stronger." June sucks in a quick breath and keeps going. "Technically, if we win, we would be establishing that it's a person's right to defect from their home world and colonize any unaffiliated planet. In fact, we would probably be opening up a land grab in our solar system—"

"Okay, thank you, June," says Nishi, cutting her off. "That's great, but if we want the Plenum to hear our petition next session, we can't miss this deadline. Start circulating the twelve drafts you've already got, so we can ask for feedback from our more politically minded members. After the amazing time we showed them last night, the least they can do is lend us their expertise. Besides, it gives them a chance to take on a more important role in our movement."

Even though she isn't saying anything *wrong*, something is definitely off about Nishi's behavior. It isn't like her to be so abrupt with someone, nor have I ever heard her sound so self-important.

"Which brings us to my next point: We've spoken with our team of scientists on Black Moon and confirmed that optimal population numbers for this first wave of settlers will be one thousand people from each House. So, House Captains, please begin the application process. And, finally—yes, Rho?"

I lower my hand. "I was just wondering, how are you finding these twelve thousand applicants?"

"Each House Captain is in charge of promoting our vision through our existing networks of members on each House. For those who are interested in joining, there's an application and evaluation process." She waves her hand in the air like it's all too complicated to get into right now. "Essentially we're looking for people with pioneer personalities, those who would thrive at building a new civilization." Her answer is so perfectly political—a bunch of loaded words strung together into vague enough sentences to offer nothing real—that it makes her seem like a stranger to me.

I've heard plenty of talk like this over the past few months, but I never thought I'd hear it from Nishi.

I raise my hand again.

"Rho, maybe you can save your questions for later—like, when they're not interrupting our meeting."

I can't move or even blink. Since when does Nishi disapprove of questions?

Ignoring my stare she looks around at the others, picking up her old thread again. "And, finally, we have a decision on the *Pisces problem*." The way she says the phrase makes the hairs of my arm stand on end. "We've spoken with our sponsors, and the final decision—*for now*, until the situation there is resolved—is to hold off on inviting House Pisces to participate in Black Moon."

I can't believe what I'm hearing.

I pan my gaze around the room, expecting people to protest, and for the first time it occurs to me that there isn't a single Piscene here, which is strange, given that the Party has been in the works for a few months, and the Piscene plague only broke out a week ago.

"Okay," says Nishi, clapping her hands together. "Let's spread out in the common room or wherever else you can find space and break into committees. Please check in with Blaze or myself with your updates before tonight's meeting; we'll message you with a time once it's set. That's all."

As everyone disbands, I pull Nishi aside. "Can we talk in private?"

"Right now, in the middle of all *this*?" she asks, sounding put out.

"Let's go to our room."

She grunts her acceptance and strides out of the office, and I follow her up the tower. "I'm sorry if I was curt with you at the meeting," she says once I've shut the door behind us. "I *really* needed caffeine before going in there."

Rather than sitting on the bed, she stands near the room's entrance, as if to emphasize that she doesn't have long to chat.

"Nish, what's up?"

"What do you mean?" she asks, crossing her arms defensively.

"Since when does unity mean *most* instead of *all*?"

"It's only for now, until the situation on Pisces is resolved."

"You said the Party has been on Aquarius for weeks. So how come there's no one here from Pisces?"

"There were a few people, but they took off as soon as news broke about the plague on their House. Just as they had to understandably prioritize their world, right now we need to prioritize this project. We really can't risk putting off the other Houses; Black Moon is in too early stages to be making divisive decisions that could weaken our members' commitment to our cause. We'll just agree on this point for now, and once the Zodai have sorted out what's wrong and developed an antidote, no one is going to oppose bringing Pisces back in."

I press my hands on her crossed arms so she'll meet my gaze. "But don't the politics here seem flawed? Favoring one group of people over another? Isn't that what the Tomorrow Party is trying to fight against? Maybe it'd be better to lose those sponsors from the cause altogether than embrace these kinds of politics."

She shrugs her arms loose to shake me off. "That's not how this works—"

"Then change the way it works!" I hear myself say, quoting word-for-word what Candela said to me on Centaurion. "Nish, I think you're compromising your values to make this the right cause for you. And I'm worried you won't like yourself when it's over."

"Look, you did things your own way a few months ago. You stuck to your beliefs and insisted on Ophiuchus's existence, even when it became clear that honesty would only hurt your cause. And that was *your* choice. But I'm not interested in wasting time fighting. I want to make progress *now*, and if that means tabling a discussion or two until later, I don't think it's worth arguing about."

I shake my head in frustration. "Are you listening to yourself? Aren't we supposed to be *changing the norm by breaking it?*"

Nishi glowers at me, her eyes burning like embers, but I blow right past her warning and say, "What would *Deke* think?"

At the sound of his name, her features harden into a mask. The fire in her eyes goes out, and she stares at me impassively, like a wall has just been erected between us.

But this time, I can't cave to her. Nishi's wellbeing—and our friendship—depends on my being brave enough to speak my mind right now. So I grab the heaviest hammer in my arsenal, and I swing.

"When was the last time you listened to Deke's final words?" I demand. Her mouth falls open, and her eyes flash with shocked fury, but I don't stop there. "He said *Don't forget me,* and that's exactly what you're doing!"

I've only seen Nishi's face look this horrified once before.

"I can't believe you."

"Nish, you're not your full self without your memories. Denying them will only twist you into someone you're not—"

"What gives you the right to be morally superior when, until last night, we weren't allowed to discuss Hysan?" she asks in a cutting tone. "Or should I just deal with my grief the way you dealt with yours for Mathias, by giving up on everything I claim to stand for and retreating into my shell?"

Her words hurt, but this argument isn't about me. "You're right. I did do that. But then I remembered who I was, and you know who reminded me?" I move closer to her and soften my tone. "I just want to help you get through this the way you and Deke helped me."

"*And look where that got us,*" she says in a low, lethal voice.

I go deathly silent, and I feel like I did that awful night on Elara's surface, when my helmet warned me I was running out of oxygen. "I begged you both not to board that ship with me," I say in a controlled voice, like I'm rationing my air. "You knew the odds, and you wouldn't listen."

"Deke wanted to fight when the Marad boarded our ship." Her features pull together in a repressed sob, and a vein bulges in her forehead from how hard she's resisting it. "And *you* didn't let him."

The same sob seems to be strangling my throat, and I grow light-headed from my lack of oxygen. "You knew the plan, Nishi. I was *supposed* to get captured," I say, my breathing strained. "I was *supposed* to be bait. And neither of you were supposed to be there."

Anger burns my belly, and it's not just over Nishi's accusation. Deep down, somewhere so far within me that she'll never know about it, I blame her and Deke for not heeding my warnings. I'm mad at them for insisting on going with me and not considering the consequences.

I'm angry at Deke for dying.

"You're right, Rho," says Nishi, as tears finally break through, and her mask comes crashing down. "*I wish we'd never followed you.*"

21

SOMETIME AFTER NISHI STORMS OFF, there's a knock on my door. I have no idea how long I've been staring at the reflection of the Aquarian planets' silhouettes in the ocean, trying not to think about the things Nishi and I said to each other.

But it's not just my best friend I feel like I'm losing.

I'd been so happy at the idea of Black Moon—the thought that in a few years I might live in a world where Nishi and I could be roommates, where Hysan and I could be together openly, where people could unite by choice instead of chance. A world where the Zeniths and Palomas of the Zodiac wouldn't need a hideout.

But instead of being the change we've been fighting for, this Party is turning out to be an upgrade on the same old politics of prejudice and privilege and popularity. Gyzer was right: Real freedom doesn't move in one direction, but in *all* of them. It isn't enough just to change things: First we have to change *the way* we change things.

The door cracks open. "Rho?" says Stan. "We're going for a walk. Can you come?"

I wipe the tears off my cheeks before turning around. "Yeah . . . sure." I grab the black coat Hysan gave me and follow him out.

We stop by my brother's room to pick up Mathias and Pandora, who are sitting on a bed talking in hushed tones. The moment he sees me in the doorway, Mathias stands.

"Coming?" I say, looking from him to Pandora, so she'll feel included.

The common room is packed with Party members; they're divided into committees, working, and I'm reminded of the bustling scene we walked in on when we first landed here a couple of days ago. I avoid making eye contact with anyone because I don't want to lock gazes with Nishi, and right as I hit the wall switch for the carpet staircase, I hear my name.

"Rho!" Imogen runs up to me, her copper-flecked eyes round. "Did you hear about Crompton?"

My friends gather around us as I ask, "What about him?"

"Untara had him arrested for treason. He's being escorted to the dungeons now—"

Before she's finished speaking, I run down the burgundy-and-blue steps. I determine which way to go by following the swarm of fair-skinned, glassy-eyed, light-haired Aquarians racing across the sandstone, whispering about the arrest.

Up ahead I spot a dozen Elders marching through a drawing room surrounding a tall man with silver hair. I hurry until I've caught up, and then I call, "Ambassador Crompton!"

The troop of Elders tries to keep marching, but Crompton stops moving, and they begrudgingly halt, too. "Wandering Star," he says, his pink eyes looking much dimmer this morning than they did last night. "I had hoped to see you before going."

He looks to one of the men around him, and I recognize grim-faced Pollus, who spares me a disgruntled glance before nodding at Crompton.

"You have five minutes," he says.

Another Elder turns to him in alarm. "We are under strict instructions not to allow him access to the Wandering Star."

"I am the senior official here, and I'm saying they can talk."

I try twisting my Ring to see if I can call to Crompton through the Collective Conscious; but I've only ever tried it with people I'm close to, so I'm not sure how to reach out for his particular essence. *Ambassador? Can you hear me?*

I don't feel anything, and when I look over, I don't see his Barer or his Ring on his fingers. He's no longer wearing his Philosopher's Stone around his neck either. They've taken his devices.

A loud whip of electricity crackles between us as an aqua blade beams out from the interconnected rings on Pollus's clenched right hand. Quick as lightning another Elder draws his own Barer, and protective shades glow around both men, similar to the one Morscerta used to wear.

"Stand down or I will have you locked up next to the Ambassador for taking arms against your superior," warns Pollus. "Supreme Advisor Untara only said they may not meet privately. She also did *not* want us to offend the Plenum, whom the Wandering Star represents. Your lack of subtlety, Revelough, is what keeps you from moving up the ranks. Now I will not repeat myself again. *Stand down.*"

Revelough looks to the others, but since no one else reacts, he lowers his blade. The whole platoon falls back a couple of paces, giving Crompton and me the smallest modicum of space.

"It seems I've failed to follow my own advice," he says gravely, in a low voice that nonetheless carries to the Elders around us. "Learn from my experience, because the Zodiac needs you far more than it does me."

"I'm sorry this is happening to you," I say, moving as close to him as I dare and dropping my voice to a barely audible whisper. "The Tomorrow Party isn't the solution I thought it would be."

"I'm sorry, too," he says, his brow creasing with more weight. "Neither is the Aquarian government. When Morscerta chose me to be his replacement, he faced a world of opposition, primarily from Untara. People from her camp said I came from too small a village, that I wouldn't be able to deal with palace politics. I guess they were right."

"How long will they keep you locked up?"

"Pollus is working on my defense, so hopefully not long. He's smart, and I trust him. He might be the last friend I have left."

"*One* of the last," I say, and I'm embarrassed to see from the warmth in Crompton's eyes that I've moved him.

"I'm sorry I can no longer help you with your search," he says sadly. "In the end I'm afraid I'm just another old politician who's let you down."

"No, you're not—"

"Listen," he says, speaking as low as he dares, "I know it will be tempting to stay here searching for your mom, but you should leave this place as soon as you can." The Elders around us begin to crowd in again, and Crompton whispers faster. "With me out of the way, Untara will not be so welcoming. She's—"

"We have to go," says Pollus roughly, cutting Crompton off before he can say more. Then the Elders swallow him in their formation, and he's gone.

✦ ✦ ✦

We leave the palace and step onto the sunny, sandy plaza, but the fresh air doesn't make my breathing any easier. Neith, Nishi, Crompton . . . lately it feels like I'm powerless to help any of my friends.

The waterfalls around us sparkle from Helios's touch, and as we walk past them, I think about last night and how much I wish Hysan were beside me right now to put my mind at ease. I twist my Ring, debating reaching out to him through the Collective Conscious.

"I think we need to abandon this stupid cause and focus on something real, like Pisces," says my brother, shattering our silence.

"I think we should find out more about this Party first," says Mathias. I look at him and he holds eye contact with me for the first time since our dance.

My skin grows soft from his gaze, and I realize I'll probably always feel a sense of security when he's around. But the pulse-pausing jolt I used to get from looking into his indigo eyes is now just a gentle breath between beats. A muscle memory.

"I spoke to my parents," he says, "and Sirna told them you reached out. Apparently the Party has been on their radar for a while because of the kind of money they're throwing around, but they're very protective of their financial records. Every politician who's donated has made their contribution public, yet the known total doesn't add up to even a small portion of how much they've been spending. Sirna wants you to see if, maybe through your friendship with Nishi, you can find out who the sponsors are."

A couple of Aquarian valets in velvet top hats pass us going in the other direction, and once they're out of earshot, I say, "Let's put more space between us and the palace."

It was a smart move on Sirna's part to send me the message through Mathias. Otherwise she would have actually had to admit that House politics are entwining with my personal life. *Again*.

As we round the corner, the Pegazi habitat comes into view on the horizon, beneath a cloudless blue sky. Across the lake, hundreds of winged horses in hides of every hue walk along the sand or lie on feathery blankets or wade in the glinting water. Helios hovers over the scene, sandwiched between the pale imprints of planets Secundus and Tertius.

I cut in the Pegazi's direction, since that's probably where we'll have the least chance of being overheard.

"*Rho!*"

A hairy creature with sharp teeth suddenly jumps out at me and roars in my face.

Shocked, I let out a piercing shriek of terror, which instinctively prompts Mathias to leap forward and smash his fist into its face.

"Ow!"

The creature emits a childlike cry, and as he rubs his bleeding nose, I realize he's a Leonine teenager with a very bushy mane of brown hair. "You animal!" he snaps at Mathias. "What kind of Cancrian goes around punching people?"

"Well what kind of person jumps out at—" I stop mid-sentence and squint at him. "*Helios*, are you Traxon Harwing?"

His outrage instantly transforms into pride, and he flashes his pointy teeth at me in a smile. "Hard to forget this face, eh, Rho?" A trickle of blood dribbles down his lip.

"*I remember you.*" Stanton studies Trax's hairy features. "You were at the international village on Vitulus. You're in that conspiracy group, the Thirteenth House—"

"Actually, it's just *13*," says Trax, wiping the blood off his nose with his sullied sleeve. He's wearing a black tuxedo that's completely covered in dirt and grime.

"Did you sleep out here?" I ask, gazing at the haphazard piles of hay and stained feather blankets strewn throughout the sand.

"Had to, since they wouldn't let me into the castle." The Leonine's face is a tangle of hair, but as he pulls his wild locks back into a ponytail, I see a broad face with multiple eyebrow piercings.

I think back to the scuffle I saw by the front doors on my way to the ball. "That was *you*," I say, frowning. "Why wouldn't the Tomorrow Party let you attend the event?"

"Blaze hates me." He says it like it's a bragging right. "I'm always blowing the lid off his new projects on my holo-show, *Trax the Truth Tracker*."

"You don't like him?" I ask.

"I don't have a problem with the man," he says defensively. "I actually admire his idealism."

"So why mess with him?" asks Stan.

"Because I'm a Truther from Leo's Truth Pride, and I believe in full transparency in all things." Traxon has the same candid way of expressing himself as Blaze, and the honesty in his speech makes him hard to write off, even if he's a bit *too much*.

"That's why I've been waiting to run into you," he says, looking at me with newfound interest. "I need you to tell me what the Tomorrow Party is planning."

"What do you mean?" I ask warily.

His eyes narrowing, he hunches his shoulders forward, like a lion shifting into hunting mode. "Blaze likes to champion progressive causes, but they're always specific to *our* House. The Tomorrow Party is far more ambitious than anything he's tried before, and he's managed to attract too many high profile sponsors in too short a time for this to be just another venture." The focus of his gaze is so constant that I'm not sure he's blinking; he looks like a predator ready to pounce.

"I know *you*, in particular, wouldn't come all this way just to play politics, which means something Blaze is doing has piqued your interest. I also know he's already shared his plans with you, or you wouldn't be here. So what is it, Rho? What's the Tomorrow Party's end goal?"

Even if I begrudgingly respect his investigative prowess, his sense of entitlement sets my teeth on end, just like it did when we first met. "Traxon, if you want to learn about the Tomorrow Party, you need to ask an actual member."

"Oh, so you *don't* like what they're up to?" he surmises, his eyes widening with surprise.

Annoyed, I just say, "Don't let the Pegazi hog the feather blanket tonight."

Then I move past him to survey the sea of colorful creatures for Candor's aqua hide. I keep a respectful distance as I approach the lake's shoreline where an orange horse is drinking and a purple one is lying beside it with its wet wings fully unfurled so Helios can dry its feathers.

"Or I can go with a different headline," Traxon calls out. "*Wandering Star Rhoma Grace attends a ball on Aquarius and spends the night with a Libran who came as Skarlet Thorne's date.*"

My body ices over with his words.

When my veins thaw and blood begins to flow again, I turn slowly, toward Mathias. He's staring at the lake, wearing the unreadable Zodai expression he used to hide behind on Oceon 6. He's shutting me out from his reaction.

I spin the rest of the way around and glower at Traxon. "You're a jerk. And that sounds more like a rumor than *truth tracking*."

"You're right, Rho." He creeps closer. "I wonder what would make it more newsworthy . . . ."

He flicks on his silver Lighter—the Leonine version of a Wave—and a holographic image pops into the air: Hysan holding my face in his hands and kissing me outside the castle this morning.

I can't breathe.

"And in case you're thinking of clocking me again and stealing my Lighter," he warns Mathias, "I back everything up. So what's my lead story going to be, Rho?"

I don't meet Traxon's stare. Hysan definitely doesn't need a dogged Truther looking too deeply into his identity. But I also can't let this nosy, bullying Leo use me. I need a third option.

"Okay," says a dreamy voice behind me. "We'll tell you."

We all turn to Pandora in surprise. Between waterfalls of auburn hair, her amethyst eyes sparkle in the sunlight. "But we'll need a private place to talk."

"Excellent!" says a beaming Traxon. "Step into my kingdom."

22

SINCE MY MIND IS AS blank as Mathias's expression, I don't question Pandora's plan beyond hoping she has one.

I grudgingly trail after Traxon as he weaves through the landscape of Pegazi, leading us toward one of the sheltered stables. My brother, Mathias, and Pandora fall behind me, and as I walk an acidic guilt eats at my guts. This wasn't how I wanted Mathias or my brother to learn about Hysan.

The sun-soaking steeds pay us no attention as we pass them, too busy eating or sleeping or drinking to marvel at the humans in their midst. They're so silent that I wonder if they have their own way of communicating through the Psy.

When he reaches the stable, Traxon turns to me and asks, "How long have you known Hysan Dax?"

I stiffen. "You know Hysan?"

"Everyone knows Hysan." The cocky Leo tilts his head. "He gets around." There's a bite in his voice that sounds a lot like jealousy. "But you already knew that, since he attended the ball with Skarlet and went home with you."

My brother arrives in time to hear Traxon's jab. "And you spent the night with a Pegazi, so what's your point?"

I snort.

"At least the Pegazi stuck around until morning." Traxon watches me for a reaction, and I feel my face blanching, until I notice his smirk looks forced. Even though he's taunting me, he's the one who seems hurt.

But why would he care that I spent the night with Hysan? I'm not getting the vibe Trax likes me that way. So if his jealousy isn't over me, then it must be about—

"Don't take it personally, Rho." The Leonine's expression hardens, like he can read the realization on my face. "I've heard Hysan rarely sticks around after getting what he wants."

Suddenly Stan yanks Traxon by his tuxedo collar and shoves him into the wall. "I swear to Helios, you better leave my sister alone—"

Mathias grabs my brother's shoulders and pulls him off Traxon, placing himself between them and holding a hand to each of their chests. The Leonine grins like he's having a blast. "You're pretty feral for a bunch of Cancrians. I dig it!"

"Just take us to your hovel," I say through gritted teeth.

Trax leads us around the side of the structure, presumably to wherever the entrance is, and I cover my nose as the smell grows unbearable for a few breaths, until we step inside. The stable has a grid of square stalls, each one stuffed with hay and feather blankets, except for the stall Traxon takes us to, which has been completely remodeled to look like a holo-show's studio set.

Stage lights hover in the corners, and a rectangular bench of hay presses into the wall beneath a holographic banner bearing the title: *Trax the Truth Tracker*.

"Okay, Rho, are you my whistleblower?" he asks, adjusting the settings of one of three floating cameras, the lens aimed at the show's title graphic. "If you don't want to be identified, I can apply a shadow filter that only shows your silhouette."

"Actually," says Pandora, bravely sitting down on the hay bench, "we want to answer your ultimatum with another choice."

She clears her throat and straightens, summoning the quiet strength she showed when we first met. "You can either cheapen your Truther brand by running a story that pries into the personal lives of people who served the Zodiac honorably. Or you can get an exclusive interview with the Wandering Star . . . *after* you've done something for us."

Traxon looks taken aback for the first time, and I could kiss Pandora for wiping the confident smirk off his face.

"We need to know where the money for the Tomorrow Party is coming from," she goes on, without waiting for his answer. "We have only pieces of the picture, but if you can get us the parts we're missing, we'll be able to pool together what we know and sort out what's happening. Then Rho can relate the real story to your viewers."

Traxon looks from her to me and back to her. It's not an ideal plan—she's still leaving me on the hook for an interview—but her strategy of making Trax work for us is inspired.

"Don't you think I've already tried to find that information?" he asks. "They're using crazy advanced encryption for their financials."

"But now you'll be incentivized," says Pandora, and when Trax glares at her, I almost smile.

"If I agree to kill one story, delay another, *and* do your legwork for you, then I need to know you've actually got something for me." His eyes narrow on me, and the good humor melts from my mood. "Give me a taste."

Without thinking it over, I hear myself reciting from memory: "Planet XDZ5709."

His adorned brows slope downward. "What will I find when I look it up?"

"A permit for scientific exploration in the Plenum's public records."

Shrugging, he asks, "And I care because?"

"The research is being sponsored by the Tomorrow Party."

Traxon cracks his knuckles, and his eyes dart from person to person, like he's trying to glimpse the catch in one of our faces. When he doesn't find it, he says, "How do I know you'll keep up your end of the bargain?"

"If you get us this information, I'll give you an interview," I say. "I swear it on—"

"I don't want you to swear," he says, picking at his unkempt beard. "I want proof I can *touch*."

I look to Pandora for guidance, but she looks back at me just as confused. "What do you mean by that?" I ask Traxon.

"Leave something of yours with me," he says, still grooming his facial hair. "Something you'll come back for."

I run through my scarce belongings in my mind. Nothing I own has any monetary value save for my Wave, and I'm *not* giving that up.

"Here." Stan tosses something small and black, and Trax reflexively catches it.

"What's this?" he asks, holding the black scorpion to his eyes and scrutinizing the red dots on its shell.

"It's an Echo." As my brother speaks, I meet Mathias's midnight gaze, and I spy a look of realization as he connects this device to Link's accusation on Sconcion. "You can use it to spy on all communications being sent nearby," says Stan, and as he explains the technology to Traxon, the Leonine's eyebrows climb progressively higher on his face. By the time my brother stops talking, Trax is staring at the device almost reverently. I have a feeling we're never getting it back.

He slips the Echo in his dirty trouser pocket and then asks me, "How will I reach you when I have something to share?"

"I'll give you my contact information," I say. "But first, tell me about House Ophiuchus."

Traxon beams like a pet that's just been offered a treat. "Before I begin, I have to preface what I'm about to disclose with a disclaimer," he says in a strangely professional tone. It sounds like he's reading from a script he knows by heart. "There's been a lot of debate and dissent in the study of the Thirteenth House, so the facts I'm about to share are based on my research and what *I* believe to be true."

His shift into host persona is so sudden that I'm distracted enough to almost forget to hate him. "Based on what we believe about Ophiuchans' biological makeup, we suspect they lived in a marshy world, a planet filled with poisonous plants and lethal wildlife—"

"What do you know about the *people?*" I ask impatiently.

"The majority of 13's members agree Ophiuchus most likely represented *Unity.* At their best, Ophiuchans were thought to have been spirited, magnetic, compassionate, and clever; at their worst, they were jealous, power hungry, and temperamental. Physically, the House had the greatest diversity of the Zodiac—skin, hair, and eye color spanned the full range of the spectrum. And when they entered puberty, Ophiuchans developed scaly skin that protected them from some creatures' bites and dangerous natural elements."

Corinthe's reptilian voice slithers through my thoughts, and a slow chill ripples down my spine. What if the molting process Risers undergo is because they're actually trying to morph into their natural, scaly bodies?

And when they can't, their soul takes its next best fit?

"You're tuning me out," says an annoyed Traxon, frowning at me. "Look, I know threatening you with your secrets was a low move, and I wish I didn't have to resort to dirty tricks just to get politicians to tell the truth for a change."

Did he really just call me a politician?

"But forget about me a moment, and think about what's best for our galaxy. There are fewer facts known about House Ophiuchus than there are about the Last Prophecy—and I'm talking about an entire *world* that was lost to our solar system, not some silly superstition. You are the only person who's had actual contact with that House—with its *Original Guardian*, at that!—so only *you* have the chance to fill in those lost chapters of our history. You could interview him, talk to him, get his side of the story—"

"What's the Last Prophecy?"

Traxon's round eyes look like they're going to shoot out of his head. "*That's* all you heard?" he blares, and I cross my arms and stare at him in stubborn silence until he relents. "Come on, you know what the Last Prophecy is. You're the Wandering Star, one of the best seers in our solar system. You *have* to know it!"

"Drop the condescension," snaps my brother, who's standing beside me.

Traxon rakes his hair back, and his finger gets stuck in a knot. "It's a prophecy that was made by an Original Guardian," he says, tugging at the tangle, "and it foretells how the Zodiac will end."

"How could something like that be around without us knowing?" Mathias leans against the wall beside the hay bench, near Pandora. He sounds as put off by Traxon as my brother.

"Because it's been forgotten," says Traxon. "No one's taken it seriously in centuries. Back in the day, people really believed in it, and there was even a myth that Zodai over the ages who saw this Prophecy would get tapped into a secret group of seers that was fighting to reverse it. Have you ever heard that old fashioned greeting, 'Light of the sun be with you?'"

The others shake their heads, but Hysan's voice echoes through my memory. He said that to me in 'Nox's nose a few lifetimes ago, when we left Phaetonis. I'd thought it a strangely antiquated saying, but nothing more.

"What about it?" I ask.

"They say the greeting originated as a way for believers of the Prophecy to test if they were talking to a fellow follower."

Again I find myself wishing Hysan were here. He must know about the Last Prophecy because he knows about everything else. But is he a believer?

"When does the Last Prophecy say the Zodiac will end?" asks Pandora.

"Sometime this millennium. I'm sure the Prophecy will be back in vogue in some nations now that we're within range of its alleged deadline; bound to be some great end-of-the-worlds parties."

I force a mask of disinterest over my features, but I spy Pandora's frightened face in the periphery of my vision, and I know she's thinking of the omen she's been Seeing, the one where our galactic sun goes dark.

"How does the Prophecy say the Zodiac will end?" I chance.

Traxon pulls at another knot in his hair. "Even I don't see how this could happen. Nor do the Zodiac's leading scientists, so there's nothing to worry about."

"This is painful," says Stan, crossing his arms like it's the only way he'll keep his fists under control. "Can you just answer a damn question without the benefit of your *expert opinion?*"

Traxon glares at my brother and waits an annoyingly long moment before saying, "The Last Prophecy says the Zodiac will end in the third millennium." Still staring at Stan, he draws out another pause, and then he finally says what Pandora has been dreading to hear. "When Helios shuts off her light."

23

HALF AN HOUR LATER, THE four of us are having lunch in a different dining hall, far from the ninth tower. Platters of food sit between us, but only the guys are eating. Pandora and I are still digesting what we learned from Traxon.

I let my head fall in my hands and close my eyes to try to focus. The Last Prophecy, Black Moon, the Marad, the master, Mom . . . my life is filling with too many more questions than answers, and the few facts I do know I can't force into any discernible design.

"The Taurian Guardian was tailing you last night," says Stan, his mouthful of food muffling his voice.

I snap my head up. "What?"

"At the ball," he says after swallowing. "When you started talking to Ambassador Crompton, she used an audio amplifier to eavesdrop." He wipes his mouth with his napkin.

Mathias frowns. "Why was she here?" he asks, abandoning his half-eaten steak. "She didn't have to come to the event if she's already sponsoring the Party. And if she was coming, why didn't *she* give the speech instead of Crompton? She's much higher profile."

"I'm not sure it'd be in the Party's best interest to publically tie themselves to her right now," I say tentatively. "She's come under fire for her defense of Risers."

But Mathias is right. Why *did* she come? Was her sole reason to ask me to lie to the Plenum for her? Shouldn't she be more concerned with what's happening on Pisces? Shouldn't we *all* be?

"I really think Pisces is the key to everything," says Stanton, his thoughts unsurprisingly straying to the same place as mine. "That's where we need to be. Whatever's happening to that world *is* the master's next move."

"But what does the master gain by wiping out every Piscene?" I ask, not exactly disagreeing, but just thinking through the theory out loud. "It's the poorest and most selfless House of the Zodiac. They share every civic duty and have no monetary system or industry. Their only 'exports' are their visions."

"It's a word of seers," says Pandora, nodding along with me, "and now the master is blinding them."

Cold air rushes into my lungs, and I exhale.

"*Helios,*" I whisper, leaning into the round table. Crompton's voice sounds in my head—*Maybe there's just something she's afraid I'll See.* It was his Sight, not his voice, that got him in trouble.

Moira was our foremost Psy expert before she was attacked, and Origene and Caasy were ranked second and third after her. Who knows how many other attacks—like the Elder assassinations, the drowning on Oscuro, the explosions on Leo—have really been targeted strikes on our best seers? Ferez believes the hit on Capricorn was really to retrieve a specific Snow Globe the master was after—so maybe every one of these large-scale attacks conceals a secret.

"What if the master is trying to destabilize the Psy to keep us from Seeing what he's planning?" I ask.

"If that's true," says Mathias, and in his tone I hear the same seeds of skepticism as when I told him my theory of Ochus on Oceon 6, "why not destroy the Fish constellation all at once, like he did with our House? Why did his attack come with a two-month incubation period?"

I think about the master's most recent attacks. They were on Capricorn and Pisces . . . and neither of them used Dark Matter.

"He needs a more powerful weapon to take out planets again," I say slowly, "and he hasn't used Dark Matter since the armada." Not since Ophiuchus told me he wanted to change sides.

I have to find him again and convince him I'm not weak. As hateful as it is to admit, I need his help—and I especially need to do whatever it takes to keep him from returning to the master's side.

"Mathias is right, though," says Pandora. "Two months is a long incubation time." She spins the Philosopher's Stone in her hand. "Having seen his army up close, the master is too organized for this kind of delay not to be deliberate."

"Maybe he wanted to lull us into a false sense of security so we'd stop searching for him," says Stan. "It's worked, hasn't it? The Plenum declared Peace."

None of us speaks for a while, and I get the impression we're each lost in our own train of thought.

"Something about the Tomorrow Party jolted me." We all look at Pandora.

"It was a word that threw me . . . *Captain*. It's probably coincidence; I mean, it's such a small, random, insignificant detail." She looks to Mathias, but his expression is still unreadable.

When she speaks again, she sounds smaller somehow, like she's had to travel to a dark place to retrieve these words. "*Captain* was what the Marad called their senior officers."

None of us says anything, but my heart starts racing like a percussive progression that's building to a drumroll. *She's right, it means nothing, it's just a word, barely a clue—*

I try drowning the realization rising within me so the words won't pass through my lips, but my heart is too loud to hear my thoughts, and they break through despite me.

"*The Tomorrow Party.*"

I sound breathless even though I haven't moved. "Stan, you said yourself the Party is only catering to the elite. Every prospective member is young and ambitious and *special*. They're being recruited the same way Risers were wooed to join the Marad—hopeful meetings about ideology that soon devolved into a darker agenda. And they seem to have unending funds that can't be corroborated, just like the Marad. The master is the *only* person we know with deep enough pockets to pull this off."

"You're saying the *master* is behind the *Tomorrow Party*?" Mathias asks, not bothering to disguise his disbelief. "*Why?*"

"Because violence was uniting us." Everyone waits for me to go on, and my heart keeps beating too hard as the thoughts in my head begin to connect. "The moment the Plenum forgave me and made me Wandering Star, we became powerful, and that made us a threat. So he—or *she*—decided to change tactics. The master is a student of history. He or she *knows* the best way to divide us is from the inside. Just imagine what will happen when this Party goes public with Black Moon. This kind of movement is bound to rile up every House's passions. It's the perfect distraction. Instead of a common enemy we can gang up on, he's making us point fingers at ourselves."

I'm reminded of something Hysan once told me—*The greater our need to unite, the deeper we divide*. "It's what happened during the Trinary Axis, and in the Cancrian poem about Ochus. By undermining our unity, we're easier to pick off."

My words of doom suffocate the conversation. I'm sure that, just like me, my friends are combing through what they know and trying to poke holes in my reasoning. But I'm certain I'm right—this sounds exactly like something the master would do. Just like he turned our own tactics against us during the armada, he's now trying to turn our brightest people against each other. He's sewing seeds of distrust to destabilize our fragile unity and ensuring his own victory by sabotaging us.

He never went away. He just found himself a new army.

My army.

"What about Fernanda?" asks Stan. "If she's a sponsor, could she be behind everything?"

I shake my head. "If she was the master, she wouldn't be so outspoken about Risers. I think she was just taken in by this Party, like the rest of us."

Pandora looks unconvinced. "The liar's best tool is his honesty," she says. "On Aquarius, there's a saying about that—*Truth builds trust, and trust blinds truth.*"

I think of Aryll, and how every time he fed me a false truth, I trusted him more. But I still don't think Fernanda is the one behind everything.

"All I know is the Tomorrow Party is a distraction, and we're playing into the master's hands, *again*," I say, meeting my brother's determined gaze. "You've been right this whole time, Stan. We need to get to Pisces and defend that House before it disappears from the Zodiac. If the master is trying to get rid of our best seers, that means his biggest move is coming."

"But if he's targeting our best seers," says Pandora softly, "why hasn't he killed you yet?"

"He's been trying to this whole time," says Stan darkly.

But I remember the Marad soldiers saying the master didn't want me dead yet. Then I think of my recent experiences with Skiff, Fernanda, and Ophiuchus, and the truth is too obvious to obfuscate. "Because he wants something from me."

And knowing he wants me alive is more terrifying than being marked for death.

24

MATHIAS AND PANDORA DON'T SEEM as confident in the Tomorrow Party's complicity as Stan and I are, but as we head back to the ninth tower, I feel a unity of purpose with my brother that feels familiar and *right*.

Our agreed-upon plan is to go back to our rooms and pack so that we can leave this planet as soon as possible. But first, there are a few things I need to do. When we reach the burgundy-and-blue cloth, Stan activates the staircase, and while he and Pandora climb up, I pull Mathias aside.

"I'm sorry about . . . earlier," I say, standing with him by the sandstone wall, in the shadow of the staircase.

"I don't want to talk about the Libran—"

"Well that's kind of a problem, because I need you to coordinate transportation with him to see if he can fly us out of here."

Mathias's midnight eyes scrutinize mine, and the acidic guilt gnaws at me again. He nods tersely. "But you and your brother need to slow down with your theories," he says, his jaw tight. "You're assuming a lot of things without proof."

"I know, but I think we've been trusting only what we can touch for so long that we've forgotten the importance of trusting our instincts, too. Maybe if we used them more, they'd be better honed."

He grimaces with disapproval. "And what of your brother's instinct to steal that device from Scorpio?"

"It proved useful, didn't it?" I say weakly.

"Rho, he's not coping well. You're not helping by encouraging him, and you can't let him lead you down his reckless path."

"I'm not. I actually think having a sense of purpose again will help him heal," I say hopefully, and to end the discussion, I add, "But thanks for looking out for us."

He nods and goes to climb the stairs, but he stops moving when I don't follow. "Where are you going?"

"Reading room." The line between his eyes deepens, and I add, "I'm thinking if we can't predict the master's next move, maybe a star can."

"Ophiuchus?" It sounds strange to hear Mathias say the name seriously and not spiked with sarcasm.

I nod. "Then I'll find Nishi and tell her everything, and we'll come get you guys once we're packed and ready to go. I just need you to arrange the pick-up details with Hysan."

"What if Nishi doesn't believe you?"

I start walking down the hall. "If the choice is between abandoning her and knocking her out, I will be carrying Nishi out of the castle."

◆ ◆ ◆

I'm relieved to find the underground reading room empty.

Standing amid the holographic lights, I stare into the rocky rubble that was once the brightest blue jewel in the Zodiac and try pushing everything far from my mind. Last night I trusted my heart over my head and it led me to Hysan. I now try letting my instinct lead me again as I sink into my Center, and when jittery Psynergy invades my lungs, I call out to Ophiuchus with my mind.

Almost instantly a wintry wind overtakes the cave. I pull on my black coat, so I don't shiver as the Thirteenth Guardian's giant icy shape takes form and grows to twice my size. His black eyes watch me impassively as the temperature steadily drops.

I think of how Traxon can set aside his personal feelings for someone in his search for the truth, and I try to relinquish my revulsion for Ochus so that I can do the same now.

If we're going to work together, I need to know more about you, I say.

Ask your questions then, he booms, and unlike the resistance I was expecting, he sounds calm, like I've finally said the right thing. *We haven't time to waste, crab.*

Before I begin firing off questions, I envision an icy wall of

Psynergy encasing my heart, barricading my emotions from infecting our interaction. The only way to have this conversation is by not making it about me.

You claim the other Guardians betrayed you because you attempted to achieve immortality—

Immortality wasn't a discovery I made, he cuts in. *Eternal life was a power given to me by my Talisman, because as the Guardian of Unity, I was meant to remain a living star among you.*

I blink. *What?*

Unity does not merely extend to the Houses; I was once the glue between man and the stars, reality and the astral plane, the past and the future. His voice drops, like he's mining deeper and deeper depths as he talks. *I was never meant to die; I was to link humanity through the ages, so that you would never again forget each other, as you had in your old world.*

Mom's necklace flashes through my thoughts, and I think of House Ophiuchus not as a thirteenth pearl but as the chain holding our whole solar system together. *So you were going to be . . . a god living among us? But how could they have defeated you if you were immortal?*

He glares at me in icy silence, and he seems to be reevaluating his decision to share anything with me. *I will share what I want you to know.*

That's not how this works, I shoot back. *Either tell me the full story, or go find someone else to help you.*

We stare at each other, and I force myself to summon every vestige of bravery in me so I won't look away. I know I'm risking pain and violence by challenging him, but it's time I hear his full story. The Zodiac can't wait any longer.

Again, I start to ask, *How did they defeat—*

When I realized the gift I'd been given, he says in a harsh voice, *I wanted to harness the power of my Talisman to lengthen human lives. I've had millennia to relive that life, and still I don't know how I was found out. All I know is the other Guardians discovered my Talisman's power, and they were outraged to learn that it was their destiny to perish and return to the stars, while I would remain on the mortal plane.*

His form shrinks a little, and the cold air is less cutting. *They insisted I share my immortality with them. I was given one year to work on a solution, and they threatened that if I couldn't manage it on my own, they would confiscate my Talisman to investigate it themselves.*

I'm so spellbound by his tale that I don't realize until he's midway through that his voice is no longer frosty and deafening, but rather it's rising and falling, sharp and soft, rushing and halting. He's talking like a human.

Only when I got home . . . the Talisman was gone. When I reported its theft to the other Guardians, they accused me of lying to keep my immortality for myself. I was charged with treason against the other Houses and sentenced to execution.

I shake my head. *But you couldn't die—*

Silence! he booms, and a blast of cold air slams into me, knocking me off my feet. Pain echoes through me as I land on my arm, and I glare at him as I sit up, my breathing shallow.

If you want to kill me, do it, I say softly, gluing my gaze to his.

The rage fades from his expression, and he looks taken aback.

Do it, I say again from the floor. When he still doesn't react, I slowly rise to my feet. *You need my help just as much as I need yours. So quit acting like you're the one in charge, and just tell me the truth. How did they do this to you?*

To my extreme shock, he answers me.

Immortality works in cycles, he begins in a toneless voice, *just like everything else in Nature. Eternal life isn't a matter of locking one's soul into an everlasting body, because all organic life dies. Instead, my Talisman functioned as a super-powered Psynergy source that enabled me to generate a new body when the one I inhabited gave out. Without the stone I couldn't regenerate. And yet my essence did not return to the stars. I retained sentience without form. I could not touch or be seen. I could only float through the astral plane without affecting anything, pulled by a different kind of gravity. I was still enslaved to mortality's master . . . Time.*

He sighs, and the sadness within him is so deep that it infects the molecules of Psynergy in the air around us. The emotion feels like a heavy blanket that's been draped over me, and my shoulders sag as even breathing begins to feel like too much work.

The Psynergy from people of every House attuned me to the changes in the worlds, making me torturously aware of time's passing. I listened to the emotional symphony of humanity, watching you endure the same mistakes over and over again, slowly forgetting what you'd learned in your exodus to this new world. You were stuck in the same cycles of hate because you were still driven by your fear and not your faith.

The mist of ice that accompanies his presence seems to fill with pieces of the past, and I feel the Psynergy around us pressing in on me, probably as he always feels it. It's like being shouted at by billions of competing voices—disembodied emotions, phantom physical pains, visions of the future—and it's hard to withstand even for just a moment. I can't imagine enduring it forever.

After being forced to watch my beloved House crushed by Dark Matter, I started to feel the Psynergy of lost Ophiuchan souls trying to Rise out of their ill-suited bodies. I hoped this time the stars might show my children mercy—but they betrayed us again. Instead of setting these Rising Ophiuchans free, fate forced them to assume slightly less uncomfortable forms, yet never the one that truly reflected them.

And as if the pain of not fitting into their own bodies wasn't enough, humanity cast my people off as completely as the stars. They ostracized Risers and subjected them to inhumane hate. I longed to stop watching, to undo time, to cease existing. Yet I could not end my life because I wasn't alive. And so, as the centuries passed, I grew to hate you.

Something small and warm cracks the Psynergy shell guarding my heart, and to my horror, I realize it's pity. But I will not— cannot—commiserate with my father's murderer. The destroyer of my world.

The being whose existence I vowed to end.

When did the master find you?

The sadness in the air has shifted into something darker and heavier. *Two years ago I heard a voice addressing me for the first time in millennia. It whispered in my ear, telling me nothing of itself but offering a way out of my condition. The voice painted a picture of my House returning to its former glory, and the other Houses suffering for their ignorance and brutality. I didn't need to know more—I only wanted the chance to exist again. So I pledged my allegiance to my new master, and when he combined his Psynergy with mine, we were able to direct Dark Matter to disturb the natural order of things. We produced forest fires on the Leonine moons, mud slides in the Hoof on Vitulus, drought in the Piscene planetoids . . . and then, one day, he told me we were going to destroy a whole House.*

His dark eyes lock on mine, and the hole that pity burned into my heart's shield repairs itself. But Ochus is looking at me curiously, like there's something I might be able to add to his unbelievable story.

How did you discover me in the Psy the first time we spoke? he suddenly asks me.

I think back to that night. *I heard voices coming from Helios, and when I touched the hologram, I appeared in the slipstream.*

He shakes his icy head. *How could a mere mortal access that dimension?*

Another Guardian's words echo in my memory—*You have been singled out, but not by the one you think.* Caasy said the person challenging me in the Psy was someone using "a timeless weapon." If Ophiuchus wasn't the one singling me out, then he was the weapon. *The master brought us together,* I say.

He stares at me like he's considering my theory. Original Guardians were the only ones who could communicate through the Psy; there's no way I could have found Ochus unless someone guided me to him. The same someone who guided Ochus's manipulation of Dark Matter.

Ever since I saw you that first time, he says, *I've been able to find you. Even when I've been hiding from him. Perhaps, in enabling us to interact that first night, he unwittingly opened a Psynergy pathway between us that he can't close.*

I nod. Vecily Matador's vision when she first became Guardian of Taurus was that a Guardian had long ago betrayed all the others, and there would be no trust in the Zodiac until that treachery was brought to light. If Ochus didn't betray anyone, that means another fallen star betrayed them all.

The master is another Original Guardian, I say, and as I accept this truth, at last I trust Ophiuchus. Like Risers, he's another homeless, hopeless soul the master has taken advantage of for his own ends.

Which other Guardians knew about the information in your Talisman?

The Talisman is a secret entrusted to one House; I would not have betrayed my people by sharing it. I have never known how the other Guardians learned of the immortality stored within it.

Can you think of anyone who could have feasibly figured it out?

Have you not been listening? he booms, the temperature dropping as his voice rises. *I have thought of little else for millennia. If there were clues in my past, I would have found them.*

Guardian Sagittarius was obsessed with time and would have been fascinated by such an object. Guardian Aquarius would have longed to use the Talisman to ensure the royal line would continue forever. The Geminin Guardians would have wanted nothing more than eternal life. *Anyone* could have had reason to steal it.

There's another Original Guardian around, I say out loud, to organize my thoughts, *and since the Talisman lets him or her change their body, it could be anyone, anywhere.*

Ophiuchus turns his back to me, and the movement almost makes him seem vulnerable. He's looking at the place beyond Pisces, where his House once was. The jittery Psynergy around us makes the Dark Matter writhe like a nest of sea snakes.

Over time, as I watched my constellation's light fade from the night sky, I also watched it fade from human memory. The Original Guardians vilified me to the Zodiac, blaming me for my world's destruction, until the last generations of humans who knew about the Thirteenth House passed on. My peers lived a handful of centuries each, and they must have agreed to erase me from their House's history, because by the time their bodies became stardust, every trace of a Thirteenth world in the Zodiac was wiped from official record. The only thing they couldn't change was art. So I snaked through time, unnoticed, hidden in your nursery rhymes and morality tales and childhood lullabies.

And now, I have become the villain you created.

I don't say anything because there's nothing to be said. I may trust his version of events, and I may even see that he's been betrayed, but I still hate him. I will always hate him.

The part I don't understand, I say, treading away from my emotions, *is how Dark Matter swallowed your House. The Guardians punished you, not your planet.*

Ochus faces me again, and his expression is so human that there might still be a heart buried beneath all that snow.

The Guardians' treachery ushered Dark Matter into our galaxy. By subverting the natural order of things and setting themselves against me, they failed to understand the fundamentals of Unity. They didn't grasp that in ousting me, the Zodiac was attacking itself—and this self-inflicted wound uprooted Unity from our solar system.

He's still wearing a startlingly human stare as he says, *Haven't you noticed yet? We create our own darkness.*

So the Original Guardians destroyed the Thirteenth House, then they hid their shame by erasing Ophiuchus from history. And if Mom's a Riser, that means I'm descended from that forgotten world, making Cancer the second home I've lost.

My Mom is a Riser. I'm not sure why I say it.

I know.

How? I blurt.

Everything is Psynergy. What you bring with you into this dimension is not your physical form, but your soul. The thoughts and memories and feelings that make you—

He stops speaking suddenly and turns toward the Thirteenth House, like he hears something. As the jittery Psynergy tenses around us, I realize Ochus is Seeing a vision. *What is it?*

I'm not sure, he says in a tone so distant, he already seems to be fading. *The Dark Matter covering my constellation seems to be . . . awakening.*

A bitter taste stings my tongue, and the rotting smell of decay invades my nose. Ochus turns to me like he tastes it, too, his black eyes wide.

Death is coming for you again, Rhoma Grace. It's the first time he's ever said my name, and I strain to hear the rest of his prophecy as he dissolves into icy mist.

And this time, you will not escape its touch.

25

WHEN OCHUS DISAPPEARS, MY HEARTBEAT is making it too hard to think, and I'm breathing like I've just run farther than I have my whole life.

My whole life.

Could this be it? Are seventeen and a half years all I'll know? It's more time than most of my classmates got.

From the moment I became Guardian, I've known that any day could be my last. But since coming to Aquarius, and learning about Black Moon, and reuniting with Hysan, I found myself facing not just a future worth fighting for, but one worth living. *Hope* came in the form of a tomorrow I desperately want to be around to experience.

But there isn't time to mourn myself now, and that means I have to wall this knowledge off and forget I ever learned it. And if Ferez is right, and free will is stronger than fate, then who knows? Maybe I'll even defy my stars.

✦ ✦ ✦

I carefully crack open the trapdoor, and seeing the coast is clear I climb onto the sandstone floor and race toward the ninth tower. As the burgundy-and-blue cloth waves into view, someone topples into me.

"Oh—sorry!"

"Rho, it's me," says Nishi near my ear. She interlocks her arm with mine and pulls me hurriedly down the hall in the opposite direction.

She cuts across a sunlit drawing room, and neither of us speaks as we weave through valets in velvet top hats and high-ranking dignitaries in aqua coats. "What'd you find?" I ask once we're out of that room.

She doesn't answer me until white mist overtakes us, and we're ensconced in the clouds of a thought tunnel. Then she finally stops moving and faces me.

I take her hand and squeeze it. "Since we're taking precautions, I'm guessing you found something?"

"I'm sorry about earlier, Rho. I wanted to prove you wrong, so while Blaze met with the Locations Committee, I went through the Black Moon population lists we've been passing around for every House."

I bite my lip to keep my mouth shut, and she sighs, like she knows everything I'm not saying. "Look, I'm not saying it was right, but we *did* block off a percentage of spots for sponsors. It's just how things get done. But that's not the point. I wanted to find the list of interested people from House Pisces so I could show you there was always a plan to bring them in eventually . . . only there wasn't one."

Her amber eyes remind me of the terrified look she wore on *Equinox*. "The Piscene plague appeared only a week ago, and these lists date back to before my involvement with the Party. So how did they know Pisces wouldn't be around to participate?"

This is exactly the kind of evidence we can use to expose the Party—and it's the proof Mathias needs to believe me. "It's the master, Nishi. He's behind the Tomorrow Party."

"But *how*, Rho?" she asks, her voice splintering.

"The Marad disappeared around the same time the Tomorrow Party emerged," I say softly. "The master is manipulating the people best suited to lead our war against him. It's a preemptive attack. We think it's a distraction from whatever he's planning for Pisces, so that's where we need to go."

Nishi's expression is so broken that I pull her in for a hug because I can't stand to see her like this. It hurts even more that I know intimately how it feels to be taken in by something so completely that you give your whole self over to it—and when it's ripped away from you, you feel like you're left with less of yourself than you started with.

"I can't believe I fell for this," she says when we pull away, her face pallid. "I really thought Blaze was a good person."

A shadow flickers over her shoulder, and I take Nishi's hand, spinning her around to my side as a silhouette presses into the fog.

"I *am* a good person."

Nishi gasps as blue-haired Blaze steps through the white smoke, his russet eyes afire. *How did he find us here?*

Fear quickens my pulse and my breathing as Nishi and I back away from him slowly. Is he alone? Are others surrounding us?

"I still want to build a united tomorrow for the Zodiac," says Blaze calmly. "And if you give me a chance to tell you what we've Seen, I think you'll understand."

"Not if it means joining sides with the master," growls Nishi, and I squeeze her hand twice to signal her to be ready.

Blaze's features harden, but not in an angry way. He looks hurt. The holographic lion on his shirt roars soundlessly from his chest. "You don't have the full picture yet, so you don't understand. But we're *saving* people. When you and I first spoke a month ago, you told me the only way to change the norm is to break it. Remember that?"

Nishi's hand goes limp in mine; the reference to Deke is like a shot to the heart. Blaze pins her with his confident stare, and even now there's something so fiercely likable about him that it's hard to picture him on the master's side. "Change isn't always accommodating, and that's why people resist it. But if you trust me, I'll prove to you why it's our best choice."

Corinthe's reptilian voice plays in my mind—*Acceptance of the new only comes with the ousting of the old.* Her motto sounds a lot like Deke's. In the wrong hands, the same philosophy can be dangerous.

Blaze's shoulders cave inward the tiniest bit, and I flash to Trax's predatory pose before he pounced on me with his interrogation.

"*Run!*" I shout. Hands linked together, Nishi and I hurtle blindly through the white fog. Sweat drips down my back as we race away from him, and I'm momentarily relieved when I don't hear Blaze's footsteps behind us.

Until I realize that if he's not following us, we must be doing what he wants.

The cottony clouds grow stringy as we approach the end of the tunnel, and hints of the sandstone wall break through the mist. I slow down to decide whether we should double back, but Nishi keeps going forward at full speed.

I yank her back by the hand. "Wait—"

Her face breaks through the cloud covering for a moment, and something small and metallic whizzes through the air, striking her forehead.

"*NO!*"

My scream splits the universe, and I reach for my best friend as she falls to the floor, the lines of her face slackening. I catch Nishi by the waist and drop with her, cradling her face on my lap, my tears sprinkling onto her skin as I check her for signs of breath.

"Nishi—please—please, you have to be okay, please wake up—"

"She's not dead."

Nishi's attacker stands over us, her twin-barreled gun trained on the same spot of my forehead. "It's a Sumber," says Imogen. "She's trapped in her subconscious."

It's only now I realize how little I trust anyone anymore. I'm not even surprised by Imogen's betrayal.

"Which pellet?" I ask in an even voice, remembering from Mom's lessons that Gemini's signature weapon has two chambers.

One barrel releases a pellet that unlocks a person's innermost dreams, while the other unleashes their deepest nightmares.

"Use your imagination."

I glare at Imogen with a hatred I didn't think my heart was capable of producing, and I find myself thinking of the Scarab wrapped around my wrist. If only I could reach under my black glove without tipping her off. But even if I could, I still have no idea how to use it.

She must spy the threat in my eyes because she swings the gun's nozzle to Nishi's forehead again. A double dose causes a brain aneurysm that's instantly fatal.

"*Don't,*" I say, hugging Nishi closer and protecting her with my body. "Please."

"Then get up."

I hold Nishi to me a moment longer, then I carefully rest her head on the sandstone. Her face betrays no evidence of what she's going through internally, and I desperately hope she's dreaming happy things.

Blaze emerges through the haze as I get to my feet. "I'll give you a choice," says Imogen, as the Leonine bundles Nishi's limp limbs in his arms.

"What are you doing?" I demand, reaching out to take Nishi back from Blaze, but Imogen's gun points at my head again.

"Shut up and come with us willingly," she says, walking over until the gun's cold metal nozzle touches my forehead, blocking Blaze and Nishi from view. "Or I'll drop you into your worst nightmares and drag you with us anyway."

"Why are you doing this?" I whisper. "I thought you believed in Nishi's leadership. You said you wanted to unite the Zodiac, that I inspired you—"

"You did," she says, and behind her, I watch Blaze retreat into the thought tunnel with my best friend in his arms. "You taught me to trust my convictions. You showed me I must be willing give my life for my beliefs, even if others won't understand at first."

Without thinking, I shove hard against Imogen's arm, pointing the Sumber away from myself, and she tumbles to the floor in her spindly heels. Then I run into the mist after Nishi.

"Blaze, stop!" I shout into the white fog, desperately searching for some sign of his silhouette. "Take *me* instead!"

Nails dig into my coat sleeve, pressing into my scars, and I yelp with pain. Imogen heaves me back with her to the clear air by twisting my arm until it spasms. When she lets go, the aching brings me to my knees.

She presses the icy metal to my forehead again and whispers, *"Good night, Rho."*

I squeeze my eyes shut, bracing myself for the shot—

The gun clatters to the floor, and I hear Imogen grunt in pain. When I look again, a hooded Aquarian in an aqua cloak has wrestled the Geminin to the ground, and they're struggling to overtake each other.

I know I should stay and help, but Nishi is getting farther from me every moment, and I have to go after her. So I dive back into the white smoke, and immediately I hear a woman's cry that doesn't sound like Imogen.

I skid to a stop. I can't let something happen to the Aquarian who saved me. Racing back to where I was, I see Imogen pinning my savior to the ground and holding a bloody knife to her chest.

Before I can think of how to help, the Aquarian rears up and knocks her head into Imogen's, dazing the Geminin enough to loosen her grip on the knife. The hood falls off the Aquarian's head as she pries the blade from Imogen's fingers, and the latter leaps to her feet surprisingly fast.

The Aquarian rises quickly, too. Imogen looks from the knife in her hand, to the Sumber on the floor, and then to me, like she's deciding whether it's worth taking us both on empty-handed. Then she dives into the thought tunnel after Blaze.

"You all right?" I ask my savior, sparing her a quick glance before I run after Imogen. My feet are already carrying me into the fog when the Aquarian meets my gaze.

And her blue stare turns me to stone.

26

HER FACIAL FEATURES HAVE BEEN edited—sharper cheek-bones, longer nose, straighter hair. But the bottomless blue eyes are exactly as I remember them.

"It's okay," she says in an achingly familiar voice that makes me gasp.

The past ten years of my life shrink down within me, until my adolescence feels as fleeting as a vision in the Psy, an illusion of mist and shadow.

"It's me."

She barely moves her lips, like she's afraid to spook me. Like she knows I'm still too small, too weak, too afraid.

"It's Mom."

Mom. The word tumbles through my mind, as if my brain is trying to place it.

She takes a single step forward and then winces, like she's injured. I look down at the gash in her cloak, where blood stains her leg. But even if I wanted to help, I can't. My body is leaden, like it doesn't answer to me anymore.

"Rho, we need to go."

At the sound of my name in her voice, my childhood fantasy comes flying back to me. I see the scene I used to replay of how I'd one day discover Mom on a far-away island looking for her long-lost memories. In my imagination, I was always so happy just to be reunited with her that I'd immediately forgive her for abandoning us.

She starts moving toward me again, her limp growing less pronounced with every step. And when her hand grips my arm, it's not her memories that come rushing back, but *mine*.

"DON'T TOUCH ME!"

My scream is inhumanly high, and the words' jagged edges slice into me on their way out.

The past decade seems to fill the space between us, and she backs away as a wheezing sound starts in my throat, like the air I'm breathing isn't making it to my lungs. A tar-like substance seems to be filling my heart, clogging my veins and clouding my mind and consuming my oxygen.

"I'm not going anywhere without Nishi," I say, my voice raspy and unfamiliar. "And especially not with *you*."

"Yes, you are," says a new voice, and I see Hysan emerging from the thought tunnel. "Are you hurt?" he asks, looking me over.

I shake my head. "Blaze and Imogen took Nishi—we have to find her!"

"We will." He slips the Veil collar around my neck but doesn't activate it. I grip his arm tightly.

"Hysan, you don't understand. They'll *torture* her, like they did me and Mathias and Pandora. We *can't* leave her—"

"Rho." He stares at me gravely, like I'm unwell. "I assure you she's too important to the Party. They won't hurt her. This isn't the Marad; the Tomorrow Party won't succeed if they use violence, and they know it." He rests his hand on mine and presses my fingers. "Your brother, Mathias, and Pandora are already on their way to *Equinox*, but right now, your mom is right. We need to go before more Party members come looking for you."

He tries nudging me forward, but my legs are still leaden. "How do you—"

"Your mom and I have been working together for a few weeks now," he says softly. His green eyes seem to be pleading with me not to be angry, but I shake my head, refusing to hear him.

"I'm sorry I didn't tell you, Rho. It wasn't safe."

He glances at Kassandra and notices she's leaning against the wall to keep her weight off her injured leg. "You're hurt," he says with concern, striding over to inspect her wound. "It's not deep, but you'll move faster if you lean on me."

He offers her his shoulder, and when she touches him, I hear myself growl, *"Get away from him!"*

She instantly pulls back from his arm, and her eyes dart to mine. I spot a familiar darkness rising from their icy blue depths, and she hops a few times as she tries to stand on her own. That limp sure escalated quickly.

Who knows if the pain is real?

Who knows if anything about her is real?

"Rho, I'm going to help her," insists Hysan, putting his arm around Kassandra and activating our networked Veils so that we're invisible to any onlookers. She doesn't resist his aid, but she keeps her gaze on me for a long time, like *I'm* the mysterious one here.

Rho, where are you? asks a musical voice in my head as we move invisibly through the castle.

I twist my Ring. *On my way to* Equinox. *Are you with Stan and Pandora?*

We're on the ship. Are you with Hysan and Nishi?

Something massive climbs up my throat, and I can't even think the words in my head, so I don't answer.

We cross beneath the stained glass constellations, and as we step onto the waterfall plaza, three massive Pegazi land before us on the sand. Their timing is so exact, it's like they've been tracking our movements.

Nishi's pink horse isn't among them.

Hysan deactivates our Veils, and when I look up into Candor's black onyx eyes, she bows. I wish she could come away from here with me.

Hysan helps Kassandra onto the white winged horse and then turns to help me. Ignoring his hand, I hitch up my skirt and climb onto Candor's back on my own.

"Rho, I'm sorry I didn't tell you—"

"Candor, *please*," I whisper, and immediately the Pegazi rears forward, speeding me away from him. I hug her velvety neck as waterfalls swell from my eyes, her warmth the only thing keeping me alive.

Cold air rakes my curls as she gallops toward the puffs of frosty steam ahead, rising from the invisible ice beneath us. There's a deafening whoosh as her wings whip outward, and then she leaps off the sand-smothered ledge and into the pink sunset sky.

We soar over a vast vista of trees that gives way to rolling green hills with extravagant estates, and all I can think of is Nishi. The broken look on her face when she learned the truth about the Tomorrow Party. The metal dart from Imogen's Sumber striking her forehead. Blaze carrying her away from me through the white smoke.

I left her.

I abandoned my best friend.

My *sister*.

A black hole opens inside me, inhaling my soul into its vortex, and I scream until I have nothing left inside.

"Turn back, Candor! We have to go back to the castle!" The hysterical pitch of my voice scrapes my throat, burning it raw.

"Please! Turn around! *NOW! I have to get back to Nishi!"*

The Pegazi ignores my desperate pleas, and every flap of her wings takes me farther from Nishi and further from breathing. I shouldn't have followed Hysan out. I shouldn't have stayed to make sure *my savior* was okay. I should have gone after Nishi as soon as I had the chance.

Candor lands on the same grassy field where we first met, only instead of the sparkly, star-shaped Tomorrow Party vessel, there's the familiar bullet-shaped spaceship that's become as comforting as a real home. I wipe my face on my jacket sleeve, and Candor bows so I can slide off her back.

"I'm sorry," I whisper as she straightens, my voice too hoarse to say more, my gaze too heavy to lift from the grass.

She whinnies so softly, it almost sounds like she's whispering back, and her hot breath blows on my hair. Before I can lift my face to hers, I feel her moist snout press down gently on my forehead.

When I look up in wonder, her heavy hooves are already clopping across the cliff, and then faster than a shooting star, she vanishes into the dusky sky.

✦ ✦ ✦

I lag a few steps behind as Hysan helps Kassandra board, and we find Stan, Mathias, and Pandora eagerly awaiting us in the nose.

"Where's Nishi?" asks Stan, staring after the Aquarian woman with curiosity but not familiarity.

I don't answer. I feel the weight of Mathias's and Pandora's gazes on me, but I can't meet them. Hysan helps Kassandra into one of the seats by the control helm, and when he steps back, she ducks her head to check out her leg wound.

Stan's eyes are on her long, white-blond locks, which obscure the ivory facial features. I'm not sure if he realizes he's moving closer to her.

When Kassandra lifts her head, my brother falls to his knees in shock. I start to go to him, but I see *her* stand, and I'm immobilized.

Everyone is silent as she gingerly lowers herself to the floor. My brother stares and stares and stares at her redesigned face, until a voice I've never heard before seeps from his lips. *"Mom?"*

The sound cuts me open.

Cautiously, she leans closer, as if she's anticipating the same rejection she got from me, and he stretches a hand toward her. When Stan's fingers touch her cheek, he inhales sharply—and then he does what I couldn't do.

He wraps his arms around our mother, burying his head in her shoulder. When she hugs him back, Stan's body begins to shudder with gut-wrenching, cathartic sobs that seem to shake the whole ship.

Like he's letting go of tears he's been waiting his whole life to shed.

27

I ESCAPE TO MY USUAL cabin and lock the door behind me.

I'm shivering uncontrollably as I pace up and down the cramped space, trying to fight off the panic eating at my organs. My mind keeps replaying the way Stanton crumpled at her touch. The depth of his suffering makes me hate her more.

It makes her unforgivable.

The ground vibrates beneath me as the ship begins its ascent into the atmosphere, and I secure myself inside the sleeping cocoon. I desperately want to know what's going on in the nose, but I can't bring myself to leave this cabin. So I take a few seconds to steady my nerves, and then I twist my Ring.

What's the plan? I ask Mathias.

We're setting course for planetoid Alamar. It's only one orbit over, so we'll be there in less than a day.

I remember that the Houses divided the five Piscene plane-toids among them and ask, *Which Houses have stationed their Zodai on Alamar?* All I know is that Libra and Scorpio are working on planetoid Naute.

Sagittarius and Gemini.

No doubt Rubi and Brynda arranged it that way. I wonder if that means they'll be there. Thinking of Sagittarius brings me right back to Nishi, and my insides grow too shaky to say more.

Do you need anything, Rho?

Nishi. I need Nishi. I can't hold back the tears anymore, and I'm glad no one can see me.

We'll get her back, says Mathias, and after a beat, he asks, *What happened?*

I dry my face on my coat sleeve. *She found proof the Tomorrow Party was never planning to invite the Twelfth House to participate. We think they knew about the attack on Pisces ahead of time. Mathias, what if—if they—*

They won't hurt her. The Tomorrow Party wants her allegiance, so they'll try to woo her. Nishi's smart; she'll know how to play the situation.

I abandoned her. I'm a coward.

Rho, please don't do this to yourself, he says, a tinge of exaspera-tion in his tone. *Can I come in and talk to you?*

No . . . I want to be alone.

I think the conversation is over, but then I hear his deep, soft voice in the back of my mind. *You're not, though.*

There's a knock on my door, and I sigh as I unzip the sleeping cocoon, letting the bed fall flat again, and get up. "I really don't want to talk, Mathias," I say as I unlock the door.

"Well, I do."

My brother stands in the doorway, his eyes small and puffy, holding a large bowl of dried fruit in his hands. "And you need to eat something."

I let him in, and we sit on the bed with the bowl of fruit resting between us. "She's in the healing pod," he says before I can ask. "She hasn't said anything about where she's been. All I know is Hysan found her. For you."

I shake my head. "I can't understand how you could welcome her back like that—"

"She's Mom," he says, widening his eyes meaningfully. "Rho, whatever happened before, whatever mistakes she's made, it doesn't matter anymore." He looks at me like my behavior is the one that isn't making sense. "You . . . you weren't there when Dad died."

His eyes grow shiny, and his nose reddens. He's been holding this in for so long. Stan hasn't talked about the day Dad died yet, and deep down I know I haven't pressed him because I'm not sure I want to hear it.

"When we survived the meteor shower, I thought the worst was over. Lodestars found us by the remains of home, and we had the chance to evacuate to an underwater shelter. But Dad and I chose to stay on the surface and help out. I kept thinking of Hurricane Hebe and how I found that infant in the wreckage. And I thought searching for survivors was the right thing to do. I didn't think about what the destruction to our moons would do to the ocean's tides, and once the tsunamis started, there were no more evacuation ships. The water pulled Dad under, and I dove in. I tried to find him, but. . . ."

"It's okay," I whisper, tears streaming from my eyes. "It wasn't your fault."

"I know," he says, clearing his throat and blinking away his pain, the way I've seen Nishi do.

"I miss Dad, too, Stan," I say softly. "*So* much. I wish I'd talked to him more, asked him more questions, gotten to know him better." I wait for my brother to say something, but there's a shift in the air, like his guard has shot back up.

He's letting himself feel his sadness, but he's not *dealing* with it.

"That's why it matters that Mom's still here," he says, adopting a parental tone again. "It means you don't have to carry the same regrets you have about Dad. You can talk to her or yell at her if you want to. The important part is she's here . . . and you're no longer alone."

It's strange how he says *you're* no longer alone instead of *we*, and I say, "I'm not alone because I have you, Stan."

The way he won't meet my gaze reminds me of how he was acting the last time I tried to have a heart-to-heart with him on Pelagio. He sits up and asks in a low voice, "What if I can't be everything for you, Rho?"

I swallow back the nausea his words awakened. "What do you mean?"

"I mean that I need to be my own person, too. I've always felt like I'm responsible for the people I love—you, Dad, Jewel, Aryll. And I need a break from lugging that weight with me everywhere. For once I just want to feel like I can do what I want without letting someone down."

Stanton has always been such a natural at taking care of us that it never really hit me that I wasn't the only child in our household who had to grow up too quickly. When she abandoned us, our mother left the parenting duties to Stan. Our whole life he's felt responsible for Dad and me because when he was just ten years old, he was explicitly assigned that role.

"I'm sorry," I whisper, fighting against the water welling in my eyes. "I wasn't there for you when she left us. Not the way you were for me. I didn't know until today how much you've been suffering, Stan, or how much I've asked of you our whole lives."

"When I was a kid," he says gently, "and Mom gave up trying to train me, I felt . . . ordinary. A few years later, when the Academy on Elara denied me entrance, I took the rejection as confirmation that I wasn't meant for greatness. So I finally accepted that I was fated to be a normal person. A caretaker. Someone like Dad."

At last he looks at me, and I stare deeply into his pale green eyes, so identical to mine.

"Rho, my whole life, you're the only person who's ever made me feel special."

Tears tickle my cheeks, but I don't wipe them. "You're the best person I know," I say.

"Then let me be that person. Believing in me is the best gift you've ever given me, so don't take it away. Just try trusting me the way I trust you, and let me be *me*."

I want to tell him this *isn't* him, though.

He's walling off his feelings so he won't have to explore them. He's so hurt by Aryll's betrayal that he doesn't want to open his heart again, so he's rushing headfirst into anger and suspicion and action because they give him a sense of control. I want to say all of this because I've been there myself.

But I'm depleted. Nishi's gone, Kassandra's back, Hysan's keeping secrets . . . and I need my brother. I want to be close to him again. So I don't argue.

Stan pushes the bowl of dried fruit toward me, and I reach in and stuff a piece in my mouth. It's the first thing I've eaten all day, and its sweetness warms my belly. I take a second piece, and soon my muscles begin to relax, and yawns roll through me like ocean waves. I didn't sleep at all last night.

At the memory of *last night*, tension returns to my body. I can't believe how close Hysan and I were just hours ago. As if he can tell where my thoughts have strayed, Stan says, "You should talk to him, Rho. I know I wasn't his biggest fan at first, but I was wrong to doubt him. He loves you. He's proven it time after time."

I shake my head. "Even if I could find a way to forgive him, I still don't see how I can ever trust him again. He's too comfortable with his secrets. Whether or not he loves me, he still chooses to operate alone . . . and I was a fool to think he could change his nature."

Stan sighs. "Why don't you try closing your eyes for a little while? I'll be here when you wake up."

"You can go if you want," I say, pulling off my black coat before lying back and resting my head on one of the pillows. "I don't want you to feel obligated to stay. Plus, you'll be bored watching me sleep."

"No, I won't, because I'll be borrowing your Wave." He opens my golden clamshell, and holographic menus beam out. "See?" he says, sitting up beside me. "There's a selfish motive at the heart of all my selfless moves."

I want to suggest he call Jewel, but I don't want to get chewed out again for being *naïve*, so I pull the blanket over me. I don't zip the cocoon so that we can share the bed.

My brother shuts off the lights, and my Wave's blue holograms dance through the air. I watch him click through them, pulling up newsfeeds and messages, and slowly I begin to doze off. I'm semi-asleep when I hear voices outside the cabin door.

They're muddled and indistinct, and at first I think they're part of a dream. Then a deep baritone says, "You're not going in there."

"You don't tell me what to do." Hysan's voice sounds so dark, I almost don't recognize it.

I feel Stan's weight easing off the bed. I try to keep listening, but my consciousness is sinking, descending deeper with every breath.

"You're not getting past me, Libran. But I've been looking forward to seeing you try."

When the cabin door opens, my eyelids are too heavy to lift, and the last thing I hear is my brother saying, "This clearly has more to do with your feelings for each other than for my sister, so take it somewhere else. If either of you were actually concerned about Rho, you'd shut the Helios up and let her get some sleep."

Then I hear the door shut, and darkness swallows me.

28

WHEN I OPEN MY EYES, Stan is passed out beside me, my Wave facedown on his chest. A carousel of blue holograms floats around us.

I close the Wave and the screens vanish, then I slip out of bed and crack open the cabin door. The ship's dim lighting is a sign that everyone is sleeping, so I venture out for a barefoot stroll.

When I enter the crystal-capped nose, I spy a tall figure with white hair sitting at the control helm. "Lord Neith!"

He doesn't react to my greeting, and when I come around to face him, I see that his quartz eyes are open wide and unblinking, reflecting a scroll of unintelligible code that's streaming from one of the ship's holographic screens. It looks like Neith and 'Nox are syncing.

The sight is unnerving, so I head back toward my cabin, only my feet carry me to a different door. It's the room where Nishi stayed the last time we were here . . . the place where we held each other through our loss.

I hear a low murmuring from inside the cabin, and I press my ear to the door. A girl's voice is reciting the Zodai chant.

"Hail mighty Helios, womb of heaven. Star maker, heat giver, doorway from death to light. Preserve our Houses now and in the ages to come."

When Pandora is finished, I knock lightly on her door; after a moment, I hear a low, "Come in."

Inside I see Deke's hologram floating through the air. Pandora unzips her cocoon, and as the bed flattens, I remember Nishi breaking down in my arms while Deke's ghost said his goodbyes. This room is haunted.

"Hi," says Pandora, and I leave the past for the present. She stands at the foot of the bed in a plain nightgown; with her auburn hair pulled back, her amethyst eyes take up most of her ivory face. "How are you?"

There's a depth in her delivery that plunges past *dullatry*; a directness that makes me think of Nishi. "I'm . . ."

But I can't talk about any of it, so instead I ask, "Why were you reciting the Zodai chant?"

She shrugs, but the intensity of her gaze doesn't falter. "Given what Traxon said, I thought it couldn't hurt to ask Helios for her protection. But I'd like to do more than pray."

"I know. Me too. Have you told anyone about your vision?"

"Just you." A faint line forms between her eyebrows. "In Nightwing, visions are sacrosanct. When someone submits a new prophecy to the Clan Elders, they read the stars to confirm it, and then it gets added to our House's Cosmic Calendar. The more major the prophecy, the more attention it attracts. And in a kingdom of seers, there is no worse affront than Seeing something others can't."

Her voice darkens with her expression. "If I'd submitted this vision, I would have been singled out, tested, questioned, and my whole bloodline would be investigated to be sure we belong in Nightwing. I didn't want to put my family through that."

"I understand."

"No, you don't. I told myself I would just wait for someone else to See the same omen, and then I'd step up to second their vision." She bows her head, grounding her gaze in shame. "I didn't want to be first."

"You were protecting your family—"

"If you'd been in my place, you would have spoken up." Her dusky violet eyes meet mine. "You wouldn't have left the burden for someone else to bear."

While I'm moved by her words, I can't help thinking of Imogen and how she twisted my message against me. I don't want to lead Pandora down a dangerous path.

"I'm not saying I believe in the Last Prophecy or anything," I say cautiously, "but I think until we learn more, it might be best not to tell anyone what you've Seen. Just in case there's truth to the myth Traxon mentioned, about people who've seen the vision disappearing."

"I don't want to stay silent anymore. I want to do something."

"Then let's at least consult someone trustworthy, like Sage Ferez and—" I want to say Hysan, but his name won't leap off my tongue, so instead I settle for, "a couple of other Guardians. But first, Pisces needs our attention."

I turn toward the door to go.

"Wait—" She walks around to the other side of the bed and pulls out two familiar traveling cases—mine and Nishi's.

"I went up to your room and packed your stuff while you were in the reading room, in case there wasn't time later."

I hadn't even thought about my belongings. I'm still wearing the Aquarian skirt and jacket I picked out in the closet archiver this morning—or yesterday. Time is once again starting to feel like a run-on sentence.

I must be quiet a long moment because Pandora starts to fill the space with words. "I just figured the both of you had already lost everything you owned, and I didn't think you should have to go through it again."

I suddenly wrap my arms around her, and from the tight way she holds me back, I realize Pandora needed the hug more than I did. I think of what the past few months must have been like for her—being torn from her old life to be tortured and traumatized by terrorists, and yet somehow finding love amid so much darkness. And when we pull away, I dig into my bag, unzipping an inner pocket, and retrieve Mathias's mother-of-pearl Astralator.

"Do me a favor," I say, pressing it into her hand. "Give this back to Mathias for me sometime."

Her amethyst eyes gaze into mine, like she intuits the significance of this gesture without needing to know the specifics. "You're certain?"

I nod and reach down for the traveling cases, trying to drown the pain that stabs my chest at the sight of Nishi's familiar lavender levlan bag. Pandora opens the door for me, and as I pass her on my way out, I murmur, "I'm sorry if I've caused you heartache."

"I've survived worse," she says, and when I turn to look at her, there's a hint of a smile on her lips. She tips her head down in a small bow and whispers, "When two people are soul-bound, I think it's natural for the star pulling their strings to sometimes get them a little twisted."

I nod, and she whispers, "But that's why we have free will, Wandering Star—so we can fix fate's tangles."

28

I REMAIN INSIDE MY CABIN until I feel that we've crossed the invisible barrier into Alamar's gravity, and then I'm too eager for my first glimpse of this world to stay in hiding.

After a quick ultraviolet shower, I change into my Lodestar suit and peek outside to make sure no one is in the hall before I step out. In the nose, Mathias is manning the helm, and I don't exhale until I'm sure he's alone.

Drying my clammy palms on my pants, I look around at the view through the glass: A colorful, apple-shaped landmass is growing larger, suspended in an ocean of blue water so pale, it looks silver.

"Hey," says Mathias. "How are you?"

"Okay. Is Stan with—*her?*"

"I don't know. The Libran asked me to land the ship so he

could finish adjustments to his android. *Equinox* is small, so we've been given clearance to use a private port in the Guardian's Holy Temple."

I remember from my studies that the Holy Temple is the House's seat of government, and it's where Prophet Marinda lives. I walk toward the window and lean into its glass, wishing I could fall into the view.

We're descending into the southernmost part of Alamar's apple-shaped continent. I see a coastal community of massive, multi-colored diamonds that look like larger versions of the crystal dome on Elara. Dozens of these Co-Ops are laid out in the curving pattern of a seashell, spiraling to a central point, which must be the Holy Temple.

Sapphire streets curl around the coils of compounds, looking like wide streams of water that have frozen over and crystalized. The Co-Ops have curved corners and semitransparent walls, and each one sparkles in a different hue; the colors are part of an organizational system for identifying each structure's designated function—housing, education, entertainment, health, and so on.

Pisces is a socialist society without a monetary system, where every civic duty is shared, and people rotate through their local Co-Ops so they can learn every trade—law enforcement, public maintenance, cooking, teaching, healing. As they get older, Piscenes can choose to specialize in one particular field by becoming Co-Op Shepherds—experts regarded as specialists in their fields who are in charge of training teens on their first rotation into their department.

We dive toward the central point of the community, a pastel-pink compound, and once we're close, a gate opens in its crystal ceiling. Mathias pulls into a private port, and the instant we land, Hysan enters the nose in his golden Knight suit.

My heart catapults into my throat as our eyes meet.

"Lady Rho," says a sonorous voice behind him, and I look up to see Lord Neith, who's thankfully looking like his usual self again. "How wonderful to see you," he says, extending his hand for the traditional touch greeting.

"You too, Lord Neith," I say, bumping fists with him. "How are you feeling?"

"Up-to-date."

Just then, 'Nox's door opens and two women run on board. One looks like a twelve-year-old with copper curls and eyes as deep as Space. The other reminds me painfully of Nishi.

"Rho!" Brynda pulls me into a heartfelt hug, and I hold her close to me to compensate for my inability to speak. "Hysan told me about Nishi," she says in my ear. "I'm so sorry. But don't worry. We're not abandoning her. We'll get her back."

When we part, small hands clasp my waist. I hug Rubi back, and after pulling away, I say thickly, "It's really good to see you both."

"Dreadful conditions," says the Geminin Twin, shaking her head heavily. "Three centuries, and I've never seen anything like this. If my dear brother was here, he would be howling at Helios."

"You have to take this antiviral every day you're here," says Brynda, handing me a tiny squeezetube like the one Mathias once gave us on Phaetonis. "It will protect you from contracting anything."

I rip it open with my teeth and suck the syrupy medicine; it takes like sea cherries. As Brynda hands them out to everyone else, I notice my brother and Kassandra have joined us.

She's still wearing her aqua cloak, and as I watch her take the antiviral, I study her closely, wondering who she's been the past ten years. She hasn't lost her memory. I don't see any physical signs of torture. In fact, she was pretty spry when she was saving my life. So what justification could she have for never reaching out, not even *once*?

"Leave your bags," says Brynda. "I'll have a couple of Stargazers bring them up." After speaking soundlessly through her Ring, she locks arms with me and leads us off the ship, through a small hangar, and into a dark hallway.

At first I can't see anything, and I'm about to say something when flashes of light begin to blast through the crystal floor beneath our feet and up along the pink walls, like lightning.

The more momentum we gather, the more sustained the brightness becomes, until it illuminates the whole tunnel. I hear Pandora gasp somewhere behind me.

"Pisces is powered by people's movements," explains Brynda in a voice that carries to the whole group. "It's a process called piezoelectric energy. Every Co-Op is constructed from special ceramic and crystal compounds that convert kinetic energy into electricity, because Piscenes don't believe in wasting anything, not even a single joule of energy."

"People generate their own power," says Mathias thoughtfully. "So when society breaks down, so does the system."

"Which is exactly what's happening now," says Rubi, looping her arm around my free elbow.

"Since Piscenes aren't moving around much at the moment, there isn't power throughout most parts of each planetoid," explains Brynda. "It's a mess."

The three of us walking side by side is a tight fit for this tunnel, but I'm glad they're here to keep me upright. If not for their forward momentum, I'm not sure I could move. Between my mother's presence and Nishi's absence, life is too upside down for me to stay right side up.

When we reach the passage's end, we enter an enormous domed lobby with semitransparent pink walls that splinter the daylight and bounce Helios's rays into the whole space. A brilliant gemstone representation of our solar system floats above us, the colorful crystal planets twinkling over our heads.

The view on the ground is far less bright: At least one hundred comatose bodies are lying on elevated beds all across the lobby, while Sagittarian Stargazers and Geminin Dreamcasters in lavender and orange uniforms monitor patients' vitals and draw blood and tissue samples from their unconscious bodies.

"Hospitals are so overcrowded that Prophet Marinda has instructed every Piscene to stay home so they'll fall asleep in their own residences," Brynda tells us in an undertone as we edge along the perimeter of the scene. "Some Disciples volunteered to be test subjects for scientists and healers to draw blood from so we can search for a cure. Those are the people you see here."

As I pass the bodies, something starts to feel *off*. I'm not Centered, but my mind feels airy, like I'm leaving the physical plane. Only my Ring isn't buzzing from the influx of Psynergy. If anything, it's becoming colder. There's a strange pull in the air that makes me think of the Nightwing seer.

"*MAMI!*"

A young girl's terrified scream cleaves the air, and we all stop moving.

She looks no older than six or seven, and she's holding tightly to the hand of a sleeping woman, whimpering softly. A prepubescent Dreamcaster tries to coax the girl away in soft tones, but she only starts to cry louder. "Please, mami! Wake up! I'll be good, I promise!"

Her cries are daggers, and my breaths grow so shallow I can hear them. If I look behind me, I'm pretty sure I'll break down with her.

The Guardians on either side of me start moving again, carrying me in their momentum, as the girl's wails drown everything else. "I'm scared! Please don't leave me, mami, *please.* . . ."

Brynda and Rubi stop moving again, and I wonder if they've finally noticed I'm not breathing, but then I see that Stan's peeled away from the group. He's going to comfort the girl.

My brother's barely taken two steps before he stops dead in his tracks. I follow the line of his gaze to a buxom blond bombshell in a form-fitting yellow dress approaching us.

But when Miss Trii registers the little girl's cries, she abruptly changes direction.

The Dreamcaster steps back as Miss Trii moves closer, and the girl stops crying as she looks into the android's otherworldly face. Miss Trii gracefully lowers herself to the girl's height and wipes away her tears with her delicate fingers.

"Would you like to cry together?" she asks sweetly, and the girl nods. Miss Trii opens her arms and wraps her in such a tender, motherly embrace that I'm instantly envious of Hysan.

She strokes the little girl's back, and when they pull apart, the android plants a kiss on her head. "When a heart is as large as yours, it's beating for more than just one person. Your mami lives in there, too. The best way to help her is by taking care of yourself to protect both your hearts. So how about you let Yana take you to eat something, and then I'll come tuck you in for a nap?"

The girl nods again, and when she embraces Miss Trii once more, I see a small Hysan hugging his android when he needed a mom growing up.

Forgetting the dangers of looking back, I turn and cast my gaze for him. He's with Lord Neith, standing apart from the group and not paying attention to Miss Trii or the little girl. They seem to be arguing. I've never seen them disagree before, but Lord Neith looks visibly upset.

"If a teenager spoke to me that way," says Rubi to me indignantly, her eyes also on Hysan, "he would be out of my inner circle. I don't care how clever that boy is—Lord Neith is too lenient for his own good."

On my other side, Brynda is also watching Hysan, but her expression holds more curiosity than judgment. Like she's catching on to something.

Hysan is becoming too overextended to protect his secrets.

"How wonderful to see you all here," says Miss Trii, who's finally made it over to our group. But her pleasant expression melts into a frown when she notices Hysan and Lord Neith.

"Hysan, are you arguing in public? *And with your* Guardian?" Her hands hook onto her hips, and Hysan stops speaking abruptly. "I hope I've raised you better than that."

My brother mouths the phrase "raised you" to himself, like it's a question he's trying to answer. Everyone else looks just as confused.

"Come here and kiss me hello," she chides Hysan, and though his ears go pink, he courteously walks over and pecks her on the cheek. Lord Neith looks at Miss Trii disapprovingly; she must be tinkering with her settings again.

"Any chance Hysan has a sister?" my brother whispers in my ear.

It's the most Stan has sounded like himself in months, and I actually grin.

"Rho, how lovely to see you again!" Miss Trii flashes me an expression full of Libran charm and tilts down to kiss my cheek.

"You too, Miss Trii."

She goes around greeting everyone except Kassandra. The android seems to disapprove of her on such a fundamental level that I can almost feel the magnetic repelling force keeping them apart. "Prophet Marinda's health is rapidly deteriorating, so healers are tending to her," says Miss Trii. "Let's get you all settled into rooms, and we'll call you when she's able to meet."

Brynda and Rubi pull me ahead again, and the bright lobby is swallowed by another dark tunnel. As the pink crystal around us lights up with piezoelectric energy, Brynda lets go of my arm and falls toward the tail of the group.

I hear her ask Hysan, "The woman you sent to be Marinda's nurse raised you? How old is she?"

After a moment Hysan's polite voice answers, "You know I have the utmost respect for your curiosity, but my personal life will have to wait. My Guardian beckons."

Brynda wordlessly returns to my side, and from the way she continues to sneak glances behind us, it's clear Hysan's diplomatic brush-off only made her more curious. But there's also something else in her expression.

She looks *hurt*.

Hysan is supposedly a friend of hers, but she doesn't seem to know much about him. His secrets keep even those close to him from ever truly knowing him.

Just like Kassandra.

We arrive at a wide balcony facing a line of door-less ceramic lifts. "Lord Neith, you'll be in Guardian accommodations," says Rubi. "I can take you if you'd like, while Brynda shows the others to their quarters."

"Thank you, honored Rubidum, that would be delightful," he says, nodding at her. "Envoy Hysan, please come along so we can finish our discussion."

"Yes, my liege," says Hysan, and as he follows Rubi and Neith onto a lift, his green eyes find mine. My Ring buzzes, and I hear his voice in my head.

Talk to your mom.

I spin away from him and join the others as they step onto a different lift, and once we're all aboard the three-walled platform, Brynda hits the button for the tenth floor.

Since the lift ascends at medium speed, we can see what each level is like as we pass it. The next story boasts an enormous room cluttered with couches, chairs, tables, Stargazers, and Dreamcasters. Since Pisces is the only House without its own signature communication device, Piscenes have technology rooms where they can send holographic communications and catch up on news. I barely have enough time to take in the wallscreens, the handheld tablets on the tables, and the semiprivate terminals in the back before we reach the next level.

The rich, earthy musk of paper rushes into the elevator, and we look into a deserted reading room that's not of the Psy variety. This is a place for reading *texts*—only unlike the holographic titles available in the suite at the Libran embassy, the stories here are tangible.

From a quick peek, I see the Piscene reading room is filled with shelves upon shelves stuffed with books of every size and color, and as the view vanishes, I inhale deeply the papers' perfume. The mingling scents of so many trees makes me sad, and I lean against the wall. I can't remember the name of the last book I read.

When we get to the tenth floor, it's just a short wing of six rooms, and each of our traveling cases is waiting outside our assigned door. Somehow Brynda's people knew not to bring Nishi's.

"Bathrooms are communal," she says apologetically, leading us to double doors at the end of the hall with a unisex lavatory sign. "This House is pretty economical with its space, so there's no closet in your rooms. But you can store your clothes in the lavatory lockers." We enter a roomy lounge lined with lockers, benches, and sinks. Past the lounge are a handful of bathroom stalls and curtained showers. A single, small mirror hangs on one of the ceramic walls.

There are no traditional gender roles on Pisces, no divisions between the sexes. Piscenes believe the body's sole purpose is to be a vessel for the soul, and as the soul is limitless and infinite, it cannot be contained by physical attributes like one's looks, sex, skin color, or body type.

"Here are the keys to these six rooms," says Brynda, handing one to each of us. "Rho, you want to hold on to Hysan's for him?" My cheeks warm, and I take it. "I've got to check in with my guys, but I'll be back." She gives my arm an encouraging squeeze, and as everyone drags their bags into their room, only Kassandra and I stay out in the hall.

I finally meet her blue eyes.

She opens her mouth to speak, but I turn away and grab my traveling case. Then I walk into the sixth room, and I leave the ceramic door wide open behind me.

30

THE ROOM IS TINY: THE bed takes up most of the space, and one wall is all pink crystal looking out at the ocean. Brynda must have chosen this room for me because it's located along the compound's perimeter so I have a view.

I stare at the silver surf until I hear the thud of my door closing, and then I wait until my breathing has slowed to turn around.

She's sitting at the far end of the bed, watching me. This room feels like too small a space to contain this conversation.

"I'm sorry I had to leave you," she begins, her tone more self-pitying than apologetic. "There was nothing I wanted more than to stay with you and your brother, but when I became a Riser, my destiny changed. For your sakes, I had to—"

"Save the performance for Stan."

She stops speaking and casts me a dark look that sends me careening back in time.

My dad and my brother always worshipped her; she had this air of feminine fragility that made them handle her with care. But even as a kid I saw through that act. I've always known there's nothing frail about her.

"You abandoned us long before you left us." My voice somehow stays even despite the feelings flooding my heart. "We grew up cut off from our extended family. You never let us know anything about them or you. You raised me in an atmosphere of fear. I want to know *why*."

"My past isn't—"

"Your past is the only thing I'm interested in hearing about," I say, cutting off whatever excuse she was about to make. I cross my arms and press my back against the window. "So if you don't want to discuss it, I have nothing to say to you."

She looks away and falls silent, the way she used to whenever my reads fell short of her expectations. The sharper lines of her Aquarian face make the expression seem more austere now than it did then, and for a moment she doesn't even look familiar anymore.

Then the blue blaze of her eyes shines on me again, and I'm face-to-face with my childhood nightmares.

"My mother was an imbalanced Riser."

I blink, and as her words swim through my veins, they chill me from the inside. If Ophiuchan blood runs so strong in my family that there's been a Riser in consecutive generations, what does that mean for Stan and me?

"Even before she shifted, there had always been a darkness in her. The changes just brought that violence to her surface. She drove most of our family away, but my dad refused to leave her. And worse, she refused to leave us." She swallows, and her voice grows softer. "Living with her was . . ."

She can't finish the sentence, and her eyes glint with what might be moisture. Only it couldn't be. I've never seen her cry, not even when Stan nearly died.

I think I'm more shocked by my mother's humanity than by Ochus's, and without making the decision to move, I sit on the bed, leaving as much distance as possible between us.

"One day, when I was about your age, I finally fought back." Her voice sounds sturdier now, either because of where she is in her story, or because I sat down, or both. "When I defended myself and realized I'd become stronger than her, I felt an overwhelming sense of *power*—and then I couldn't stop myself. To this day, I don't know if she was still alive when I left her."

The water in her eyes freezes to ice. Pity and revulsion fight for control of my heart, but even stronger than those feelings is my astonishment. Who is this woman who calls herself my *mother*? How much of her story did Dad know? I twist toward the window, no longer sure that sitting down was the right move.

"I jumped into the family schooner and sailed it as far as it would take me. That night was the first time I Saw myself Rising into an Aquarian."

"Where did you go?" I ask, my voice scratchy, my face still turned away from her.

"I found an island where I could be comfortably anonymous, but I was a teenager without family, so I was conspicuous. I knew I needed a place to belong. I slept in my schooner at night, and during the days I'd scrounge for food at the local market. And that's where I met your dad."

The first spark of light warms her narrative. "He sold nar-clam pearls at his parents' stand. He was by far the youngest salesman, and though he had no actual salesmanship, people appreciated his honesty and the quality of his pearls. He was also kind. When a woman couldn't afford the pearls she wanted for her wedding coronet, Marko would often loan them to her for the ceremony."

In a Cancrian wedding, a woman's coronet means more than her ring or her dress because she creates it herself. It represents the person she's been up to this point, on her own, and the instant she's wed, her partner removes it.

"We watched each other for a while before speaking, and our courtship escalated quickly. But before asking him to marry me, I made him promise never to ask me about my past. So at our wedding, we took a vow to live every day in the present and never look back."

As I picture everything she's describing, I start to miss Dad so much that even breathing becomes painful. Moments I haven't thought of in years suddenly creep up through the crevices of my mind's memory walls. The evenings when Stan would go out, and Dad and I would sit on the couch watching my favorite holo-show together while splitting a bucket of sugared seaweed. The mornings when he'd take me to school, and he'd go the long way because he knew how happy it made me to sail past the sea otters on Calliope Island.

"But when he introduced me to his parents, they disapproved of our vow and distrusted me for refusing to discuss my past." The spark in her voice is snuffed out by her inner winter. "They never warmed to me and eventually, a rift formed between your dad and his family. So we set out to start our own family, alone."

On Kalymnos we had the smallest plot of land because we owned a single bungalow. Our neighbors, the Belgers, had about eight of them, and they lived surrounded by Jewel's maternal grandparents and aunts and uncles and cousins. I always wanted a big family—and now I know why we never got to have one.

Kassandra needed an identity, and she used Dad to get one. He became her camouflage. She pulled him away from his family, and a decade later, she abandoned him and us.

"I know how monstrous this must sound to you," she says softly, "but I loved your dad. He was the best person I'd ever met, and I hoped his influence would save me. I didn't need the stars to tell me I would Rise. I've always known I harbor my mother's darkness in me."

Glaring at her, I ask, "So what made you decide to direct that darkness at me?"

The emotion fades from her eyes, like clouds clearing from an icy blue sky. "Not long after you were born, I had a vision of Helios going dark and our solar system coming to an end. I looked for corroboration in the Collective Conscious, and I discovered an ancient myth called the Last Prophecy that I vaguely recalled hearing about when I was younger. The very next day, I was on the porch nursing you in the hammock and gazing at the sea, when a hooded woman appeared before me. She said she was part of a secret group of seers who had Seen the Last Prophecy, and she invited me to join their ranks.

"They call themselves *Luminaries*, and they are devoted servants of the sun who have been searching for ages for a way to stop the Last Prophecy from happening. She wouldn't tell me more until I joined them, but she warned me never to speak of this vision into the Psy again, or I could be putting my family in danger. I thought, as much as I didn't want to leave you, that maybe this would be for the best. I would become a Riser one day, and I couldn't put you through what my mother did to me. But I've never made a decision without first consulting the stars, so that night, I read my Ephemeris, and what I Saw made me turn down her offer."

The intensity of her stare takes me back in time to Stanton's tenth birthday and to a week later when I saw her for the last time. It's the look that heralds storms.

"I Saw that someone from my bloodline would be the harbinger of the Zodiac's doom."

I swallow hard.

"Stanton was a funny boy who didn't like to slow down. He was a child of the present. But you had your father's quiet, introspective disposition. You were just four years old the first time I tried teaching you to Center yourself. And *you did it*. I instantly knew you were the one from my vision, and so I knew I had to use every moment we had left together to prepare you for the stars' plans."

"Great job," I growl, and at last, the sculpted ivory of her face cracks with remorse.

"Rho, there was nothing I wanted more than to stay by your side for all the trials you were fated to face. But more than ever, I knew I had to go. My being a Riser would only be a hindrance to you." She leans forward without sliding closer, like she wants to bridge the distance between us but knows better than to try. "I know I was hard on you, but I had to be sure you would be strong enough to endure all that was to come."

"Couldn't you have stayed a little longer?" My voice sounds as small as I feel, but I can't silence the cries of the little girl anymore. "You weren't showing signs of the shift when you left. You could have at least tried sticking around. Maybe you wouldn't have become your mom. We *needed* you. You took off right after Stan recovered from the Maw bite—"

"That was why I had to go," she says in an equally pleading tone, sliding up a little on the bed toward me. "I believe the Maw's attack was an omen. That's when I reached out to the hooded woman and made plans to leave. I worried they would cast me out when my transformation began, but those fears went away when I met other Luminaries and saw that there were Risers among them. They accepted me completely, and I've been with them ever since.

"But after the attack on Cancer, I became restless and anxious with worry, and I wanted to find you. Only, if a Luminary leaves— or reveals her identity to an outsider—she can never return."

She blinks a couple of times, and I suddenly realize she had a true home among the Luminaries. That's why we never heard from her the past ten years. She liked her new life and didn't want to risk it. Being away wasn't a sacrifice for her the way it was for us. *She was happy*.

My thoughts grow dizzy, and I feel dazed from the conversation. I pull my traveling case closer and pry out the black seashell from an inner pocket. "If you've really been with the Luminaries this whole time . . . how did the master have this?"

She digs her fingers into a pocket of her aqua cloak and pulls out an identical shell. "What you have is a fake. I don't know the master."

"But—the master knew about Hurricane Hebe. How could he know these things if not from you? He must have a source—"

"*You're* his source," she says gravely. "He knows everything that matters to you because he's in the Psy, and what you bring with you to the astral plane is your soul. Everything that's dearest to you is exposed there."

It sounds like what Ochus was starting to tell me when we spoke on Aquarius. This whole time, on every level, it's been my *heart* betraying me.

"I'm proud of you, Rho." Kassandra has now slid close enough to touch. "You've lived your life honestly and stayed true to yourself, two things I could never do. Despite the darkness around you, and within you, you have channeled only light."

"That's why you never wanted me to subscribe to *happy hearts start with happy homes*," I whisper. "Because you knew one day we would be broken. And you didn't want that to break me."

Her breath blows into my face as she says, "All I wanted was to give you everything you needed before I had to go."

"All I wanted was a childhood."

"You didn't have time for childhood, Rho." She takes my hand in her cold one, and my heart pumps twice as hard. "You are a flame that burns too bright."

She suddenly presses her cold lips to my forehead, and the gesture smashes the dam that's been holding back my feelings. A sob shoots up my throat, and Mom pulls me into her chest as I cry, the way I always hoped she would when I was little.

But she doesn't smell like water lilies anymore.

31

BRYNDA BURSTS INTO MY ROOM, and I sit up and pull away from Mom, suddenly embarrassed by my outpouring of emotions. Especially when I still don't know how I feel about her or about any of the things she's shared with me.

"We're having a Guardian meeting in ten minutes, and we unanimously voted to invite you to join. Can you come?"

"Of course," I say, eager to share what I've learned of Ophiuchus and the Tomorrow Party.

"We'll talk more later," Mom says, and I nod as she leaves the room. I'm about to follow her out when my Wave goes off.

Thinking of Nishi, I tell Brynda, "Give me one quick moment." She steps out, shutting the door to give me privacy. My hand shakes as I snap open the clamshell to accept the transmission, and a holographic, puffy-haired Leo with decorated eyebrows beams out.

"Mrs. Dax."

My whole body deflates. "Traxon, I don't have time to be extorted by you right now."

"Well, *that* was rude." He must still be on Aquarius because the time lag is slight. "At least *my* greeting was a compliment. Now say something nice about me, or I won't tell you what I found."

I roll my eyes. "You're . . . not hideous."

After a brief delay, he frowns. "And you're not very good at this."

"Just tell me what you found. I'm serious, I don't have time."

"I found the answer to your question. You know, the one you extorted me into answering. You wanted to know who's backing the Tomorrow Party, right?"

"Yes, we want a list of the major donors."

"You don't need a list," he says, his hologram flickering. "One person has been financing almost ninety percent of the Party's expenses since its founding."

"*Who?*"

The Leonine leans in and arches a pierced brow. "Supreme Advisor Untara."

◆ ◆ ◆

I pay little attention to where we're going as I follow Brynda to the Guardians' meeting. I don't know why Traxon would lie to me, but

I also can't see how Untara could be the person behind the Party when she was so set against it—unless she was protesting to disguise her involvement.

Did Crompton discover what she was up to? Is that the real reason she had to get him out of the way? Is that what he wanted to tell me when he was being carted off to the dungeons?

We take a different elevator to the thirteenth floor and enter a round room with pink crystal walls. Just like the lobby, half the space faces the ocean, and the daylight outside has dimmed to a gray dusk. Alamar is a small planet and its quick rotations make the days here rather short.

A round table takes up most of the space, surrounded by thirteen chintz chairs: Four are empty, two have humans in them, one has an android, and seven are inhabited by holograms. Transmitters are embedded into the seatbacks, and though the holographic Guardians look slightly blurry, they're somehow operating in real time, as though they were transmitting from nearby.

I feel the influx of Psynergy in the air, and as my Ring buzzes with its presence, the Guardians' faces come into focus, and I realize what's happening. The technology is *Psy-powered*. To travel faster than the speed of light, the holograms are taking a shortcut through the Psy Network.

The fact that there are no Advisors here is probably another precautionary measure, since trust is always the first casualty of war. It feels almost intimate, being in this room with only Guardians, without any entourages or audience members. On their own, the

Guardians look smaller somehow, like actors in a play. Humans playing at gods.

Only one of them might actually be a god.

"Welcome, Wandering Star," says Prophet Marinda in a weak voice, her delicate, feminine features making her seem too frail for this war. When she rises a little higher in the air, I realize she's in a medical hover-chair. I met her on Phaetonis during the armada; she's in her late twenties, but right now her drooping eyes, emaciated body, and paling brown skin make her look much older. "Please, have a seat."

"Thank you," I say, taking the spot between Brynda and Lord Neith. To his other side is Rubi, and beside her is Sage Ferez's hologram. He bows his head at me, and I bow mine back, and then I notice the misty, gray-green eyes of the white-haired woman next to him.

"Holy Mother Agatha," I say, bowing my head at my Guardian. "It's so good to see you."

Before she can respond, a strong male voice rings out and takes control of the meeting. "Wandering Star, we haven't met yet. I'm General Eurek."

The holographic Guardian of Aries sits across from me. He looks to be in his early forties, and he has black skin and orange-red eyes that glow like embers. "I look forward to a better introduction in the future," he says, "but for now, we all have busy schedules, so let's focus on the task at hand."

I nod, studying him closely. What do we really know about the Ariean Guardian? He's supposedly been under house arrest for years, locked up by his House's junta of warlords—but how can we be certain that's true?

I pan my gaze from him to Marinda to the olive-skinned, mossy-eyed hologram of a Virgo Advisor who must have replaced Moira for the time being. If the master is an Original Guardian, he or she could be in this room right now.

Ophiuchus said immortality works in cycles, so age is no indication. It could be anyone.

Eurek looks pointedly at the two empty seats. "Guardian Fernanda and Supreme Advisor Untara will be unable to join this meeting because they are in flight."

I sit up at the mention of Untara, and Brynda leans in and whispers, "It's a new precaution Guardians have to take when we go into Space, since our capture could be devastating to our Houses. We have to travel with shields up, so we can't communicate or visit the Psy."

Fernanda is probably headed home to Taurus, but where exactly is Untara going?

"Should we reschedule?" asks holographic Holy Leader Aurelius of Leo, who in his youth was the most famous leading man in Zodiac cinema.

"There's no time," says Eurek. "We'll fill them in later."

Beside Aurelius is the hologram of Chieftain Skiff, whose red eyes are watching me closely. The Scarab around my wrist seems to tighten as I stare back, and Skiff's gaze drifts away.

Until I know who the master is, *none* of these people can be trusted.

"I've collected updates from every Zodai team on Pisces," says Eurek in his powerful voice, "and at last count, seventy-five percent of the Piscene population is unconscious. We've found a link among those who haven't shown sign of infection yet. They were recently off world, helping out another House after an attack, so they have less of the virus in their system. This seems to confirm the theory that the attack on Pisces's communication system from a few months ago was some kind of biological strike with a lengthy incubation period."

Stan was right from the start. He knew this was the master's work and that we never should have backed off on our pursuit of his army.

"It gets worse," Eurek goes on. "Those Piscenes in comas aren't *sleeping*. Their bodies are actually shutting down, just really, really slowly. The first few people who were diagnosed have shut down completely. They're being kept alive by technology, but they're technically brain dead. And it's going to start happening—soon—to everyone else."

I look at Marinda in horror, and she whispers, "Helios help us all."

"Stridents are working to reverse the effects," says Eurek, "and we hope House Scorpio will have progress to share soon." Skiff doesn't react.

"Is there any lead on the Marad or its master?" asks Brynda.

"The trail has been dead for weeks, and the Risers in custody have yet to say anything," reports Eurek. "However, Lord Neith may have a new lead to share with us."

"Thank you," says the sonorous voice to my left. "There is a new political movement some of you may have heard of called the Tomorrow Party that might well be connected to the master. My Knights began suspecting them when they showed a lot of money right from the outset, similar to the Marad. When we tried to access their files, we found them to be hiding behind encryption similar to what we discovered on the Marad ship we captured. However, Wandering Star Rhoma Grace has been on the ground with the group and will probably have a more thorough report to share."

Everyone turns to me, and I swallow, my mind scrambling to find a place to start. If the master is in this room, I have to be careful what I say.

Or maybe not.

If the person behind the Marad doesn't want anyone to know the truth, this could be a way to lure them out. And if the master is Untara or Fernanda, then this might be my best chance to share this information without their interference. Either way, Traxon is right—the Zodiac deserves to know Ophiuchus's story.

"Thank you, Lord Neith. Given that I had to leave Aquarius at gunpoint, I have no doubt the Tomorrow Party is connected to the master."

Agatha and Marinda gasp, and Ferez and Eurek lean into the table with concerned interest. Brynda is the only one who's unsurprised, probably because Hysan already told her.

"But before I share that story, I owe you a different one. We have to begin at the *real* beginning, a time when there weren't twelve Houses in the Zodiac, but thirteen."

I inhale deeply, and I think of Vecily, and how a millennium ago she tried to deliver the same message I'm about to give, and I hope I'm making her proud.

"Ophiuchus was betrayed by another Original Guardian who wanted his Talisman, because it held the power of Immortality." Astounded silence greets my words, and I search every pair of eyes in the room for a sign of recognition.

"This Guardian vilified Ophiuchus to the others and manipulated them into sentencing him to execution. And then while everyone was distracted, this Guardian—*the master*—stole the stone for him or herself. It was this betrayal that ushered in Dark Matter and undid the Thirteenth House."

Everyone is wide-eyed. Ferez looks as fascinated by my words as I always am by his, and it feels strange to be amazing someone who amazes me. I wait for someone to say something, but nobody says a word—which I guess is an improvement over the reactions my incredulous announcements have received in the past.

"Ophiuchus was trapped in the Psy for millennia, and then a few years ago, the master spoke to him. Just as he manipulated the Risers of the Marad, he coerced the Thirteenth Guardian into helping him wield Dark Matter as a weapon against the Houses. Together, they've been attacking our worlds . . . until Ophiuchus changed sides."

"Then this is the solution to the riddle of Risers," injects Ferez, his voice distant, like he's thinking out loud. "They must be descendants of the Thirteenth House. That's why they have a reptilian makeup." He looks at me like he's awaiting confirmation. "They are trying to return home."

I nod.

"*Holy Helios,*" whispers Brynda beside me, and everyone grows inwardly focused, like they're doing the math for themselves to make sure it adds up.

"The Original Guardian who betrayed Ophiuchus is the mastermind behind everything that's happened. Not just in recent times, but *all* times," I say softly, my eyes on Ferez, since he's the only person in the room who holds my gaze. Everyone else's stare is unfocused, like they're still processing these revelations.

"This person was a *star*. He or she predates everything we know and has been among us since the Zodiac's colonization." I look from Eurek to Marinda to Aurelius to the others, and everyone's eyes are glassy with fear. I'm not getting *master* vibes from anyone in here.

"We're going up against someone who knows us intimately," I go on, "who's seen all our behavioral patterns, who's studied all our strengths and weaknesses, and who can predict tomorrow eons before we can. And our only advantage is that until now, we've acted exactly how he or she has predicted. But if we can do the thing the master doesn't expect—if we can set aside our prejudices and come together in trust—maybe we can surprise him or her."

Everyone starts asking questions at once, and I end up relating in detail different parts of my conversation with Ochus. I then tell them about Black Moon and Nishi's discovery that the Party knew about the attack on Pisces ahead of time.

When I mention my best friend, Brynda squeezes my arm under the table. There's only one thing left for me to share.

"The Tomorrow Party is terraforming a new planet, and their plan is to select a thousand people from each House to create an experimental society made up of every race. It's called Black Moon, and as I was coming to this meeting, I discovered who's been funding it: Senior Advisor Untara."

I clear my throat, and I add, "I think there's a chance she could be the master."

Brynda, Rubi, and Agatha square their shoulders like they're ready to arrest Untara right away, while Ferez and Eurek keep still like they're weighing my words, but Skiff and Aurelius furrow their brows disapprovingly.

"It's unseemly and absolutely unacceptable to accuse an acting Guardian of such heinous crimes when she is not here to address the charges," cries Aurelius.

"Who cares if it's *seemly?*" snaps Brynda. "The only thing that matters is whether it's true!"

"How do you know she's been funding the Party?" asks Eurek.

"I have a source," I say, deciding against mentioning Trax's name so I won't get him in trouble with his Guardian. "I also know Untara has had Ambassador Crompton arrested, and I think it's because he knows something."

"Do you have any more information about the Party's plans beyond this Black Moon project?" asks Ferez. "Something that could point us to their next move?"

I shake my head. "I only know part of the story. But I think you guys know the rest." I look at Ferez, and only him, because he's the Chronicler of Time among us. "I need to know . . . is the Last Prophecy true?"

From the way his expression falls, I know this isn't the first time they've discussed the Prophecy. And it hits me that they've probably *all* seen the vision. They are Guardians, after all.

"At first the Last Prophecy was a secret passed on from Guardian to Guardian," explains Ferez, "that the Zodiac would one day end with Helios going dark. In time, other Zodai started Seeing it, and so the Prophecy grew to mythic status. But none of us has ever believed we would live to see the Zodiac's last day."

Rubi jumps in. "But when Cancer's destroyed, the Piscene people are asleep, and a Thirteenth House is rising from the ashes, it's hard not to think that the End Times have begun."

"If the master is the one setting this Prophecy in motion," I say, "then maybe he can also stop it."

"I'll have trackers locate Untara's ship." Everyone's face whips to Skiff, who's broken his usual silence.

"Stridents will be waiting to arrest her wherever she lands. If she's behind this, we'll know shortly."

The whole room seems shocked for a moment. This might be the first time in history that Scorpio has shown Cancer any support.

"I think we should read the stars," says Marinda, her voice even weaker now. "It's a full moon on Alamar tonight, and we have a Quorum. That means that in one hour, we can channel enough Psynergy to See more than any Zodai has Seen in centuries."

It takes me a moment to remember the word Quorum from my studies; it was a practice the Guardians employed back when the Zodiac was under galactic rule. When at least four Guardians were present in one place, that constituted a Quorum, and if they channeled their Psynergy together in the Ephemeris, they could synchronize their reads, Seeing the same things and reaching further into the future.

"I think that's wise," says Ferez. Now that it's night out, his dark skin and black robes blend with the shadows of the room, making the golden star in his right iris stand out. "Placarus," he says to Skiff, "let us know what you find. I will search the Zodiax for more clues from the past that point to the master's identity. If it's an Original Guardian, there are only thirteen suspects."

I'm about to say *twelve*, but then I remember Gemini's Guardians are always twins, so there would have been two.

"This is good progress," says Eurek, and his commanding voice fills the air with purpose and resolve. "Let's agree to meet again in six galactic hours for general updates and specific reports on Untara's questioning, the situation on Pisces, and what the Quorum Sees in the stars."

As the group disbands, I turn to Lord Neith.

There's just one last conversation I need to have tonight.

32

MISS TRII COMES TO TAKE Marinda to the medical bay, while Brynda and Rubi check in with their troops, leaving me free to go with Lord Neith back to his quarters.

"Hysan and I thought you were superb in there," says the android as we step into an elevator.

"How do you know what he thinks?"

"He was inhabiting my mind during the meeting."

"Oh." It takes me a moment to process that visual, and then I ask, "Is everything okay with you? Hysan seemed worried the other day on Aquarius."

"I'm not sure, Lady Rho." His quartz eyes look as sad as any human's as the lift ascends past different levels. "It's my judgment that my existence is now a level-red threat to him and House

Libra, and he should destroy my parts immediately. But he refuses to accept. I could use your help convincing him."

"Lord Neith, I'm sorry, I can't—"

We reach the Guardians' lodging level, and I follow him into a round space with twelve rooms, each door painted the color of the House it represents. Before unlocking the yellow door, he turns to me.

"Wandering Star, as an artificial being who is able to see your species with some degree of objectivity, I have observed something." He rests a warm hand on my shoulder, and drops his voice. "The happiest people are the ones who have mastered life's hardest lesson." His quartz eyes gaze deeply into mine as he says, "They've learned how to let go."

Hysan opens the door, and Neith straightens. "I will use this time to charge," the android announces as he strides into the room.

"My lady." Hysan holds open the door for me with his elbow. There's a smudge of grease on his cheek, and strands of hair poke into his eyes; he shakes his head to dislodge it. "Sorry," he says, wiping his greasy hands on his coveralls. "I was just finishing some work . . . ."

His voice trails off as I reach up to comb his golden locks back for him, and his eyelids sag as my fingertips run across his head. "You . . . talked to her?" he asks, his voice husky, his face inches from mine.

I nod, but I don't say anything yet. Being this close to Hysan is like entering a magnetized zone, and I can't resist getting pulled in. But for right now, I need to exist inside this force field, so I can look at him without being blinded by his light.

The first time I gazed into the green galaxies of his eyes, all I saw were secrets, and they frightened me.

Now, I see an unknowable universe whose worlds I could spend eternity exploring. And that frightens me more.

Ferez's wisdom flits into my mind, how he said we only see a person clearly when we appreciate their many sides, even the ones we're afraid we won't like. I can't be in love with only the best parts of Hysan; if I'm going to be with him, I need to accept all of him. Only I don't know how—or *if*—I can live with so many secrets.

"How did you know she was a Luminary?" I ask, still standing too close.

"I guessed," he says vaguely.

His gaze drops to my lips, and I realize this buffer between us won't last much longer. So I force myself to step back, and Hysan blinks.

"Should we sit?" I ask, turning to survey the suite; we're in a living room that's pastel yellow with silver accents, and a hall in the back leads to the rest of the place.

"Can I get you anything?" he asks.

"I'm good, thanks."

"I'm just going to wash my hands," he says, and while he enters a lavatory, I head toward the back and notice a door ajar. Inside, Neith is already lying on a bed, his eyes flickering with data, and various wires are hooked into the veins of his arms. A knot forms in my stomach.

"He hasn't completely recovered from his misfire a few months ago." Hysan is behind me, a soapy, citrusy scent clinging to his skin.

"Will he be okay?" I ask.

"Of course." But he turns around as he answers, avoiding my eyes, and I follow him down the hall to another door. We step into a second small bedroom, and Hysan's tools are scattered over the yellow bedspread.

"What do you think is wrong with Neith?" I press.

"He's been working too hard, and it's delaying his recovery." He busies himself with collecting the tools from the bed. "I haven't been around him enough to do proper maintenance, but I'm fixing that." Once the mattress is clear, he gestures for me to sit, and once I do, he does, too.

"What did you mean you *guessed*?"

"I've Seen the Last Prophecy—most Guardians have—but since we can't just abandon our posts to become Luminaries, many of us have a secret contact among them," he says, hinging his elbows on his lap.

"It occurred to me that the one thing all Luminaries have in common is that to disappear, they first had to die. I thought of the memory Aryll used to manipulate you about your mom, how she predicted a hurricane would hit a location no one else expected, which is rather rare. Throw into the mix the fact that her daughter is our most powerful seer," he adds, his tone growing tender, "and I thought it could be a possibility that she'd joined the Luminary's ranks. It was just a guess, but a couple of months ago, I reached out to my contact and said I wanted to get a message to Kassandra Grace, if she was with them.

"Then a few weeks ago I was contacted by a different Luminary who asked a lot of questions about you. I started to hear from her more frequently, and we finally agreed to meet. When I confirmed she was truly your mom, I offered to take her to you. Leaving the Luminaries' ranks is an irreversible act, but she didn't hesitate."

"And you knew the Tomorrow Party wasn't what it appeared to be because the technology was like the Marad's?" There's a sour note in my tone, and he hears it because his expression dims.

"I went to Aquarius to gather more information. I stole Blaze's Lighter for a moment while Skarlet distracted him, and I slipped it to Ezra and Gyzer so they could download the data and send it to 'Nox. Neith is working on decrypting it."

"Ezra and Gyzer are helping you?"

He nods. "I hired them to attend the ball and spy on high-ranking Party members. I'm also working with Ezra to refine the device she created to see if we can use it to trace the Marad's original broadcast to its source and locate their main outpost."

I'm both impressed and incensed, and I can't tell which direction I'm leaning in, so I say the words out loud to hear how I sound. "You knew the truth about my mom *and* the Party when we were together that night?"

The light retreats from Hysan's features, like his inner sun is setting. "I wasn't certain about the Party yet, but . . . I'm sorry, Rho."

He slides closer to me on the bed, but I drop my gaze to the floor, and he keeps his distance. "I didn't say anything because I wanted to keep you safe. You're, well . . . you're not the best liar. Blaze would have seen through your doubts, and I didn't want to put you in any danger."

He waits for me to say something, but I keep focused on the ground, trying to work out how I feel without the distraction of his eyes.

"Hysan, I know you were coming from a good place, but I needed your honesty more than your protection. It might have taken me longer than you to see the Party for what it is, but I did eventually see it. And Blaze still came after me."

"You're right, Rho." He doesn't defend himself, and I know he's still waiting for me to look at him. Only I can't.

"Twain told me that to be a people person, you probably can't let others get too close," I say. Sadness softens my anger at the thought of the brave Virgo who gave his life for me. "And I think he was right." I finally lift my gaze to Hysan's. "Everyone trusts you, but you trust no one."

His eyes widen with surprise. "I trust you, Rho," he says in a heavy voice.

"Only when you're the one in control."

"What does that mean?"

A herd of accusations stampedes out of me. "You waited until we were on the Plenum stage on Phaetonis to tell me about the Psy shields you and Neith manufactured for the Houses, just like you waited to tell me about the students coming to meet us on Centaurion until they'd already arrived, just like you waited to tell me about my own mother, even after I told you I'd had a vision of her—"

"Yet when I warned you about Aryll, you didn't trust me."

His words silence mine, though there's no reproach in his voice. Rather than upset, he sounds raw, like he's admitting something he feels deeply.

"Most people think Librans' ability to read faces is practically inhuman, but it's precisely our ability to be so human that allows us to get inside another person's head. Being perceptive isn't reading minds—it's absorbing emotions. We're taught empathy from a young age so we don't simply understand what someone else is going through—we *feel* it." His eyes are as gentle as his voice. "So, sometimes, I'll take into account what I know about a person, and I'll make a judgment call. But I admit I don't always make the right one."

He slides closer until our knees are touching. "I thought it was your mom's right to share her own tale, but I still should have told you I found her. I guess I have to work on opening myself up more. I'm just not used to having someone to—"

"Report to?"

He takes my un-gloved hand in his warm one, and my skin cells tingle. "*Depend on.*"

His features blur as he begins to lean in, and for some reason, at this moment, I hear Traxon's voice in my head. Right as Hysan's mouth meets mine, I whisper, "How do you know you won't get bored of me and resume your playboy ways?"

His mouth twists into its crooked smirk, and his eyelashes brush my skin. "My lady, if *you* don't know what the future holds, then I'm afraid no one does."

"Be serious." I think of Mathias and his steadfast devotion, so like Dad's and Deke's. Cancrian care is complete and uncompromising. But what do I know of Libran love?

"How can I be when there's nothing serious about the question?" he asks lightly. "You're asking for a guarantee no one could give you, because even if I swear that would never happen, it wouldn't be enough. You're looking for proof you can touch."

I stand up because he's right, and I'm embarrassed, but I'm also scared and in need of reassurance. I don't know his world or his life or anything about who he's been for most of his existence. All I know is what I feel for him in this moment. And I don't know if that's enough.

"So here's what I *can* offer you," he says, his voice seductively soft. "*Facts*."

The levity in his expression has been replaced by vulnerability, and he stands. "I've been alive eighteen years, and in all this time, I've loved exactly one person." He walks up to me, his green eyes never straying from mine. "I've met thousands of people in my life, from every House, and you're the only one I've ever trusted with my secrets."

His thumb brushes my lower lip, and his fingers rake my hair behind my ear. "I've visited every inhabited planet in our solar system, set foot on every world . . . ." His voice drops to a husky whisper. "And I never had a home until I touched you."

He presses his mouth to mine, and the kiss erases everything that's happening in the Zodiac, reducing the universe to just the two of us. As I breathe in Hysan's cedary scent, my fingers find the metal tab of his coveralls' zipper. "I should probably help you change," I say, tugging down.

We're still kissing as Hysan steps out of his coveralls, and my fingers rise and fall as they run across his sculpted arms, chest, abs. My breathing grows heavy as his hands find their way inside my tunic, and my Ring buzzes.

We're meeting in the Cathedral in fifteen minutes.

Hysan must have received the same message from Brynda, because we both slow down. "We need to stop," I say, forcing myself to step back and readjusting my suit.

Hysan looks as disappointed as I feel when I sit down on the bed. "I hate this plan," he says.

"So you heard everything I said at the Guardians' meeting, right?" I stare at the shifting lines of the muscles on his back as he pulls on his golden Knight suit. "What are your thoughts? What do you think the master's plan is? You're too smart not to have a theory."

"Flattery is so underrated," he says, and I hear the smile in his voice. "Neith and I might have found a pattern that could explain why certain Houses have been targeted." He turns around, his tunic still partly undone. "We think the master might be targeting the Zodiac's swing votes."

"The what?"

"Back when the Zodiac was under galactic rule, there was a certain predictability to the way some of the Houses voted, and eventually a political scholar came up with a chart that generalized how each House behaves based on whether it's a Cardinal, Fixed, or Mutable world. And it seems like the master has been causing the most damage to the Mutable ones."

"Mutable . . ." I furrow my brow. "I've never heard of that. I mean, I obviously know Aries, Cancer, Libra, and Capricorn are Cardinal signs. But what does that have to do with anything?"

"This chart claimed that the people of each category have a tendency to act a certain way. Cardinal worlds are filled with leaders—people who won't back down and who will look out for those around them, regardless of time and place. You could usually count on the Cardinal Houses to vote for whatever was in the best interest of their people.

"Then there are the Fixed worlds—Taurus, Leo, Scorpio, and Aquarius. They are considered equally definable: Slaves to their own moral codes, it's said they often make for the best second-in-commands because if they believe in someone, they can be depended on to follow their lead loyally. They were considered to always vote with their passions.

"But the Mutable Houses were wild cards. There's no way to know which way they'll fall. Virgo, Gemini, Pisces, and Sagittarius—if you study the Plenum's records, you'll see their votes are the least predictable. What better way to control how they'll act than to control their activation? Take away Virgo's homes, and they're lost. Take Gemini's hopes, and they're vulnerable. Take away Pisces's agency, and they're blind."

Hearing Hysan's brilliant deductions always makes me wish I could rifle through the files of his mind. It seems like such a fascinating place to visit. "What about Sagittarius?" I ask.

"The Marad's first act of war took place on a Sagittarian moon. The army's first galactic address threatened the Guardian of Sagittarius. Whatever they have planned for the Ninth House, maybe we haven't seen it yet."

The thought of Nishi enduring more pain makes me nauseous. "And Cancer?" I whisper. "Why us?"

"You're the sacrifice," he says, and I think back to the words

I exchanged with Fernanda. "Of all the Houses, Pisces's Sight isn't what poses the greatest threat—it's Cancer's heart. Cardinal Houses are unmovable. Cancrians are nurturers who won't abandon anyone. For you, the loss of one life is equal to the loss of thousands. So you're the one world the master could never hope to convert."

He cups my cheek in his hand. "But even if I'm right about the pattern, I still don't know why he's doing this, Rho. I know which votes he's targeting, but I still don't know the question."

I turn my face and kiss the inside of his palm. Then he finishes getting dressed, since we have to get going to the Cathedral. While he straps on his belt with the ceremonial dagger, I ask, "What do you think of Untara?"

"She's strange, a little hard to get a read on. I have Miss Trii looking into her. Who's the source that put you on to her, by the way?"

"Traxon Harwing."

Hysan stares at me in surprise. "I didn't realize you knew him."

"We met briefly on Vitulus, during the celebration. And the past few days he was hiding out in the Pegazi stables outside the palace because Blaze wouldn't let him into the ball."

Hysan laughs. "Sounds like Trax."

I frown. "What does he have against you?"

"Why? What did he say?"

"He just . . ." I clear my throat. "He saw us the morning after the ball, when we were sneaking back into the palace." Hysan's face slackens with surprise, and he sits down at the edge of the bed.

"And he decided to remind me that you've never liked being *tied down*," I say, adopting the same phrase Hysan once used to describe himself.

"Rho . . . I can't change my past."

"I know. I just wondered why he said that to me."

"You'd have to ask him," he says vaguely, his ears turning pink. His shy reaction confirms my theory; Hysan's probably picked up on Trax's feelings for him, but he's too much of a gentleman to say anything, so I drop the subject.

"There's just one final thing I need your help with," I say, slipping off the black glove to reveal the Scarab around my wrist.

"Chieftain Skiff gave me this, and I don't know how to get it off—"

Hysan grabs my hand and brings the bangle up to eyelevel. Light emits from the golden star in his right iris as he scans the Scarab. "Why did he give this to you?" he asks tersely.

"I'm not sure. I think he maybe meant it as a token of trust."

"Did he show you how to operate it? Or explain how to remove it?"

"No."

"Then how is this a good thing?" he demands, a sharpness in his voice that's unlike him.

"Do you know him well?" I ask as he tests the bangle for pressure points.

"No. He's the Guardian I know least. He makes it incredibly difficult to get an audience, and I prefer to keep Neith a good distance from him anyway, just in case, since he's the best inventor in the

Zodiac." Hysan doesn't find any hidden keys, and sweat forms along his hairline, his forehead scrunched up with worry.

"This isn't a normal Scarab," he says tonelessly. "There are no visible controls. That could mean someone else controls it."

He runs out of the room so fast that it takes me a moment to realize he's gone, and I go after him. Hysan rips out the wires connected to Neith, unhooking him from every device, then he activates the android.

Neith sits bolt upright and blinks a few times. "Charge incomplete," he announces in his booming voice.

"Forget that," says Hysan. "I need your help removing that Scarab from Rho's wrist."

Neith follows Hysan's gaze, and he rises to his feet, holding his hand out for mine. I rest my wrist on his palm, and he inspects the bangle. After a few moments, he says, "Removing this Scarab will require a key we don't possess."

"Then we'll saw it off—"

"Any attempts to forcefully remove a Scarab can result in the device turning on its wearer. It could sting Lady Rho with its poison."

My body goes cold.

"Then tell me how we get it off!" Hysan yells.

I've never seen Hysan lose his temper like this, and my stomach is so knotted I can barely keep upright. "It's okay," I say as calmly as I can. "Hysan, this can wait—"

"We can't let someone have control of Rho's life," he says to Neith, ignoring me. "Skiff could activate the poison any moment if he wants!"

"We are being called to the Cathedral," says the android regally, unmoved by Hysan's tantrum. "We will find a way to extricate Lady Rho from this situation after the Quorum."

"No," says Hysan decisively. "We're not going anywhere until this is off her wrist."

"Hysan." Neith adopts a deeply authoritarian tone I haven't heard him use before. "You must put aside your emotions; they cloud your judgment. Nothing has happened to Rho yet, so there is no reason to believe she is in danger. We can return to this problem after the Quorum."

"I can't take that chance. She's more important."

"No, *I'm not*," I say. "The Quorum matters much more—so let's go."

Hysan finally looks at me. "Rho, you don't understand. *Skiff could be the master.* If someone was going to pull off the kind of technological feats the Marad has accomplished, I can't think of anyone more qualified in the Zodiac."

"You heard him at the meeting," I say. "He trusts me—"

"And since when has Scorpio ever defended you? His support could just be a way of deflecting suspicion."

Behind him, Neith begins to shake, his teeth chattering like his body is experiencing an earthquake.

Hysan wheels around just as the android's eyes go blank, and in a terrifying voice completely unlike his usual one, he says, *"I SEE YOU."*

33

NEITH'S FIST SWINGS AT HYSAN, who reflexively ducks his head. The punch blows a hole through the ceramic wall instead.

Hysan beams a light from his Scan and tries to sync it with Neith's eyes, but the android swings at him with his other arm, and Hysan is forced to duck once more.

Neith's fist connects with air, and the force of his strength spins him around enough to notice me. His blank stare fixes on my face, and my heart bruises my chest with its beating.

I scramble backwards toward the hall, but he lunges at me with his superhuman speed, and I scream. His fingers graze my shoulders as he crashes facedown on the floor.

I stare at his long body in bewilderment, and the only thing I can hear is my heavy breathing. A gold stem sticks out the back of Neith's white head.

"Are you okay?" asks Hysan, holstering a small golden weapon into a suit pocket. He holds my face in his hands and surveys my eyes, like everything he needs to know is in their depths.

"What happened?" I ask, aghast.

Hysan's voice hardens, but his expression grows sad. "The master has discovered my secret."

✦ ✦ ✦

I have to run to keep up with Hysan. He leads us to the door-less lifts and hits the button for the top floor. From his focused brow, I can tell he's communicating with someone, most likely Miss Trii. She's the only one who can help him with Neith now.

Floors flicker past, and the furrow of Hysan's brow steepens the higher up we go. Losing Neith will be like losing a real parent for him.

I take his hand in mine, and he squeezes my fingers. When we reach the top story, it's completely dark, but a muted light fades up as soon as we step off the lift. A collection of shoes is lined up against a wall, and Hysan begins to pull off his boots. As I do the same, I remember what I learned about the Cathedral in my studies: It's the place with the highest concentration of Psynergy in the Zodiac.

Hysan takes my hand again, and we enter a semi-dark, domed room that spans the length of the Holy Temple. One must be barefoot to walk inside because the floor is made entirely of human bones.

Every Disciple donates her corpse to this Cathedral. Since the Twelfth House believes the body matters less than the soul, they crush their bones beneath their feet and place their focus on the stars. That's why above us is the Zodiac Solar System.

All twelve constellations blink down at us, and Helios glows in the Cathedral's center, providing the only light in the space. Pisces has a satellite with a telescope that projects back this magnified 360-degree view of the Zodiac into this room. It feels like we're stranded on a cadaverous island on the clearest night in history.

Stan, Mom, Mathias, Pandora, Rubi, Brynda, and Marinda are already here, in a circle beneath our galactic sun.

"Where's Lord Neith?" asks Rubi.

"He's asked me to come in his stead," says Hysan. "He has House Libra business to attend to."

"But the Quorum—"

"I think we'll be fine," says Brynda, watching Hysan knowingly. He looks back at her, and in that instant it's clear she knows his secret.

"Yes, Lord Neith has recalled Miss Trii to his side, so it seems serious," says Marinda kindly, her voice frail. "Let us leave him be."

The door to the Cathedral flies open, and someone new rushes into the room. "I'm sorry I'm late," says Fernanda, running over in an olive green suit, her boots still on.

"She's one of the Tomorrow Party's supporters!" Stan calls out accusingly.

"Yes, I *was*," she says breathlessly. "But only to get close to them." She looks at me. "Something about their recruitment methods made me think there might be a connection to the Marad, and I thought by getting involved I could find out who was behind it."

"Untara," I supply.

"That's what I thought." Her hawk eyes narrow on my face suspiciously as she adds, "Except she's dead."

34

"DEAD?" ECHOES BRYNDA. "HOW?"

Fernanda shakes her head. "I don't know. That's why I was late. The Elders just found her body. She's been dead for weeks, and someone else has been masquerading as her hologram."

I think of when Dr. Eusta's hologram approached me at the Hippodrome and ordered me home. It wasn't Ochus who forged my Advisor's appearance. It was the master. Just like he did with Untara. *So who is it?*

Fernanda's fierce gaze finds me again, and for a moment I think she's going to accuse *me*. But before she can speak, a soft voice asks, "What's that up there?"

I look at Pandora and follow her line of sight into Space. In the area past Pisces, where House Ophiuchus used to be, lights are starting to flicker. Like stars peeking out from behind a heavy cloud covering.

It's the thirteenth constellation.

Tendrils of electricity streak across the solar system like lightning. At first I think we're still seeing what's happening in Space, but then bolts of light begin striking the bones of the Cathedral floor.

"What's happening?" shouts Stan over the buzzing sounds of the electricity. He shields Mom; Mathias grabs Pandora; Rubi, Brynda, and Fernanda gather around Marinda; and Hysan grips my hand tighter.

Suddenly the screeching sound of Psynergy that used to herald Ochus's arrival overtakes me. I cover my ears, and Brynda, Rubi, Marinda, Fernanda, and Hysan do the same, the six of us falling to the bone floor.

My soul feels like it's being ripped from my chest, and I press my hands to my ribcage as the Psynergy attacks me.

Only my Ring isn't buzzing—it's *cold*. I flash to how I felt in the Piscene lobby, and by the black tent on Nightwing, and suddenly I understand what the master is doing to House Pisces.

He's Psyphoning their Psynergy.

Just like he's channeling ours now.

I squint up to see what's happening, and the lightning above us begins to form a shape, like a constellation being outlined in the stars. As the brightness dims, I make out the man and the snake.

It's Ophiuchus.

When the pull on my Psynergy finally subsides, I feel weak and sickly, and my brain buzzes. Hysan and I slowly get to our feet, and so do the other Guardians. And suddenly a man's gut-wrenching screams fill the air.

Ochus's icy face is in agony as his frame shrinks and begins descending through the lights, like a constellation of shooting stars. Something is happening to him as he falls: Black hair sprouts from his head, and his icy body grows a layer of thick skin unlike any I've seen before.

Then he falls to a heap on the bone floor, naked and facedown. And *human*.

"Rho." Hysan's grip on my hand cuts my circulation, and I look to him in horror as he says, "The thirteenth Talisman is *here*."

And so is the master.

35

THIRTEEN MARAD SOLDIERS IN WHITE porcelain masks storm into the Cathedral and surround us. They train their black cylindrical weapons on our chests—the same ones that stopped Deke's and Twain's hearts.

Two more people walk in behind them, a Stargazer and a Dreamcaster. I recognize the Geminin—Yana—from earlier; she was tending to the little girl who was crying out for her mom. They both stand at either end of the Marad soldiers, and there's little doubt they're the ones who let them into the Holy Temple.

"Samira?" asks Brynda in shock, staring at the Sagittarian. "*Why?*"

The Stargazer says nothing. Rubi looks just as betrayed by Yana, but she seems too speechless to speak.

Suddenly one of the Marad soldiers steps forward and removes his mask. He's a teenaged guy with a face unlike any I've seen before: His skin is gray and grainy, like levlan, and his irises are yellow and oval shaped. He's Ophiuchan.

"The Thirteenth House thanks you for your donation," he says with a wide smile. His voice has a raspy edge.

He tilts his head back and looks up at the blinking lights just past Pisces—the first few Ophiuchan stars that have returned. "Our home is calling us back. Looks like there's a place for us in the Zodiac after all."

"Where is your master?" demands Hysan, his strong and brave voice cutting a gash through the atmosphere of fear.

"How do you know I'm not he?" asks the teen. "Youth can be deceiving, right, Rubidum?" He winks at the Geminin Guardian, who is still standing with Brynda and Fernanda, protecting Marinda.

"But why am I saying this to you?" he asks Hysan. "You know better than most just how deceiving youth can be."

"So are you or aren't you the master?" I snap, my heart jumping into action before the Ophiuchan can reveal Hysan's secret.

"What do you think, Rho? Am I master material?" He spins around for us like he's modeling his white Marad uniform. "And please, don't spare my feelings just because I've got a dozen Murmurs pointed at you and everyone you love."

That must be the name of the cylindrical weapon.

"If you have your House back, what do you want from us?" demands Stanton. Mom instinctively pulls him closer as the Ophiuchan stares at my brother.

The soldier steps toward my family, and I move closer to them, too. He brings the hand not holding the weapon up to his neck, like he's looking for something, and then drops it suddenly.

The incomplete movement feels familiar, and goose bumps race through me.

"*Aryll.*"

He turns to me with his widest smile yet. "Rho wins this round! I'll get to you in a moment, dear. First I want to say hi to Stan. Hey, buddy."

My brother is pale, his eyes lost. "Aryll . . . don't do this." Stan's emotions are so imbalanced that his heart has swung to the opposite extreme, and now pity has gotten the best of his anger. He still wants to think there's good in his former friend.

"Wait, wait, wait, don't tell me!" cries Aryll, clasping his hands together as he studies Mom. "Is this the *Grace Matriarch?*"

His yellow eyes grow darkly delighted. "Bang up job you did with these two! You could write a book on parenting! I've got your title right here: *How to raise kids with such crippling abandonment issues, they can't even give up on a guy when he's about to murder them.*"

"What have you done to the Piscene people?" asks Hysan, still speaking with the authority of one who's in control.

Aryll whirls around to face him, intense dislike lining his features. "What have you done to *your* people? My master has been around enough millennia to have studied everything. Machines are no match for him."

"So where is he then?" I ask, again trying to deflect the attention off Hysan.

"Pretty protective of your man, aren't you, Rho? How does Mathias feel about that?" He looks to where Mathias is standing, his arm on Pandora's shoulder.

"Well, he bounced back fast."

From the floor, Ophiuchus lets out a long, torturous wail and curls into himself.

"What's happening to him?" I ask.

"It's an excruciating transition to take on corporeal form," says a new voice. "I only experienced it once, when we Guardian stars became mortal, three and a half millennia ago. But I'll never forget the pain."

I look up at the tall man who's entered the Cathedral, and my whole being hurts with disbelief.

"*You*," says Fernanda, and I realize he's the one she was about to accuse earlier. He's the reason she was eavesdropping on me at the ball.

"*Me*," says silver-haired Crompton, holding a diamond-bright stone in his hands. "I am Aquarius."

36

"IT CAN'T BE YOU," I say, shaking my head, nausea working its way up my throat.

"Life is a dance of illusions, Rho," he says warmly, speaking as though nothing has changed between us when everything has. "With the right distraction, you can make a person believe anything."

I flash back to the first and only time Crompton and I ever traded the hand touch, and I remember the buzz of electricity that shot through me. It was the same one I got from touching Morscerta's shade. I think of the reel of holographic captures of every Ambassador that's ever held his office, and a sickening realization spreads through me.

They're all the same person.

Aquarius has been handing down the ambassadorship to himself ever since he created the position.

"How—"

"He manipulates the Psy," says Hysan, his voice heavy with judgment. "He creates the visions he needs to get his way. But how did you create Crompton while you were still Morscerta?"

"I think I'll be keeping my secrets today," says the Original Guardian, and he's cut off by another torturous wail from Ophiuchus.

"*You're* the one who betrayed him three millennia ago," I say. "You stole his Talisman."

"I did."

"Why are you taking Psynergy from Pisces?"

"Bringing back the Thirteenth House requires Psynergy from the nearest constellation . . . and a Quorum of Guardians." He looks around the room, pleased at how everything worked out the way he planned. Like always.

"And why are you bringing back House Ophiuchus?" asks Brynda.

"Why should that matter now?" he asks pleasantly. "The Zodiac is coming to its end. The Last Prophecy is real. And *I'm* the star who prophesized it."

I cast my eyes around the room, realizing none of us are making it out of here alive, and the Death omen fills my mouth again. Every single person I love is in danger.

"Then tell us when it will go dark," commands Hysan, addressing a god in the voice of a king.

"When Rho agrees to join us," says Crompton, ignoring Hysan and keeping his pink eyes on mine, "you will know more."

"That's never going to happen," snaps my brother.

Crompton tosses something at me, and probably thinking it's a weapon, Hysan reflexively reaches out and catches it first.

When he spreads his fingers apart, a strand of silver seahorse hair glints in the starlight, linking a dozen pearls together. Crompton recreated the necklace with real Cancrian nar-clam pearls, and every stroke of Mom's calligraphy is just as I remember it.

As I remember it.

My perfect memory has been my enemy this whole time.

Ferez once said memory can be an enemy you fear or a weapon you wield. But the master has been using mine against me all along. I've been bringing my deepest secrets with me into the Psy, and he's been collecting them.

"Take her now," Crompton commands.

"NO!"

Stanton, Hysan, and Mathias jump in front of me, blocking my view of what's happening.

My heart racing, I bring my hand up to wipe the sweat off my hairline, and I notice a small light flickering from my Scarab. My body's response to danger must activate its controls, and since this is the first time it isn't covered by the glove, I'm only just noticing.

Suddenly Mom shrieks, *"Get off me!"* And too late, we realize I'm not the person Crompton wants. It's Mom.

If he's truly been hunting down Luminaries for millennia, then by asking him to help me find Mom, I practically gave away that she's one of them. If Hysan put it together, there's no doubt Crompton did, too.

Aryll grabs Mom by her upper arm, and Stan shouts, "Let her go!"

My brother leaps across at him, and they fall onto the bone floor. Mom manages to free herself while the guys roll around, each one trying to get the upper hand.

Hysan and Mathias run over to intervene. Stan punches Aryll, but he barely flinches; his thick Ophiuchan skin seems to compensate for imbalanced Risers' weaker bone structures.

Suddenly Aryll pushes Stanton off and manages to roll on top of him. Quick as lightning, he straddles my brother's torso and presses the Murmur to his chest.

I don't hear the gun go off.

I only see Stan's head roll to the side.

The light in his pale green eyes has gone out.

37

AN OTHERWORLDLY CALM COMES OVER ME.

Mom looks like she's screaming, but I can't hear her. A couple of soldiers step forward and inject her with a needle until her body goes limp. My friends are trying to help, but the other soldiers have their weapons trained on them, so they have no choice but to watch as she's carried out.

I still can't hear anything as I watch Crompton and Aryll go. A handful of soldiers point their Murmurs at us warningly as they file out.

I raise my wrist, and I see a little red arrow blinking along the black band, pointing in the direction the dart will fly if I press down on it.

Aryll is almost to the door when I close one eye and line the arrow up with his back.

Then I press down.

Sound explodes into my head as he crashes onto the Cathedral's bone-ridden threshold. The soldiers raise their weapons threateningly at me, and Crompton turns back in alarm, staring at me in shock, like I've finally surprised him.

Chaos breaks out as Mathias pounces onto the soldier closest to him, blasting the Murmur out of his hands as the two of them tumble to the ground. Another soldier runs over to help his companion, but Hysan leaps across the room and bashes his first into the soldier's mask, knocking him off his feet.

Brynda's Arclight shoots fiery bullets at the rest of the soldiers to keep them away from Marinda, Pandora, Fernanda, and Rubi. In the fringe of my vision, I spy Crompton, the Dreamcaster, and the Stargazer slip out behind the soldiers who took Mom, and I chase after them.

I race into the dim hallway, and as if he senses my presence behind him, Crompton turns around. The Dreamcaster and the Stargazer stand guard on either side of him, while the soldiers carrying Mom run ahead, and I flash back to Blaze taking Nishi away from me.

"Let my mom go," I say in a voice too even and empty to be mine.

The Stargazer raises her Arclight to my chest and the Dreamcaster points her Sumber at my forehead.

"Don't kill her," Crompton warns his bodyguards, even as I raise the Scarab and line up the arrow with his face.

"Go back inside, Rho," he says, his voice somehow still managing to sound warm and soothing, despite everything he's done. "You're not ready to come with me yet."

Hot sweat drips into my eyes, and I blink to clear my vision. Ochus was right . . . this time, I won't escape Death.

"I'm never coming with you," I say, and then I press down on the Scarab to fire—right as I hear a gun discharge.

And the world goes dark.

◆ ◆ ◆

THE END OF BOOK THREE

◆ ◆ ◆

ACKNOWLEDGMENTS

Like each House of the Zodiac, I am just one pearl in a long and beautiful necklace. This series would not exist without the following Zodai:

You, dear reader—Thank you for joining Rho on this journey. Every time I hear from you on social media, or meet you at an event, or stumble across your posts about the books, my soul sings with happiness and my heart floods with gratitude. You are awesome, and getting to know you is the best part of this whole crazy experience.

Stargazer Liz Tingue—You have been my soul's Center for the first three books of the series. I will *always* be grateful to you, Liz, for making my dreams come true.

Promisary Marissa Grossman—I think the stars have long been

conspiring to bring us together, and I am so very excited to discover what our future holds!

Ben Schrank and Casey McIntyre, Guardians of House Razorbill—Thank you for always having my back. I am profoundly proud to call myself a Razorbill author.

Lionheart Vanessa Han—The way you manage to top yourself with every cover inspires me to dig deeper to write stories worthy of your art. You are my muse.

My Guide, Laura Rennert—You are my guiding star, and I am grateful every day that I can call you my agent. Thank you for making me feel like I'm not alone in this.

All the bright lights at Penguin—The whole Razorbill team; Kristin Smith and the design team; Kim Ryan, Tony Lutkus, and the international team; Emily Romero, Erin Berger, Anna Jarzab, and the marketing team; Shanta Newlin, Elyse Marshall, and the publicity team; and Felicia Frazer, Jackie Engel, and the sales team: Thank you for channeling your star power to make this series shine.

Del Nuevo Extremo—Tomás, Martín, y Miguel Lambré, somos familia y los quiero muchísimo. Vane Florio, sos mi hermana y te extraño demasiado. Jeannine Emery y Martín Castagnet, son un par de genios. ¡Gracias al equipo DNX por TODO!

The publishing teams at Michel Lafon, Piper Verlag, Karakter Uitgevers, and AST Mainstream—I am constantly amazed by the level of care and creativity you put into your editions of the books, and I'm thankful for all the love you give the series on social media. *(Ediciones Urano Colombia, ¡son los reyes de las redes sociales!)*

Bookbloggers, booktubers, bookstagrammers, etc, across the globe—You bring our fictional worlds to life. You are the bridges between books and reality, writers and readers, Earth and the astral plane. Thank you for sharing your magic with us.

Scribblers—You will always be my favorite writing university. Lizzie Andrews, you have such a pure soul that I'm confident you'd be the best seer in the Zodiac. Nicole Maggi, my twin brain: Thank you for supporting me, advising me, and above all, putting up with me. You and I are the definition of *soul-bound*.

The Armstrongs, my west coast family—Thank you for welcoming me to your family and for coming to all of my local events. I love you guys. Caden (aka Clary Fray), I absolutely adore you!

My family and friends and writing companions—I wish I could list every single one of you, but then I'd probably miss my deadline for the fourth book! Whether it's a phone call, or a writing date, or a meal, or a movie, or a sob session, or even just a quick text, your friendship and encouragement is *everything* to me.

Knight Russell Chadwick—Until you, I never thought I'd meet someone who could understand me even when I can't, who could believe in me even when I can't, or who could put up with me even when I can't. Thank you for being my best friend, my favorite brainstormer, and my Center.

Mis abuelos, Sara y Berek Ladowski—Baba y Bebo, nadie en este mundo se compara con ustedes y los extrañamos todos los días. Fueron los mejores abuelos del universo.

My siblings, Meli and Andy Garber-Browne—You are my best friends and favorite couple. Andy, I've always wanted an older brother, but I never imagined I'd get this lucky. Meli, you are my entire world, and you're the inspiration behind Rho. *You are an everlasting flame that can't be put out.*

Papá, Dr. Miguel Garber, mi héroe y mejor amigo—Todo lo que hacés para ayudar a tus pacientes me llena de orgullo, inspiración, y esperanza. Gracias por siempre apoyarme y hacerme sentir que puedo lograr todos mis sueños. Te quiero tanto, pa.

Mamá, Lily Garber, mi ídola y mejor amiga—Sos la persona más fuerte, inteligente, y capaz que conozco (además de ser la más hermosa). Gracias por ser un ejemplo a seguir para Meli y para mí. Sos la mamá más grande del universo y te quiero tanto.

And finally, all the booksellers, librarians, and teachers around the globe who are the gatekeepers to new worlds—You are kindlers of hope, and you save more lives than you'll probably ever know. On behalf of readers everywhere, THANK YOU!

TURN THE PAGE FOR
A SNEAK PEEK OF

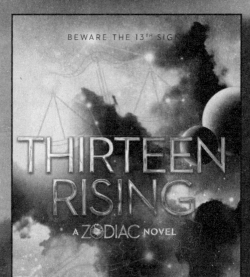

BEWARE THE 13TH SIGN

THIRTEEN
RISING

A ZODIAC NOVEL

ROMINA RUSSELL

THE STUNNING FINALE OF

THE ZODIAC SERIES

AVAILABLE AUGUST 2017

PROLOGUE

WHEN I THINK OF MY brother, I hear his comforting voice.

Stanton's words have always been my lifeline: They have the power to soothe me, guide me, even save me from my nightmares. I especially love what I call his *Stantonisms*—catchy one-liners he came up with on the spot whenever I was afraid.

"Don't fear what you can't touch," he told me the night Mom abandoned us. I used to think it was the smartest thing I'd ever heard, but now I know better.

Everything touches us eventually.

The day Mom left us, I stayed up late with Dad and Stan, the three of us huddled on the couch, pretending to watch the wallscreen while we waited for her to come home. At some point I must have dozed off, and Stanton probably carried me to bed. The sky was still dark when I awoke to the sound of my own scream.

The door to my room opened, and my ten-year-old brother's familiar voice said, "Rho, it's okay."

His weight settled beside me on the mattress, and his warm hand closed around my clammy one. "You're safe. Everything's fine."

My entire body was slick with sweat, and my breaths were coming in short spurts. I could still feel the spot on my shoulder where the Maw from my nightmare sank its fangs, the same place where the real Maw had bitten Stan the week before—only in the dream, Mom didn't swim swiftly enough to save me.

And as the monster carried me far from my family, its eyes were no longer glow-in-the-dark red.

They were a bottomless blue.

"Is—is she back yet?" I whispered as I fought to free myself from the nightmare's hold.

Stan squeezed my fingers, but the pressure felt faint, like I hadn't surfaced to full consciousness yet. "No."

"Is she . . . coming back?" I whispered even more softly.

He was quiet a long moment, and I grew fully awake as I awaited his answer. Then he slid up and rested his back against the bed's headboard, sighing. "Want to hear a story?"

I exhaled too as I nestled under the covers beside him and closed my eyes in anticipation. I'd take a Stan story over pretty much anything on the planet.

"There once was a little girl whose name I can't remember, so let's call her Rho." His comforting voice wrapped around me like a second blanket, and I felt my heartbeat finally slowing down. "Little Rho lived on a tiny planet that was about the size of Kalymnos."

"But how can a world be that small?"

"Are you telling the story, or am I?"

"Sorry," I said quickly.

"Let's try this again: Rho lived alone on a very small planet, in a different galaxy where things like small planets were possible, and if you worry too much about the science, this story will end. Anyway, little Rho knew everything about her world: the name of every nar-clam, the shape of every microbe, the color of every leaf. Her home was her heart, and her heart was her home, just like Helios belongs to the Houses and the Houses belong to Helios."

His words painted pictures in the black space of my mind, burning up the darkness with their light. "But one day," he went on, "a huge storm rolled through her planet, and little Rho was blown into the atmosphere, caught in a whirlwind that tossed her about the cosmos and stranded her on a strange, much larger world."

"But what about her home—"

"It sounds like you don't want to hear the rest of the story," he said, sitting up suddenly, "so I guess I'll just go."

"No, no, I'm sorry, I want to hear it," I pleaded, tipping my head up on the pillow to stare at Stanton's gray profile.

"Then no more interruptions," he warned, settling back against the headboard, and I mimed sealing my lips shut. "Anyway, she landed on a new world, and instead of the sea surrounding her, she stood on a field of feathers."

"*Feathers?*"

"Huge feathers. They grew from the ground like grass, and they were every color and design you can imagine. When Rho walked, the feathers tickled her bare feet, so she couldn't keep from smiling with every step."

I squealed with laughter as something soft suddenly brushed the soles of my feet, and I curled into myself and shrieked, *"Stan, stop!"*

"Yeah, she reacted just like that," said my brother, and I could hear the ghost of a smile in his voice.

"Only every time she laughed," he went on, "Rho's mind forced her mouth back down into a frown. She *shouldn't* be happy, not when she was so far from her home. She had to get back. She had to be serious."

"Were there people on that planet who could help her?" I asked—and then I cringed as I suddenly remembered I wasn't supposed to be asking questions.

"Actually," said my brother, "almost as soon as little Rho started walking across the field, she ran into someone. A purple bird that was human-sized and wore a wreath of flowers around its head."

"Whoa."

"Yeah. That's exactly what Rho said. And then the bird spoke to her."

"It *spoke*—?" I asked, awed.

"In a normal—if not slightly squeaky—voice, it said, 'Welcome, friend. Why do you fight yourself?'" I giggled at Stan's high-pitched bird impression. "Little Rho's shock at meeting a talking purple bird turned into confusion as she considered his question, and she asked, 'What do you mean?'

"The bird pointed with its beak to Rho's feet. 'I can see the ground pleases you, yet you won't allow yourself to feel pleased. Why do you resist the pull of the present in favor of a pain that is clearly past?'"

"That sounds like something Mom would say," I blurted, and then I sucked in my breath at my own boldness.

Stan paused only a second, and in that instant it occurred to me that he probably didn't want to sound like Mom right now.

"Little Rho's shoulders sagged with the weight of her sadness, and she said, 'I'm upset because I've left my home, and now I don't know how to get back.' The bird frowned. 'But why should that be upsetting? Every bird must leave her nest, and once she does, she can never return. The nest dissolves because she doesn't need it anymore.'"

A sense of unease settled in my stomach, and I went from enjoying Stan's tale to not wanting to hear its ending. "I don't like this story. Let's start a new one."

"That's not how life works, Rho," murmured my brother, sounding older now that he wasn't speaking in character. "It's like in a game when you're dealt a hand you don't like, you don't get to ask for a new one. You have to change your hand for yourself."

"How?"

"By playing through it."

I didn't understand what he meant because I didn't want to try. There was only one thing I was waiting to hear from him. "Is Mom coming back?"

He was quiet for a stretch, and in our silence his breaths grew louder, until they rose and fell in rhythm with my own. When at last he spoke, his voice was so low I barely heard it.

"I think our nest is gone."

Tears spilled from my eyes, because I knew my brother wouldn't lie to me. Mom wasn't coming back.

Stan crushed me to his side as I cried, and he continued narrating his story in a tone as soft as my sobs. "'That sounds like a terrible life,' little Rho said to the bird, horrified at the thought of never seeing her home again.

"But the bird's beak widened as it smiled and shook its head. 'Judging is a waste of time, because most of what happens in our lives is out of our control. The only choice we get is what we do *right now*, with this moment. Every second is a choice we make.'"

I sniffled as I slid my face up on his shirt, which was stained with my tears. "So little Rho can choose to smile or frown as she walks through the feathers," I said.

"Exactly," said my brother. "You can get through anything, Rho. You just have to let go of your fears and keep moving forward."

"How?" I asked.

He was quiet a moment, and then he said, *"Don't fear what you can't touch."*

I sat up a little, sounding the line out in my mind. There was something empowering about it, and I loved how neatly it declawed the monsters I couldn't fight, like my visions and my nightmares. And I knew then that I would survive the loss of Mom because I had Stan.

My brother was my strength, my guiding star, my anchor. It wasn't just the times he saved me from my nightmares—it was the love and faith and patience he showed me our whole lives.

With Stan by my side, the monsters couldn't touch me.

As long as my brother was safe, my fears weren't real.